Time's
Mouth

Time's Mouth

A NOVEL

EDAN LEPUCKI

COUNTERPOINT
BERKELEY, CALIFORNIA

First Counterpoint edition: 2023

Library of Congress Cataloging-in-Publication Data
Names: Lepucki, Edan, author.
Title: Time's mouth : a novel / Edan Lepucki.
Description: First Counterpoint edition. | Berkeley : Counterpoint, 2023.
Identifiers: LCCN 2023003296 | ISBN 9781640095724 (hardcover) | ISBN
   9781640095731 (ebook)
Subjects: LCSH: Time travel—Fiction. | Family secrets—Fiction. |
   Communal living—Fiction. | Women—Fiction. | LCGFT: Novels.
Classification: LCC PS3612.E66 T56 2023 | DDC 813/.6—dc23/
   eng/20230201
LC record available at https://lccn.loc.gov/2023003296

Jacket design by Nicole Caputo
Jacket image © iStockphoto.com/dimitris_k
Book design by Laura Berry

COUNTERPOINT
2560 Ninth Street, Suite 318
Berkeley, CA 94710
www.counterpointpress.com

Printed in the United States of America

10 9 8 7 6 5 4 3 2 1

For my dad, Bob Lepucki,
whose license plate reads: ORGONE

Time's
Mouth

You've wondered about me. When a decade passes as quickly as a year, when you look up and see that life is half over, that it's almost over—that's when you wonder: How did it all pass so quickly? You try to conjure the past, and yourself in it: that thing you used to feel, what you wore, how the bed felt in the dark, how you carried your body through space, the depthless mysteries the world created only for you. It's as if those versions of yourself still exist. Somewhere, on another plane, you're sure of it. If only you had access to them.

You close your eyes, and you can almost touch the past. That's you, grasping with tiny hands at the scruff of the family dog. Or you're doing cartwheels with your sister. Or you're getting a popsicle at the store down the block. There's your dad. Or you're in a low-ceilinged room you'll never see again, listening to someone whose voice you'll never hear again. Or there's a baby in your arms, and that baby is already the only person you can't stand to lose.

You can almost touch what's been lost. Almost—

That child isn't a child anymore. Neither are you. This moment is gone and this one is too. It's slurped away from you.

I guess I do the slurping. Not that I have a mouth. Or I'm all mouth, or mouth-like. I'm not time, but I hold it. Again and again, on and on, I witness how people return to the past in their minds or avoid it altogether. Build an altar or dig a hole, pray or bury, try to relive or forget.

I am a space that precious few have been able to inhabit for more than a moment.

Those who can? Those who can slip the membrane and visit those moments again?

Well—

I want to tell you about them.

Part
ONE

1

LET'S BEGIN WITH URSA.

She is Ray's mother—though, in 1938, when she is born in the caul like a mystic in Mystic, Connecticut, that lineage is yet to be written. Her name isn't even Ursa yet. It's Sharon.

At first, Sharon is only a beautiful baby, and then an adorable little girl, living with her parents in a creaking clapboard house with a narrow staircase and the faint tickle of mildew in both bathrooms. On a chair by the front door her father's hat settles like a mound of dark soil.

Imagine Mystic, Connecticut, back then: the brick post office, the ships in the port, the sea salt in the air. Imagine young Sharon, the child she used to be, bows at the end of her pigtails, saddle shoes on her feet, porcelain dolls lining her bedroom shelf. Nothing amiss. Or everything.

Imagine her a few years older: slipping into reverie during a dull classroom lesson, or riding her bike through town, or biting her nails.

Picture her at sixteen years old, lying on her twin bed in her room.

It's a Wednesday. About five in the evening. Mid-October.

It was chilly out, but because Sharon didn't want to have to re-make her bed, she lay very still atop her pink chenille bedspread. There was a hole in her left sock, and she wiggled the exposed toe before tucking it back into the white cotton. She was tall, and her feet reached the end of the mattress. Downstairs, her mother cooked dinner, and Sharon could smell the pot roast and the mushy carrots, no doubt too much food for a widow and her daughter.

She felt bored—desolate with it. The lamp on her dresser cast a sallow glow across the pale blue wall and the painting of the teddy bear that had hung in her bedroom for her entire life. The bear's black marble eyes were beseeching and needy, but if she took the painting down, its absence would reveal a darker rectangle of blue on the wall, and what then?

Sharon was a high school junior and hated everything about it except slamming her locker shut between classes, and afterward, tossing her majorette baton high into the sky before catching it in her fist. Right now, she wanted a cigarette, yet she didn't dare steal another from her mother. The widow had begun counting them.

The days were getting shorter, and within weeks the trees would be spindly and bare. At the thought of the red and orange leaves fluttering from the trees to a soppy ground, she closed her eyes. She held her breath for as long as she could before letting it out in a rush like a swimmer coming up from the deep.

It was then that she felt it. Something. It brushed her as a breeze might—it wasn't a breeze. It was like a spirit, only not one. It was like an invisible butterfly tickling its wings against her skin, or like a stirring. What was it? Nothing like this had happened before.

Her eyes remained closed. The nubby roses on the coverlet nudged her spine. She didn't consider herself spiritual, or mystical, and she wasn't much curious about the unseen. No matter. A lack of interest isn't the same as prevention.

She took a shallow breath. Her body prickled with goose pimples.

She—went.

She found herself . . . elsewhere.

Her backyard, at night. In the dark, the tall trees bordering the lawn had turned into craggy monsters, the moon a fingernail clipped against the black above. A few feet away, she saw herself, kneeling on the grass, as if praying.

How could she see herself? She could feel her own body, back in the bedroom, but she was also here in the backyard, without a form. She was a floating consciousness. This other self, the one on the grass—Sharon recognized herself. Three years in the past. She was thirteen. And, still, sixteen. Here and there at the same time.

This was the night of her father's funeral. The best day of her life. Her younger self wore the new black dress her mother had purchased for the service. With effort Sharon had zipped it up herself that morning, and now she never wanted to take it off. If she could wear it forever like a new skin, she would have.

Even though she was only watching herself from afar, she could feel the top of the zipper's teeth against the nape of her neck and the grass poking her arms, just as she could also feel the coverlet in the bedroom and the hole in her sock.

For a moment, Sharon opened her eyes, and she was once again on her bed, in her room, with the portrait of a teddy bear begging. She was also watching herself in the yard. A palimpsest of two realities. She had no word for this.

In the bedroom, the yard began to dissolve and she closed her eyes to will it back. Already she wanted more of this—whatever *this* was.

The Sharon in her funeral attire had flung herself on the scratchy lawn, the air around her humid and heavy, and she was running her arms up and down as if she were doing snow angels. She was smiling to herself. This Sharon was staring up at the stars, at her favorite constellation, the big bear, feeling free for the first time in her young life. Her father was finally dead. The feeling returned as she watched herself: a kind of full-body throttle, a drunkenness, the *whee!* of a balloon released into the windy sky.

Sharon tried to get closer to herself on the grass—she wanted it so badly—and quick as a snap she was back in her bedroom with the smell of overcooked meat in the air, the sallow light, and the hole in her sock. The other world was gone. She felt exhausted, and then terribly woozy. Her head was heavy as an anchor, the stink of dinner too much.

As she vomited onto the carpet, her mother called up from the kitchen, "Sharon? You all right up there?"

She didn't answer. She hated that name.

She wanted to do *that* again. That *thing*. As soon as she figured out how.

∞

By the time Sharon packed her knapsack and ran away from home, she had been doing the thing for a year.

How was she able to do it? And why, on that autumnal evening, bored out of her mind, dreading dinner with the widow, had it begun?

Sharon didn't have a name for what she did, let alone a reason for how it worked. She only knew that something had called her to the past, and that it respected her enough to not pull her too far backward, to the horrors she so assiduously kept out of her mind. She wasn't used to being respected.

Even so, these were the early days. Traveling made her ill afterward, and she couldn't do it on command. In the beginning, she felt no purpose, especially since she could only return to moments in her own life. It wasn't as if she could help anyone. Including herself.

And yet. It showed her that anything was possible. It's what gave her the courage to run away.

She decided the only place for her was California; she had seen pictures of San Francisco and Hollywood, and of ancient trees wide as houses. There had to be others like her there.

She left in the middle of the night and hitchhiked across the country. Bad things happened to her, that's what she expected, as if she were marked for trouble. She told no one where she was going. The widow had no idea and that was how Sharon wanted it. If her mother had loved her, even in her own deranged way, why hadn't she protected her? It didn't matter that Sharon's father was dead, not unless her mother had killed him. She hadn't; a stroke had. No, her mother had cooked that man breakfast and lunch and dinner and served him his drinks and starched his shirts. She left that chair by the door for his hat. And all along she knew what he was doing to Sharon.

He was—

No. She did not go there.

As she crossed the border from Nevada into California her old self became unreachable, the name her parents had given her just some word. She was different now. She would call herself something else. She was Ursa. Nothing would hurt her.

According to Ursa, her story begins here. Although she was seventeen, the years before that might as well not exist. Ursa struck them from the record. Sharon was born in 1938; Ursa wasn't. She arrived, fully formed, in 1955.

Ursa, tall, broad-shouldered, breasts like a bulwark, hair black as a beetle's back, steps out of a stranger's Buick in San Francisco with only a knapsack and fifteen dollars and an idea of herself as untainted and free. It's half past nine o'clock in the evening at the end of September. Almost a year since Ursa discovered what she's capable of.

The man driving the car leans toward the open passenger window and asks if she needs a place to stay.

"I do not," Ursa says and walks away as if she has somewhere to go. No one has to know that she doesn't.

∞

It took only two nights of sleeping outdoors and one frantic run from a police officer before Ursa secured employment as a maid at a large white hotel on Market Street. The tourists were pouring in, the manager said, and they needed strong and punctual girls like her to make the beds and bleach the toilets. It wasn't awful. There were stale dinner rolls to eat, and she liked how stiff the sheets were, and she occasionally discovered spare change behind the dressers. She was required to wear a uniform, which meant she did not have to buy any more clothes, or not right away. She kept to herself. She didn't have a safe place to go backward and so she stopped herself from doing so, which was the hardest part of running away from home.

One night, a few weeks into her new life, Ursa walked from the fancy hotel where she worked to the shabbier motel she was staying in. It was late, nearly midnight, she often got the late shift, and the block Ursa hurried down was deserted; it was the kind of street where humanity evaporated as soon as the sun set and the shops closed. Ursa had almost reached the corner when a man in an expensive suit and the broken capillaries of a drunk stepped into a streetlamp's pool of light.

"Good evening," he said in a nasally voice.

Ursa said nothing, only clutched her pocketbook tighter, just as her mother used to whenever they were in a big city. She hated herself for being like her mother and let go a bit.

"I have a proposition for you," the man said.

They stood beneath a sign that read FISH DINNERS, its neon extinguished.

"I have to go," Ursa said and tried to step around him.

The man stepped forward, blocking her, and the fear was a drip into her spine.

"What do you want?" Ursa asked.

"I'll give you ten dollars for your soiled undergarments."

"That's it?" She meant, *Will you also hurt me?*

"All right, I'll give you twenty."

She glanced at the fish sign over their heads and couldn't help but laugh. A cackle, really. It seemed like something someone named Ursa would do.

The man didn't follow.

"Give me the money first," Ursa said.

He sighed and pulled the twenty-dollar bill from a brown leather wallet. A crisp bill. Ursa plucked it from his hand, and he waited as she put into her purse.

"Now," he said when she was finished.

He watched her with his tongue peeking out of his mouth as she removed her hosiery and then her panties. She looked away and emptied her mind, trying to do the thing—to go backward, to get out of this moment and into another, better one. It didn't work. She was out of practice, and, besides, it was never convenient like that.

Once he had her panties she ran past him, her bare legs cold in the night air. She ran all the way to the motel. Once she was able to calm down, she felt exhilarated. The rich drunk had her sweat-soaked undergarments but she had his money.

She was able to rent a permanent room in North Beach with one small window sheltered by a bay tree, and here, she was able to do the thing. Unlike the motel, the room was safe and private. It was in a Victorian house that had been cut up and reassembled to accommodate her and eight other tenants, all women except for an older man on the top floor who rarely left his bedroom. There was rumor of a chamber pot.

In her room, furnished with a twin bed and an armoire, Ursa locked her door, pulled down her window shade, and practiced. She did it as much as she could, which wasn't very often because it always made her sick, and she had to stay well enough to work. She managed it about once every month; she had gotten so much better at it since coming to California.

Why was that? Perhaps it was the cool air and the thick fog, and the gnarled rocks jutting out of the Pacific Ocean, which struck Ursa as so much more powerful and dangerous than the ocean she'd known all her life. The fat seals, slick yet pocked, lolled about on those rocks. The city had been built on sand dunes—and on a landfill too. The bright buildings and homes were so young, built after the earthquake a mere fifty years before. This place was proof that you could not only recover from destruction but emerge better and more beautiful than before.

Ursa decided that there was no darkness here—no brick, no drab colors. The women wore fabulous coats in pink and red and turquoise, and once she'd seen a lady in yellow pumps the same bright shade as the yarrow blooming in people's front gardens. There was a restaurant that had once, a century ago, charged gold dust instead of dollars. Chinatown was strung with paper lanterns and packed with antique stores and curio shops, and there were Chinese people, crowds of them, Ursa had never seen so many Chinese people before. Downtown, the cable car terminus wasn't far from the hotel, and sometimes she watched the motormen push and pull the trolleys around on the turntable until they faced a new direction, as if the cars were stubborn horses. Down the street from her house were jazz clubs and cafés, the tables of which were crowded with bearded men in corduroy coats, smoking and talking. The girls wore no makeup. Once, Ursa had seen a woman in black-and-white-striped pants and a crisp black top, and bare feet, and she was drinking coffee at eleven o'clock at night, as if she had no plans to sleep, as if she didn't need shoes, or anything at all, to protect her.

Here, everyone was seeking their own transcendence, and the and-you-should-too atmosphere was a seduction Ursa couldn't deny. She loved California and San Francisco within it. It wanted her to explore the thing. It was as if it whispered to her its encouragement. The tree outside her window smelled of nutmeg.

And so, in her room, she experimented. At first, as in Mystic, Ursa couldn't make it happen at will, and sometimes, when she was tired, or grumpy, it would begin unbidden. Once—only once—did she slip into a time too far back, and she found herself in the kitchen with both of her parents. Her father's voice, his heavy gait—*no, no.* It took everything she had to get yanked out of there.

Eventually, Ursa got better, more deliberate. Even if she might never understand why or how it worked, or why she of all people could do it, she did know that she had to relax her body to properly find the hem of time. It was like feeling for a doorknob in the dark. She figured out that access to the past got stronger the more time had passed. She couldn't reach anything that happened in the last two years; experience needed to marinate. If she tried to drop into the same moment more than a few times, it turned blurry, degraded as a moth-eaten sweater. And she still didn't have a body inside these moments—only that roving consciousness that felt everything her old self felt.

Every time she traveled back, Ursa tried to bring her body with her. She wanted to move through the space, have her way with it, and she told herself she'd figure it out. She had so much drive, so much confidence. Her past was a secret black hole at her center that pushed her forward—and backward.

She was a wise girl, nearly eighteen, living alone in a big city. If she ever made a friend here, she would tell them what she did and see if they had ever heard of such a thing. How would she describe it? *I can only return to my own past, no one else's.* She could say, *It's nothing, and everything.* She could ask, *Can you help find others like me?*

∞

One afternoon, on her day off, Ursa lay on the floor of her rented room, breathing carefully. She was trying to relax so that she could go backward, but her body wasn't cooperating. Her legs wouldn't stay still, and her breath was shallow, panting like a dog's. She felt more vulnerable than usual, a hermit crab without its shell. She would begin menstruating the next day, and perhaps it was this—the monthly shedding of her uterine lining, the egg flicked out with the home the body had begun to make for it—that made her feel defenseless. She longed for something to envelop her, to surround her. Moments before, she had tried getting into bed, crawling under the covers and placing the pillow over her face, but all she'd felt was hot and stupid. The floor, its opposite, hard and cold, was no better, and Ursa wished she had a car or an elevator, something to cradle her as she whooshed backward. Like a man in a science fiction movie, she needed a machine.

She sat up and, looking across her room, got an idea.

Ursa removed her two maid uniforms and her four outfits from the armoire. As she laid her clothing on the bed, her wrists buzzed with promise. Something within her felt viscous, permeable as an egg yolk, and the empty armoire, doors open like arms, welcomed her. She wanted—needed—an enclosed space to keep her steady.

She climbed into the closet and, after some difficulty, cursing her height, with her knees pinned to her chest, her head grazing the top shelf, she closed its heavy double doors.

Inside the warm dark: a hush. It smelled of cedar and the bag of mothballs the landlady had placed in the back corner. And of Ursa, of her exertions.

She held her breath and let it go.

As if turning a switch, she went.

This time, it felt different. She knew where (when) she was going, and, as if driving a car, Ursa took herself there. She was in the department store in Hartford, the one her mother favored when they went to visit her father's aunt. Christmastime. Ursa was fifteen. She was sucking on a candy cane while her mother shopped for a new pair of shoes. The peppermint tasted as sharp as the candy's tip, lathed to a sword by her tongue.

It was a random moment, nothing significant about it. What was important was that Ursa had beckoned it to her, that she stepped inside it as if it were a ballgown. She felt as she had back then, the boredom and the rage and the candy on her tongue. She experienced everything anew. The past was present. It felt so good.

When Ursa emerged from the armoire, she was weak, the familiar nausea rising. She was also buzzing, already jonesing to do it again.

Imagine the power she felt, the awe.

A gift.

Also: a curse. Not that Ursa knows that yet.

∞

It was in this stage of discovery, this age of private thrills, that she met Karin. And Charlie.

Ursa, a year into living in San Francisco, had no life beyond the hotel and her room. She had always been solitary, her aloneness a fact of life, a background hum she noticed but rarely minded; only now, that aloneness felt lonely. It surprised her, and it pulled her toward the café closest to her house, which wasn't as crowded as some of the others, in part because, after dark, the proprietor expanded the seating to the sidewalk next door, below the neon words WATCH REPAIR.

It was beneath this glowing red sign that she had caught sight of the barefoot woman in the striped pants. Tonight, the woman wore blue capris and sensible leather shoes, and smoked a hand-rolled cigarette. She looked elegant and self-assured. She looked fun. She drank black coffee from a black cup and saucer and nursed her cigarette, smiling at the passersby. Ursa's stomach flip-flopped as she slipped into a table next to her. She wanted this woman to be her friend, and she wanted one of her hand-rolled cigarettes.

"I hope you don't mind me asking . . ." Ursa said.

Karin was only seven years older than Ursa, and yet, at twenty-five, it seemed as though she'd already accrued a lifetime of knowledge that Ursa never would. Karin could quote Emily Dickinson and read palms and play the harp, and her nails were painted blood red, which seemed to contradict her bare face and her wild, curly hair.

That evening, they talked and talked until Karin moved to Ursa's table and ordered more coffee, along with some biscotti. When Karin asked Ursa where she was from and Ursa said, vaguely, "Back east," Karin did not press. She was good at reading people.

"You'll fight for what you believe in," Karin said cryptically an hour later, after they'd left the café and were at a bar drinking Pernod, which Karin had described as licorice on wheels.

"I suppose I would," Ursa replied.

Karin said she had a barely used apartment in the Outer Sunset and that she was married to a man named Henry.

"Henry is old—ancient," she said. "I love him, and he's very ill. Right now, poor thing is in bed up in Ben Lomond. I have to head back tomorrow."

"Ben who?"

Karin hooted, leaning back on her leather barstool. "It's a little town outside Santa Cruz. Ever been?"

Ursa shook her head.

"It's my family's home. The property isn't in Ben Lomond. Near it. Really remote."

Most of her family had come to California during the gold rush. She said one of her grandmothers was half-Chinese, that her great-grandfather had built the railroad.

"My other great-grandfather plundered the land, trying to get rich," she said. "He succeeded. I was born there."

According to Karin, the house was in the middle of the woods.

"It's unfindable," Karin said. "Unless you know how to find it."

And then Karin looked up and shouted, "Charlie!"

Ursa turned from her glass of licorice on wheels to see who Karin was waving at.

He was at the other end of the bar, sipping at an amber-colored liquor, no ice. He wore his long blond hair braided down his back, his beard reddish, his large eyes brown.

Charlie heard his name and grinned at Karin. When he noticed Ursa, his eyes lingered, his face softening to a shy smile. He signaled something to the bartender.

In a moment, Charlie was standing next to them, and Ursa was thinking only of him and his big brown eyes, his large hands that gripped his glass, the braid of his hair like a rope. She never had a lover before. She'd never been with a man she wanted.

Unfindable until you find it, et cetera.

∞

Charlie left the bar not long after meeting Ursa; friends of his pulled him outside by the arms, they had somewhere to be, apparently, they were in fact late. Ursa and Karin giggled, watching Charlie being pulled backward, away from them. He dragged his feet as if being carried off to the gallows.

"I'll see you soon, Karin," he called out, helpless, but he was looking at Ursa when he said it. She gave him a little nod and prayed it telegraphed enough.

She and Karin stayed up until dawn, and as the sun rose, they found themselves in Karin's apartment, which was swallowed by a gigantic mattress. There was a faded rug beneath the bed, red and brown, a pattern of geometric shapes, which Karin said was from India.

"I want to go there someday," she said.

"I could not even find it on a map," Ursa admitted.

"Remind me not to make you the navigator then."

They sat on the bed as Karin rolled them a joint. She said they would smoke the reefer and then she'd cook them a big breakfast of poached eggs and toast, and then they would fall asleep.

"I love dreaming under the influence," Karin said.

"I've never smoked marijuana before," Ursa said, once Karin had licked the joint sealed and held it up to the light for them both to admire.

Karin did not, as Ursa had feared, laugh at her new friend's inexperience.

"Don't worry, you'll love it. This crop turns me ponderous. Two nights ago, I ventured deep into a memory."

Ursa's stomach dropped. She knew Karin wasn't talking about doing the *thing*. Even so, she hoped they might smoke together and cross into the past at the same time, side by side. It was a childish wish. She couldn't help but wish it.

Being under the influence wasn't at all like the *thing*. She wasn't anywhere but here. It was more like a dip, a shift, an *aha*. She moved down to the basement level of her brain where the chug-chugging happened. She was stoned enough not to be disappointed that she and her new pal weren't traveling. At least there was this. The orange gloopy yolk against the white plate and the way the sun hit the wall. How funny this big bed was.

"Is it happening?" Karin asked.

Ursa nodded. It was.

∞

A month later, Ursa found herself in the passenger seat of Karin's baby blue Chevrolet Bel-Air, its wheel wells gunky with mud. "I don't drive the truck because I despise it," was all Karin said when Ursa asked about the dirt.

Ursa's year of solitude had quickly been replaced with this friendship, and she felt dizzy with it. Karin *was* fun. She was also smart and worldly, and she had told Ursa about all kinds of obscure foreign things, like chanting and meditation, and about practical things too, like how to get a diaphragm. Ursa longed to tell her about the armoire, about the thing she could do. What if Karin knew others like her?

They took Highway 1, the edge of the world, a slow drive on account of the steep cliffsides and the mammoth ocean, unbearable in its beauty.

Ursa had asked for two days off to see Karin's house, and she prayed that some runaway wouldn't steal her job in her absence. If the management weren't so desperate for help, they might've already fired her. She had called in sick the week before to go on a picnic with Charlie. And then, the next night, she'd left the hotel an hour early so that they could attend a poetry reading. Charlie had caught her suppressing a laugh at the shirtless man on stage, croon-talking, "Sweet lover, oh sweet lover," in a terrible falsetto, and he cupped her elbow sweetly as if leading her to a church pew. When in fact he was leading her to bed.

Charlie's apartment was above a club called Arabian Nights and was filled with dirty ashtrays and unwashed undershirts and many books. He was interested in all sorts of things: the dharma and negro spirituals and poetry and communal living. When he spoke, Ursa wanted only to listen. The first time, he took off her dress and slip and bra, and then, before he took her breasts in his hands and bent down to kiss them, he asked, "Is it all right if I—?" No one had asked before. She gave in to him, and that permission was the greatest pleasure of all. Standing naked before him, with her body in his hands, Ursa didn't care about the thing. Or anything. The music from the club below pulsed through floorboards into Ursa's feet and up her legs.

"I'm glad you got the diaphragm," Karin now said as she blew her cigarette smoke out the open window.

Karin turned off Highway 1, and in minutes the landscape changed. The ocean was no longer visible, and with it went the sand and the scrubby brush. Karin rolled up her window. Here, the greenery was lush, the primordial trees clotted close at the edges of the road, and in places their leaves canopied overhead, shutting out the sunlight.

Ursa caught a glimpse of a stream with shaded boulders at its edge, which she imagined were icy to the touch. A hawk soared across the sky before plunging toward some unseen prey.

They passed through the town of Ben Lomond with its general store and post office, and Karin described the watering holes nearby and the perfect water of the San Lorenzo River, clear and cold, which began in the Santa Cruz mountains.

"It has magical properties," Karin said.

They wound their way out of Ben Lomond and deeper into the woods. The road curved, curved again, tapering, sharp as the tip of Ursa's long-ago candy cane. They drove and drove until Ursa began to wonder just how far from that charming town they could possibly go. She was about to ask when Karin slowed the car and turned off the paved highway onto dirt. Ursa could not see a road, or even a driveway. It was like they'd been swallowed by the woods.

Now Ursa understood how the Chevy had gotten so muddy, for Karin was driving it over uneven, wet ground. Tree boughs, soaked from a recent storm, slapped the windows, and the glass was streaked with their soggy leaves. Rocks pinged off the wheel wells.

And then, after another few turns, Karin crested an incline, and the house came into view.

A pause here, for the house—

It was massive, three stories tall, with a wide front porch and ornate carvings along the eaves, and a turret whose metal tip pierced the sky. Its gray exterior echoed the overcast clouds above, and as Karin nosed the car down a grand, unpaved driveway, lined on either side by redwoods, it was as if the house waited patiently for their approach. Though its porch and carved panels resembled the Queen Annes in San Francisco, it was far bigger than its urban counterparts, far more majestic. Solemn too. Ursa had never seen anything like it.

Karin rounded the house to park behind it, and Ursa saw that something blighted the home's elegance. A bulky, honeycomb-shaped dome was attached like a growth to its left side.

Oh, Ursa thought.

Karin seemed to read Ursa's mind. "That's the eastern wing," she said. "Henry and I built it right after we married. It was for his yoga practice."

The other day, Karin had explained to Ursa what yoga was.

"I know from here it looks as ugly as a stepchild," she continued. "Don't be fooled. Wait until you see it from the inside."

At that, Karin skipped out of the car, already getting their things from the trunk, calling out Henry's name as she carried them toward a side door. She had explained to Ursa that when she went to San Francisco, a night nurse came to care for Henry, empty his bedpans, that sort of thing. He didn't want anyone at the house otherwise, and he didn't mind Karin leaving for a day here or there, to see the world. She was young whereas he was old, and dying of cancer besides.

Ursa worried it might be creepy, being in this big house with her new friend and her dying husband. Yet as soon as she was through the mudroom and had taken in the enormous kitchen with its long pine table and the pots and pans hanging from the ceilings, even a giant fireplace, she knew this house was special and that she'd love it here. In the parlor were stained-glassed windows and damask walls and glistening wooden floors beneath their feet. The staircase was as wide as she was tall, a red and blue floral carpet draped over its steps and held in place by gold metal rods. It wasn't only its grandness that Ursa loved; the place felt alive, the way some houses do.

"Oh Karin," she said.

Here, in this alive house, in the middle of nowhere, would be better than in some cheap closet. She hadn't ventured into the armoire for weeks, and now she felt the urge. It was as if there was a door nearby, and someone was knocking. Or the door itself was knocking. All Ursa had to do was open it.

Ursa followed her friend upstairs, until, at the bedroom that was clearly Henry and Karin's, Karin made a gesture like, *Go on.*

"I'll just be a while," Karin said and disappeared into the sickroom.

Ursa wandered respectfully, as if on a tour of a castle that had been turned into a museum. She counted four bedrooms on the second floor, two furnished, one empty, one filled with junk: papers and furniture covered in sheets, and even old lawncare equipment. The empty bedroom was painted purple and had a window seat. All of them had chandeliers. Ursa discovered a dumbwaiter and admired the wainscoting on the walls, running her fingers along it, humming to herself. There were two bathrooms, both with clawfoot tubs and toilets with chain flushes.

The staircase to the turret was on the third floor. Ursa was surprised by how dizzy the rounded room made her feel. It was wood paneled and punctuated with windows, the glass of the windows thick. A solitary leather chair and ottoman waited, as if for her.

This place—confined, at the top of a house—would be a good place to do it.

Ursa's wrists tingled. The door was knocking.

If she went and Karin found out later, she might view it as a betrayal.

Ursa had to tell her first.

It's why she needed a friend, wasn't it?

Instead, she went to the windows to look out at the world below. Even from up here, she couldn't make out any roads or other signs of civilization beyond. There was only green: moss and olive, emerald and sage. It wasn't only the shades of color, it was their character too: rugged, slick, fleece, crumbling, clay. If she could lick them, each would feel different on her tongue.

She imagined bringing Charlie here.

Unfindable until you find it, she thought.

She couldn't wait any longer.

Ursa rushed out of the turret and down one set of stairs, and then another, and another, her breath snagging on a nail inside her as she hurried down the first-floor hallways. She thought she might go outside—fresh air would help, wouldn't it?

That wasn't where she was led.

The hallway angled abruptly to the right until it ended at a door that someone had painted baby blue. Here she stopped, gasping for air. She pushed the door open, and on the other side was the eastern wing.

It was a nearly empty hexagonal room. Nothing in it except a few hard-looking pillows scattered on the floor. It smelled stale—like its most devoted visitor was dying in a bed upstairs. There were no windows except the skylights above, and the light that fell through them was different than the milky-weak sun that rendered the rest of the house dim. Here that same light felt bright and rich. Ursa felt her body calm, her inhales and exhales slowing.

Karin, as always, had been correct: the room was special. There was something else here. The shape didn't set her off balance as the turret had. It energized her. This room, this *wing*, was not only the promise of safety and privacy but the result of it. A mansion hidden in the woods could have a honeycomb dome jutting off its side if you wanted it to. Out here, you could do whatever you pleased.

"It's groovy, right?" Karin asked from the open door. Ursa startled.

Ursa nodded, her eyes on the skylights above. Now, she thought, she should tell her now. Instead, she asked, "Why did you build this room if you already had so many?"

"Henry said the other rooms had too much history. And you know what? He was right. This place is a baby soul. The energy flows. You feel it, don't you?"

She did. It wasn't contained like the armoire, or even the turret, and yet she felt something gathering here, welcoming her. It wanted her to go back. To do so here.

"Does the door lock?" Ursa asked.

"Certainly." With a sly smile Karin walked over to the door and kicked it closed with her foot. When she turned the lock, it made no sound.

Ursa never thought she'd do it without warning, and she would have told Karin what she was about to do if she had the proper—or any—words for it. She didn't, and Ursa *had* to go, she was going, she was sinking to the floor, right in the center of this strange room, beneath the largest skylight, which was shaped like an almond or an eye. The room didn't let in the green world like the turret had, and that seemed, somehow, significant. The eastern wing wasn't high above, it was rooted to the ground, its beauty a secret. It was an underestimated place, and that's what made it spectacular.

"What's going on?" Karin said.

Ursa reached the floor and lay curled on her side. Karin might have thought her friend had fallen ill were it not for the looseness of Ursa's limbs, the way she surrendered to the wood slats beneath her, were it not for the way the room seemed to shutter and tilt before righting itself as Ursa gasped for air and held it in her rounded cheeks. The tilting happened imperceptibly, but Karin was perceptive, and she perceived it right away. It was as if the eastern wing were a film that lost focus and then found it, sharper, so sharp it could cut you. Ursa let out her breath, and her eyes, open, went blank as a sheet of paper, then closed.

To Karin, it was as if the room filled with a new kind of light. Milk turned to honey. It was like stepping into a warm bath, the way it made her nerves shimmer and purr. Karin thought she might die of bliss.

Ursa slipped into the yolky membrane. Back, back. It was easier than ever before. It had to be the influence of the eastern wing, where she remained, even if she was also here, four years earlier. Age fourteen, summer. Eleven months after her father's death, and she was running through the woods behind her house in her green bathing suit, bug bites spotting her legs. Ursa watched as her younger self ran. The tree branches were scratching her torso and the bug bites stung. Ursa could feel their calloused centers, their scabby peaks. Her knotted black hair was falling down her back and her mother would be upset to see it. She was running to swim because it was so hot. Her lungs might explode.

Imagine going back like that. Not only to conjure it—that isn't sufficient—but to live it. Can you imagine that?

Ursa could, especially here, in this big house, unfindable in the forest. When Ursa came to, Karin was on her knees, crying. Ursa felt, as always, that she was going to retch, her head pounding. She'd never stayed so long or felt it so vividly.

"Where did you go?" Karin asked.

Ursa said, "More like, *when* did I go?"

She tried to find some words to describe what she could do. "I usually do it in my closet, in my room. It's why I came to California."

"I'm so happy you did."

Ursa said, "Do you know anyone else like me?" and when Karin replied, "No," Ursa tried not to give away her despair, which seemed so pathetic. How could she have been this naïve?

Karin, who could read Ursa like a bus schedule, said, "Oh honey, it'll be okay. Better than that. This room shifted to some new plane! You have no idea. Do you think I entered a sort of timelessness just by being here with you? I must have. I mean, even the weather felt different."

She said Ursa had tapped into the powers of the goddess. The whole process lasted only a few minutes, and yet, Karin said, she would be irrevocably changed.

They were still on the floor beneath the largest skylight; neither made any move to leave.

"What do you call that?" Karin asked as she stroked Ursa's hair. Ursa was feeling a little better now; she would keep her breakfast down.

Ursa only shrugged.

"A transport," Karin said.

"I transported," Ursa said, smiling.

"You have a purpose," Karin continued. "A higher calling."

"I'm not sure about that," Ursa said, though she felt herself blushing and couldn't smother her relief that Karin hadn't run off.

Karin thought Ursa could do more with her transports, even help others. After all, Karin said, it felt so good to witness. She wanted to assist Ursa in any way she could.

"I was going to take you to meet Henry," Karin said. "Not right now, though. He wouldn't understand. Men never do, or they want it for themselves. You didn't show Charlie, did you?"

It had not even occurred to Ursa, and she said so.

"Good. It would be reckless to reveal this to a fling."

∞

Following this weekend outside Ben Lomond, a weekend that included meeting Henry (kind, old, sickly), and bathing in the creek (cold, glittering, exhilarating), and which did not, due to Ursa's nausea and headache, include transporting a second time though the two friends discussed it at length, Ursa returned to San Francisco, and to Charlie. To her surprise, the house receded from her mind as soon as they were back in the city, as did the eastern wing. It was as if it had been a dream. Charlie, on the other hand, was real.

He took her fishing, and as he folded a worm onto a hook for her, he said that back home in Idaho he preferred hunting for fish with a spear and a net.

She assumed he was kidding. He wasn't.

"A fishing net is beautiful," he said. "Empty or full."

Ursa didn't give one lick about transporting then.

They began to spend all their free time together, and Ursa was sure that Charlie's love—his lust too—would last forever. As would hers. When they could, they stayed in bed all day, and then, at night-fall, they went out to find a meal, and after they ate, they would walk for hours, and he would tell her about Idaho or about what he was reading and writing. She never tired of him; she wanted him.

Maybe, Ursa thought, Karin had been wrong about her purpose. Maybe it wasn't to use her gift, if that's what it was. Maybe it was easier (or harder) than that: it was to be happy. To be with Charlie. To feel safe. Charlie had never taken anything from her. That was the most important thing. Together they would shrug off the materialism of this world. Live a life like those described in his books. She was prepared to give up anything, everything, for him.

Three months later, when Henry died, Karin called Ursa on the telephone and said, "I'm going on a journey and I'm giving you my house."

Ursa was standing in the downstairs hallway; another tenant was trying to get past her with bags of groceries. Ursa nodded an apology and moved closer to the wall, phone cord wrapped around her torso.

"You can't leave," she said into the receiver. "I'll miss you too much. And you can't give me a house!"

"Fine, you're borrowing it," Karin said. "Better? Go to the eastern wing. Take care of everything while I'm gone. Promise me you'll cre-ate something magnificent there."

Ursa said she would. She was already imagining showing Charlie all the rooms. What they could do with them. Together.

That evening, Ursa told Charlie her plan at the same café where she'd met Karin, under that same red neon sign that read WATCH REPAIR. She described the house, the rooms, the privacy, the turret, the creek. She did not mention the eastern wing, remembering what Karin had told her about men.

"The property is amazing. They've even got reefer." This last word she whispered. "We could grow more, Karin said. To make money. Karin's going to India. For Henry, to honor him. She said she might not come back, not for years." She paused. "The house will be ours— to take care of, to have, basically. Imagine what we can do there, Charlie."

At first, he didn't answer.

"Charlie?"

"You know I'm an explorer," he finally said. "I thought you knew that."

Ursa, although young and naïve, understood like a punch to the face that for Charlie there was no *we*. He would never come to the house with Ursa, and because she had even mentioned it, he could not continue to see her. She had soured their sweet dalliance with her expectations.

"You understand, don't you?" he said.

"Of course," Ursa lied.

They parted ways amicably, or so Charlie assumed. To him, Ursa was just another young woman, taller than most, breasts larger than most, stranger and quieter than most, but simply another lover.

Ursa, on the other hand, wanted to die. If only she could transport to Charlie on their first night together, then she could be with him again and again and live in those days until it killed her. She couldn't, thankfully, it was too recent, and so, instead, she rushed home to the armoire and shut the doors. She transported until she vomited all over her new black shirt and black pants and then she cleaned herself up. Raked with nausea and a headache, she put on lipstick and curled her hair, and she headed to a club to find a man who would want her. Her diaphragm remained at home.

∞

Ursa arrived in the woods beyond Ben Lomond a few weeks later, her few belongings in a bag by her feet. Her menses was late.

A consequence.

Tucked inside of her womb, like a penny in a pocket, was Ray. He would be born the following autumn.

2

In 1955, two years before Ursa moved to the house outside Ben Lomond, it rained and rained until the banks of the San Lorenzo River overflowed, causing the deadliest flood in the county's recorded history. Ursa had no idea, only that the trees on the land were greener than green. She also didn't know that the mountains she so admired had been tunneled into to make way for a railroad, which had, less than a century later, been dismantled, piece by piece, to make way for a highway, which would defile the mountain even further.

Ursa was too focused on her own story, as small as it was.

All she knew was that she'd been living alone in a beautiful house for half a year, growing bigger each day, more orb than woman, speaking to nearly no one. She knew that Karin had left for India and that Charlie didn't love her. That she was carrying a stranger's baby who made her sicker than transporting ever could, which made transporting, her main reason for leaving San Francisco, impossible. And that she would soon be an unwed mother, her own mother's worst nightmare.

Ursa was, once again, alone.

Soon after moving into the house outside of Ben Lomond, she'd rolled up the staircase's floral carpet and unhooked two of the chandeliers and drove them into Half Moon Bay in the truck Karin so despised. She sold them to an antique dealer.

Was this what Karin meant by creating something magnificent? Certainly not, but Ursa needed the cash. She had nothing. She had no one.

This was the story she had always told herself, wasn't it?

∞

Not six months later, Ursa's myth of herself as a solitary creature was cracked in two by the arrival of a woman Ursa had never seen before. The stranger showed up one morning in the driveway, so tiny between the rows of redwoods, like a sprite among giants. For better or for worse, that's how Ursa would forever think of Mary: as a sweet, weightless thing.

She seemed to emerge out of nowhere, a woman appearing among the trees like an apparition, and as she got closer to Ursa, who was seven months pregnant and sweating on one of the porch's rocking chairs, details revealed themselves one by one: the straw bag on her shoulder and the bouquet of lavender in her hand—an offering, she later told Ursa. She wore a man's shirt and a man's dungarees, like she was prospecting for gold.

"Are you Ursa?" the woman asked when she reached the porch. She was probably twenty, twenty-two, and gorgeous, with green eyes and long orange hair, freckles everywhere. Mud splattered her pant legs, and she was out of breath. "If you are, these are for you." She thrust the lavender at Ursa, who did not take it.

"Who are you?" Ursa asked.

"I'm Mary. Karin sent me."

Mary placed the lavender on the porch railing and pulled something out of her straw bag. Ursa tried to keep her face neutral when she saw that it was a postcard of the Taj Mahal, the same one Karin had sent to the post office box in Ben Lomond. How could Karin send them the exact same postcard?

Mary told Ursa to turn the postcard over and read it, so she did.

If you feel lost go to my house.

A girl named Ursa is there taking care of it for me. She'll help you. She has a gift.

A girl named Ursa. Was that all she was? Karin said she had a gift. Did she? She could barely recall transporting, it had been so long. Even now, sitting still on the rocker, her last meal—a bowl of rice— was settling badly. Acid rose in her chest. She suppressed a burp.

"Karin didn't say you were pregnant," Mary said.

Ursa chose not to mention that Karin had no idea of the pregnancy.

"What do you need help with?" Ursa asked finally, handing back the postcard.

"What do you mean?"

"Karin wrote that I could help you. But what do you need help with?" Ursa placed a hand on her stomach. "Clearly, I'm in a pickle myself."

Mary told her she was living with a man, a farmer, outside of Los Gatos. That these were his clothes, actually. That she didn't speak to her parents anymore.

"They're in Santa Barbara. But it's the dreams I need help with."

She ascended the porch steps and sat in the empty rocker next to Ursa.

Mary's green eyes glittered, teary. "Griffin—the guy I'm going with? I had him let me off in town. I didn't want him to know where I'd gone. I walked here. It took a long time, but I just knew I had to come alone, without the aid of a vehicle. I felt pulled here."

"It's the house," Ursa said as she struggled out of the rocking chair. "It pulled me in too."

"Like a magnet," Mary said.

She said that she had turned off the road and wound her way along the path through the woods until she hit the hill and trudged up it, and when she saw the enormous house waiting for her, she had wanted to sink to her knees, crying out in gratitude.

"The house coaxed you forward, didn't it?" Ursa asked

"How did you know?"

Ursa hadn't, it just seemed like an interesting thing to say. She was now standing, revealing her full height, towering over Mary in her rocker. Her head blocked the sun, a border of light behind her like an angel's halo.

"It's also *you*," Mary replied. "You're the pull."

Ursa wanted to push Mary's puny bunch of lavender off the porch railing and, right at the last moment, thought better of it. The hormones—they were a possession all their own. "I bet you wish your man were here to drive you home," she said.

"The opposite."

"You should know that my gift isn't happening right now. Pregnancy won't allow it."

"Are you planning to be pregnant forever?"

A fine point, Ursa thought.

"It's a good thing the farmer didn't come with you," Ursa said, "because men aren't allowed on the property unless absolutely necessary."

There it was: Ursa's first rule. She liked how it felt.

Mary raised an eyebrow and nodded at Ursa's belly. "No men, huh?" She laughed, a little twinkly fairy bell laugh, and Ursa couldn't help but laugh too, and she sat back down in her rocking chair.

Ursa paused. "I don't know anything about dreams."

"What do you know about?"

"Once this baby is born, I'll show you."

∞

Mary moved in. Ursa had already taken the third floor and didn't want anyone up there with her. She showed Mary the rooms on the second story and told her to take her pick.

Mary chose the first door by the stairs. Ursa was relieved she didn't pick the largest room with the window seat, which was painted purple. She wasn't sure why, only that her gut told her someday it would have other uses.

"I hate to sleep alone," Mary said.

"Maybe others will join us," Ursa said.

Mary laughed her tinkly fairy laugh.

After that, she took over many of the house duties that Ursa, in her state, had neglected. Mary worked in the garden and did all the grocery shopping. She found Ursa a midwife who would trade care for reefer. And she agreed to meet with Lee, the man who had overseen the marijuana for Karin and Henry.

The marijuana was planted at the back of property, bordered by the live oak trees on one end and the creek on the other. Lee tended to it and harvested it too. It was a tiny operation, if it could even be called that, yet it did bring in money.

"Have Lee teach you how to do everything," Ursa told Mary.

"What about you?"

"You'll teach me."

"It'll be easier if you talk to him too."

Ursa refused. "It should only be me if absolutely necessary." Another rule.

When Lee pulled into the driveway, Ursa went up to the turret and turned the deadbolt. To hide, some might say, though Ursa thought of it as keeping watch.

∞

From her perch in the turret, Ursa oversaw developments on the property below. Mary turned out to be a whiz at marijuana cultivation. After Lee gave her a final tutorial, Mary bedded him, becoming pregnant, unbeknownst to Lee, who would never meet his child, let alone know he had fathered one. Not long after that affair, the first contraction squeezed Ursa's womb, a signal either from or for the baby that his arrival was imminent.

"Breech," the midwife said, as Ursa squatted on a red towel in the downstairs parlor, her body stretched stem to stern; she was a rubber band about to snap.

Forty hours after the first contraction, Ray emerged bottom first. His mother imagined him scratching her insides with his fingernails on his reluctant exit.

Ray. The love of Ursa's life. Here he is, squawking, pink, hair sopping with amniotic fluid. Ursa thinks he is the most beautiful baby to have ever been born.

Those first tender weeks of Ray's life were heavenly in a way Ursa didn't expect: his eyes gray and glossy as marbles, umbilical nub drying to stone at his navel, the godly seam of his testes, Ursa's breasts smarting with milk. She knew that one day she would transport back to these weeks, and she wished she didn't have to wait, for already Ray looked different than he had the day before. Perhaps, she thought, the true purpose of her gift was to return to a younger version of her child.

Any mother would do it, if she could. Wouldn't she?

When Ray was a month old, Ursa led Mary into the eastern wing. It was finally time to show Mary what she could do. Ursa didn't feel quite ready—she was so tired from the nursing, and afterbirth still soaked the pads the midwife had sewn for her—but she couldn't put it off any longer.

It was the full moon of November, and right then, facing the eastern wing's blue door, Ursa decided another rule. If she could still transport—it had been months, after all—she didn't want to be asked to do it all the time. And what if she wanted to do it on her own, privately?

"I can only do it on a full moon," Ursa said. A third rule.

"May the moon be open," Mary replied.

It was cold that night, the baby bundled in three blankets and the women in baggy wool coats they discovered in an upstairs closet; they resembled bedraggled soldiers who had wandered from their infantry.

They had wrapped scarves around their necks and wished they had something to cover their noses. Their breath was smoke.

Mary was wise enough to be patient, not to pry, to light the candles in silence, the shadows from their lit wicks flittering against the wall. She opened her arms to Ursa, and Ursa handed her bundled Ray, his face scrunched up against the cold.

Unencumbered, Ursa sat cross-legged on one of Henry's pillows, the green one, and shook out her arms and shoulders. She closed her eyes. The day before, she realized that enough time had passed since she'd arrived in California; she could return to those moments if she wanted to. And she did want to—badly. It had been so long since she'd done this.

She took a breath, and as the air expanded her lungs she sensed the buzz, the yolk, the drippy place. It was far off, but it was there.

Baby Ray began to cry. A weak mewl at first, nothing Ursa couldn't shut out as she hurtled away.

Ray's cries grew louder and more insistent, and they brought Ursa back into the eastern wing. She opened her eyes. It was cold. Her nose was cold.

Mary was pacing with the baby, jiggling him. She did not even seem interested in the transport.

"He wants his mama," she said.

"That's only what you perceive. Put him upstairs. Come right back before you miss it."

When Mary returned, Ursa was already going, she was gone, and if Ray was crying, the women couldn't hear him from behind the closed door of the eastern wing.

By then, neither of them cared. Ursa was crossing the bridge, she was at the darkest spot, all shade and metal, Treasure Island brambly below, her hand grasping the car door, whereas Mary was bathed in her friend's timelessness, the eastern wing wobbling once then straightening, tightening, brightening. The room filled with what Mary thought was moonlight, starlight. She felt a rush. Her scalp tingled.

This was what Karin dreamed of, Ursa thought later. Something magnificent.

And Ray? He was fine. He was safe. He fell asleep in Ursa's warm room on the third floor.

Taking care of children requires being tethered to the present, to an endless parade of daily tasks, to the *now*. That wouldn't work for someone with this gift.

Thus, another rule, which Ursa announced the next morning over their bowls of millet porridge: No children—not Ray, not Mary's baby, who would be born on the property in eight months—would be allowed in the eastern wing. Ever.

"Whatever you want," Mary said, her spoon aloft.

It was into this world that another woman arrived, and another, then another. There emerged a whole universe of rules, an order to this house in the woods.

∞

Let's skip ahead. Time sometimes works like this, doesn't it? It slips by so fast you can barely keep track of the days, they flow together, blurring, one into the next and the next.

Let's slip past Ray learning to sit up, to eat, to walk. Past the four women who arrive that first year—Joan, Natasha, Rose, and Annie. Most come alone, with little more than a sack of clothing and a few worthless trinkets, maybe a bottle of alcohol. Natasha arrives with ten pounds of ground beef and a six-month-old. Annie gives birth in a clearing by herself at dawn. Two more women arrive as Ray is speaking in full sentences, and then there are five other children: Tara, Hawk, Amethyst, Dom, and Baxter. Ray and his mother sleep in the large bedroom on the third floor, down the hall from the stairs that lead to the turret. The others board in the rooms below. Bunkbeds have been purchased.

By now all but one of the chandeliers are gone, as are the sideboard from the parlor and the tufted two-sided mahogany courting chair, curved like the letter *S*, that the antique dealer in Half Moon Bay said was also called a gossip couch. The little bedroom off the kitchen, which had once been Karin's father's office, is now known as the dressing room—the desk sold. Inside this room, clothing drifts into piles, and the women—the kids call them the mamas—venture in for what they need, picking over tops and overalls and dresses like birds at a dump. Ursa's clothing is folded neatly with Ray's in their bedroom bureau; she says she is too tall to share with the others. The kids belong to all the mamas, except Ray, who belongs resolutely to Ursa.

More women arrive. When Ray turns two there are eight of them.

Men come to pour the foundation for the addition, to be erected on the western end of the house when Ray is two and a half, as far from the eastern wing as possible. For four months, the children are commanded to stay inside, sequestered in the purple room on the second floor as the construction progresses. The men cannot see them, or count them, or know them, Ursa tells Mary, who tells everyone else. "We're keeping them safe" is what the mamas tell each other. A new boarder, her daughter is named Liesl, is directed to watch the children, and two weeks before the construction ends, she and Liesl take off. It's an inconvenience rather than a crisis; the woman was new to the property, not right for this place, the sort of temporary visitor the addition is being built for. She was just a boarder, a mother not a *mama*—she hadn't even been invited to a transport. Ursa won't let just anyone in.

As for the transports, the same rules apply: only on a full moon, mamas only. The children have no idea what happens in the eastern wing. They don't know that Mary lights the candles before they begin, and that Henry's pillows remain. That there are now blankets for when it's chilly.

There are also stones, because the second winter a woman showed up with nuggets of pyrite. This woman offered two handfuls of this fool's gold and claimed its gravity stimulated the intellect, that it aided physical vigor. The next transport, Ursa did indeed feel stronger, and, by the next full moon, the mamas had lined the edges of the eastern wing with pyrite. Later, they added turquoise for protection, followed by agate for perception, which Ursa doubted helped all that much. They looked pretty, however, and it was imperative to impress newcomers. A little theater.

A little theater. The phrase popped into Ursa's head one afternoon as she watched the mamas washing the stones to prepare them for another transport in the eastern wing. The mamas witnessed Ursa go back in time on every open moon, and between these transports, they played music, bathed in the creek, and danced in the forest. There was also gardening and cooking to do, and a mansion to clean. There was brush to clear, and a road to maintain. Mary taught them how to pick the marijuana and sort it and pack it. Their fingers bled. They had to go out and sell.

They did it all without complaint because of those nights in the eastern wing. Every one of the mamas said the room changed when Ursa transported, and that *they* changed; it was like being lifted off into space. Ursa untethered them from whatever was keeping them here, keeping them small and powerless. The following days, every mama felt a little stoned. Cheekier and joyous. They felt lighter because they could still recall what it felt like to be unburdened by time.

They weren't wrong.

Ursa did occasionally transport by herself, in the hen house or in her room if Ray was outside playing. Always secretly. She would visit her baby's first year, the moment he was brought to her breast. His cradle cap like a net over his scalp. The first time he vocalized, *dah dah dah.* These private transports were pleasurable; yet, to Ursa, they seemed shallower. Ursa needed an audience.

A little theater, she thought.

∞

Time passed in this way, a fairly happy era for Ursa, with Ray, who built forts out of the kindling and learned to weigh the reefer for

Mary. The mamas had begun to drink fresh mint tea every morning in silence, a kind of communion, they called it, a way to relax into the possibility of timelessness, and Ursa found she enjoyed it too. Soon enough it became another rule: the morning ritual. The occasional postcards from Karin said things like *You're the power of the goddess!*, and although these slogans were a poor substitute for friendship, they did at least offer Ursa a jolt of pride. She had made something magnificent here, hadn't she? The property boasted two additions by now, as well as the expanded marijuana plot, and twelve mamas, nine children, and always one or two boarders. Ray turned three.

It wasn't until an unseasonably warm January morning, just after dawn, when the sound of a car engine pulled Ursa out of sleep, that things began to go sideways.

That morning, Ray slept diagonally beside his mother, his hair wet with sweat, his thumb in his mouth, which was raspberry pink and shimmering with spittle.

Ursa sat up at the sound. A car, definitely. Approaching. There was supposed to be a mama on watch at all times, but last night they had all stayed up late drinking. Whoever had fallen asleep in the new lookout cottage on the path to the driveway would get an earful.

She locked Ray in her bedroom and climbed the stairs to the turret to get a better look. Unless it was an officer or someone coming to rob the weed, they'd be fine. Men rarely showed up here unannounced; even the kids who had daddies saw them by appointment only. Ursa hated when women arrived at odd times, not that it could be avoided; desperation didn't keep regular business hours.

The car came into view. It wasn't police and it seemed to be driving too carefully to have criminal motives, and as it pulled in front of the house and parked, Ursa thought she could see two people in the front seats. If there was a man, someone would have to come down with the airhorn and tell him to shoo. Get the gun if he didn't. Locals knew the rules, though occasionally someone was an idiot. Ursa didn't mind if a man came by—someone's daddy, someone fixing a pipe—as long as it was necessary. "Is he relevant?" is how the women put it. And they had to be on the calendar. No surprises. They needed enough time to herd the children into the purple room, and Ursa usually went up to the turret. The mamas said her absence made outsiders fear her, it intimidated them, and the women laughed about how she used it to her advantage.

It was in this self-satisfied reverie that the driver stepped out of the car.

It was Charlie.

Charlie.

He looked as handsome as ever in his plaid shirt and tan trousers. He didn't have the braid anymore; his hair was still long, and he wore it loose like tangled straw, parted in the middle, his scalp white. He wore the same big beard, coming in copper here and there. Ursa couldn't wait to smell it.

Charlie didn't approach the house. Instead, he walked to the other side of his car, a white Ford berried with rust at the wheel wells. Ursa held her breath.

He opened the passenger door like a goddamned chauffeur.

A woman got out—more like a girl. She was very, very pregnant.

Ursa reared back from the window as if burned by the glass. The pregnant girl looked young—no older than twenty, probably more like eighteen. Her brown hair was tangled like his was, parted in the middle like his was. Her dress was a blue sack that strained at her belly and at her breasts. She wore boots.

Charlie helped to steady her, and from the window Ursa watched as he placed a hand on her belly so tenderly, and with such familiarity, that she knew at once that this was his baby. Ursa let out a little squeak. Rage like a fist closed over her throat.

Ursa left the turret and hurried downstairs. She emerged through the front door with a smile pasted across her face, her long nightgown sucked between her thighs as she strode across the porch and down the steps to where Charlie stood with the girl.

Ursa was naked beneath the nightgown, which left her breasts to hang pendulous beneath. She hoped Charlie would remember how they felt against his face, how great his cock felt nestled in the deep cradle of their cleavage. Her nipples were two dark shadows behind the white muslin fabric, her pubis the third, and she wanted him to remember that too.

Charlie seemed put off by her state of deshabille, though wasn't it just after dawn? What did he expect? He kept his eyes on her face.

"Ursa! I knew it would be you!"

He didn't touch her at all, not a hug or even a handshake, not even after she left to grab a robe and her child, to introduce them, no matter that it was against house rules. Charlie *did* shake Ray's little hand and when he said, "Pleased to meet you," he did so genuinely. If Charlie was at all concerned that the boy was his, he hid it well; it looked as if the curious timing of Ray's existence had never crossed his mind, so far from his thoughts was Ursa's naked body.

The girl's name was Ruth. The couple had driven in from Stinson. They'd loved living there, Charlie said, but it hadn't worked out, and eventually they'd go back to San Francisco where a friend said they could crash. As Charlie explained this, Ruth shrugged, then smiled, and when Mary appeared from inside the house, asking Ruth in her kind murmur if she'd been to a doctor or a midwife, Ruth remained untroubled. More self-assured than Ursa liked. This was not how pregnant women typically arrived.

Charlie said, "When I heard someone named Ursa was running a house for women out here, I knew it had to be you."

"That's not what this is," she said, trying to keep her voice light.

"Ruth can stay," Mary said. "You'll have to go."

Charlie did not argue. He took a small suitcase out of the trunk and handed it to Mary.

"I'll be back," he said to Ruth, and kissed her neck, rubbed her belly.

"Why not take her to a hospital?" Ursa asked coldly.

"I have to see my brother in Idaho," Charlie said, pulling himself away from Ruth. "I need to take care of some business. You can help Ruthie while I'm gone, can't you?"

∞

Ruth was from some shit town in Kern County, near Bakersfield. She didn't call it that—a shit town—Ursa did, in her mind. Outwardly, she made herself charitable. Mary had tried to show the girl a bed in the western addition, next to the other boarder, Anna, and Ursa said they should make an exception. Put her inside the big house, with the mamas. She was about to pop, she said. They needed to watch over her. Mary only squinted at Ursa for a moment before agreeing.

As the mamas showed Ruth around the property, Ursa imagined Charlie coming back and seeing his girl magnetized to this place. Would Ruth even want Charlie anymore? Imagine that. Ursa would use the girl to break his heart.

Only it didn't work.

Ruth was not a seeker, Ursa realized. Not like the others. The other women believed Ursa had a gift, and her presence comforted them. Even the boarders who didn't know what was going on in the eastern wing wanted to be near Ursa. They wanted her to heal them.

Ruth didn't want to be healed because she wasn't hurt. She came from people who loved her. Her mother was a babysitter, and her father worked the oil fields. She had a younger brother who was touched. He wore a diaper at age fifteen and barely spoke; Ruth's grandmother took care of him during the day, and he was cherished by everyone, as Ruth was. The worst thing that had ever happened to her was becoming pregnant because she couldn't tell her parents what she'd done. She had written her mother and father a letter to tell them she was all right and nothing more; she knew they worried.

Someday, she told the mamas, she and Charlie would return, married, with their child. She hoped she would be forgiven.

Ursa couldn't figure her out. She didn't want to call them mamas, or sing songs with them, or learn about the garden, or smoke any reefer. The only thing she seemed to want were cherries. And it was January, so there were no cherries.

Ursa took pleasure in denying her this one thing, at least.

It shouldn't have been a surprise, when, two weeks later, Mary handed Ruth her bald baby, crying and covered in vernix, and Ruth said, "Hi, baby girl. Hi, Cherry."

Ursa hated Cherry from her first breath.

Loved her too, in some twisted way, because she looked just like Charlie.

∞

Cherry was nine days old when Ruth took off in the middle of the night. The mamas were surprised. Why didn't she wait for Charlie?

Ursa told the mamas she woke up and found the baby by the door.

She told the mamas they would care for Cherry until Charlie returned.

It took two months for them to receive the letter at their post office box that said he'd been shot in a bar fight in Idaho. He'd been dead longer than his daughter had been alive.

At the news of his passing, Ursa's anger, her despair, grew bigger and taller than the house and the redwoods leading up to it, than the mountains whose beauty so astonished her.

She came home from the post office and ordered the mamas to find a new place to store their clothing. The little room off the kitchen, she said, would belong to Cherry. The orphan deserved it, she explained.

Her instincts were twofold: She wanted to make sure the poor child never felt a lack. And to make her cry in a room by herself.

After Charlie's death, Ursa felt only rage and unhappiness. At first, she could barely eat, and then a switch flipped, and she couldn't stop; for a week she consumed an inordinate quantity of food, stuffing herself, as if it might pack the wound. One morning, she yelled at a boarder for trying to join them in the morning ritual before being invited to do so and had the woman exiled from the property. When Mary let three pounds of potatoes rot, Ursa nearly slapped her. That was on a Wednesday morning, just after the teacups had been washed and put away and they were alone in the pantry.

"You need to transport," Mary said finally, once Ursa stopped yelling. They would head to the eastern wing in two nights.

"So you perceive."

"I perceive you need to transport."

"I perceive I need a bullet to the head."

"Who was Charlie to you?" Mary whispered.

Ursa began to cry, the humiliation as fresh as it had been that morning when Charlie put his hand on Ruth's pregnant belly. As fresh as the night he'd told her he didn't care to move to the woods with her and she'd gone and fucked a stranger in foolish revenge. She didn't matter to Charlie, nor did Ray. And now Charlie was dead.

"Was he Ray's father?" Mary asked.

"I wish," Ursa replied, surprising herself. Mary, who knew full well that Ursa could have lied and hadn't, loved her all the more for it. She took the moldy potato out of her friend's hand and, plopping it into her apron pocket, said, "You'll transport to him. To a happier time."

Ursa had no desire to do that, to transport at all. What was the point? Her past had been as hopeless as her present—as her future.

"It's loss you're feeling," Mary said.

"I know, I'm not an idiot."

"You don't get it. Loss is why we're all here. You said it yourself."

Had she? She had. In the eastern wing.

"The mamas need you," Mary said. "So does Ray."

That was true. Ray was only three and he'd been worried about his mother, had asked the other mamas to get her soup or something because Mama Ursa seemed sick.

"Use your loss to go deeper into the past," Mary said, her hands on Ursa's shoulders.

"It's not like you to be so bossy," Ursa said.

Mary shrugged and drew a hand through her orange hair. "Let your loss guide you."

Wiping her nose with her sleeve, Ursa imagined how wretched she must look, screaming at Mary over potatoes. She was exhausted. For two months, Ursa had slept with both Ray and Cherry in her bed; now the baby was downstairs in a crib the mamas had purchased in Santa Cruz. Without Cherry, Ursa's bed felt too big, and so cold. Charlie would never return to find them.

And so, two nights later, at the next full moon, Ursa told herself the transport would be different because *she* was different. She would heed Mary's words.

The children were locked into the purple room. She had to admit, walking into the eastern wing, she felt a little frisson of energy. The desire hadn't, in fact, disappeared, it had simply been hiding from her grief and anger. Now, encircled by the mamas—nine of them, their faces bisected with sage ash (another recent development)—the pyrite glittering along the walls, Ursa felt certain that the transport would be changed by what had happened. By her loss. She wasn't a fraud. She wasn't a thing to hurt or abandon. She was a woman, a mother.

She shut her eyes, whooshing into the membrane faster than ever. The eastern wing began to glow and tremble; it shook so viciously that Judith worried it was an earthquake until the room stopped to a stillness she'd never experienced before. The bliss overtook them like a drug.

Ursa hammered into the past she wanted. Charlie. Meeting him. Before this night, she had always held back from transporting here: to Karin shouting his name, and her first sight of the man across the warm bar, sipping his whiskey so calmly.

The bar, here it was.

Here—

At once it felt different.

What was it?

Ursa's body. Her body was here. Translucent as a ghost, flickering like a candle, but nevertheless present.

The place felt as vivid as it had the first time: the bar surface bumpy with white tiles as tiny as gum chiclets, the shelves of glass liquor bottles along the wall, and the handwritten sign that read CHILI DOGS, ¢ .40. The broken clock by the cash register—its hands always pointed at XII.

Even if Ursa glowed, even if no one in the bar could see her, Ursa could see and feel herself, and she felt as solid as ever.

By the bartender there waited an open jar of goopy maraschino cherries, red as an iodine tincture. In the eastern wing, the mamas moaned.

Ursa was no longer bodiless, no longer merely an invisible eye, floating without direction. She was present in a way she hadn't been before. Her heart was here: gauzy, yes, yet pumping. Her see-through tongue moved in her see-through mouth. Finally, finally, she had brought her physical form—or at least some spiritual version of it—to the past. Just as she'd always hoped to.

Ursa turned to get a better view of her younger self staring at Charlie, who was saying something to the bartender. Translucent Ursa felt the swoop in younger Ursa's belly. She kicked at the stool legs, nervous. There was that fateful glittering Ursa remembered, only now it wasn't memory but a living fact, inside of her once more, the warmth spreading across her skin, the fur of desire.

Ursa wanted to touch her own shoulder. What would happen?

In the eastern wing, the mamas gasped—it felt more intense than usual, and they didn't understand why.

Ursa's limpid, jellyfish hand slipped right through her solid, younger self, impaling her without making a mark, and the scene wobbled. Ursa, sensing the danger, let her hand drop by her side. She would observe. She would behave.

With her body present, she could take in more of the moment, control what she focused on: she could see behind her younger self, and step closer to Charlie (she didn't dare touch him), and smell him, and see herself from his side of the bar. If she stepped too far from them, trying to view the world beyond her experience, the image wobbled again and went dreary, threatening to disappear, so she stopped. She told herself to just observe and feel. She didn't want to get ahead of herself.

Ursa was still in the eastern wing, lying on the floor, held there by the ring of mamas. Even as she stood in the bar, she sensed the women around her; she heard them breathing, felt their heat, smelled the bark of their womenhood. But she was also a body in the past. Embodying that past.

She was *here*.

When Ursa returned to the present, the mamas wanted to do it again. They begged her; the next day, they were all sick, headaches like an epidemic.

A gift.

A curse.

Once they were recovered, Ursa told Mary the house needed to be even more well-hidden than it already was. Consider the reefer, she said. Consider what goes on in the eastern wing. She and the mamas needed more security.

And so Mary hired a construction crew to remove some boulders and uproot trees, and the machines they brought carved a path that would spit strangers back onto the road. Off the main path sprouted other, narrower paths; these roads spread across the land like tentacles, paths upon paths, and only one reached the house.

Three months later, the mazes were finished.

Now only the mamas knew which path was the right one; a mama would have to invite an outsider to the house and lead him to it.

Ursa was finally unfindable.

3

YEARS PASSED, TIME'S ACCRUAL AT ONCE GRADUAL AND sudden. Somewhere along the way, Karin had gotten word that the women were raising children in her big house. By the time she shipped the iridescent moth wings from Thailand, Ray was nearly eleven and Cherry was seven. Karin had taken to sending the kids little gifts. The message accompanying this one read *They sparkle!*

After Hawk suggested they decorate the redwoods lining the driveway with them, a newish mama named Gertie showed him how to mix the crushed-up wings with rubber cement, and all the kids went out with paint brushes to slop the rough red bark with their sparkle. The trunks now glittered.

"Nice!" said Taz, who at age four had only about fifteen words, *nice* being one of the better ones.

"Looks like magical snot," Cherry said.

"Like Mama Ursa's snot," Hawk said, and they all laughed, including Ray, even though he knew his mother's snot didn't sparkle.

Later, when Mama Ursa saw the trees glowing from the porch, she remarked how mysterious and wonderfully strange they looked. Ray heard her voice shift into pronouncement-mode as she said, "Let the children do this every month before the open moon."

The kids were pleased because, for the first time, they would possess a ritual of their own. They hoped Karin would send them a bigger package eventually; this supply would be depleted by spring.

A lot had changed in seven and a half years. Not that the kids could remember what life had been like before Cherry was born, before Ruth fled and Charlie died. It was as if they'd always known the tentacles leading off the main path so that any stranger trying to find the house would fail and likely be led back onto the road. They had no idea that there used to be boarders here, regular as hotel visitors and that women would just drop by, asking for healing. Nowadays, someone new came to live with them very rarely and with much fanfare, only after the mamas had met with her many times off the property. The kids knew the eastern wing was for mamas only and only on an open moon, and that for a few days afterward, things were, as the kids called it, bad-good. Bad because the mamas were usually sick. Good because they seemed happy despite their headaches and diarrhea. They laughed easily and would hug the kids tighter, sing them whatever songs they requested, even bake a cake if they had the sugar.

At ten, Ray was more curious about what the mamas were doing in the eastern wing. Tara was convinced they were doing drugs, Hawk thought they were probably kissing, and Cherry had decided it was special praying. Ray pointed out that the mamas did all those things freely outside of the eastern wing. Mamas were known to get frisky with one another during or after a fiddle session. And they smoked plenty of the reefer, not to mention the mushrooms they steeped as tea, or the tabs of acid they'd place on their tongues on special occasions. Drugs weren't verboten. So why shut themselves up to do them privately?

The only clue was in the morning ritual, when the mamas fell silent, breathing deeply, sipping their mint tea, until Mama Ursa, speaking into her empty mug, said, "We are timeless" and they all held their hands in prayer, or they grinned and said *awomen*. The kids weren't invited to the morning ritual, though it occurred in the kitchen so anyone could catch pieces of it.

"How can someone be timeless?" Ray asked his mother one night in their bed. He assumed he was old enough to be treated like an adult.

"It's just something we say," she said, "so as not to be tied to this earthly plane."

Ray tried not to be disappointed by her reply, so vague as to be more feint than answer. It was late, and he had fallen asleep before his mother's getting ready for bed pulled him from a dream. In the low light of the Tiffany table lamp, in the watery unreality of half sleep, he felt newly courageous to ask what he wanted to know.

"Can you tell me what happens in the eastern wing?"

Mama Ursa, mammoth in her long white nightgown, reached to turn off the light, bathing the room in darkness. "We're meditating," her voice finally said from the other side of the bed.

The way she said it, imperious yet tender, closing the door to more questions, told him she would never reveal the truth.

His mother must have sensed his dissatisfaction because in the dark she whispered that she had another secret to share with him.

"You promise me you won't tell a soul?" she asked.

He promised.

"My first name," she whispered, "before I became Ursa, was Sharon."

He wanted to say *who cares?* though he was smart enough not to. Instead, he thanked her for telling him.

"You must never say it aloud," his mother said.

After a moment, he told her that after tonight he'd be bringing a twin mattress up to their room. There was plenty of space for it.

"You don't want to be in the beddy-by?"

"I'm growing up," he said.

"I see," she replied.

Ray hadn't intended to hurt his mother, though if she had told him the truth about the eastern wing, he would have waited to bring the second mattress into their room. It wasn't until later, when he and

Cherry had run from the woods and the mamas and, especially, his mother, that he realized this was where their break had begun.

∞

At school in town, Ray whispered not a word about the other kids on his property, and he shed the ways the mamas spoke as soon as he could taxonomize what was normal and what was not. When his mother didn't show up for conferences or holiday shows, he explained she was too ill to do so. His teachers assumed she was bedridden but not dying, and Ray let that assumption follow him from grade to grade. Ray was careful never to get into trouble, and he aced fewer tests than he could have; if he was too smart, he knew, they would attempt to contact his mother. Good luck with that: the phone number on the forms was a string of made-up digits. The line Karin had installed had been dead forever—Ray imagined his mother cutting the line as soon as she'd arrived here. Now it was used only for games. Once Mama Mary had picked up the receiver and said, "Hello? Hi, yes, can I please exchange my bosom for a larger set? Thank you!" The mamas sitting around the kitchen table shrieked with laughter.

A few years before Ray learned his mother's name, the university in Santa Cruz opened, and suddenly their nearby city wasn't as sleepy. There would be more interest in this land, and the vulnerable bodies on it, Mama Ursa warned. There would also be more buyers for their product—college students were a goldmine. Ray thought he might want to be a college student someday. He and Mama Mary met one of them, a guy who called himself Code, every other Tuesday in the woods of Henry Cowell. Code sold their reefer on campus, and he often had books sprayed across the car's front passenger seat. He'd told Ray he was majoring in English.

"We read novels all day," he explained.

Now that Ray went to school, he was allowed to go on errands like this; it was the girls his mother seemed to worry about most.

"Watch yourself," she warned Tara when she slipped off her dress at the creek, revealing what another mama named breast buds.

Tara looked down at herself. "Watch for what?"

"I'll tell you later," Mama Ursa replied, and Ray thought it had something to do with "vulnerable bodies." His body wasn't as vulnerable, he guessed.

The other kids were occasionally allowed to leave the property with a mama, but only to go to boring public places like the store, and never as a group. Mama Ursa was afraid people would have questions about what went on in their house. That was why only Ray went to school. If any of the children left the property, to go to the beach, maybe, or down to the post office or Harold's grocery store in Ben Lomond, it was always solo, with one mama. And you had to brush your hair first. You had to wear shoes.

Ray taught the older ones to read, though none of them seemed to get very good at it, nor did they really have the opportunity to improve. It wasn't that they were stupid or ignorant; their knowledge was just different. All of them knew the names for plants and trees, and the older ones knew how to play the fiddle or the guitar and how to drive the truck. They knew how to grow and cook their own food and how to forage for mushrooms.

They knew everything about marijuana. They were good at math, addition and fractions in particular, because the reefer sales required it.

The first color they learned was purple, because of the purple room.

Sometimes, waiting in that room with the other kids as a daddy visited or an electrician fixed the faulty wiring in the parlor, Ray imagined scratching the paint off the walls until every trace of purple disappeared. Call it something else—the prison, maybe.

In that room, he and Cherry looked at books, the pathetic, spine-snapped rejects from his school library. As the younger kids took turns wrestling with Hawk, who never seemed to stop moving unless a mama gave him some wine, and as Tara and Dom did handclap games, and Baxter completed a hook rug, Ray read to Cherry. She often grabbed his hand, mid-line, to ask him a question. "Which one is your favorite?" she might say, pointing at Sleeping Beauty's trio of fairies. They could not choose the same one, she explained, and so he pointed to the chubby blue one, prepared to pick another if pressed.

"I'm Aurora and these are the mamas," she whispered, and it was true, she did look a little like the princess with her blond hair and big eyes.

"Aurora begins with *A*," Ray said, mimicking what they had done for him in school.

"I perceive that as well," Cherry replied, and then said, "Read," as if she hadn't been the one to stop him in the first place.

When Cherry had turned five, Ray told his mother Cherry should go to kindergarten. "Absolutely not," she said. "We'll educate her here."

"I'm doing well at school, and so would Cherry."

Nope, nope, nope. If anyone found out there were this many children here, his mother said, the government would intervene. The additions were not up to code. And school, with its paternal expectations, its conventional requirements, would be too much for the mamas: their lifestyle would be questioned, if not outright rejected. She told Ray the mamas needed the protection of the woods. He had the sense that there was more to it: that his mother couldn't stand the idea of any of them leaving—like Cherry's own mother had.

"Cherry doesn't have a mama, though," Ray reminded her. "You're almost like her mother."

"I certainly am not."

The conversation was over.

It was probably because Ray was in school, followed by chess club, and then homework in his third-floor bedroom, alone with the door shut, that he failed to notice how things had changed with the mamas—and with the kids. A kind of rot had begun to spread, as if the house he'd been born in were a beautiful peach in a fruit bowl that had been left too long in the elements. Pick it up, and on its hidden end you'd find a gummy sag, the blue-black of decay.

Ray was in the sixth grade, twelve years old, about to graduate
from grade school and move to the large junior high—not that anyone would attend his commencement—and he returned home with
his black graduation robe and the mortarboard hat in its paper wrap-
ping. He was rushing upstairs to store what felt like sacred vestments
in the dresser for safekeeping when he met Hawk on the stairs. He
carried Cole in his arms. The little boy was naked and slumped into
Hawk, whimpering. He smelled of poop.

Ray didn't want anyone to see the graduation gown. If Hawk
spotted the hat, he'd want to try it on, or toss it across the field behind
the house like a boomerang that wouldn't come back.

Ray rushed past them, not even nodding, and Hawk said, "Skip
your homework this once. We need your help."

It was Wednesday. Some of the mamas would be at the farmers
market in downtown Santa Cruz, selling herbs tied with twine, soap
hairy with herbs, and a more expensive herb in a little baggy, if you
knew how to ask. This was often how they met new mamas too.

"Where are the others?" Ray asked. The full moon was two nights
ago. All the mamas were no doubt feeling better by now, and they
wouldn't begin preparing the eastern wing for at least another three
weeks. "Why don't you find Mama Mary in the packing room?"

"She's in the eastern wing."

"Now? Why?"

Cole let out a wail that bounced off the stairwell walls, and he
flung his torso backward, writhing from Hawk's grasp, nearly falling
out of his arms. Hawk hushed him and brought him to his chest.
"Hey man, hey." To Ray he said, "Mama Gertie's been in there since
the open moon. Won't come out."

"Why does Cole care?"

Hawk sneered at him. "He doesn't. He found a tab in the parlor."

"Oh—oh no."

"Licked it like a stamp." Hawk stuck out his tongue and pretended
to lick the top of Cole's head as if he were a cat cleaning her kittens.

"Mama Ursa told them to make sure to clean up after a trip," Ray said.

"They were trying to lure Mama Gertie out with it, I guess."

After he'd tucked the package away in his bedroom, Ray found the kids in the parlor, the older ones surrounding Cole, who sat calmly on the chartreuse couch. He wasn't sobbing anymore, but the silence that replaced it was more unnerving because he stared without focusing, empty-eyed as the dead, or the undead. Someone had found some shorts for him that were at least two sizes too big, and they reached his ankles, the waist so loose that his little penis wagged out the front. His bare ass was no doubt hitting the velour seat cushion.

"Did anyone clean up his excrement?" Ray said.

"Just say *shit*. You mean shit," Hawk said. "And yeah, Cherry did."

"The bravest nine-year-old in the world," Amethyst said, and Cherry smiled. She had a big bowl in her hands, and Ray tried to make out what it was.

"Where's Dom?" he asked.

"He took a tab himself," Hawk said. "On purpose. He's in the western addition laughing his head off."

"He'll be fine," Amethyst said.

The other kids, the ones as young as Cole or younger, and Lily, who was about a year older, were making a racket; Martha, the baby, was crying on the ottoman, and Sammy, who was not much older than Baby Martha, had crawled under the side table, perhaps not knowing how to get out. The twins were throwing pillows. Taz was stuffing a pillow into his pants.

"I'll take them outside," Tara said.

Hawk was not going to leave Cole, that was obvious.

"The mamas should be here," Ray said.

"Eastern wing's locked," Cherry said. Her bowl was full of chocolate pudding, the kind they made from a powder and kept in the cupboard for Amethyst's daddy, Ricardo. He came every third Saturday, if he wasn't on tour.

"Cole needs to eat," Amethyst said, nodding at the bowl on Cherry's lap. "That helps if you've got a bad trip. Remember Mama Wanda last year? That bread solved everything."

"Hawk wanted to give him wine," Cherry said, "and I told him it wasn't happening."

At that moment, Mama Ursa and Mama Mary entered the parlor.

"Oh dear," Mama Mary said when Ray told them what had happened.

"Cole needs to be tucked back in his pants," Mama Ursa said. "Mary, get him some clothing."

Ray didn't move. He'd been told to never touch anyone's body, just as he'd been told to never touch the LSD tabs. The mamas had taught all the kids these lessons—and yet the mamas didn't care to make sure they complied.

Mama Mary returned with a smaller pair of pants. She used the bigger shorts to wipe Cole's face clean, and as she did so the child winced. He had begun whimpering again, and Ray worried it would soon be followed by that ear-piercing cry.

"What is this?" Cole was saying. "What what what no no."

Hawk was nearly in tears himself. "You'll be all right."

"Yes, he will, though this was unfortunate," Mama Ursa said. Turning to Mama Mary, who now carried Cole in her arms, she said, "Let's put him in with Gertie. They both can sleep it off."

"What happened?" Ray asked once Mama Mary and Cole were gone. "Why wouldn't she leave the eastern wing?"

Amethyst, Cherry, and Hawk were pretending not to listen, but it was obvious they were. Amethyst began shoveling the pudding into her mouth.

"The . . . meditation," Ursa said. "It was too much. She didn't want it to end."

"Why not?"

"She was in quite a state."

"What do you mean?" Cherry asked, and Ray was so happy to have her on his side. For once, another kid wasn't afraid to ask questions.

"Someday we'll find out," Amethyst said, mouth full. "We'll be mamas. Right, Mama Ursa?"

"Only when you're much older."

"What about me?" Hawk said. "Will I?"

"You'll be a man, stupid," Amethyst said.

They all turned back to Mama Ursa to discover that she had already left the room. What a coward, Ray thought, and the anger that came with it surprised him.

Was this when he began hating his mother?

Not yet. But almost.

∞

Graduation—

The grade school auditorium, constructed only two years prior, was large, and it was packed. From the dais on the stage, the principal reminded the students and their loved ones that the word *commencement* meant "a beginning," no matter how much they might want to frame it as an ending.

They were only twelve years old, thirteen at most, and they had long lives ahead of them.

Though everyone had made small talk about the unseasonably cold weather for an evening in June, the large auditorium, filled with families, was stifling and hot, and by the time they were handing out the diplomas, Ray had sweated through his shirt and his robe and the lining of his funny hat too. So much for sacred vestments.

An acquaintance's father had agreed to drive him from the ceremony to downtown Ben Lomond, and as Ray left the car, Mr. Brown said, "Get yourself a bath, son," as if Ray didn't know any better, as if he didn't have anyone at home to instruct him. And he didn't. He was walking home alone, wasn't he? It would take over an hour.

It was as cold as everyone had warned it would be, fifty degrees
in June, and it seemed to get colder the farther from town Ray got, as
the road pinched, its edges unpaved and muddy, a brief dip and he'd
fall into a tangle of trees. A dead oak lay on its side at the lip of the
forest, as if in warning. But of what? He could choose to read it as a
beginning, he thought, not an ending.

Ray had a flashlight for the trip home, though occasionally he
thrust it under his graduate robe to walk in the dark and warm up his
hands. Whenever he spotted approaching car headlights, he stepped
off the road into the woods, his black robe flapping behind him. He
was good at being invisible.

He wanted nothing more than to take off his shoes and sit down.
He would first give his mortarboard hat to Cole. A gift. The boy
seemed to be doing okay, as far as Ray could tell. Mama Gertie hadn't
left her bed. She slept like an ill person and the mamas were worried,
including Mama Ursa. Someone called Mama Gertie depressed.

Mama Ursa said only a visit to the eastern wing would cheer her
up. They needed to snap her out of it.

"She's addicted," Ray overheard a mama say.

Addicted to *what*?

He'd heard the mamas were going back into the eastern wing
sooner than planned. There wouldn't be another open moon for three
weeks, but no matter. Gertie needed it, Mama Ursa said.

That morning, when Ray reminded his mother about his graduation, she congratulated him and asked when he would return home;
she did not offer to pick him up and he knew better than to ask.

By the time Ray reached home, it was after ten, and his feet were
leaden. The house at the end of the driveway was nearly dark except
for the windows of the purple room, which were lit with low light.

He trudged forward and entered through the mudroom.

"You're finally back."

His mother. She stood in the kitchen. Around her shoulders was
draped a bright blue shawl. Her hair was brushed to a glint.

"You waited up for me?" Ray said.

He straightened his robe, but his mother didn't seem to notice he was wearing anything out of the ordinary.

"The mamas are gathering in the eastern wing," she said.

So that was why she'd met him here. She wasn't going to ask about his night.

"We need you in the purple room," she said.

Ray's stomach growled as she led him to the second floor. The commencement had begun at seven, and it was only when they were lined up in the music room, readying the procession, that he realized everyone had just come from dinner. Before leaving for the commencement, Ray had downed some kefir in the kitchen. Now he was starving.

"Be good," Mama Ursa said before she locked him in.

The purple room had two twin beds and a pile of cots for the younger kids. Cole was asleep on one in the corner. Ray tucked the mortarboard under his pillow and hoped Cole would wake up before some older kid snatched it from him.

How the child could sleep was a mystery; the room was crowded and loud. Ray hated it in here: the dark purple walls scratched and stained, the cushionless, punishing window seat, and the window itself, with its warped glass that looked out over the porch. The room was stuffed with children. A bunch of broken toys. A few books with broken spines and ripped pages. Someone had recently nailed a banana peel to the wall; it was rotting brown now, turning to jelly, and no one had removed it, not even Cherry, who usually cleaned up after everyone.

The door was locked. They were prisoners.

The younger kids sprawled across the floor, drawing on months-old newspapers with some old crayons; Baxter had a pen and was drawing on Amethyst's arm. Hawk was sitting by the window, bouncing a little as he always did, vibrating with energy, a flask in his hand. Dom and Tara were drinking beers that a daddy had bequeathed to the house. Cherry sat cross-legged on a bed, braiding her own hair. Baby Martha lay next to her. How was it that Cherry was only nine? She was so mature, she seemed like everyone's babysitter.

"Want a beer?" Dom asked as he dove onto the other bed, his open can held out in front of him, the ocean foam of beer dripping down the side and onto his hand. He nearly kicked one of the little kids in the mouth.

Ray shook his head. He wasn't sure if any of them realized that other kids their age, normal ones, didn't drink.

No one in here noticed his graduation robe either.

In the corner was a little table they used for all kinds of things, from snacking to painting to Bunko games. Tonight, there was nothing on the table except a random ball of yarn.

"There anything to eat?" Ray asked.

"Nope," Hawk said, finally turning from the window. He was listing a little, clearly drunk. "But let's go grab something."

"How?"

"He's got a plan," Dom said.

"We can get out of this window pretty easily, I think," Hawk said. "Get onto the roof here and shimmy onto the porch."

Ray didn't say that he'd had this thought before.

"Why would you do that?"

"I want to find out what they're doing. Don't you?"

Hawk wanted to scale the roof of the eastern wing. He heard the mamas talking about the skylights; he would peek in from above. See what might be in there.

"You're drunk and it's cold out," Ray said.

"I told you he wouldn't want me to," Hawk said to everyone else in the room.

"I didn't say that," Ray said, looking around.

"Come with me then," Hawk said.

Mama Ursa always told Ray she would kill him if he tried to get into the eastern wing. What would she do to the kids she didn't love?

"No thanks," Ray said. "But you go ahead."

Hawk gave him a look like he'd predicted as much and stood from the window seat. "As soon as I piss in the bucket, I'm gone."

"Wear a coat at least," Ray said.

"I forgot to bring one. Can I borrow that?"

He gestured at Ray's robe.

In the split second that Ray hesitated, Hawk said, "I'm kidding. Anyway, I'll move better this way." He paused, swaying a little, glossy-eyed from whatever was in the flask. "You won't rat on me, will you?"

"You think I would?"

Hawk didn't reply.

The plan was for Hawk to climb through the window and spy on the mamas. He would drag the big ladder over if he couldn't scale the eastern wing. Afterward, he would hide in the western addition, and when the mamas unlocked the purple room, they'd have no clue what happened. One of the kids would retrieve Hawk, and in thanks he would reveal what he'd seen.

It was their secret. For once the kids would keep something from the mamas.

Before he went, Hawk asked Ray once more if he wanted to come too. "We can get some food after?"

Ray looked at Cherry, who shook her head.

"You know I can't," Ray said.

Hawk was slurring by the time he pushed himself out the window and scrabbled to the edge of the roof. He climbed down the porch post. Ray refused to watch, but he could tell it was successful by the excited sounds the older kids made.

The air blowing through the open window was a shock. It must have been forty degrees out; not terribly cold, but cold for June, and Hawk was wearing only a T-shirt and cords.

They didn't know what happened next because they were locked in the purple room.

Ray should have gone after him. Hawk was drunk, and it was cold.

Instead, Ray fell asleep next to Cole on a too-small cot.

Later, they pieced it together.

First, Hawk slid off the side of the eastern wing as he was climbing to the roof. He hurt his ankle. Maybe it was the injury, or the cold, or the amount of alcohol in his system, but that was when he started to feel bad. Queasy, freezing, dizzy.

This was only at the start. He somehow managed to get the ladder and drag it to the eastern wing. He got onto the roof. He crawled to the skylight. He looked in. At the mamas and their secret world.

What did he see? The kids didn't know because something happened. He must've been tossed off the roof. He must've hit his head. There was a cut there.

Just after dawn, Mama Annie found him outside, not far from the side door. He was crawling in the dirt like an injured animal. Shirtless. He was barely awake but crying. Moaning, really.

He told Mama Annie he needed a mama. Or perhaps he had said "I need *my* mama," even though only Ray said it that way.

By the time Ray woke up and went downstairs, Hawk was in the parlor, shivering with fever, his lips blue, his skin a greenish pallor. Delirious, he was goose bumped and sweating on the chartreuse couch. He didn't speak except to say his ankle hurt, his head, that the light bothered his eyes, and then he grunted in pain.

In the next moment he seemed lucid. He caught Ray's eye and said, "The eastern wing was shaking."

The mamas hushed him.

"It was hot to touch. The roof was melting."

"It's okay," the mamas said, sharing worried glances.

There was no thermometer in the house, but the boy's fever had to be very, very high.

Mama Mary washed him with rubbing alcohol and sang to him in a whisper. She asked everyone to bring blankets, and she was the one to tear them off him when he cried out at the heat. His injured ankle was swollen and purple; it looked like a balloon filled with water.

Did he even feel the injury as the fever pillaged the rest of him?

Later, Ray would think of this time in pieces, because to remember it head-on was too painful. Mama Mary wringing out the red washcloth, the smell of rubbing alcohol that pervaded the room. The sight of Hawk, limp as that washrag, when he was usually so wild and electric. The kids crying, confessing his escape and his plan to get on the roof. The wind that picked up that afternoon as the temperature rose and the house got warm. The sound of pine needles hitting the stained-glass windows above the couch like someone tapping to be let inside.

Who suggested they take Hawk to the hospital? It was a kid first—Cherry, maybe. A few of the mamas thought it might be a good idea to go, even if Hawk had never been to a doctor, even if the world beyond their plot of land didn't know he existed, even if it brought attention to the mamas and what they had going on out here.

"It's worth the risk," Ray remembered himself saying—at least he'd done that.

Mama Mary said Hawk would be okay, she was sure of it, though the next morning, once he started to vomit and writhe, his fever as high as ever, she'd gone up to the third floor to talk to Mama Ursa. They both came downstairs. Ray was sitting in the corner. He hadn't eaten since the night before last. Someone had tried to give him a bowl of scrounged-up lentils and he refused. His stomach felt inverted. An inside-out sock. His whole body felt like that, his heart a seamed, raggedy ball, threads dangling.

Ray remembered this:

Mama Ursa bent over Hawk, who lay on the couch, as everyone else looked on. She put a hand on his chest. She agreed he felt hot, very hot.

"Hawk," she said.

He didn't answer.

"*Hawk*!" Mama Ursa's voice rang across the room, reverberating down the hall, into the kitchen. Ray imagined the word soaring across the property.

Hawk opened his eyes.

"Hawk," Ray's mother said, smiling. "How are you feeling?"

Hawk hadn't spoken a coherent word in hours. Even before Hawk answered, Ray knew he would be coherent. For just this moment. For Mama Ursa.

"I'm okay," he said, and everyone cheered.

Was he performing for Mama Ursa, for fear of getting in trouble? Mama Ursa, satisfied, stood and left the room.

Mama Ursa didn't return that day—or if she had, Ray didn't remember.

He didn't remember a lot after that.

Hawk's fever did not abate. No one took him to see a doctor. Years later, Ray asked himself why he hadn't carried Hawk out of the house and put him in whatever truck was closest and taken him to the ER. None of them had.

Why—oh, he knew why. There was only one person powerful enough to take the child to get help. Instead, at the end of the second day of his illness, the mamas carried Hawk outside, hoping the fresh air would revive him. Someone put a turquoise stone on his navel. As if that would do anything.

The mamas sang and played the fiddle to the setting sun. The little kids ran around with sticks; the big kids surrounded Hawk, who lay on a blue quilt on the ground, beneath the largest live oak. Ray hoped the spiky leaves weren't cutting through the blanket and into his skin.

Mama Gertie kissed every woman on the mouth, crying, probably guilty that she was the reason they went into the eastern wing the night before. Mama Mary looked at the sky and reached for the pink spreading across it. Ray didn't realize then that this was a sort of ceremony for Hawk. Not a commencement. A memorial.

Hawk was dead before sunrise.

His had been the most vulnerable body of all, it turned out.

He was eleven years old.

∞

What happened to Hawk's spirit?

Ray hoped it had soared away, to somewhere safe. Somewhere beautiful.

Hawk's body, Ray knew, was buried under that live oak. Mama Ursa came downstairs and directed the mamas to dig the hole. Once they had done so, they dragged Hawk's body into it and then shoveled the displaced dirt over him. As soon as they were finished, Mama Ursa directed the mamas into the eastern wing.

"Does the open moon mean nothing anymore?" Mama Annie said.

Mama Gertie nodded vigorously. "Look what happened when I—"

"There has been a loss," Mama Mary said, her words starched.

"Let's go," Mama Ursa said, taking Mama Mary's hand, and together they led the other mamas away from the tree and the buried body and the clumps of children watching. Taz was already down the driveway yelling, "Shit!" and Baby Martha was sitting in the dirt, crying, until Cherry lifted her up.

The mamas locked themselves in the eastern wing for two days. They didn't care what the kids did. During that time, Ray drank a bottle of whiskey he discovered in Mama Ursa's bureau. Drunk, he watched from the porch as Cherry picked eleven rocks—one for each year of Hawk's life—and placed them in a circle on his grave.

Who died of a fever in 1970, *anno domini*? Ray didn't know what to think.

His mother had always warned them not to go into the eastern wing. Or even try to. She said she would kill him. And now Hawk was dead. Was it because of what he'd done?

For those two days following Hawk's death, the children heard wailing and other strange sounds coming from the eastern wing. Tara finally took the truck to Santa Cruz and traded a bag of weed for a bag of hoagies.

When the mamas emerged, they looked sick and drained but resolved. There were no tears. One of them went to the market and another took a trip to her favorite herbalist for more tea and shampoo. They needed to get the house back on track. A few went into the packing room to return to work.

No one said Hawk's name.

The next day, when Mama Ursa discovered the rocks on his grave, she came barreling into the house, demanding to know who had done it.

"It was me," Ray lied.

"No, it wasn't," Cherry said. "I did it."

Mama Ursa demanded she go outside and get rid of the rocks at once.

"If anyone finds out what happened here," she began. She did not finish her sentence.

Cherry did not stay for Mama Ursa's speech. She had already left the room, and through the window Ray watched her kneel beneath the tree and gather the rocks in the front of her dress.

This—of course *this*—was what finally severed Ray from his mother.

∞

After that, Mama Judith left with Tara and Sammy. Baxter and his mama took off, too, because Baxter said he would run away if they didn't, that he would drown himself in the creek. Ricardo came to get Amethyst and her mama, and then Taz and Dom packed up with their mama.

Within a month, almost all the children had disappeared. Or died. Of the kids who were left, only Ray and Cherry were old enough to remember Hawk and what happened to him.

That must please Mama Ursa, Ray thought.

Where did Cherry put those rocks, he wondered. Sometimes he imagined them in the room Cherry slept in by herself. He pictured them in a circle, under her bed. Or lined up, under her pillow. Wrapped in a scarf at the back of her closet.

Did she touch them once in a while?

He wondered if Cherry thought Hawk had been cursed for seeing into the eastern wing.

Once everyone was gone, Ursa said she wanted Mama Mary and the others to find new mamas to replace those they'd lost. Women they could depend on. There was a new rule too. The women could not have sons. Only daughters. Really, no children at all would be preferable.

∞

Ray was correct—this place was rotting.

It wasn't only the house's exterior, with its flaking and peeling gray paint, or the rat infestation in the attic, or the leak on the third floor that meant, during rainy season, three buckets and one crystal punch bowl (Karin's grandmother's) had to be placed in the turret to collect the water eating the roof and the ceiling. It wasn't the chains hanging from every room where a chandelier had once been or the gouges in the wall of the purple room. It wasn't the mess of finger paint on the second-floor landing or the empty shelves in the larder. It wasn't the room of unmade bunk beds or the pile of clothes where occasionally a toddler might pass out. It wasn't the packing room with its cloak of skunk, the lighting harsh, long tables covered in seed and tacky with resin. It wasn't the two big scales and the cardboard boxes of packing materials. It wasn't the twine the kids learned to tie the bags of weed closed with before they learned to tie their shoes. Or it wasn't only that.

It was something else that Ray couldn't name. The mamas now shut themselves inside the eastern wing for over twenty-four hours at a time. And still Ray and Cherry didn't know what was going on in there. It was the new mamas who came, usually childless though occasionally with a baby daughter. How they hung on Mama Ursa.

How they had Cherry hold their infants as if she weren't a kid herself. These mamas were more damaged than the ones who had come before. Their hardness wasn't only in their eyes. It was in their very beings: they were all need and disappointment.

It was the way Mama Ursa told Cherry to get the kids into the purple room when a man came. How Mama Mary warned Cherry to be careful whenever she went to town.

It was how they never spoke about Hawk. How he had been erased. Tara too, and Baxter, Dom, Amethyst, Taz. All gone.

Ray was relieved when summer ended and the school semester began. He fell into his classes. By the time he entered high school, he knew he would get away as soon as he graduated. He would go to the university in Santa Cruz; Mama Ursa would allow it. That would be the first step before getting a job, a good one that required a college degree.

He'd go somewhere far from here.

Ray was well aware that there was no school for Cherry. There was no place for her to go, nothing to distract her, nowhere she could pretend to be someone else. She had to stay on the property to take care of the kids. She had to handle the reefer and help garden. She had to scratch Mama Gertie's back, fetch the eggs before dinner, scrub the tubs.

Ray told himself he couldn't think about any of that. Cherry would become a mama, he told himself. Someday she'd enter the eastern wing and be lost forever.

It was best to let her go now.

4

SIX YEARS SINCE HAWK'S DEATH. RAY WAS EIGHTEEN, A senior in high school, already admitted to UC Santa Cruz with a full scholarship. Cherry was fifteen. If she ever read a book, he didn't know. He had no idea what she did all day aside from hang out with the mamas and the children. He had no clue if she liked her life. Ray wasn't around enough to ask; he made sure to help Mama Ursa, to be present enough that she didn't ask questions; otherwise, he was gone.

That day, just after high school graduation, he was home to help paint the trees with the younger kids. The open moon was tomorrow, and the mamas were preparing. As they had when Ray was ten, the kids mixed the wings into the rubber cement, just as Mama Gertie had shown them. And like that first time, the wings glowed supernaturally against the rough red-brown tree trunks.

Mama Ursa told the children that the circles weren't supposed to mean anything, that they were simply pretty. Didn't matter: the kids all had different ideas about what the tree paintings symbolized. Jewelry for trunks. Portals to a fairyland. Ray had begun to think of them as eyes, watching.

That day the kids lost interest quickly, and after the second tree, Ray and Cherry were the only ones left. They'd started at the porch and worked their way down the eastern row. When they reached the last tree, they would cross to the other side, and paint their way back to the house.

It should have been obvious something was going to happen.

If there were a lot of kids, there was usually no method, just find a tree and give it a circle; either paint over the previous one or add a new one somewhere else on the tree. Ray and Cherry, though, were taking turns, sharing a single paintbrush. One of them would watch as the other worked. They were discussing where the circle should go, how big. Taking their time.

"Are you looking forward to going?" Cherry asked him when they reached the end of the driveway. She meant college. Ray had convinced Mama Ursa to let him stay in the dormitories.

"Honestly?" Ray said.

"Honestly."

"I can't wait."

They were kneeling. They wanted to make a small circle at the base of the tree, and Ray held the brush between his fingers. He looked at Cherry, holding the bowl of goopy sparkling cement in her hands. Her round cheeks were glittery with the bug dust, which brought out the flecks of gold in her eyes. He felt the sudden need to apologize for his plan to leave—to leave *her*.

Instead, he said, "You've got bug wings on your face."

She blushed, embarrassed, and he realized she had taken it wrong.

Before Cherry could bring a hand to her face, he leaned forward and kissed her.

Ray had kissed a few girls at school, random classmates at parties, but this felt unlike those others. What was it? Was it that he'd never imagined it before? Not with Cherry. Was it that he knew Cherry better than the other girls? And that she knew him. Was it Cherry's lips? They were so soft. Her tongue, like an animal inside of her mouth.

She pulled away and she didn't say anything before dropping the bowl and running.

Later that night, he realized kissing Cherry felt different—felt better—because he was in love with her. He loved her.

Ray was afraid he'd offended her. Worse, that he had scared her. After all, Ray was a man now, and the mamas always told her to watch herself. If Mama Ursa found out, she might exile Cherry. Where would Cherry go? She had no mama to run with. Ray's stupid desire, his love, was a threat to Cherry. He didn't want to want her. Pretty soon she'd have to hide from him in the purple room.

He left for Santa Cruz but was sure to return every other weekend so that Mama Ursa didn't get nervous and tell him to drop out. He could tell she was proud of him; she called it "the university" and told the mamas, in front of Ray, that her son's education would help protect them from the "tyranny of legalese" that might someday befall them when a "Capitalist fascist" came knocking at their door. Ray knew the truth: his mom was okay with the other mamas' kids being illiterate, yet she couldn't stand the idea of her own not getting an education.

Plus, he was the one selling the reefer on campus now; Code had long departed for his hometown, a place called Hercules, California. Word of Ray's supply spread among the students, and he found it an easy way to move through the world. He was no one's friend and everyone's dealer. He went to class and sold reefer, and that was it. He just had to do well enough, he told himself, to get a good job when it was all over.

When Ray came home, he and Cherry avoided each other as best they could. There were so many kids now—twelve, thirteen—and fifteen mamas. It was easy to never be alone.

The next time they kissed was a year later. Cherry was sixteen, Ray nineteen, now living in downtown Santa Cruz. Unbeknownst to Ray, Cherry's period had finally come—so late the mamas worried there was something wrong with her. Now her pits stunk, and she had a full bush, and there were stretchmarks spiderwebbing across her thighs. Tiny breasts still, but there were no bras in the house anyway. She knew she was pretty because Mama Ursa told her so, and said it was a bad thing.

"We can't protect you forever," she said.

Cherry wondered why beauty needed protecting.

She and Ray met on the landing of the back staircase, Ray with a patchwork bag on his shoulder and a sunburn across his nose. He looked different. Older.

"Cherry," he said, startled.

"Hey yourself," she said.

Later, Cherry told Ray that she had run from his first kiss because she liked it, and she didn't know what else to do but reject such a feeling. If the mamas knew, she'd die. They wouldn't want her to want Ray. Or any man.

Ray thought he could smell Cherry, musty with a hint of sweetness, like cinnamon. It was a scent as familiar as his own, as his mother's, and yet he craved it.

Nevertheless, when Cherry stepped forward and put her hands on his chest, and then kissed him, he was the one to stop her.

What would happen, he thought, if they got caught? He couldn't do that to Cherry.

He stepped back, and, humiliated, Cherry rushed upstairs.

The third try, another six months after that, each of them counting the days like beads on an abacus, was the charm. They were outside under a full moon and drunk off mulled wine.

The other kids had fallen asleep, and the mamas were busy in the eastern wing. Ray had come home unexpectedly; he'd run out of weed, and there was a big party tomorrow—he'd forgotten to check on the moon. Ray helped Cherry get the kids in their beds and then he brought out the wine.

They would both claim the other started it. Like a fight. And it was sort of like that, the two of them wrestling on the ground in the woods, grabbing at each other—as Hawk used to, though neither was thinking of death as they struggled and laughed and tugged at each other's midsections. Cherry let out a shriek when Ray pushed up her dress. They both stopped, their heavy breathing the only sound.

He undid his jeans and pushed himself into her.

Cherry didn't know how it worked. Until she did. Watch yourself, the mamas had said. And all this time, she'd been watching Ray.

Later Ray would lie and tell Cherry he lost his virginity to a girl in his dormitory. In truth, this was his first time. The moon was an overripe peach above them, and an owl flew across it, its wings *thwapping*. To Ray, Cherry was the moon and the owl and the whole night sky.

Afterward, he felt the guilt like a coat of paint covering his body, drying him into a kind of cast. How could they have done that? Cherry had not watched herself. He'd let his urges overtake them both.

"Don't tell anyone," Cherry said when he got in his truck.

"Same to you," he said.

Cherry was at the driver's side window. She was so beautiful.

"I'm sorry," he said, but already he knew he'd be back.

∞

Three years of meeting secretly: down by the creek, in the packing room, even in the turret when Mama Ursa had gone on a rare farmers market outing to vet a new woman the others wanted to bring in. That time at dawn in the pantry, Cherry facing the herbs drying like clothes on a line as Ray got to her from behind. His mouth on the back of her neck and the little blond curls there.

He told himself they should stop. He told her they should stop, and she agreed. Yet they couldn't. He finally admitted he loved her.

"I love you," she said, like an echo, and he wanted to cry.

How private and true their love was. No one else could know about it—it was to be nurtured, protected: from the demanding children and from the suspicious eyes of the mamas, who perceived the worst in humankind.

Were he and Cherry the worst? Maybe they were, he thought.

But how could they stop?

When Ray was home, he would leave stalks of yarrow in the pocket of the apron Cherry favored, and she would reply with two smooth pebbles dropped into each of his work boots. Sometimes, she'd tuck little drawings into his wallet for him to discover once he was back at school. They were observational doodles that he treasured because they were from her, and because they captured, with a few lines and shading, the world no one at school knew about. Once she'd drawn the stove in the kitchen, the outline of a mama next to it; another time, the door of the purple room. He imagined her, locked in there with all those kids, sketching with some chewed-up pencil, and he crumpled the little paper in his fist. And then he smoothed out the drawing and kept it with the others. He treasured them all and didn't dare leave anything for her that someone at the house might trace back to him.

After a week apart, their first moments alone together were breathless: fumbling buttons, giggling, nudging necks like two horses. Ray would always take deep breaths into her skin. He wanted to remember how she smelled. He felt himself stiffen and hated himself for it.

Ray told Mama Ursa that coming home helped him concentrate on his studies, and he began to drive from campus more often. He made less money selling reefer and made up for it during the week as best he could. And every full moon, no matter what day of the week, he returned. Usually, Mama Ursa, preoccupied in the eastern wing, had no inkling of his visits.

On those nights, there was more time, and they could talk. At the creek's edge in the middle of the night, the kids fast asleep in the house, the mamas doing who knows what, Cherry would plumb Ray for details about her mother, Ruth. He would tell her he didn't remember a thing.

"I was only three," he'd say, and Cherry would reply with the saddest look.

Neither of them knew a father, but that was true for lots of kids; it didn't matter in the same way and they both knew it.

It was on one of those full moon nights, the two of them talking and kissing, that Cherry asked, "Do you ever think about Hawk?"

"All the time," Ray said, and she grabbed his hand.

She told him she'd been invited to the morning ritual.

"You're becoming a mama," he said.

"Never," she said and pulled him to her.

∞

It was Ray's final semester, and his mother expected him to move back onto the property as soon as his lease on the house on Ocean Street ended. He hadn't told Mama Ursa that he had gone to a career fair on campus and applied for a microfiche sales position. The job was in Los Angeles.

"Ell Ay," said the man who took his application materials.

Ray hadn't told Cherry either.

The job probably wouldn't have excited any other college senior, but Ray had never known anyone who worked in an office, had never worn a suit. He would have a salary.

The man called Ray at his little ramshackle house in downtown Santa Cruz to tell him the good news, and Ray's voice trembled when he accepted the offer.

"You don't need any time to think it over?" the man asked.

Ray still hadn't told anyone about the job.

No one, not even Cherry, knew that for over a year he'd skimmed money from the weed sales. It would be enough to buy a used car and a couple of suits and get to Los Angeles. Find a modest apartment and keep his number unlisted.

Why didn't he tell Cherry?

He couldn't quite explain it, except that he couldn't imagine Cherry away from the house and the property. She was the creek and the sparkling redwoods and the mazes that led to and from the road. She was connected to everything he vowed to leave. The place was rotting, and yet Cherry, whom he loved, was inextricable from it. How was that possible? He would have to give her up in order to fully get away.

Besides, she had joined the morning ritual. She described to him her tasks of picking the mint and separating the leaves from the stalks. Placing six leaves in each mug and then stepping back for Mama Mary to pour the water. Cherry didn't mention anything about the ritual itself and Ray didn't ask. She didn't say whether she'd been invited to the eastern wing, and, again, Ray didn't ask.

What if he told her, and she didn't want to go with him?

If he was going to leave, he had to really leave. Everything and everyone. It was one thing for him to move to LA, but to take Cherry with him was another matter. He didn't think he could do that to his mother.

After another failed attempt to confess to Cherry about his job, Ray returned to school. It was nearly finals, and he was at the grocery store buying cereal; he wanted to study and eat raisin bran, at the same time preferably. He opened his wallet to pay, and inside, he found the piece of paper folded up next to his bills. A new note from Cherry.

He didn't open it immediately because he was at the register, and with a pang he thought this might be the last one he got from her. He must savor it.

Outside in the parking lot, he balanced the paper bag on his hip and fished out the note. This time, there was no drawing. Only a sentence. Cherry never did that; she said she was embarrassed to write because couldn't spell. Which was true, but he didn't care.

The note said: *My mensees stoped what now.*

Ray looked away from the note. The parking lot was packed— three on a Sunday afternoon, everyone getting their groceries for the week. A car honked. There was the ugly crashing of carts against one another. Someone slammed a trunk closed.

Once upon a time, Ray planned to abandon his lover at his mother's cult in the woods for the big city of LA, for a suit and a salary and something resembling normalcy. And then his lover revealed she was pregnant, and he knew he would escape with her. With her and their baby. They would become a family. A *real* one.

Part

TWO

5

————————

RAY AND CHERRY REACHED LOS ANGELES IN THE SUM-
mer of 1980, the baby inside of Cherry only a little bigger than a
coffee bean. Her name would be Opal, though they hadn't decided
this yet.

They fled in the middle of the night like criminals. The mamas
had gone to bed early because the following evening the moon would
be open, and they needed their rest for the eastern wing. Ray wanted
to wait until the mamas were occupied to flee, but Cherry worried
the kids, under her care, might sniff out her nerves. Also, it might be
bad luck.

Sooners beter, she wrote to him.

By the time she crept out of the house, all the kids were asleep
except for Sage, who cried as Cherry passed the western addition.
With a pillowcase doubling as a getaway bag slung over her shoulder,
she kneeled to soothe the little girl back to sleep, and as she hushed
her and rubbed her back, she felt desperate for Sage to quiet down so
that she and Ray could make a run for it.

He was waiting on the porch in new blue jeans and a new black
shirt. He wore his old jean jacket, faded and soft as flannel, with
the metal buttons that got cold in the cold. His hands were in his
pockets, his flashlight around his neck on a thick leather cord.

Seeing him like that, with his worn jacket and stiff jeans, his hands hidden, Cherry was overcome. It was a feeling of need. She needed to have him.

As she approached, Ray mouthed the word *Okay?* and she nodded. He took his hands out of his pockets and removed the flashlight, traded it for her heavy pillowcase.

Their new car sat hidden in the maze, in the second tentacle, as it was called. Ray had cut the lights and engine and walked off the path, through the woods, to reach the house on foot. That way, Mama Alice, on watch in the cottage, wouldn't hear. The car was fifteen years old, with over two hundred thousand miles and an oil leak that meant they'd have to refill it in Coalinga. That was a town full of cows headed for slaughter, Ray explained. It was halfway to LA; he showed it to her on the map. Three canisters of motor oil sat in the trunk, as well as his suitcase. The car was a piece of shit, Ray said, but it would get them where they needed to go.

It felt romantic to be huddled on the threadbare front seat as the old car trundled back through the second tentacle, onto the main path, and then off the property. It was as if they were the only two people awake in a sleeping world. Once they reached the highway, Ray briefly turned to her and grinned. "We're gone," he said.

They drove for hours until all that existed beyond the cocoon of their car was dark farm after dark farm. They stopped in Coalinga for no more than thirty minutes, the stink of cow so strong it made their eyes water, and when they got back in the car, Ray told her she should nap if she could. Cherry slept through the sunrise, drooling against the passenger window; she woke to find Ray wide awake at the wheel, tapping fingers against the steering wheel. She loved the way he looked as he changed lanes, his eyes darting to the side mirror and back to the road. Speeding up. He drove with such confidence; he kept her safe as she slept.

Ray wasn't tired because for the past week he'd prepared for the trip by sleeping during the day and staying up nights.

"How is it being an owl?" she asked. The clock on the dashboard read 7:00 a.m.

"Sunrises are nice, but otherwise I don't recommend it."

He leaned across the seat and gave her ear a little tug. It tickled.

"What was that for?" she asked, laughing.

He shrugged and returned his hand to the wheel, a silly grin on his face. "I just like your ear is all," he said, and Cherry felt her ears on the sides of her head going pink.

Daylight revealed a new world. The surrounding brown mountains curved like hips, dotted with scrubby brush and anemic-looking trees, the occasional bright gasp of wildflowers, electricity poles, and even a runaway truck ramp, which looked like a road to nowhere, gray concrete poured into brown dirt. Where had the green gone? From afar, the land appeared smooth as suede, and yet, as the car streaked by, Cherry saw it was rough and rock strewn, covered in grasses that could cut.

The highway narrowed, and Cherry held her breath as they sped alongside hulking big rigs and trailers fishtailing in the wind, the mountains close. Before she knew it, they had descended, and the land opened up and flattened out. There were signs for 76 stations and McDonald's, billboards for accident lawyers, more powerlines. It was uglier than any place she'd ever been, but the ugliness was also a comfort because it meant that she and Ray had said goodbye to their old lives. At least here it was all out in the open; nothing was hidden in trees. For a few miles the landscape was a desert, and in a sandy field by the freeway stood a single oil pump. It dipped and lifted its head like a giant metal bird.

In a short while, they were in LA; it happened gradually and then all once, and then traffic caught them in its net. There were so many lanes in either direction, and theirs, southbound, was snarled with cars. Cherry had never seen so many cars. She felt a bit woozy at the sight. Next to them, a red sports coupe carried a woman with a buzz cut. Hair so blond it was white.

"You might be an owl," Cherry said, "but that woman is a polar bear."

Ray glanced over and laughed. Then, almost to himself, he said, "You've never seen it before . . ." Shaking his head. "Girls at Santa Cruz do it sometimes. I hear if you keep the bleach on too long it'll burn everything off. Scalp too."

The woman, as if sensing their gaze, glanced at Cherry. Cherry wondered what she saw. A young woman with a tangle of long blondish hair, no makeup, a chipped front tooth and another one gray, a hand-knitted green sweater far too big for her. Did she see a runaway? An escapee from a compound of women? An awestruck country girl? None of the above. Truth was, the woman barely registered Cherry, who was a nobody in a poor person's car, and she didn't care to know her story.

Cherry had been so focused on the woman that she hadn't really taken in the landscape. Now she looked. Not far, a mass of skyscrapers rose like towers a child might build. "Downtown," Ray said. It couldn't compare to the vast expanse of modest buildings and lots everywhere else. Self-storage. Office space. A parking lot of school buses. There were bushy palm trees close to the freeway, and in the distance, their taller and slimmer cousins, all trunk. Cherry spotted a few jacarandas, explosions of purple in the flats. Those trees grew in Santa Cruz too, a reminder that she and Ray hadn't traveled far, even if it felt like they'd landed on another planet. The freeway signs here were only slightly different from the ones up north, but they were different enough: a more muted green, and dirty-looking, as if dipped in soot. Streets upon streets sprouted off the freeway. This place had no beginning or end. It stretched forever.

Cherry felt suddenly ill. In Coalinga, they'd eaten the cheese and alfalfa sandwiches Ray brought, and the lingering smell on her hands, mixed with the car exhaust, was giving her an upside-down feeling.

"Are you all right?" Ray asked as he nosed forward. They were headed to Hollywood, to a motel where they could stay until they found permanent lodgings.

Was she all right? Cherry didn't know. Morning sickness hadn't struck, if it was ever going to. Anyway, this wasn't that. There was only this new world, the pocked and stained asphalt beneath their tires, the cinder block walls that separated them from the city itself, the polar bear woman. Back home, the mamas would be finishing their morning ritual, energized by the promise of the eastern wing. *The sun summons us. We are timeless.* And Cherry wasn't there.

A motorcycle gargled past, startling her. Cherry loved the morning ritual; she could admit it now that she wasn't ever going to do it again. Ray had promised her, "We're gone," and he was right. They were gone. Mama Ursa wouldn't find them, would she?

"I thought it would be sunny," was all Cherry said. The sky was an overcast white, though nothing like the fog at home, which was so thick it not only covered the world, it obliterated it. This was a mere blankness.

"So did I," Ray replied.

When Cherry thought of Los Angeles, she stupidly imagined movie stars and convertibles, a future baby wrapped like a tiny monarch in purple crushed velvet. She didn't think of Mama Ursa's name for it—"the smoggy morass." Until now.

"I'm scared," she said.

"Don't be," Ray said. And then, as the car chugged off the freeway and into the city, he said, "I'm scared too," and she thought she'd never love anyone as much as she loved him.

The city went on and on. She opened the window and let the rushing air calm her. It helped. They were heading to an area a bartender in Santa Cruz had mentioned to Ray, with plenty of cheap and convenient motels. As he drove, Ray assured Cherry that everything would be fine. His mother didn't know any of his college friends, and anyway, they weren't *real* friends. He hadn't told anyone of the plan, so there was nothing to divulge. He'd purchased the car from a stranger, with cash, and parked it down the block from his house until it was time to go. There would be no trail to follow.

"We're gone," Cherry said.

"Exactly."

The motel they chose was on the second floor above a coffee shop. They were given room number four, the keychain a diamond-shaped strip of orange plastic that read TROPICANA. As soon as they got into the room, Cherry felt shy. She and Ray were alone. Alone in a car was one thing, but alone in a room, with a large bed and heavy orange curtains lined with rubber and a door that locked, was another. They had never shared a bed, not for sex, not for sleep—that was not allowed under the rules of the mamas. Never. For all their wildness, they'd been afraid of men, of boys, too, of what they might do. Even Ray.

Well, the mamas were stupid, Cherry thought, because you didn't need a bed for what she and Ray had done.

This one had two pillows and a slinky orange bedspread. Cherry tried to conjure how she'd felt when Ray came to retrieve her the night before. The jeans, his hands in his pockets, the dark sky, the cold, cold buttons of his jacket, her hunger for him. *Watch yourself,* as the mamas said. The memory was nothing but a relic, another lifetime ago, another body ago.

"I'm not tired yet," Ray said from the other side of the bed.

"Me either," she said. She could tell he was as nervous as she was.

"Want to go outside?" he asked.

"Do you think it's safe?"

"You'd have to be an idiot to mug us poor hicks."

They walked through Hollywood for hours, up and down the seedy boulevards and into the chintzy shops, so sleep deprived it felt like something from a dream. A man walked by holding a transistor radio to his ear like a seashell, another wore a tinfoil hat, ranting. On Hollywood Boulevard, stars stamped the glittery sidewalk. They were printed with the names of people Cherry had never heard of, but that wasn't saying much. She hadn't seen a movie in her life, never watched a television show, not even a commercial. Sometimes a women's magazine might appear in the parlor as if washed ashore from a shipwreck, and she would read every wrinkled page, pore over every photo.

Until now, she had never been outside of Santa Cruz County. Until now, she'd spent her days in one rickety house, on a single piece of land, unless she was given permission to do the shopping in town or work the farmers market. All of it a few miles away. Until now, the most exciting day of her life was going to the Boardwalk three years before to ride Logger's Revenge with Mama Rose. She still nursed the memory: the way the fake log shook and nosed the chute as they boarded, the bleachy stink of the water, how her stomach jumped into her mouth as the log shot down the flume's highest drop. The view of the cliffs and the ocean on their ride down.

That was nothing compared to this. LA.

The big streets—Santa Monica, Sunset, Hollywood—stunk of fried food, car exhaust (always car exhaust), and piss, and so they wandered away from the noise, up into the curving canyon streets above. Cherry's feet in her rubber sandals ached and smarted but she didn't complain, for here was the smell of jasmine, the sound of someone's band practicing far off, a woman's squealing laugh, a big splash into what had to be a swimming pool. Cherry imagined its turquoise water; it went with the convertibles and the movie stars. Later, they ate premade sandwiches from a corner liquor store and Ray watched her drink her first Pepsi, so bubbly it was almost spicy, but actually it tasted sweet as a vein of gold. Ray watched her as the Pepsi went down, and she could tell he liked watching her.

When the sun was setting and they got so tired they could barely string together a sentence, they returned to the motel room. People were being loud a few doors down—it sounded like they were drunk or high or both. The pungent cloud of reefer on the stairs to their room made Cherry afraid; for a second she worried the mamas had found them. But no. It was the partiers. Even so, Ray must have had the same fear because he used both locks on the door. Cherry pulled the heavy curtains. They began to get ready for bed. In the bathroom, they stood side by side before the sink, meeting each other's eyes in the warped and rusted mirror. Cherry felt exhausted and sunstricken, and yet she wasn't sleepy. Anticipation coursed through her. In the mirror, Ray's forehead was pink and glossy with sun, and the color made his dark eyes appear darker. His new black shirt was now wrinkled. He pulled at the collar.

Cherry had never, in her nineteen years, used store-bought toothpaste, and though she'd seen the boxes on the grocer's shelves, she never imagined what it might be like. Ray's toothpaste came in a tube with a ribbed white cap that felt pleasing between her thumb and index finger. It tasted as blunt as metal, fizzy as the Pepsi she'd loved so much. It was called Crest—like the highest point of an ocean wave, like the feathers on a bird's head, a crown that communicates. Now, like toothpaste.

"Can I get my teeth fixed sometime?" she asked.

"A dentist," he said. "Sure." He'd been the only kid on the compound to see one, and they both knew it.

They were pretending it was normal, to be brushing their teeth at a motel sink. They couldn't stand here forever. Aside from holding hands on their walk, they had barely touched each other's bodies since before the escape. Cherry knew that would change as soon as they got into bed. They would not be too tired for that; they had to do it, she thought, otherwise why had they run away together? It wasn't only to get away from the mamas. To take their baby far from there. It was because they were in love. Ray took off his wrinkled shirt and the sight of his broad back made the feeling inside her rise—the hunger. It was a comfort to feel it.

He took her hand and led her to the bed. One of the side table lamps was lit, and in its meek glow he undressed her, first her shirt and then her pants; there were no brassieres at home, and rarely clean underpants, and so in half a minute she was nude, and Ray leaned back to look at her. Her nipples were already a darker shade of pink, and her breasts were swollen. Did Ray notice? He didn't usually see her completely naked. There was never time, there were too many chores or little girls about, or it was too risky.

Even though she wasn't showing yet, he cupped the space beneath her belly button as if she were. Inside was Opal.

With his touch Ray told Cherry that they didn't have to be furtive anymore. This city was huge, and no one knew their story or where they came from. They were a couple now, like any other. And, soon, they would be a family.

∞

After a week at the Tropicana, they found the rental. They didn't call it a house, even though that's what it was. A ten-minute drive from the motel, in what the listing called the Fairfax District, it was one of the thousands of little Spanish-style places in LA with a stucco exterior and a tiled roof and a front lawn. The backyard was a carpet of grass, brown and scrubby, with a lemon tree in one corner, and telephone wires stitching the sky above. Inside, the living room's tall ceiling curved at the corners, and down the hall were two small bedrooms and one bathroom with lavender-colored tiles. They rented it immediately. Although it was built in the twenties, the rental felt brand new compared to what they were used to; home seemed ancient by comparison. That house and this one couldn't be called the same thing, Ray said, they were just too different.

They bought a mattress and some dishes, and the landlady, Mrs. Vartanian, who explained that the neighborhood was a destination for young people like them, left a card table and two folding chairs in the dining room. The baby would be born in February; there would be time to furnish the rooms and prepare. They both wanted the baby to have a crib and one of those spinning things hanging over it. Ray wanted a nightlight, shaped like a star, and Cherry wanted a stuffed animal, its fake fur softer than a rabbit's. Nor far from the rental, a construction crew was tearing down a children's playland to build an enormous mall, to be called the Beverly Center, and Ray said he wished it were finished and open already, so they could go shopping. Cherry, who had never been to a mall, was nervous about the idea.

Instead, she took to haunting the consignment shop around the corner on Fairfax, where elderly shopkeepers swept the sidewalks. Their stores sold nuts or Shabbat candles or kosher pizza, and in the consignment shop women in wigs and headscarves chatted at the register while Cherry searched for what she and Ray needed. On the weekends they took the car out, looking for garage sales. It seemed that everyone in LA in possession of a front lawn displayed, at one point or another, their unwanted wares for people on a budget. Cherry imagined having her own garage sale in a couple of years. A baby grew fast; nothing fit or made sense for long; she'd have to sell the old to have money for the new. She could almost see it: the stuff organized by category, their baby toddling around the piles, babbling, and their new life, flowing along.

Cherry liked the rental and the dumb sunlight that poured through the living room window every afternoon. In the hallway was a built-in desk called a secretary, and in the bedrooms French windows. She liked the wide-open backyard and its lemon tree, and she liked the neat avenue out front, lined with sycamore trees. She liked the four-way stop signs at the corner; it could be a neighborhood anywhere. Most of all, she marveled at how little she had to do. It wasn't boredom. It was freedom.

The mamas treated her like a servant, she realized. Back home, there were always rooms to clean and hallways to sweep, the garden to weed, a dress or romper to mend. There were meals to prepare and children to mind. The harvesting of the weed made her fingers bleed, and packing it once the girls separated the leaves from the shake was a real headache. The labor never ended—and the mamas were creating more for her. Although they had finally invited her to the morning ritual, which she loved, it was so peaceful, after a week it became her job to prepare the mugs and put on the kettle and then clean up once it was over. Cherry didn't complain because it felt like a test. For a year the mamas dangled before her the promise of the eastern wing.

Soon, Cherry, soon, they said. Soon she would be invited behind that door.

What did the mamas do in there? The kids used to debate it constantly. They knew it was something big. Probably scary. Likely dangerous. After Hawk, Cherry was sure of that. After Hawk, they stopped their conjecturing altogether. Hurt too much.

Whatever happened in there, the mamas gave up everything for it.

Once a month, the mamas grew frantic, readying their supplies of ash sticks and candles. In a basin outside, they washed the stones that lived in the eastern wing: the pyrite, the agate, the turquoise. The mamas said the stones could not be dusty. Why not? Cherry wanted to know. She was afraid to know.

The secret ritual in the eastern wing made what the mamas did together in the mornings seem insignificant. Just some tea. Some little slogans. *We are timeless.* Okay, sure. Even so, Cherry felt something special in those morning rituals. A bit of magic. The eastern wing had to be another level, a mountain she never got to climb.

Soon, Cherry, soon, they said. Only to yank it away.

Every open moon brought the same excuses. Cherry was needed with the girls. She wasn't ready. She wasn't a woman yet. Bleeding didn't make you a woman, or not only that.

Then what did?

If they knew she'd been with Ray. A man. Would that change things?

Maybe having this child would finally make Cherry a woman.

Not that she wanted that life anymore. She was going to be a mother. Not a mama. Never.

"The goddess will tell me when it's time for you to join us," Mama Ursa was fond of saying.

To Ray, it was absurd. More than that, he said. It was cruel.

Cherry was inclined to agree, as much as it hurt to admit that the mamas didn't love her. They merely found her useful.

If the mamas came looking for them, Cherry knew it was Ray they would want.

She did not let herself think what Mama Ursa might do if she learned of the baby. Just picturing her child back home with the mamas made Cherry's blood freeze.

So she didn't picture it. There was no need. They were gone. They were okay.

∞

For the first few weeks the skies in Los Angeles were white until noon, and then they transformed into a cloudless blue. Before it got too hot, Cherry would go outside and sit on the spongy earth beneath the lemon tree. In its shade, she closed her eyes, trying to mute the helicopters and the car horns and the ubiquitous growl of leaf blowers.

Despite her best efforts, she missed home. She missed its trees—oh how she missed its trees, the pines and the Douglas firs, and the redwoods especially, which could survive fires, go on growing like nothing bad had ever happened to them. Their trunks, charred and hollow in some places, gave them away. To her surprise, she also missed the dank stink of weed: growing out of the earth, then harvested, then smoked. And the vegetal smell of henna, which a few of the mamas used to dye their hair. They would lean over the edge of the creek, rubbing the mud-like substance into their locks, the skin at their hairline stained orange. "You're next!" one of them might joke.

Home smelled like life, sweet and musky. Here it was cut grass and wet concrete after the sprinklers. The motor oil for their car.

But they were okay.

The baby was coming, and Ray liked his job at DataComp, which paid decently. Each day he left the rental in one of his three suits. His clients were big corporations: banks, insurance companies, even movie studios. Rather than print on paper, Ray explained, which was expensive, these corporations had their data printed on microfiche.

"You can fit two hundred pages on one little fiche card," Ray said.

His job was to sell DataComp's services, talk up how fast they were, how cheap. After he signed them up, someone from his company would come and pick up the client's tapes. DataComp transferred the data from the tapes onto the fiche overnight, and before dawn a guy in a pickup truck delivered it back to the client. Ray described the microfiche in the cab, bundled together with thick rubber bands, the largest orders wrapped in packages the size of shoe boxes. After his first week on the job, he took Cherry to the library to show her a bank of fiche readers. A woman was leaning into one, squinting at a column of black that looked stenciled with words.

"It's a tiny photograph of a newspaper story," Ray explained.

On his first day of work, Cherry stood on the porch as the car got farther and farther away, until she couldn't see it any longer. Then she was alone. Inside, she washed the breakfast dishes and mopped the floors. She cleaned the toilet. She showered and dressed. It wasn't even ten o'clock and she and the rental were spotless; there were no more chores to distract her. She walked through the rooms, thinking of what to do next. The quiet lay heavy as smog.

"Hello," she called through the empty house. "Helloooo."

Her voice sounded tinny and pathetic.

It would be like this from now on, she realized. She had hours ahead of her, and she would be alone. Tomorrow, and the day after that, and the day after that. Hours alone. To do what? Wait for Ray. Wait for the baby to be born.

She imagined holding the baby, making raspberries at it, dressing it, bathing it. That would be nice.

With the mamas she was isolated, but there was activity and noise. Now she was by herself in a city bigger than some countries. If she had a question, there was no one to answer it. If she was hurt, no one would know.

Then again, her whole life she hurt and nobody but Ray noticed.

At the kitchen table, she drew one of the cartoon pictures he liked, this one of their baby, naked save for a diaper, climbing a palm tree.

For a while, she cleaned the already-clean tile grout in the kitchen. She swept the front porch.

Eventually, she took a walk, finally daring herself to turn right on Melrose, with its streetlights and boutiques, the cars swerving toward suddenly available parking meters. She passed punks with foot-high Mohawks and spikes drilled into their vests; they were begging for change, their mutts on ropes sitting sentry. "Spare a quarter," they called to her, and she sewed a tight-lipped smile on her face and moved on. Another polar bear woman, white-blond hair to her shoulders, stepped out of a store dedicated, as far as Cherry could tell, to selling dog collars to humans. She passed a vintage clothing shop called LEO RISING in sparkling silver letters; through the front window she spotted a baby sitting atop a mountain of clothing. Cherry could see the mother—she presumed she was the baby's mother—leaning against the counter nearby, talking on the phone as she made goofy eyes at the child.

No one noticed Cherry. She was young but not as pretty as the other young women, who seemed to know how to hold their faces, how to walk, how to *be*. Other women wore dresses and jackets that gave them sharp angles and tiny waists, leather boots in bright colors, and leopard-print belts. They wore ties, too, when all along Cherry had assumed ties were for men. They wore big dangling earrings; Cherry didn't even have pierced ears. She wore the plainest clothes that drew zero attention, boring oversized T-shirts and elastic-waist skirts that would stretch as the baby grew, and comfortable white shoes the salesman called *tennies*. That day on Melrose, she passed a woman wearing lace lingerie as a blouse, and then a man ran past her in too-short linen pants and dark loafers with socks white as the fog she missed so badly. He stopped and laughed at someone behind Cherry. She saw that there were a trio of friends at the end of the block, laughing at his antics. When she turned back around, he was doing cartwheels down the street.

Cherry went back to the rental to wait for Ray. He was home by six. He had his suit on, and she loved the way he looked in it, especially with the jacket off and flipped over his shoulder, balanced on two curved fingers. He could walk down Melrose like that.

Ray was spilling details about his day and then he kissed her and asked how she did on her own, a little concerned, protective as always. She described the cartwheeling kid.

"He reminded me of someone," she said, and Ray didn't have to ask who.

"Let me show you something," she said, as soon as he'd changed into jeans and a T-shirt.

At the back of their closet was her pillowcase from home. Nearly empty. She grabbed it and told Ray to follow her to the yard, where the sun was still bright, almost manically so, and an airplane was drawing a line of white across the blue.

From the pillowcase, she pulled out the rocks. Eleven in all. Ray didn't look so much surprised as reassured. The rocks were on the ground between them until he picked one up and held it in his fist and Cherry picked another and did the same. They handled each until their blood warmed it, and then they encircled the lemon tree with them.

Now Hawk was here, too, even if she and Ray would never say his name. They wanted to say it, they both did, but they would have to practice the not-saying before the baby came, just as they had to work to get their house set up, and learn LA, and figure out how to live without the mamas. Ray and Cherry sat beneath the lemon tree and held one another, in grief and relief, the ring of stones a reminder, a talisman, an altar.

The child could know nothing of what they'd left behind.

∞

A little over seven months later, Cherry went into labor.

The year is 1981. The month February.

Picture Cedars-Sinai Medical Center, the new location, only five years old by that time. Picture the bland yet colossal building, the Stars of David on its west and east exteriors, the Datsuns and Oldsmobiles parked in the lot outside. Picture Cherry in the maternity ward, lowing and moaning like a cow. She's on all fours, in a hospital gown, on a plastic and metal bed, as Ray leans over her, rolling a cold can of Pepsi up and down her lower back. Picture the can. It says CATCH THAT PEPSI SPIRIT! in diagonal lettering. Later, when the baby is asleep in the hospital nursery, Cherry will crack open this soda and drink it. Picture the beige hospital room, its large double-paned window, its smell of bleach and antiseptic failing to override the smell of Cherry's sweat and exertions. Her breath is a dead animal, and she has no idea, and she wouldn't care if she did because she is in labor and thus beyond shame. Picture the New Wave haircut on the youngest nurse, her mane like a cockatoo's (a crest), her long nails squared off and painted magenta. Picture the cornstarch dust inside the doctor's latex gloves. Picture the baby, tunneling toward the light. On the street below, an RTD huffs by.

When it's over, and Opal is born, the nurse with the cockatoo hair whispers *what a beauty* as she wipes the fluid and vernix from the baby's purplish body. Cherry, spent and elated, eyes half-closed, asks if everything is okay, and the nurse says, "Your baby is perfect. Better than perfect. Her light shines so bright."

It does. This is indisputable.

Cherry saw it as soon as the nurse placed Opal in her arms. Down below, someone was stitching a wound, but on her chest lay this perfect tiny child. A girl. Safe with her parents. Only one mother. It would now be the three of them. It was as if Cherry and Ray had been running from a flood. Picture this: their higher ground.

6

THE DAY URSA FOUND OUT THAT RAY AND CHERRY HAD run away together was more than seven months before this. June 1980. June 21 to be exact, the summer solstice.

When Ursa woke that morning, just after dawn, her back aching, she didn't realize this date would be forever branded in her mind with a hot hiss. No, that morning, she was tired, nothing more. In the half-light, the dresser beamed, and the pink peony in its green vase showboated. The dresser was at once fussy and imposing, from the mid-nineteenth century, one of the few pieces of furniture they hadn't sold. There was nothing as nice in the rest of the house, and it pleased her to think this.

A few minutes later, she headed downstairs for the morning ritual. In her mind, Ursa could already see the mint steeping in the hot water, how the scent would open her sinuses and the mug would warm her hands. She stood in the first-floor hallway, at the place where the finger paint greened the wainscoting. Cherry's door was painted bright yellow.

"Cherry," she whispered.

Cherry prepared the morning ritual with Ursa or Mary: picking and storing the mint, filling the tea kettles, lining up the mugs, the others shuffling in, yawning, good morning, ready for another day, praise goddess. Then Cherry cleaned it up.

"Cherry," Ursa whispered again, and pushed open the door.

She still felt tired, a little dreamy. Her back hurt. She was running through the day's tasks, barely seeing what was in front of her. The transport—the big one, with the mamas watching and holding her—was tonight. The summer solstice transport was always special and there was a lot to prepare. The women were wound up last night. "I can feel the fizz," Rose said more than once.

Ursa was so busy mentally going over the preparations for the transport (candles, matches, sage, water jugs, barley tea) that she didn't initially realize Cherry wasn't in the room.

"Cherry?" Ursa said again.

The quilt was bunched up at the foot of the bed, clothes scattered across the floor.

Perhaps, Ursa thought, she was already in the kitchen. She would be plucking the mint off its stems, bringing a leaf to her nose, eyes closed in minor ecstasy. Ursa could picture her in one of the aprons, standing straight, so serious.

It was then that she noticed the bare pillow. Where was the eyelet pillowcase that she bought Cherry at the antique mall in Half Moon Bay? She doesn't yet understand.

Downstairs, there was no water singing in the kettles. There was no mint evenly distributed into each mug. There was no Cherry. Only Joan, goofy Joan, in a ratty bathrobe, Roo suckling at her breast.

"Goddess bless this day," Joan said, which is what they always said in the mornings.

"Where's Cherry?" Ursa asked.

The morning ritual commenced as usual, save for Cherry's conspicuous and troubling absence, the mamas sitting at the table and on the counters, or cross-legged on the floor. They sipped their tea, humming gratefulness. The sunlight funneled into the windows and covered the room with gold. *The sun summons us*, the mamas said. *We are timeless*, Ursa replied.

But where was Cherry?

All the other kids were much younger than her; the next oldest was Tova and she was only seven. That morning, one of the mamas, maybe Faye, gave Tova some pickles and told her to take everyone outside until the women were done with the tea.

Now Ursa stood up from the table, startling Bernadette, who let out a little gasp and banged her mug on the table.

"Cherry is missing," Ursa said.

The mamas were so inside their gratitude that no one responded, or they didn't do so fast enough, and Ursa pushed her way out of the kitchen, stepping over Pamela sitting in the doorway.

The kids congregated at the edge of the driveway. Hanna wore Roo on her back and was growling like an animal. A few were throwing rocks. Sage was humming. It was cold out, and one of the little girls, they called her Kitty but that wasn't her real name, Ursa didn't care what her real name was, had the giant jar of pickles tipped into her mouth, and she was drinking the juice. Ursa was aware that she should feel bad for not caring about Kitty—but she couldn't summon any emotion for the child. Kitty wasn't wearing shoes and it was cold out. Maybe that was why they called her Kitty, Ursa thought, because she had paws instead of feet.

"Go find Cherry," Ursa called from the porch. "She's on the land somewhere. Or hiding in the house."

The girls scattered like birds. They thought this was another game, which was how the mamas got the youngest ones to do anything. Kids were quite good at labor if you pretended it was something else.

They yelled Cherry's name as they searched the big old house, all its hidden corners, as they crossed and recrossed the creek.

There was no sign of her. It wasn't like her to play a prank.

"She's either gone, or she's been taken," Pamela said. The latter seemed unlikely, but it was enough of a possibility that Ursa decided to drive into Santa Cruz to get Ray's advice.

Ursa knew as soon as she saw his empty driveway that he was gone for good. A mother's intuition, perhaps. Through a window she saw his open bedroom closet, as bare as the mattress on the floor. She ran along the other side of the house, where he kept the garbage bins. Nothing to do but search them. She lifted open the first bin, wondering what to feel. She wasn't worried or angry so much as confused. Where was her son?

He had thrown out nearly an entire fridge's worth of food, folders upon folders of old schoolwork, pennies and chewed-up pens, a ratty towel.

She found the keys when she kicked over the second trashcan. That old blue rabbit foot she stole for him when he turned eight. One key was for her truck, and the other three for her house: front door, side door, lookout cottage. Ray didn't need them anymore and so he tossed them away in the same way he did the statistics homework and the meat he wouldn't eat. This was the trash of someone who had moved away, who was looking ahead. It was the freewheeling discard of one life as you anticipated another.

Ursa put the rabbit foot in her mouth and locked her teeth down like an epileptic anticipating a seizure. The tiny bones crunched. How could he leave? She felt herself falling to the ground. She closed her eyes.

Focus. Breathe.

The membrane between *then* and *now* was out there. Nearby. On the tip of her tongue. It was like feeling for the opening of an envelope—not that it would rip apart as easily as that: she wasn't in the eastern wing, or inside an armoire, or inside, period. She was out in the open, unprepared, on the side of a house in downtown Santa Cruz, in full sunlight. Someone might walk by at any moment. No place for a transport.

Ursa didn't care. She wanted it.

She breathed in, and *focus, focus*, she found the edge of the membrane. Slipped in. Her stomach cramped, and her head felt crushed.

Whoosh.

Ursa went backward. Her lungs, her chest, oh it was crushing.

In the bedroom, full moon framed by the open window like in a children's book, the air humid. She is naked, in labor. Her every nerve and muscle and joint twisted and crushed, this pain a tornado she's been sucked into. The midwife and Mary bustle behind her and Ursa wants them to go away, get a doctor to cut this thing out, leave her with a scar like a zipper from her belly to her womanhood, fine, whatever. Anything to make this stop. The pain sears and the white heat of it obliterates everything else, the room and the midwife and Mary too. No more unreal human pain. She is an animal what a horror what a balm.

Ursa slipped out of the moment before Ray is handed to her, before the torture of his birth recedes and the other, tender feelings sweep in. She was back in Santa Cruz, lying on the ground with a cheek to the dirt, the keychain still between her teeth.

She spit it out. She wanted to vomit and so she did, right next to where she lay. She looked up, as woozy as she ever was as a teenager in San Francisco.

Things felt wrong. The air syruped. No wind to speak of. Too still. Deathly.

The birch tree at the edge of Ray's front yard—what was the matter with it? The white trunk was blistered with black and the branches were bare, its fallen leaves a ring on the ground, as if the tree had dropped its skirt. A few feet away from the tree lay a crow, limp and dead, a puddle of black on the green grass.

Still feeling weak and ill, Ursa forced herself to stand, surveying the street. At least no one had seen her transport. Only the tree, apparently.

Ray skipped town. She knew this, just as she knew, somehow, that Cherry went with him.

Where did they go? And why?

The last time she saw Ray, they discussed how she would bring the truck over to help him move. He was a man, sure, but he was her son, and he would live in the house with her and the mamas. She still wasn't used to his hair, newly shorn after it had always been long, his ears pale white and delicate, tiny pimples on the back of his neck. Other than that, nothing seemed different.

She saw Cherry last night. The girl came up to Ursa's room to say goodnight and before leaving opened her arms with a shrug. Ursa laughed because they rarely hugged and opened her arms back. The girl leaned against her, resting her head on Ursa's chest. So that had been *goodbye.*

Ursa got back into the truck; once the door was shut, she closed her eyes. She breathed deeply, searching for the membrane a second time. Here it was. She was at the edge and she wanted back in. The door wasn't knocking, it was locked, and she was the one doing the knocking. She was banging on the door. She would kick it down. *Focus focus in in in—*

She slipped through with a cry.

This time she transported haphazardly, searching for Ray and Cherry together, as recent as she could get, though she could never get anywhere recent because the membrane still wouldn't allow it, no matter how experienced she got.

Ursa wanted a clue. She saw Cherry again and again, though only briefly: her growing interest in the morning ritual; sorting the edibles; tallying them after this or that festival; sewing a pair of pants and mending the children's clothing; playing cards with Darcy's youngest; hushing another baby before a transport, Ursa having to tell Cherry to get the brandy to calm her, the mamas were about to begin. She kept transporting. Ray was hardly there, he was at school, and when he was visiting, he wasn't anywhere near Cherry.

She scooped herself out. There was that bad feeling again, the air viscous and still. On the radio, cracks spiderwebbed at the red dial line. Ursa turned the knob, and the red dial didn't move.

"Well shit."

She started the truck but kept it in park, her hands shaking on the steering wheel, no music or radio news to blunt the truth, which was that there weren't any clues in the past because she hadn't paid enough attention to them—to any of the children.

She put the truck into reverse and backed out of the driveway without looking behind her.

Cherry. She was naïve and kind. She wasn't very smart. She was sensitive. She would have been the first of the daughters to age into the transport, and the others thought her presence would be powerful, though Ursa was skeptical. Ruth had been so dismissive, and Cherry came from Ruth.

Well, now Cherry was with Ray. Ursa was sure of it.

If the girl was unhappy, if she longed to see the world out there, she never let it show. And why go with Ray? Some of the younger kids were attached at the hip, spoke in secret codes, shared beds and their special pretend games. Ray and Cherry were never like that. They were rarely together. There was no bond between them.

Unless.

Ursa knew what it meant. Cherry and Ray—

She shook the thought from her mind as she sped through town. She couldn't bear to think it. The thought was too much.

If Cherry and Ray were only friends, Ursa would have seen it. They hid what they had together. What they *did* together.

Were they in love? Her child with *that* child?

The road tightened and curved, bending into the forest. The ancient redwoods blurred past, swipes of paint. Ursa thought she might vomit again.

It wasn't love. No. Couldn't be.

She reached the property without realizing it, and it was as if she came to with a gasp, her truck pushing through the first tentacle of the maze, and then the second, tree branches whipping at the windshield. She gritted her teeth. She bore down on the accelerator and gunned the engine, the truck bucking forward. *Thunk, thunk* went the tree branches in her way, she wanted the trees dead. She turned off the second tentacle and onto the third, which was hard to get through and minimally maintained. It was used for walking, a private trail for the mamas and the girls, though now Ursa wanted it differently. She wanted everything different.

Ursa sped the truck through the path, snapping tree branches, squashing ferns, bursting huckleberries as she went. A ground squirrel ran across the passage and Ursa nailed the gas pedal with her foot, her hands squeezing the wheel. She hoped she killed the little animal.

She was headed to the eastern wing. She needed it. She would get in there and lock the door and transport to her son. Where had he gone, and why?

Tell me, tell me, Ursa thought, her brain as brambly as the forest around her.

She rounded the curve to where the third tentacle met the first. There was the lookout cottage, where Alice was last night, allegedly keeping watch. How did she not hear Cherry leaving? Or Ray coming to fetch her? Alice was useless. Worse than useless.

The truck rammed into the cottage door. Ursa backed it up and did it again for good measure, her neck snapping back against the seat as metal hit wood. No one was inside the cottage: lucky them, too bad. Her neck would be fine, a touch sore. The cottage door was crumpled like a crying child. Ursa imagined the truck's front grill was gnarled too. So what. She needed the eastern wing.

The sounds of her destruction pulled the women out of complacent stupors. She heard whistling and then the airhorn, and when she rammed the truck down the front driveway, the only child she spotted was Roo in Annie's arms as Annie ran into the house, the screen door coughing shut behind her. In front of the house, a few of the mamas stood guard. Mary held one of the hunting rifles, Joan the airhorn. Gertie had a shovel. They looked confused. They had expected an intruder, a man, and here was Ursa.

She got out of the truck, and Mary passed the gun to Gertie and came running.

"Are you hurt? Was there an accident?"

Ursa pushed her off. "We need to be in the eastern wing."

"It's only ten. The moon doesn't open for hours."

"*Now.*"

"What about the children? Cherry isn't here to—"

"I don't care about the fucking children! Lock them up if you must."

Ursa went inside, striding through the kitchen and down the hall-way, where Alice stood, looking terrified and then confused. As Ursa passed her, she slammed into Alice's stupid meaty shoulder, the urge to transport rising. She was almost to the eastern wing.

She unlocked the door and entered.

Here it was. The energy gathered like storm winds. Ursa felt strong, stronger than she ever had. The membrane had already been loosened. Now it *was* an envelope and she the letter opener.

Ursa slipped out of her clothes and kneeled on one of the pillows that waited for her at the center of the room. The stones in the corners breathed. Sunlight fell through the skylights above, and the top of Ursa's head, her chest, her navel, shined in the glow.

Her eyes were already closed, so she didn't see the women entering the room, only heard and sensed them. She didn't know that Mary was upstairs, hushing the children, many of whom were crying and asking who had trespassed, what he wanted. At least Mary had the sense to bring a jug of water and a fresh loaf of bread before padlock-ing the door from the outside. It would be hours before anyone came to let them out.

Mary made it into the eastern wing right as Ursa was slipping into the membrane.

Whoosh.

The glow through skylights grew stronger and stronger until it hummed. The mamas weren't encircling Ursa as usual; they crowded the room's many edges, leaning against the walls, hugging the pil-lows, or holding each other's hands. A few covered their eyes and mouths. They were nervous, and some were scared because this wasn't how it usually went. Ursa was breaking the rules.

Ursa transported, and the eastern wing pulsed like a wound until the mamas felt the familiar bliss descend. The room pulsed and so did the mamas, their bodies tap-tapping as the good feelings flew in. Ursa slicked through the past until she found Ray. She was holding him to her breast. She was burping him on her shoulder. She was rubbing strings of lint out of his tiny fists.

And then he was learning to crawl, pulling his body across the parlor like a soldier in the grass. Now he was saying his first words. *Mama, milk, bird, need, moon, hi.* She smelled the top of his head. Now she was placing his first rose quartz in his hand, asking him if he could feel it calling to his heart; she was watching him bite into a peach; she was feeling his back rise and fall as he slept beside her. She was a good mother.

In the eastern wing, the room vibrated, and the mamas moaned in pleasure. It felt better and better as Ursa went deeper and deeper into the membrane.

Here it came, the rush—

The transports always had a rhythm, like a dance or the tides of the ocean, and the mamas sensed that the moment when Ursa paddled her way back to them, to the present, was just up ahead. The intensity would soon recede.

Except, this time it didn't.

Ursa was far away, leaning over a little sleeping Ray, who smelled of breastmilk and crackers. Now she was watching him dip a toe into the creek water, squealing.

She was a good mother.

Ray, trying to cut his own hair with a paring knife.

Ray, laughing at his belly, covered with creek mud.

Ray, eating a bowl of oatmeal, bleary-eyed with sleep.

Ray. Ray.

Ursa wasn't paddling back to the mamas.

On the floor of the eastern wing she writhed and moaned, and the room pulsed until it shook, and it felt like too much, like a roller coaster ride that wouldn't stop, the pleasure flipping to pain. The women felt it in in their bodies: a tight throat, a stomach cramp, a bolt of pain through the brain. It was that same sick feeling they experienced after every transport, except this wasn't the aftermath, the transport kept going. Ursa was still inside it, and unless she came to, the nausea, the headaches, the diarrhea would hurtle through every one of the mamas. It was already happening. Mary's head hurt so bad she wanted to scream. She did.

"Ursa! Come back!"

Ursa, tucked into a ball, the pillow kicked away, was halfway across the room. She spoke unintelligibly, as if in a dream. The light shined as bright as ever and now it hurt to look at it. Mary tried approaching Ursa, but she had to cover her eyes, it was too much, and then she couldn't see where she was going, and her stomach rollicked, as if socked. Gertie vomited.

Ursa transported until the membrane grew cloudy with her sweat and the dust of her sloughed-off skin cells. She pushed harder and harder, ignoring the calls of the women on the other side of time. Telling her to snap out of it, to please stop, please.

She kept going. Back, back.

Where had she gone wrong? Didn't Ray understand that she loved him?

She dove deeper, searching. She went backward. To the beginning.

Ray. A baby. She was holding him, felt his peach fuzz cheek against her own.

She pushed harder.

She loved him. Didn't he love her back?

The eastern wing pulsed, and pulsed again, and Ursa went back still.

The first moment.

She held a slippery, amniotic-glazed newborn to her bare chest. His first hair sponged to his tiny unknit skull. The umbilical cord snaked them together, and it was still warm, still sending oxygen and blood, though he didn't need it any longer. He was pressed against her chest, eyes closed.

In the eastern wing, a flash of renewed euphoria throttled through the mamas, a pleasure so deep it would warp them. The room seemed to buckle, it would crack open like an egg; the walls shimmered until a small fissure appeared. Inches away, Alice swayed. The crack braided the wall, crawling up it like an insect. It was as if Alice cracked too, and she fell to the floor, collapsing with a horrible flesh-slapping, bone-pounding sound.

The pleasure vanished as fast as it appeared. The sight of Alice, broken on the floor, was enough to pull the rest out of their hazes. They surrounded Alice, who lay comatose on the floor, deranged by something, her eyes half-closed, fish-like.

"We need to get her out of here," Bernadette cried. "All of us do!"

Joan and Darcy grabbed Alice's legs, and with Bernadette's help, they dragged her body toward the door, the others following, a few crawling, too weak to stand. Alice's head slid through Gertie's pool of vomit, leaving a sour trail across the room, and her limp hand, a dead fish, caught on the pile of discarded clothing, towing Ursa's dress with her.

Mary stayed in the eastern wing. She couldn't leave Ursa. Despite the pain in her head and her cramping stomach, despite the bright light, she tugged at her friend.

"Ursa! Come back!"

Mary slapped Ursa's face. She punched her stomach.

Ursa kept hurtling. She'd wanted to get away, find Ray, and so she had. Ursa knew she was being destructive and selfish, and she didn't care.

Here was baby Ray. Here was Ray at three, at six, at nine. At one. At two weeks old.

Ray, Ray, Ray.

Upstairs, locked in the purple room, the children cried and fought and fell silent, frightened by the sounds coming from the first floor of the house. That night they would be sick with hunger, and still no one would come to unlock the door.

In the parlor, Alice lay on the same couch where Hawk once lay suffering before he died.

Ursa didn't come to until the next day. By then she was covered in her own urine and shit, her tongue bleeding. She wasn't in the eastern wing anymore.

"Wake up!" Mary said. She stood over Ursa in Ursa's bathtub, and the water pouring over Ursa's head was cold and mean.

Mary saw that Ursa was back. Between tears, she told her that Karin was on the next plane out of Bangkok.

∞

More than two decades after she left California, Karin came back. The afternoon Karin returned, Ursa sat on the porch, a quilt wrapped around her shoulders. It wasn't cold out and yet she felt chilled. Mary kept taking her temperature to be sure there was no fever. There wasn't, only a cold fatigue down to her bones. The transporting levied its tax and now she was paying it.

Ursa hadn't moved for nearly a day; she took her meals there, getting up only to use the bathroom. Everyone except Mary was avoiding her, buzzing about in the kitchen or acting as if the reefer needed to be dealt with right away. That or they were officiously tending to Alice, who lay in one of the bedrooms, lights off and curtains drawn. So far, she hadn't spoken a word, only moaned, as if ill with a malady she could not or would not name. She seemed so fragile. She had to be carried to the toilet.

"What did you do to her?" Mary asked once Ursa was able to talk.

Ursa shrugged; she honestly had no idea, though she didn't exactly feel contrite. "Alice had it coming."

From where Ursa sat on the porch, she could see the children painting the trees. They seemed perfectly fine, running between the redwoods with their paintbrushes. It didn't take kids any time at all to bounce back. She didn't see what the big deal was. They hadn't been hurt in the purple room, they were fed as soon as the room was unlocked. If anything, they'd been spared.

The sound of the blue truck's engine broke Ursa's revery; at the noise, Tova began to holler, and a few of the youngest ones, seeing her panic, began to cry. Okay, maybe they weren't fine.

A mama, hearing the truck, called the children inside, and Ursa watched as they picked up their palettes and paintbrushes and bounded past Ursa into the house. She tried not to cower at how they displaced the air with their movements. She would trade every one of those kids to have Ray back. She willed herself not to tip into another transport. She told herself to wait for Karin.

The person emerging from the truck cab looked nothing like the friend Ursa remembered. This Karin, the Karin of 1980, was not only older; she was thinner, more severe looking. She was bald. She wore unflattering khaki pants and a T-shirt that read THAILAND, with a drawing of an elephant.

"Ursa," she called out.

Ursa stood to get a better look at the woman, who was now helping Mary with the luggage in the truck bed.

"You're bald," Ursa said, once Karin was facing her on the porch.

"You don't have to tell me it makes my nose look gigantic because I am well aware." Then she squinted at Ursa, took her in. "What in the fuck have you done to yourself?"

And Ursa knew she was the same old Karin.

"I'm home," Karin said, looking up at the house with reverence. Ursa had nearly forgotten that Karin was born in the house and that her father died here. Her husband too. Karin narrowed her eyes at Ursa. "Why the mazes? The—uh—tentacles?"

"Let's go inside," Ursa replied.

"Mary told me you wrecked the smallest tentacle, the one you can walk through, and I saw more than a few ruined trees on the one we drove down. How could you? And that little house—the casita?"

"The cottage."

"You rammed your truck right into it like a drunk."

"I know," Ursa said, dropping her quilt, straightening her posture. "In case you've forgotten, the front door is this way."

She led Karin into the house. The other women congregated in the entryway to catch a sight of the visitor; they had finally worked up the courage to get closer to Ursa. They used to love when she transported to her early days with Karin in the city, to the parties and the hikes and the drives to Inverness to eat oysters. When Ursa came to, the mamas would tell her how the air turned springy, that everything felt full of promise; the optimism carried for days afterward. Now they treated Ursa like a dog with rabies, afraid she'd bite them.

"You must be the mamas!" Karin said. "I love you already."

Ursa let everyone introduce themselves, and then she instructed Mary to give Karin a tour. "Not that you need one, seeing as this is your house."

"*Was* my house," Karin said. "Much has changed."

Ursa guessed that meant Mary had filled Karin in on everything.

Mary showed their guest how they'd set things up to accommodate everyone: the two big tables in the dining room and the third one in the kitchen. The sideboard full of plates and cups, two drawers stuffed with cutlery. The closets filled with clothing and shoes, all the bandanas and hats for gardening. The two hammocks in the parlor.

"And the reefer?" Karin asked. "Where's it growing?"

"Still by that live oak you always loved," Ursa said. "Far from the road."

"Production happens in the basement," Faye said. "Or in the kitchen if we're making edibles."

"Do you want to see the eastern wing?" Mary asked with a carefulness she didn't even try to disguise. "We cleaned it after . . . what happened . . . but I'm not sure it's a good idea."

"Let's wait on that," Karin said. She looked at the group surrounding her. "And the mama who isn't feeling well?"

"Alice," Mary said. "In bed, recovering."

"She just drank some chicken broth," Faye reported.

"She'll be fine, I'm fine," Ursa said.

No one answered.

They returned to the parlor; Pamela went to fetch the brandy while everyone else found a seat. Karin was still looking around, taking it all in.

"One other question," she said, looking at Ursa. "Where are the children?"

"They took off three days ago, who knows where."

Karin flashed her a pitying smile. "I didn't mean Ray and the girl."

"Oh," Ursa said, and she knew she was supposed to feel embarrassed but felt nothing of the sort. "They're upstairs."

"So quiet?"

"They're—" Bernadette began.

"They're hiding," Ursa said.

It was house policy, Ursa tried to explain. It came out sloppily. She felt annoyed at Mary for not discussing this part ahead of time. The men, she tried to say. The lookout cottage, the mazes, the purple room. This time, she *was* embarrassed.

Karin was not pleased by any of this. "This doesn't feel good," she said. "What you can do, it feels good. There's a bad feeling in this house."

"Please keep your voice down," Mary said, gesturing to the ceiling, to the kids above.

"Why?" Karin asked.

"They'll perceive you."

Later, when it was just Karin and Ursa sitting under the live oak, passing a joint back and forth, Karin said, "You haven't lived up to your promise."

"That's obvious."

"You transported yourself sick over Ray leaving." She took a drag from the joint, closing her eyes. She opened them. "That poor Alice is bedridden and mute. And you obviously don't give a shit about the other children." Karin couldn't believe they never joined the transports, that, in fact, they were not allowed to know what the mamas did in the eastern wing.

Karin said it was unkind. "For the children to be here, but not be *here* with you—to not even know about the transports. They experience it as a primal rejection. Even Ray. How could you not tell your own son?"

"I didn't want to scare him."

"Bullshit."

"It didn't belong to him."

"Well now he's gone, and he left without even an inkling of what you can do."

"I need to find him. And Cherry."

"Maybe you should let them go." Karin lay on her back, and her breasts flopped into her armpits. The elephant on her shirt was tusked. Karin held the joint above her, waving it through the dappled light. "My former guru—ugh, what a lecher—he had a lot to say about this. It was basically if you love something let it go, et cetera."

"Ray is my child."

"He's an adult."

"There's something else you should know," Ursa said. Her head felt like lead, but her legs were weightless, they had disappeared. She wanted so badly to transport, if only to get away from this moment.

Karin sat up on her forearms. Without her full mane of curls, she looked unwell. Her skull was knobby.

"It's about Cherry," Ursa said.

"What about her."

"Cherry is Charlie's daughter."

"Who's Charlie?" Karin asked.

Ursa was stunned. How could Karin not remember Charlie? And

yet, that was the point. Why couldn't Ursa forget Charlie like everyone else had?

Then Karin was laughing. She said it was all coming back to her.
She said, "Oh, Ursa, you were always so stupid about that man."

∞

Ursa took Karin into Santa Cruz to look for Ray. No one at the university had any information. His landlord hadn't talked to him, nor
had the neighbors. Ursa had no idea who his friends were or where he
hung out when he wasn't in class. Dead ends everywhere.

"Should we hire someone to find him?" Karin finally asked when
they were driving back to the house. "He can't be hard to trace. This
is 1980. He and Cherry can be tracked down."

"I want him to come back on his own," Ursa said.

Ursa waited for Karin to assure her that he would. She didn't, and
so Ursa said, "He'll come back. And when he does, I'll tell him about
my gift."

By then, Karin had been there for a week, and she hadn't allowed
Ursa to transport. The mamas explained all the rules, so she knew
that it wasn't an open moon, that it wasn't the appropriate time.

"You know better," she told Ursa, who could feel her desire growing. A jonesing.

"But I want to."

"Don't you understand how much you've upset everyone?"

Alice was able to walk now, though she still hadn't spoken. "I'm
sure she wants to leave," Karin said, though Ursa didn't believe it.

Karin said Ursa should never again do what she'd done: transport
without control. She should always do it at the appointed time, with
the women there to support her. "Don't ever do it alone," Karin said.
It was too dangerous, she said. It was addictive.

Karin moved into Ursa's room. She slept on Ray's twin mattress.
Every morning, Ursa found her sitting cross-legged on the floor, meditating, often with her eyes open, staring at some invisible point on

the wall. Her hair was growing in white, like she'd dipped her skull in salt. She wore some of Ursa's clothing, favoring the loose dresses, and in them she looked more like the Karin whom Ursa knew in the fifties.

"Goddess bless this day," Ursa would whisper from the bed in the mornings upon waking, and Karin would turn to her, beatific.

Curiously, during the day, Karin seemed most interested in the kids. She asked them about the tree painting, if they liked the beetle wings she sent. She traipsed across the land with them, playing hide and seek and tag and red rover. She followed them into the hen house and the garden. She assisted them in the basement as they rolled the shake over the screens so it would be ready for baking; when she emerged, she seemed impressed. "They know a lot about reefer," she said. She asked Tova if she wanted to go for a walk. She gave Sage a bath. A couple of times she put Canary, the baby, down for her nap.

"That one's got a rotten tooth, no?" she said, nodding at Kitty, who was wincing as she ate a plum. Ursa shrugged. No one had cared about the children's teeth before, and Karin gave her a look.

Nearly a month passed before Karin called for Ursa to come down from her bedroom.

"The mamas want to talk," she called from the landing.

It was only an hour after morning ritual, and Ursa was changing out of her nightgown. Now she hurried to dress and braid her hair into a coil at the top of her head. The new moon was in four days. Surely, they would be going back to the eastern wing and this was what Karin wanted Ursa and the mamas to discuss. She would want them to reset the ground rules, make sure everyone felt safe and prepared. Ursa would promise to behave. She would even apologize to Alice if that's what was required.

The children were no doubt scattered across the land. For meetings like these, a mama would tell them it didn't matter what they did, as long as they remained outside and far from the house. As Ursa looked for the women in the parlor, she caught sight of Kitty with Baby Canary through the front window. They headed down the driveway; the girl, barefoot as always, held the infant on her hip, and under Canary's weight, Kitty tipped at an awkward angle. She couldn't be older than four herself.

The mamas weren't in the parlor, or the kitchen, or down with the reefer. Ursa's heart puttered as she reached the eastern wing. She hadn't seen it since that day. The second morning Karin was there, she took Ursa's key away. "For your own good," she'd said.

Ursa came to the open door. What if a child saw them?

They were waiting for her, though it was obvious no transporting would take place. The mamas had carried in chairs from the dining room, and they were set up without pattern or design, as if for a lame rec room party. In the corner, Gertie sprawled across one of the old blankets they used for picnics. She was eating pistachios, shelling them with great effort, intent on not looking at Ursa. The room smelled of new paint. Someone had spackled up the crack and painted everything so that the walls glistened new.

"Smells like the first day of school," Ursa said, trying to keep her voice light.

No one answered at first, and then Mary blurted out, "Alice left. For good."

"How did she tell you she wanted to go, if she can't even talk?"

"It's easy to communicate fear and distress," Karin said coldly. "Did you know she's been crying out in the night? Her toenails are black too. They will fall off, and she can't bear the sight of them. I had Bernadette drive her to Half Moon Bay, to her cousin. She was happy to go."

"Good for her then."

"Why don't you have a seat," Karin said.

"I'll stand." And yet she held onto an empty chair for support. After a moment, she let herself sit. "The new moon is coming."

"Ursa," Karin said. "The other mamas are leaving."

"Not me," Mary said quickly.

"This can't be," Ursa said, glancing around her.

"You frightened everyone," Mary said.

"So you keep telling me."

"They feel violated," Karin said.

"Oh please," Ursa said. "Don't talk to me about being *violated*."

"You broke all the rules and made the women feel unsafe."

"Everything's changed," Mary said.

"They realize the transports will always be yours," Karin said. "Not theirs."

Karin went on. About how, aside from how the mamas felt, it wasn't right for kids to be here. That being kept from everything that was sacred would, over time, damage them. That it probably already had. That Ursa's gift was being perverted. How she needed a smaller community to do her work, one less dependent on her. How Karin took some responsibility for leaving the country for so long. "I should have stayed to help you," she said.

Ursa tried to get someone besides Karin and Mary to look at her. No one would, or their glances were brief and apologetic, flicking away after a moment like mosquitos who had taken only an instant to steal her blood before flying off.

"You want to send the mamas and the children away," Ursa said.

"It would make it easier for you," Mary said gently.

"They *want* to go," Karin said.

Ursa waited for someone else to say something. To apologize for going or to thank her for their years here. To express their sadness, their rage even, at what happened in this very room less than a month ago. They must be so angry at her. Yet they couldn't show it. No one ever got mad at Ursa. Not on this land, not in this house. She was the boss. Or used to be. The mamas said nothing, only occasionally nodding when Karin spoke. Karin must have instructed them to remain silent.

The mamas were sheep to the end.

She waited for her anger to rise. She should stand and throw her chair. Scream. Demand that Karin leave. Who was she to make these decisions, to boss everyone? After all Ursa had done for these mamas? But the anger wasn't there. Instead, she felt tired. Sad. More than anything, she was embarrassed. The mamas had seen her lose control. And now they were leaving her.

"All right then," Ursa said and pushed herself up from the chair. She wanted to get out of the room before they saw her cry, and yet she willed herself to walk out slowly. She would not lose control entirely.

At the door, she turned. The room might have been newly painted, might have smelled of vinegar from someone's overzealous mopping, and still it was itself. It was the eastern wing. It was the room she ran into at age eighteen to unleash her power. She would keep returning.

"I can already feel the energy gathering here," she said, letting her eyes fall on the departing mamas, one by one. Pamela bit her lip and Gertie crushed an empty pistachio shell between her thumb and index finger. "You will miss it," Ursa said.

The meeting was so quick, so unceremonious, that Kitty and Canary were still on the redwood path when Ursa rushed back to her bedroom.

∞

Karin let the open moon pass without a transport. She said it was unclear when Ursa would be ready for another. Ursa felt like a prisoner and tried to wish the resentment away.

Within a few weeks, nearly everyone left. It was at these goodbyes that the mamas finally cried and asked Ursa to forgive them for leaving and thanked her for changing their relationship to themselves, for showing them the power of the goddess. She barely paid any attention.

It stung her pride to see everything she'd built for two decades dissolve so quickly. "Some cult," she said to Mary wryly, who was offended; she did not consider herself a member of a cult.

Ursa was also relieved by the departures. Karin, in the end, was right. It would be better this way. The children were a burden; so, too, were the women. All that *need*. Now that Ray was gone, and gone for good, Ursa only had room for her own pain.

By the time the moon was fattening once more, the house was quiet. It felt so large, most of the bedrooms empty and bare, the hallways hushed. In the absence of a transport, the energy had nowhere to go, and so it thickened, goopy, wherever Ursa went.

Alone before dawn, Mary and Karin asleep, she would wander the house like a ghost, sliding her hands across walls, grasping doorknobs gone cold overnight. If Ray ever came back, she thought, he would be surprised to find this place so changed.

And charged.

Ursa would put on some boots in the mudroom and go outside. Into the gray predawn. The first birds chattering. No moon, no sun.

Whatever happened when Ray and Cherry had left, when Ursa transported without permission and killed the birch tree and the crow, then broke the truck radio too; when she wrecked the mazes and the cottage; when she spent too long in the membrane, going back to her first moments with Ray—it bent her. Or fixed her. She wasn't sure. No matter how she wanted to look at it, she couldn't ignore the fact that the universe was rich with her power. The land felt bigger than ever, its trees massive, its creek loud. She couldn't wait to transport with Mary and Karin.

There were no children to decorate the redwoods. That was fine because that ritual was bullshit anyway. Just a thing to get the children to go away for a while.

Mary said she didn't even think to go. Karin said she would not be stupid enough to leave a second time.

"We will find Ray and the girl," she said. "And you will stop keeping secrets."

Ursa agreed, though she didn't know if she was capable. Her whole life was about secrets.

In the newfound quiet, the energy gathered. The air in the eastern wing prickled with expectation. The moon would be opening soon.

7

At first, Opal was wormy and long fingered, and then all at once she became a real baby, cute and chubby and bald, drool glistening her chin, snot scabbing her nostrils. Her dark eyes, which were Ray's eyes, looked and looked, curious and astonished; she would never be so beholden by the world again. She was a beautiful baby. But all babies were beautiful. How had Cherry not understood until now how miraculous they were? A baby gets a scratch and the next day it's gone. Teeth tear open their gums and there's no blood. Living on milk alone, getting fat on it, even. The aura of a baby, Cherry decided, was clean.

She thought she'd never be so happy again, and she was right.

At the baby's bedtime, she and Ray liked to sit on their bed, now outfitted with a solid pine headboard, their child between them. In the beginning, Opal lay on her back, and later, as she got stronger, she sat up. Cherry sang lullabies and Ray made shadow puppets on the wall or thought of a rhyme on the spot: *The ribs in the skeleton go clickety-clack, he's bouncing in the truck, way at the back.* Cherry might pick up Opal and keep her nose to her daughter's baby's head, breathing in her sweet scent. A miracle.

It was in these moments, the sweetest ones, that she wondered about her own mother. Ruth. Her name was about all that Cherry knew. For too long she'd resented the lack of information; she hated that none of the mamas knew much about Ruth or seemed interested in talking about her. For years, she was angrier at them than at her mother. Mama Ursa liked to say that Cherry was lucky. "You have ten mamas and counting!" It wasn't true. Cherry didn't have ten mothers, she had ten snaggle-toothed, limp-haired wet nurses, a league of women who hugged her sometimes, tolerated her usually, bossed her always. Cherry only needed, she only wanted, one mother. She had exactly zero. And now she was supposed to be Opal's.

How could she be a good mother if she'd never had one herself? It wasn't merely about taking care of Opal. *That* Cherry could do—at least she had experience with that. Cherry fed Opal. She cradled her when she cried. She bathed and dressed her, and she changed her soiled diapers. Once a week she raked the pink baby comb through a tub of coconut oil purchased at the health food store on Beverly and then ran its greasy teeth through Opal's scalp, dislodging the lace of cradle cap from her scalp. Every few days she trimmed Opal's baby fingernails with her own teeth.

It was not enough. It would never be.

The child was taken care of—impeccably. To look at her on the bed between Cherry and Ray, sucking on her fist, her eyes on her parents as they sang and clowned before bedtime, was to see a baby loved and protected. Cared for. But wasn't there more to it?

A child required something beyond mere presence and attention. What Opal needed, Cherry decided, was more complicated than a clean diaper or a lullaby. Her needs went deeper, unfathomably deeper, because that's what a child was: a vast network of unending and connected needs. A child needed to take you for granted. They needed you to be there in the middle of the night when they heard a sound you couldn't explain. They needed you to tell them *Everything's going to be okay.* They needed you to understand the world and translate it for them. And Cherry didn't understand much except that she was damaged. Ruth had damaged her.

What if Cherry damaged her own daughter because of what she didn't know and never had?

What if Cherry couldn't give Opal what she required—whatever it was—because Ruth had never given it to her?

How she resented Ruth, who gave Cherry her name and then left.

Like Cherry, Opal was also named after an object. But an opal was precious, a rainbow gleam in a fissure of marl. It wasn't something you ate, spitting its pit into the garbage.

"That's not how your mother meant it," Ray told her as their baby clapped her drooly hands in her new pajamas. Cherry wanted so badly to believe him. She didn't want to think what her mother's leaving had done to her. Cherry tried to tell herself this wasn't her bad life, it was Opal's good one. Cherry would give Opal the life, and the mother, she deserved. Could she? She didn't want Opal to have any idea how lucky she was.

∞

Mornings before Ray went to work, the three of them would sit out on their front yard so that Opal, now nearly eight months old, could spot squirrels and dogs and wave to the neighbor jogger named Cindy who wore nylon shorts and ankle weights. Ray would imitate the crows to make Opal laugh, and she loved it almost as much as she loved the garbage trucks that thundered down the street every Wednesday. Cherry shared her daughter's delight; that they would never have to take their trash to the dump themselves, not ever again, was a gift she would always be grateful for.

One morning, outside on the porch, Opal was crying. She didn't want to nurse, and Cherry's rocking didn't seem to help either.

"I perceive she's gassy," Cherry said.

The words were out before she could stop them. She noticed the surprised look on Ray's face; they had agreed not to use those words. Mama language is what Ray called it. Opal was too young for it to matter, she had to be, but might the phrase get stuck in some pristine place, seep in like a slow-drip poison?

For Opal's sake, the words of the mamas were to be stricken. Ray told her what it was like being the weird new kid at school, how he'd eventually learned to talk like everyone else. How freeing it was. It made sense to Cherry, and she wanted to be able to do what he'd done so that she could unhook herself, and their daughter, from that past.

She was trying.

She would remind herself not to say *I perceive* or *praise goddess* or *the sun summons us* or *may the moon remain open*. She would tell herself to say *period* instead of *menses*. *Vagina* instead of *womanhood*. *Bra* instead of *brassiere*—and wear one. That there was no such thing as a *morning ritual*. To avoid the word *ritual* altogether. To say *pot* instead of *reefer*. *Dinner* instead of *supper*. *Penis* instead of *manhood*. *Supermarket* instead of *grocer*. To pretend she'd never heard of *millet*. To never again say something like *luck visits upon you*.

To not, under any circumstances, say certain names. *Ursa, Roo, Karin.*

Hawk.

To say *calisthenics* instead of *movement*. *Boobs* instead of *bosom*. *Pantry* instead of *larder*.

She would not say *Mama*. She would be *Mommy*.

Cindy jogged by and waved, though Opal was too cranky to care. "I think she's gassy," Cherry said. "I think."

"Me too," Ray replied as he waved back to Cindy. "I think so too."

Opal was still crying, a wheezy little gasp, and she kept crying as the crows lifted like a black veil from the sycamore tree, cawing. There were so many of them, their eyes little hard bubbles, their feathers black as the motor oil that leaked out of their old car before Ray traded it for a newer model. The birds darkened the sky with themselves, moving as a locust storm overhead, their caws louder than Opal's cries, the pink-flesh of their open mouths like secrets. Mama Ursa once told Cherry that crows remembered people. If you angered one, it wouldn't forget.

Opal cried on, the crows circling, Cherry's arms aching.

"Let's take her inside," she said.

Ray left within the hour, already late for work, and then Cherry was alone to care for Opal. Ray would come back at six. Almost nine hours. Time stretched before her as it had when she was pregnant, the day a great yawn in sun-strained Los Angeles.

This wasn't what she expected. Cherry had waited months for her baby to arrive so as to give her hours shape and meaning, and here, finally, was Opal, and the days, if anything, felt longer. Today, Opal was cranky, not wanting to be put down, refusing sleep, unhappy in her own mother's arms. Cherry took care of plenty of children on the compound and it never felt like this: unrelenting, thankless, boring, painful. Her neck and back hurt. Her nipples stung, and her voice was hoarse from lullabies. The worst part was that she couldn't make Opal feel better. Did Cherry understand her own child?

At two in the afternoon, Opal finally passed out, and Cherry laid her gingerly on the bed, too nervous she would wake if carried to the crib. Opal sighed in her sleep; arms flung above her head. Cherry regarded her. How would a stranger see her? The baby wasn't even cute.

Cherry imagined herself walking right out the front door with only the clothes on her back, not even a purse—no money, no house key, no name. She would be free.

Was that how it was for Ruth?

Opal's nap lasted two hours. Her stomach settled, if that's what it was, and she was in a better mood by evening, entertaining herself on the kitchen floor with the two plastic cups she liked as Cherry prepared dinner. What a relief. Fatigue hollowed Cherry's bones like a dog licking its food bowl empty, and she wanted to take a long bath before dropping off to bed. At least the sun was setting, the air turning cool.

"Should we play music, baby girl?" she asked, trying to sound like any mom. Sweet and easy.

Ray recently brought home a record player and some albums he thought Cherry might like to listen to when she was by herself with the baby. At the very least, he said, she should hear them so that she might know something of this new world they inhabited.

"There's a lot out there," he said the first time he put on a record. He'd had arty friends in Santa Cruz and was making a few at work too; the younger salespeople liked him, and the music they listened to was odd and discomfiting.

"It sounds like they're playing under a blanket in a cave," she said.

Ray would be back from work soon and Cherry thought the vision of their tiny rental, lit up in the dusk, windows open to let in the cross-breeze, music wafting into the street, would cheer him. She wanted it too.

She set one of his favorites onto the player and dropped the needle as Ray taught her. The record crackled and then the drumbeat came in, persistent.

The band was called Joy Division; Ray explained the name, though she wished he hadn't. The name felt appropriate, at least, dark as it was. The singer had hanged himself last year.

"Music!" she cooed to Opal and then she set to work, moving to the song as she did so, trying not to think how awkwardly she danced. The previous weekend, Ray took them to a coworker's barbecue; the hosts served something called teriyaki drumettes to the kids—apparently for Cherry, too, since she ate about fifteen, astounded by their flavor. As the sun went down, a few people started dancing. They moved with such ease, bouncing and swaying to the music, the embers of their cigarettes like fireflies in the dark. Cherry tried not to stare. She tensed as a man leaned toward a woman and gave her a deep kiss. No one cared. It was normal. Men weren't scary. Kissing was normal. Cherry was the one who wasn't normal.

A few feet from the dancers, Ray stood with Opal on his hip as she gummed a drumette. How mundane this world would seem to their daughter. To Cherry, it would never stop being strange. The perfectly groomed people who smiled as they shopped, who looked beautiful as they danced or jogged, as if an imaginary camera were catching their every graceful moment. Saturday mornings, the Orthodox men heading to synagogue with their fur hats and coats in ninety degree weather. The giant Marlboro Man being erected on Sunset Boulevard; he would ride his gigantic horse over the Chateau Marmont, which itself was a hotel meant to resemble a castle. A restaurant shaped like a hot dog. Another shaped like a hat. The searchlights crisscrossing the sky at night—another movie premiere. Though LA would never belong to Cherry, it already belonged to Opal, who would have to leave to see how mystifying it was. But why would she ever leave?

The singer's voice—the dead singer—was a monotone, less singing and more insisting. Cherry liked the drums but not anything else, it gave her a low feeling.

Tonight, dinner would be spaghetti and a jar of tomato sauce, a culinary development that brought tears to Cherry's eyes. Did the mamas know about it? The sauce didn't taste much like tomatoes, it was far too sweet, but at least it was red, and so easy and quick. Also, Opal loved it, and Cherry figured that should matter most of all.

She stopped to watch the baby, who was knocking over the cups with a chubby foot. Cherry should interact with her. She should pick her up. Dance with her. The drums kept beating, the bass behind them. The man, insisting.

Cherry picked up Opal, who immediately wriggled out of Cherry's arms, uninterested in her mother. She didn't seem to like the music either, and so Cherry put her back down on the floor with her things that had become toys. A baby could make anything into something. A miracle. Cherry would change the record.

On the stove, the pasta water was nearly boiling. If the music weren't playing she might hear its hiss. She should deal with that first, put in the pasta.

She heard the car pull into the driveway; it was the new (used) car, and the smell of motor oil would be somewhere deep in the vehicle and not, thankfully, on Ray's hands.

She decided to let the song play. For Ray. Let him enjoy a moment of this not-actually-idyllic scene before she told him how bad the day had been.

The front door opened and closed, and in seconds Ray was crossing the dining room, dropping his suitcoat and briefcase onto a chair. He approached the open kitchen doorway, yelling hello over the music, cupping his hands at his mouth as if it were louder than it was. And yet the music *did* seem louder. Cherry wanted to turn it down, turn it off.

The water on the stove was angry now, big bubbles rising and popping, rising and popping.

Suddenly, there was a scent of burning, and beneath that, a sourness. The dinner wasn't burning, though—so far it was only this pot of water. Had Opal thrown up? *Oh no*, Cherry thought, *not the flu*. She turned to the baby and the kitchen wobbled. An earthquake? Couldn't be—the tremble was only inside this room. Or inside Cherry? Everything beyond remained unmoving, untouched, even Ray, who stood in the doorway.

It was as if Cherry and Opal were caught inside something: a current, a bubble, the boiling water. The cabinets shimmered like the freeways here did when it got really hot, like they were about to melt; when Cherry shook her head, they righted themselves. Back to normal. What was happening? Cherry reached for the counter to hold herself up. The water was still roiling. It would suck itself into steam.

And Opal—

Something was wrong with her. There was no other way to put it. She sat stiffly, unmoving, unnaturally. Her gaze was empty; it was as if it had slipped away to some unreachable place. She sat there unblinking. Like a doll. Or a mannequin. Or like a corpse, Cherry thought, and immediately unthought it.

"Opal!" she cried, and Ray looked to see what was so alarming.

The baby's legs were thrust in front of her, as unnaturally straight as her spine, her toes pointing at the old water stain on the ceiling, the one shaped like an eye.

Ray stepped into the kitchen, popping the bubble skin. Like it was nothing. Did he not feel that? He bent down and clapped his hands—once, twice. Nothing.

"Opal," he said.

He clapped a third time.

Cherry found that she was crying. Dread crawled up the back of her neck. Something was wrong with her daughter. Or with her.

Ray clapped a fourth time.

A fifth.

This time he also stamped his foot, so hard that the record skipped. How could that be? The player was in the other room.

"Opal!" Ray called, and the shimmer, the sliding feeling, ceased.

The spell finally broke. The baby shook her head like a wet dog and smiled. Then she reached for the cup as if nothing had happened.

The music, after its hiccup, brooded forward.

"She's returned to Earth," Ray said, picking her up. He kissed Opal's neck until she shrieked with laughter. Cherry couldn't take her eyes off them, a picture of normalcy. The water was still boiling; she should put the spaghetti in, and yet she didn't move.

"Hey," Ray said softly, coming toward her. "She's okay, she's okay."

Opal reached for her mother, and Cherry stepped away from the stove to take her from Ray. The child was not a doll, nor a mannequin. She was normal.

"Please stop the record," Cherry said.

Two hours later, after they'd sung and rhymed on the bed and lay Opal in her crib and walked backward out of her room, Ray and Cherry went outside to sit under the lemon tree with its circle of rocks. They did this occasionally. A nod toward the yard was all it took. To Cherry it reminded her of home, the way they might exchange glances across a room crowded with mamas or other children, saying so much without a sound.

It never got dark in LA, there were too many lights, and so tonight the sky was a nubby gray, an airplane's wink their only star. Under the tree, Cherry leaned against Ray and said she was still freaked out.

She told him how hard the day was, how, maybe, what happened in the kitchen meant Opal was seriously ill. All day, Cherry had missed the signs. "She was crabby from the moment you left," she said. "She was trying to tell me!"

Ray thought Opal seemed fine. "She ate a bowl of pasta, and she fell asleep right away."

"You saw her in the kitchen though, right?" Cherry stopped there. What would she say? *The room was wobbling. The baby and I were stuck inside a bubble.* It would sound nuts, like she was the one who was ill. "That's what I get for waiting until I was six months along to see the OB." *Oh Bee.* She had learned some things at least. The mothers said those letters at the park as if they'd been saying them all their lives.

"We had to wait for insurance to go through. Besides, we didn't know how it was done."

"I was afraid."

"I know you were."

"The needles and the paper gown."

"The nurses were so gruff, I remember."

"I had to pretend I knew what blood pressure was."

"You fooled me."

"It's not funny, Ray."

"Opal is fine, Cherry. More than fine. She just had bad gas. You had a bad day, and she was tired."

"But what if something's wrong?" She didn't say *With me.*

"Call the doctor, then."

"You think I should?"

He didn't reply. They would never wait too long to call a doctor— of course they wouldn't. It would never be too late for Opal. But why draw attention to themselves? They were careful not to create a paper trail. On the birth certificate their child's name was Opal Jones. That was Ray's new last name; he'd changed it a few months before. It was forgettable, a common name. It was Cherry's first ever last name. Opal's father was listed as Raymond Jones, and Opal's mother was listed as Cheryl Jones, as if Cherry were just a cute nickname. In this way, they made themselves unfindable.

"I won't call the doctor," Cherry said.

That night, long after she and Ray went to bed, she woke. Was that a shadow looming in the doorway? Was that the phone ringing at this still hour? No and no, and yet something *had* woken her. What was it?

Careful not to wake Ray, she crept out of bed and headed to Opal's room. The baby was sleeping on her belly with her bottom in the air, her arms curled into herself, a little loaf of bread. Nothing was wrong. Opal was perfect.

Cherry crawled back into bed, and Ray rolled over to take her into his arms.

"It's okay," he whispered.

How did he know? He didn't.

She didn't dare say this to Ray because she feared what he would say. Or he wouldn't say it, because he loved her, but he would think it. She was being ridiculous. It had been nearly a year and a half since they escaped the mamas, and no one was even looking for them, and if they were, they wouldn't find them. They were safe. It was time to stop hiding, stop being traumatized and afraid.

Nevertheless, the next night, and the next, at 2:00 a.m. when Opal cried out for milk, Cherry was already awake, covers clenched to her fists, the light under their bedroom a leak.

∞

After that, when Ray was at work, Cherry tried her best to keep them out of the house. It was stupid, but she worried the rental was haunted. What else could it be but a ghost, haunting her and Opal? She considered calling Mrs. Vartanian, the landlady, to ask if someone had died on the property; she couldn't seem to work up the courage.

Instead, every day for a week, she took Opal on walks in the stroller she'd found on the street a few weeks after giving birth, a FREE sign taped to its handle. She was afraid everyone could tell as much by the cracker crumbs rooted in its crevices, bite marks in the oddest places. Opal didn't mind, though, and so they'd take it out for hours. It was the only thing that seemed to work, the only time they both felt content. Anything to keep them okay, busy.

On these walks, Cherry found it easy to point out the world for Opal's admiration: a pigeon's glittering gorget, the spinning of a cement mixer, a poodle trotting by. Opal sat happily in the stroller, and Cherry pushed until her legs tired and her mind emptied. She didn't want to think about what had happened in the kitchen.

She usually walked them south, toward Beverly Boulevard. On the corner was the small health food store where she bought Opal's coconut oil. The place was called Erewhon, and it reminded her of stores in and around Ben Lomond, with its tickly smells of wheat grass and vitamins, the body odor of the woman behind the counter with her tank tops and hairy armpits, the bins of beans, and the aisles of natural peanut butter and sugar-free candy. Hippie country. The guy who made the juices told her that Erewhon was an anagram of the word *nowhere*. Cherry liked that, like each visit was a trip to oblivion.

At Erewhon, Cherry bought Opal a piece of fruit before heading east. There was the retirement home with the old ladies sitting on the porch in their stockings, speaking in Yiddish. There was the triplex movie theater with its ornate box office that Ray called Art Deco, and there was Bargain Fair, a warren of a store with a billion kinds of dinner plates and juice pitchers. Across the street, tourists lined up outside CBS studio to watch a taping of *The Price Is Right*. That was a gameshow.

On these walks, Cherry understood LA as a string of neighborhoods. This one was hers. Walk south and she'd hit the 10, a freeway. Walk north and she'd reach the hills, which separated LA from the valley. It was hotter there. Nothing happened in the valley, Ray said. Nothing seemed to happen here either. No secrets. The autobody shops painted in bright yellows and blues shined against the white haze, and the billboards advertised 95.5 KLOS, Chevys, Newport cigarettes. Walls of ivy and jasmine obscured the golf course and the

nicer houses. Cars sped by. On the sidewalks, they passed no one except the occasional dogwalker and housekeepers headed for the bus.
Cherry and Opal were no one, they were nowhere.

In Santa Cruz, college students and surfers and burnouts crowded
downtown, and in the little towns beyond there were hippies and
country people, a recluse or two. A cult of women. No such people
here. On these walks, Cherry felt like she belonged, like she could
be anyone else in LA; those who didn't show up in this town to be
famous came to disappear. On these walks, Cherry could manage
Opal. She could love her in the right way. Capably, correctly. Undam-
aged. They were simply a mother and daughter in this enormous city,
enjoying the sights.

Today they walked through Hancock Park to see the mansions,
and by the time they got home, Cherry was sweating and the muscles
in her thighs pulsed, and Opal was woozy with sleep that she would
not accept. She didn't nap in the stroller and wouldn't now. All at
once, in the cool, darkened house, Cherry felt desperate for a break.
From what? Being in here, with Opal.

Cherry carried Opal to her and Ray's bedroom and placed her on
their bed to change her diaper. She longed to take off her shoes. Her
tennies. Her feet throbbed. She hadn't been sleeping very well and
exhaustion was building. Her back, tense. A sting in her eyes.

Now that she was home, the thoughts rushed to the front of her
mind: Opal catatonic on the kitchen floor. Her unseeing eyes and stiff
legs. The boiling water. The way the cabinets melted and then jerked
back to normal. Opal frozen and unresponsive. Cherry thought again
she should call Mrs. Vartanian.

She realized she was so preoccupied by her thoughts that she was
barely looking at Opal—now, as she was, in this moment. The bedroom was silent, as if uninhabited, and her baby watched her like
she was on a television. But Cherry wasn't on TV, she was here. The
mother. She should act like it. "Hey baby girl," she said, and in her
head her voice sounded fake. "Hey cutie."

The bedroom's French window swung open, as if by a strong wind, as if answering Cherry. It banged against the wall, the muslin curtain rippling like a flag.

The hairs on Cherry's arms stood. The skin all over her body prickled.

The window was now wide open.

Cherry craned her neck to see beyond the crosshatching of the screen. There was a strip of dirt out there, and the neighbor's wooden fence. There would be nothing. Unless something crouched beneath the window. An animal slinking. A person.

Cherry sucked in her breath, and her nipples went hard, scraping against the cups of her bra, and then they tingled, and her breasts turned to stone. The letdown. The milk dribbled out of her as if summoned, wetting her bra. Cherry left Opal lying on the bed and rushed to the window. She kicked it closed, her forearms pressing her chest to stop the milk. *Come on, Cherry*, she told herself. No one's there. It was just a breeze. She had to feed Opal.

Opal—

The baby lay on her back. She hadn't conjured the milk with a cry or even her desire to eat. She was stiff. Unmoving. Eyes unseeing. A doll, again. Unreal.

The milk was seeping beneath Cherry's bra now, sticky on her sweat-soaked skin. It dripped down her stomach, pooling into her navel.

Cherry picked up Opal, and the child was stiff in her arms, like a piece of plastic.

The bed looked like it was made of plastic too, like a doll's bed, plastic comforter and plastic bedsheets and two plastic pillows, hard as Cherry's own breasts before the letdown, and the bedroom walls— what was happening to the walls? They were seeping. Like milk was dripping down them, like rain beading on glass. The window was wide open again—what had opened it?—and it went *tap-tap* as it hit the wall. *Tap-tap.* The wall looked soft now. She could poke it with the tip of her finger. Step into it. Where would it take her?

The milk was drying cold on her midriff. The child stayed stiff in her arms.

The dread bounced into Cherry's throat. Her instinct was to put down the baby and run. Get out of here. Get away from Opal. But she couldn't trust herself. Not now, maybe not ever again.

She did the opposite of what she wanted; she squeezed Opal to her chest. Her breasts ached from the pressure. The child, as if yanked from a deep sleep, cried out, a high-pitched and loud screech that hurt to hear. It was a sound of pain. As she cried, her body softened, and she flailed, and Cherry held onto her hard so that she would not fall to the floor.

The baby's cries went on and on and Cherry thought of the crows darkening the sky above the house. They must be there now, trapping them inside.

Cherry was crying too. Her daughter was a block of ice, thawing. She was leaving Earth and coming back. She was trying to get away from Cherry.

As suddenly as it began, Opal stopped. She was calm. Subdued, even. Her eyes were wet, and she rubbed her face on Cherry's shoulder as Cherry tried not to move, her own tears still coming. They fell into her mouth and she swallowed them. Her bra was soaked.

The room looked like itself again. Just a room.

Cherry carried Opal out into the living room and sat her down on the couch. From her perch, Opal, serious, stared out at the room, her gaze alighting on one object and then another.

"You okay?" Cherry whispered, drying her own face with the back of her hand.

Opal's eyes were so wide and dark that Cherry was afraid.

She got Mrs. Vartanian on the first ring.

"This is your tenant Cherr—Cheryl Jones—at 609?"

In her melodious Armenian accent, Mrs. Vartanian exclaimed, "Cheryl, Cheryl, yes! Good afternoon!" She asked about the baby, inquired how the new fridge was doing.

"I'm sorry to bother you," Cherry finally said. "I wondered . . . did anyone die in this house?"

Mrs. Vartanian was silent for a moment. "Died? Why? Do you smell animal? Maybe dead skunk under house? Is there bad odor?"

"No, no, nothing like that. I mean, in the past. A human. A previous tenant?"

No, the landlady insisted. No one had expired in those rooms. She had all the records.

"Why?" Mrs. Vartanian asked. "Are you inspired by one of those Old Hollywood tours? Clark Gable is a ghost on Hollywood Boulevard, is that right?" She was laughing.

That night, Ray told her to call the pediatrician. "It'll make you feel better."

Dr. Mortimer was a cheery doctor who said Opal had probably just been tired. He said her eyes looked good, as did her reflexes. She was responsive. She was reaching her milestones, right? She had not once tipped over and hit her head or gone limp, had she? She hadn't foamed at the mouth? Cherry shook her head. She could tell the doctor thought she was a clueless mother, barely old enough to be one.

"There are more tests we can do, but they're easier to do, and more effective, when the child is older," he said.

Ray didn't think it made sense to go to other doctors to do those tests the pediatrician mentioned. At least not until Opal was older.

Cherry could tell he wasn't worried. Then again, Cherry hadn't told him everything about the episodes. That's what Cherry called them. *Episodes*.

Here was her own language, for her own world.

She didn't tell Ray how the world was transformed when Opal went under. She kept her mouth shut because she didn't want Ray to think of her any differently. To think her demented. Paranoid. Calling Mrs. Vartanian like that. A bad mother. Damaged.

With every passing month in LA without word from home, with no one to come looking for them, Ray relaxed further into their new reality. The more she talked about what might be wrong, the more she pulled him away from the life he wanted.

LA belonged to him too.

∞

What were the episodes?

Instead of drawing any more cartoons, Cherry ripped off a sheet from the DataComp-branded notepad and wrote down her theories, a diary entry without a diary:

> *some kind of disease*
> *a tumor*
> *eppalepsy that doc test didn't see*
> *im crazy*
> *im not meant to have a baby*
> *ghost in the house*
> *an angry spirit*
> *LA? Smog? Cars? Noise?*
> *A sign its wrong here*

When Cherry finished writing and reread it, the list seemed not only damning but also stupid, her handwriting childish above Data-Comp's tagline THE FUTURE OF FICHE in bold black letters at the bottom of the page. Cherry flicked on a stove burner and held the paper over the bluish flame until the fire ate the paper and stung her fingers, the kitchen hazy with smoke.

Ray could not discover it.

Opal, who'd turned nine months old the day before, was crawling to the kitchen cabinets. She had become mobile in the past week; it was as if the episodes aided in her development.

"Maybe the episodes are a positive?" Ray had asked the other night.

When Opal saw her mother fanning at the smoke with her hands, she laughed and waved. Cherry froze. She realized she was holding her breath. Waiting for another episode.

"We gotta get out of here," she said.

She remembered the vintage shop on Melrose, Leo Rising, the one with the baby. That kid couldn't be more than a year older than Opal, and maybe they were far from home too.

Before Opal became too crabby, Cherry got them ready. Her white pedal-pushers were out of style, but they were clean, and they didn't scream *weird isolated hippie girl* like so much of her wardrobe. She put Opal in her purple onesie, the one that Cherry had sewn into a shirt when it got too small to snap; it wasn't crushed velvet, though with its ruffled sleeves and ribbon rosebud at the collar it was more elegant than anything Cherry had seen on a baby before. She swept Opal into her arms, kissed her cheek, and strapped her into the dirty stroller. The baby stared at her, then smiled knowingly.

"Let's make some friends," Cherry said. Her face felt warm just thinking about it.

Opal stopped smiling.

"What? You don't think we can make friends?"

Opal sucked a finger, regarding her mother. Wind is invisible until it blows the leaves off the trees and so was Opal's regard: Cherry felt it as a force, like her child had shoved something inside her.

"Let's go, wise one," Cherry said and directed the stroller toward Melrose.

As they walked, she practiced what she'd say to the woman. "Your baby is so cute! How old is—He? She?"

From the stroller, Opal was fascinated by a fallen palm that blocked their way.

"Dat," she said as Cherry maneuvered the stroller around the frond, jagged at the edges, coarse-haired as a pig. "Dat, dat, dat." Opal would turn one by Valentine's Day.

It took only a few minutes to reach their destination. The shop's security gate was still accordioned across the display window. Cherry checked her watch and cursed herself. It wasn't yet ten. The sky was a gritty tan-blue and cloudless.

Just as Cherry was about to wheel the stroller away, the woman was at the entrance, unlocking it from the inside, mouthing something. She wore mechanic coveralls cinched tight at her waist with a yellow scarf. Cherry wondered if she'd sewn in the shoulder pads herself.

"Here I am, here I am," the woman said. She had an accent that made her sound fancy.

Cherry could see the woman's baby behind her on the floor, crawling on bare knees, wearing a onesie and a sweater. Not even socks. Its legs were so dirty they looked bruised.

"I'll be open in a few," the woman said.

"Your baby's so cute."

The woman glanced at her child for a moment, then back at Cherry. She looked at Opal.

"We don't carry clothes for children."

"Oh, that's fine," Cherry said. Why was she so awkward and weird? "That's fine. I just—"

What was she going to say? That she had no friends. That she was a homesick country bumpkin. That she sometimes couldn't sleep at night, she was so worried about Opal. About herself. That she didn't feel connected to her child. Her own baby. That she was perhaps having a psychotic break herself. The doctor said Opal was a healthy baby, but what did he know.

"Do you sell that outfit?" Cherry asked, nodding at the woman.

The woman raised her eyebrow. "Why?"

"I can't afford it," Cherry said quickly.

"Nor can I," the woman said with a smile. Her first. "I'm stealing it from myself, technically." She gave Cherry a careful look and then stepped aside, opening the door wider. She nodded at her baby. "Can you mind him while I set up the till?"

"This is my daughter Opal," Cherry said as she pushed the stroller into the store, answering the question before the woman could ask it.

The baby's name was Gareth. His mother was Emmy. Emmy came from a city in England Cherry had never heard of, but Cherry had only heard of London, so.

"I just moved down from Ben Lomond," Cherry said. "Or not there exactly. Outside there." Emmy's face was blank. "It's near Santa Cruz."

Emmy knew what Santa Cruz was.

"My husband went to UC Santa Cruz," Cherry said. She and Ray weren't married, but they told everyone they were.

The store was larger than it looked from the outside, with clothes displayed like paintings on the walls: a fedora here, a lace wedding dress there, and there a pair of overalls and a plaid shirt, paired with a skeleton mask—a Halloween costume that Emmy hadn't gotten around to taking down yet, Cherry figured. A huge Union Jack flag had been nailed to the wall above the dressing rooms.

Cherry put Opal on the floor with Gareth, who was still crawling at nineteen months.

"My neighbor says it's because I don't walk around with him," Emmy called from a back room. "You know, holding onto his finger or whatever, but that's nonsense."

Cherry nodded, though she did wonder if sinking the boy into piles of clothes all day had delayed him a bit. Not that she would say that. Cherry had never made a real friend before, no one who hadn't grown up in the house with her, but she wasn't stupid. Anyway, Gareth seemed fine. He was a smiley baby, his hands blackened with dirt, raspberry guts smeared across his cheek.

On the floor, Opal leaned forward and patted Gareth's head.

"Gentle, gentle," Cherry said.

"Opal is a great name," Emmy said, walking to the counter with a vellum pouch under her arm. She drew a roll of coins from it and looked up at the ceiling, as if calculating something. "But there's no way she was born in October."

"February. Why?"

"Opal is the October birthstone," Emmy said.

Cherry didn't know what that meant—did some people get a stone when they were born? Mama Ursa had said the stones, the minerals that Mother Earth made with Her own heat, were for all of us. Cherry made something like a murmur.

"They say opal is bad luck unless you were born in October."

"That true?" Cherry said and looked down at her daughter, who was patting Gareth with the flat of her hand. A blade of fear sliced into her. "Gentle," she said again.

Emmy laughed. "I was born in October. That's how I know."

"Her dad too—on the tenth," Cherry said.

"Well there you go," Emmy replied distractedly, as if that explained it. She finished with the register and looped some ugly scarves over a mannequin. The store smelled like the very back of the hall closet back home, where they kept the clothes waiting to be mended.

"Want to help me go through this bin?" Emmy asked as she walked toward the counter. She nodded at a pile of clothing in a metal laundry cart. "We just got this load, and I'd love another pair of eyes."

"I don't really know fashion."

Emmy glanced at Cherry's outfit and snorted. "Okay, maybe not, but it'd be nice to have another adult to talk to as I sort." She nodded at the children on the floor. "Makes me realize it's mostly just me and him, you know?"

"Oh, definitely," Cherry said, relieved. Maybe Emmy understood what it was like: all the hours to fill, your baby a stranger.

Emmy held up a blue lace negligee, squinting, and Cherry said, "Sometimes I think I'm losing my mind. A baby is so hard to take care of."

Emmy didn't balk or call her crazy. She only set the negligee aside and nodded. "Same." Then she crossed her eyes, stuck out her tongue, and tossed a black velvet beret at her. "Put this on. It'll make you feel better."

The hat hit Cherry in the face and she giggled. In the mirror, she saw herself put on the beret. She stood before her reflection. For the first time in her life, she looked cool, like a young woman on Melrose in a jaunty cap, her waves framing her face, headed somewhere fun. She wasn't French, she was Californian.

"I love it," Cherry said and cocked her hip like she remembered a woman at Ray's work barbecue doing.

"It's yours for free." Emmy winked. "Consider it your compensation."

Cherry grinned, and the cool version of herself in the mirror grinned back. "Thanks," she said. "This is fun."

"This?" Emmy said, and Cherry saw that Emmy wore a ridiculous puffy dress, lime green, tugged tightly over her outfit.

Cherry hooted. "It's perfect for the nightclub."

Emmy shimmied her shoulders and cackled. "Pass me the cocaine, will you, Gareth?" She laughed and then so did Cherry because the boy, as if on cue, reached his hand out to his mom, like he really did have something to give her, a louche little druggie.

"I should get him into acting, yeah?" Emmy said, and Cherry agreed. So here was a friend. How easy.

As the women tried on more clothes and rejected others, the children played happily at their feet, talking gibberish, exploring. Cherry felt lighter than she had in months.

"What's she up to?" Emmy asked, nodding at Opal.

As Gareth crawled in circles and babbled at everything and nothing, Opal sat there with that telltale empty stare, arms stretched outward like she was conducting an orchestra.

No, Cherry thought. Not now. Not here—they weren't even at home.

Cherry imagined her burned-up list.

~~Ghost in the house.~~

How naïve and shortsighted of her. Here was Opal, in this shop with two near strangers, falling into another episode. There wasn't a ghost in the house—it was in Opal.

"She's intense," Emmy said.

Cherry tried to smile, all the while the alarm in her body growing like a flame and heating up her insides. "Well, her aura *is* bright," she said.

Emmy snorted. "Aura?" She said the word with disdain. "I don't go for that hippie stuff."

Shame rocked through Cherry. Don't say *aura*.

Cherry hoped Emmy would shift her attention elsewhere until Opal shook herself out of this and they could move on. This time, Cherry told herself, she would let it pass, not freak out. She would keep herself from going under with Opal.

Opal was fine. Nothing was wrong. It was just a phase. A little thing.

But Emmy was still focused on Opal, and as she approached the infants, she asked, "Does she want to be picked up?"

"No, no she's all right . . ."

Emmy bent down.

The room began to tremble. Didn't Emmy feel it?

"Don't," Cherry said.

The walls—were they slanting inward? They would all be crushed. "Please don't."

A clothing rack shook, as if something were hidden underneath, yanking on its wheels. It tugged on the shirt sleeves. The back of a dress, unzipping. Something, someone, was hunched there, about to pounce. It was the same feeling as in the bedroom: an animal, slinking just out of Cherry's vision.

But no one was there, there was no way, and Emmy didn't seem to notice anything besides Opal, who was stiff as the dead, eyes wide and unseeing.

"I said *don't*," Cherry repeated.

The walls were definitely slanting, the room narrowing.

The moment Emmy's hands hooked under Opal's arms, Opal let out a sound. It was much worse and louder than a shriek, as eerie as the snarl of a cat in heat but deeper and lower. Cherry felt it in her molars and in her scalp. She thought she could see it, too, like a wave moving across the shop. The sound kept coming, dug out from some terrible grief place. Like something was being ripped away from something else: the wall from a house, a heart from a chest, one person from her entire life. It kept moving, toward the wood-arched ceiling that resembled the ribs of a pirate ship. The clothes on their racks quivered in its wake. The invisible animal crouched.

Emmy must have let go. That, or Opal wrenched herself away, because the baby was on her stomach. The shriek crumbled into a cry. But it wasn't Opal who was crying, it was Gareth.

The episode was over, not long after it started. No more trembling, no more slanting walls, no more shriek. No more haunting. Opal was back. She looked on, drained, but also, Cherry saw, somehow majestic. The baby was changed by what happened.

Emmy rushed to pick up her son. She had already unbuttoned her coveralls and shoved her nipple into Gareth's mouth. As he sucked his eyes roamed to Cherry, alarmed, and then settled back toward Emmy. His lids lowered as he took in the milk. It was like she was drugging him.

When Opal nursed, did she ever look as blissful? Her daughter was born with a light, Cherry would never forget it, but maybe it shined outward, toward the world. Away from Cherry.

She didn't dare touch Opal, who had rolled onto her back like she was stargazing.

"The fuck was that?" Emmy asked, nodding at Opal, and Cherry said she didn't know.

"It's something she does."

Emmy blew the bangs out of her eyes. "You should see a doctor, yeah?"

"We have," she said. She took a deep breath and pulled Opal up to sitting. The baby did not protest this time. Opal began pointing at things. *Welcome back to Earth*, Cherry thought, and with another exhale, she picked up the child. She left the beret on the counter.

"We should probably let you get back to it," Cherry said, standing. Emmy didn't stop her. On their way out of the store, Emmy called, "You feel that, right?"

By now Gareth was in one of the clothing bins behind the counter, safe among piles of skirts and polyester shirts that smelled of other people's lives.

"Feel what?" Cherry asked, but she knew what she meant. It was as if the store were trembling.

"*Something,*" Emmy said and nodded at Opal. "Something . . . is *wrong.*"

At the door, Cherry only nodded like an idiot as Emmy called out, "Flip that OPEN sign over, will you?" Cherry complied.

She pushed Opal in the stroller so fast that the baby was hooting as if it were a game, a roller coaster thing. As soon as she got home she gave Opal an apple to suck on and called Ray. She would tell him an episode happened outside of the rental. That it wasn't something confined to the house. That Emmy thought the baby needed help. It was true, Opal did need help. So did Cherry. She would finally confess to Ray what else happened: the walls, the trembling.

She could count on her hands the number of times she'd dialed a telephone in her lifetime. Hopefully when Opal was old enough to be conscious of such things, Cherry would be able to do it without keeping track. *This is the eleventh time I've ever dialed a telephone.*

Call it a *phone,* Cherry.

The receptionist at DataComp, Ebony, said she'd patch her through. Cherry loved Ebony, who was always so friendly, and she loved her name. Last fall, when Cherry suggested that she and Ray call the baby Ebony if it was a girl, Ray laughed. "Oh there's just so much you don't get," he said.

Cherry heard a click. "Raymond Jones," Ray said into the receiver. In the background, phones rang, people murmured, and some sort of office machinery whirred

"I need you to come home," Cherry said. Her voice sounded odd, even to herself. Like a pigeon's coo, a warble. Another person's voice. "It happened again. Another episode. We were at that clothing store, Leo Rising, trying to make friends with the owner and her baby."

"That's great! You need to meet other moms."

"Something is happening to Opal, and it isn't right. It's more than just her stiffness, her blank eyes. The store felt wrong. I swear it was like someone was there with us, hiding. Whatever it was, it was going to hurt us, hurt her. Like a ghost. It was there and also not there. It sounds crazy but even the woman—Emmy is her name. Emmy was the one to mention it, the feeling. The walls were closing in on us. She doesn't even believe in auras so it's not something she would say. I was worried maybe—"

Someone at the office was talking to Ray, a man with a smoker's voice. Cherry could hear him talking until she couldn't, and she was certain Ray had put his hand over the receiver's mouthpiece. He might as well have put a hand over her own mouth.

After a moment, Ray said, "Sorry, baby." It was his turn to sound different. It was his work voice, she guessed. Maybe the smoker co-worker was nearby, eavesdropping. "I can't get there right away. Probably by three? Oh wait, I have something. I can be home at four, or four-thirty at the latest, the client's in Northridge."

She didn't answer.

"Cherry?"

"You know I don't know where Northridge is." Ray didn't reply and she said, "We'll just see you tonight at your regular time."

"You sure?"

"I'm sure."

"It'll be okay," he said.

He hung up so quickly that Cherry was left with the phone on her ear, hearing nothing. He didn't get it. Now she wouldn't even be able to take Opal outside. They couldn't go on their walks. Couldn't get away from here. No matter what, the episodes would follow them. They were stuck.

Cherry hung up and looked at Opal. The baby sucked the apple to sauce, her dark eyes glimmering.

8

OPAL, LYING IN HER CRIB, STIFF AS A CORPSE, SEEING nothing. Opal, sitting in her highchair, frozen. Opal, on the grass in the backyard holding a lemon in her hand like a baseball, eyes as hard and piercing as screws boring into a solid wall.

And Cherry. Cowering.

Opal, come back to Earth. Opal.

Ray only witnessed Opal's first episode, and no one else but Emmy and baby Gareth witnessed another, and who knows where they went, maybe back to England. A month later, Leo Rising became Banana Vinyl, a record shop.

Cherry made more appointments.

They tested Opal's blood. At the first appointment, the doctor massaged Opal's little neck; she said she was palpating the main arteries to see if it might cause the child to faint. "If she does, it's vasovagal syncope." Whatever that was. Opal did not faint. Her electrocardiogram, which another doctor explained would test for irregular heartbeats, didn't report anything out of the ordinary either.

For her next appointment, Ray and Cherry brought Opal to the neurologist at 4:00 a.m. The doctor wanted her asleep for the tests; then he had Cherry wake her so that the doctor could give her what was called an electroencephalogram, a word Cherry tried to memorize until she realized everyone else called it an EEG. A nurse pasted the nodes onto Opal's head, and from them flowed a medusa mane of multicolored wires. The neurologist explained that they would read her brain activity. They translated it, too, into wavy lines that the doctor could decipher.

Opal's brain activity, he said, appeared normal.

The doctor said to make sure the child ate enough. Slept enough. He said if the events continued, the tests could be administered again. He said Cherry should remain vigilant, but calm. That Opal shouldn't be left alone in water, in a pool or even a bath. He said that when Opal got older and learned to ride a bike, she should be monitored more closely than other kids, in case an episode occurred while she was riding. But that she would probably grow out of them within a year. He was confident that she was fine.

He said to bring her back if it happened again.

"Better yet, call 911," the doctor said. "Get those vitals as close to the event as possible."

After Opal's next episode, Cherry followed the doctor's advice. The medics clomped with their big brown boots into the rental's beautiful living room while, outside, the firetruck slid its red eye across the sidewalk, the road, the lawn. The burly men listened to Opal's heartbeat, took her blood pressure, shined a light into her eyes. Nothing amiss.

"Cute kid," one of them said, and then, because there was nothing extraordinary or concerning that they could measure, they left.

∞

Cherry spent every weekday alone with Opal, waiting for Ray to return from work, and every weekday she waited for another episode. The anticipation was nearly as bad as an episode itself. Cherry would look up from the banana she was peeling, or tread carefully into Opal's room after a nap, and steel herself for what was sure to come. That now-familiar doll gaze. The corpse feeling. The room transformed. That presence at the edge of the room, the sense of someone watching them. Cherry was afraid all the time.

In the stillness of the night, unable to sleep, she tried to slow her breath and make out her surroundings. There was Ray, snoring softly beside her. There were his shoes by the dresser, tossed on the floor like bricks. She knew that was her robe hanging from the closet door.

She would slip out of bed. Opal's star nightlight, the one Ray had hoped for since before she was born, lit the hallway, and its soft glow led Cherry to Opal's door, left wide open because Cherry couldn't bear to think of her child trapped in the dark. And there was Opal, fast asleep in her crib. Cherry would stand over her, cataloging the facts: her daughter's panting breath, her cheek pushed against the mattress, the pink satin ribbons of the crib bumper glinting in the dim light. Opal was fine. When Cherry was a girl, no one had ever come check on her like this. Not that it mattered what Cherry did. It wasn't enough.

She didn't tell Ray about these nighttime vigils. She tried not to talk too much about the episodes anymore either. What would she say to make him understand? Ray nurtured a myth that he'd rescued Cherry from the house in the woods, but now he was the one who needed protecting. From her. From whatever was wrong with her.

He has a client in Northridge, Cherry told herself. *He has a client in Northridge.*

In her crib, Opal grumbled and rolled over, and Cherry hurried out of the room and back to bed before Ray perceived her.

∞

Turned out, the ambulance visit was pricey.

"We don't have the money for this," Ray said when the bill came in the mail. He still wore his blazer because it was December and cold. In two months, Opal would celebrate her first birthday. Two weeks had passed since the last episode, and the weather changed in the meantime, a crispness in the air, dusk a deep dark blue. Everyone hoped for a rainy winter.

"I was only listening to the doctor," Cherry said and opened the

Celeste pizza boxes. She and Ray would each have their own personal cheese for dinner. A salad, too, iceberg lettuce with tomatoes. Thousand Island dressing, orange as a fox.

Ray picked up Opal and kissed her until she squealed, and over their daughter's joyous sounds, he said, "I want you to see a doctor."

"We've been to so many already."

"Not for Opal. For you. You need help."

He wasn't wrong. After every episode, Opal appeared unscathed—even peaceful. She was nearly walking. She had one word already. *Daddy.* Whereas Cherry was a mess, frightened and jittery, and sometimes her head hurt so badly after an episode she needed to take a painkiller.

"I want you to see a psychologist," Ray added.

She knew of the word—psychologist—but she wasn't sure what it meant. She hated waiting for Ray to realize she didn't understand something, especially these days, with her locked up at home with Opal and him out in LA with all kinds of people, all kinds of exciting experiences. Last week he sold microfiche to a pornography production company in Reseda. In the San Gabriel Valley, he tried Chinese food—real Chinese food, he said, as if Cherry knew what even fake Chinese food was. He had friends. A life. She was only dragging him down.

"It's a doctor that you talk to," he said, finally. "Sometimes it's called a therapist." He sounded impatient.

She remembered how slowly he undressed her on their first night in the Tropicana motel. Now, if they were intimate at all, it was brief and silent, before Opal woke in the morning. "A quickie," Ray called it, before he got into the shower and ready for work.

"You tell your therapist your feelings," he was explaining. "Tell them what you're anxious about. They'll ask about your upbringing."

"You want me to tell them about—" She could not even complete the sentence.

"If it helps, yes."

She could only stare at him.

"And if you . . . need . . . meds . . ." He was speaking delicately now, slowly. She could tell this was a prepared speech. "You can go to what's called a psychiatrist. They prescribe drugs for mood disorders." Here was the biggest pause before he added, "Hallucinations."

"Hallucinations," Cherry repeated.

He swallowed. "Yes."

"The episodes are real," she said.

"To you, maybe."

"They're real to Opal too."

"The doctors never find anything," Ray said.

"Doesn't mean something isn't there."

"Why not get her a psychic then?" Agitated, he hitched Opal higher onto his waist. "Or, I don't know, a priest to perform an exorcism? Or, hey, how about a fucking medicine woman?" His voice was loud now, and he focused his dark eyes on her. "Would that feel better for you?" He looked angry, but also confused by his anger, like he wished he wasn't so upset, like he wished she were different. Cherry could barely breathe.

"It's been a long time since anyone's been mean to me like this," she said softly.

"Is it a comfort?"

She didn't know how to answer such a question, and that was fine because he kept talking. "It's been hard letting go of the mamas, is that it?"

The very word made him go pale as a ghost. She could hear him breathing.

"Don't say *mamas*," she growled. How could he? Opal was right there.

He seemed to come back to himself. "I'm sorry. I'm sorry."

"I need to make dinner," she said. "Please leave me alone."

Without another word, he took the baby out of the room. She heard him say, "Let's give Mommy a break, okay, my Opalina?"

The frozen pizzas, unsheathed from their plastic wrappers, waited dumbly before her on the counter. She picked at a sliver of the sparse, balding cheese and popped it into her mouth, let its icy salt sting her tongue.

"Daddy," she heard Opal say.

She wanted to scream.

The episodes were an inexplicable phenomenon. They were unspeakable. But they were real.

If Ray wanted her to find answers, she would.

The next morning, as soon as Cherry could no longer hear Ray's car engine, she plopped Opal into her playpen with a couple toys and went to the hallway secretary, where the big phone books were stacked next to the second telephone. *Say phone.* Cherry picked up the newest one and flipped its wrinkled and translucent pages until she found what she was looking for.

There were a lot of psychics in Los Angeles.

Cherry shut her eyes and slowly drew her finger down the thin, slippery page.

Down, down. Down.

She opened her eyes. Her finger was on the last psychic listed. Xilomen—a single name. Cherry had no clue how to pronounce it, didn't know if they were a man or a woman. Xilomen's shop was in downtown LA. She looked up the address in the Thomas Guide and saw that it was in the Toy District.

After Opal's second feeding and first post-breakfast snack of rice cakes, Cherry said, "Let's go see where toys are made."

Opal, cleaned up after her snack, pulled herself to standing at the edge of the coffee table, and she grabbed the remote control for the new TV. "Put some shows on during the day," Ray told her after he bought it. "Keep you company." But the television was loud and bright, *vulgar* was the word she imagined Mama Ursa using, and so Cherry kept the set dark during the day. It would become another object for her to dust.

"Let's not play with Daddy's remote control," Cherry said now.

Opal eyed her suspiciously. "Daddy," she said.

"That's right! Daddy's remote control. I know we haven't been out in a while. We have to go, though. You'll be good, right?"

Ray and Cherry went downtown only once, before Opal was born, on a Saturday afternoon, to drive around and see the new skyscraper, the fifth tallest in the world. He said an art museum was being constructed, and more office buildings, but that no one lived there. That at night, only criminals and roaches scuttled about in the dark. His coworker said a decade or so ago the city disassembled the last two houses on Bunker Hill and moved them to some other place in the city. No idea where. One of the houses was called The Castle. Cherry wished she could see it.

She and Opal would have to take the RTD downtown because it was too far to walk, at least with Opal in the stroller. The bus didn't intimidate her; she took it a few times when she was pregnant, and she preferred it to being inside a tinny car, stuck in the crush of others just like theirs. She appreciated how the bus drivers simply asserted themselves into the flow of traffic.

It was 10:00 a.m., and it took some time for the bus to make its way east. Cherry hadn't thought to call Xilomen. Did psychics take appointments? As the bus groaned along, Opal squirming in her stroller, pulling at her safety straps, Cherry wondered if they should have just stayed home and called one of those dollar-a-minute hotlines instead. Too late now. In her mind, she told Xilomen they'd be there by eleven at the latest. The bus was now full, and a few people stood in the aisle, holding onto the leather handles above their heads. Cherry was grateful she had found a seat and room for the stroller.

Opal was fussy enough that Cherry worried someone would complain—or, worse, that Opal would have an episode here, on this crowded bus. Would there be an accident? She imagined Opal turning stiff and the bus tipping over, the windows rippling and cracking, the passengers flattened, bloody. And Opal, when she came back to Earth, would stare at the carnage, resplendent.

Cherry took Opal out of the stroller and jiggled her on her lap, pointing out the window things that might've wowed Opal a few weeks earlier. A dog on the corner. A pickup truck stuffed with lawn-mowers. A police car. LA looked grimier, more crowded, the farther east they drove. How could people not live downtown? Did the apartments, the little corner stores, just stop? She wondered where Xilomen lived when she wasn't working.

Cherry bent over Opal and whispered into her ear, "People say psychics can read the future, but that's not exactly right." Opal stilled, as if she understood her mother's every word. "They can intuit more than anything. Read another person." As Cherry continued, Opal flapped her arms up and down like a bird trying and failing to fly. "This psychic will tell us what's happening to you. And to me, too, I guess."

It took another twenty minutes to get down First Street, and when they hit Los Angeles Street, they got off. Pedestrians wove around piles of unpacked boxes and vendors, and Cherry struggled to find a space to check her bearings and get Opal strapped properly into the stroller again. If Ray was correct, by nightfall, most of downtown would be empty except for the junkies and the indigent; before then there were shopkeepers making deals, people loading items onto carts and furniture dollies, elderly women weighed down by plastic shopping bags, men in suits like Ray wore, a nurse in scrubs, a mail carrier, countless delivery men, and even other mothers, hurrying their kids along in Spanish, Chinese, Thai, Tagalog.

Cherry was rarely around so many strangers, and once Opal was settled, Cherry squeezed the stroller handle as she pushed it forward. Opal leaned in her seat, rapt, pointing at one store's giant bag of inflatable rubber balls and then at a window piled high with plastic baby dolls, then a table of Christ figurines, blood weeping. Piñatas hung in almost all the shops: magenta and yellow donkeys, white angels, blue stars with streamers exploding from every point. They watched as a woman brought one down with a big hooked stick. A block later, a bright yellow sign read CURIOSIDADES, and behind the storefront rose a brick building with fire escapes, like the apartments on the TV shows Ray watched. Cherry spotted another bright sign, two doors down: BAÑOS $.25. They passed an ornate white cage filled with parakeets.

"Dat, dat, dat!" Opal cried.

Cherry didn't stop until they finally reached the address. Xilomen's shop was in the Atrium, Suite 4.

They stood before a tallish and unremarkable building. A vinyl sign blocked a bank of windows midway up, advertising rooms for rent—SE RENTAN CUARTOS. On the ground floor was the atrium of shops, or so Cherry assumed; the entrance was flanked with tables selling more of the same junk they'd already seen: generic plastic dolls, combs of all colors, paper folding fans, transistor radios. When the old Asian women behind the tables saw Cherry and Opal approach, they stood and called out, "Big sale!" and "Pretty baby!" Cherry kept on.

They found themselves in a wide and dark hallway with lit-up storefronts on either side. Cherry looked up. The green glass ceiling above was pocked with leaves and other debris, dirt ribboning the edges. There was just enough light to show off the dingy linoleum floor. It felt like they were inside an abandoned aquarium. This was an atrium?

Cherry was busy searching for the word *XILOMEN*. She pictured it in neon red above the outline of a blue hand. Was Xilomen a palm reader as well? Cherry hoped her twenty-dollar bill would be enough.

They passed a pupuseria where an older woman in a hairnet stood forlornly behind the front counter, waiting for customers. Across from it was a school for barbers called Francisco's Beauty Academy. Opal pointed at the Styrofoam heads stacked in the window. Beyond the open door, a young Hispanic man was using clippers on another young man. The sign in front said HAIRCUTS $1.

The barber school took up two shopfronts, and behind the next window, a Black girl who looked like a teenager, not much younger than Cherry really, skimmed a razor across a balloon slathered with shaving cream.

"Look at that," Cherry said. She imagined describing it to Ray. *The balloon was blue, and the girl looked nervous it would pop!*

She felt a mournfulness then, knowing she wouldn't breathe a word of this to him.

Xilomen, it turned out, did not possess a neon sign. Instead, at the end of the hallway, a department store mannequin in a rhinestone-studded gown held a poster board.

XILOMEN

PSYCHIC & MEDICINE WOMAN

READINGS $10 OBO

So Xilomen was a woman. A medicine woman.

What was OBO? Didn't matter—Cherry had enough money. She pushed open the curtained door with one hand and backed the stroller into the shop.

There were quite a few psychics in Santa Cruz, and one in Ben Lomond too. On the bus ride, she'd imagined a dimly lit room draped with scarves, a crystal ball sitting on a circular table. Tarot cards too. Maybe some music resembling wind chimes. She also thought, briefly, of the eastern wing back home. Mama Ursa wasn't a psychic though—at least as far as Cherry knew. Mama Ursa was, as the other mamas put it, "influential."

Xilomen's place was just a square room, with bright, impersonal lighting and low ceilings. A dining room table loomed at the center, too large for the space, its legs a little fussy, flaring out before tapering into dainty paws. There were four chairs, and they were just as heavy and ornate as the table, all of them crowded on one end. A lone sage smudge stick lay discarded on the other end. Cherry remembered something Ray's boss had said to her, about how poor people's furniture was always ridiculously grand, as if they were furnishing a manor rather than an ugly apartment. She and Ray didn't fall into that trap, at least.

"Hello?" Cherry called out.

That's when Cherry noticed a second mannequin, also in evening wear, standing in the corner. One of her molded hands rested against her tiny waist.

Behind a door at the back of the room she heard two voices, murmuring. Panic feathered her throat. What if this was a drug front? Or a brothel?

"Anyone here?" Cherry yelled.

She thought she heard the clatter of silverware against a plate and then a girl came out of the door at the back of the room. She was Hispanic, probably about ten. Cherry took in the girl's pink shorts and white T-shirt, her brushed black hair, and let out a breath. This girl didn't appear to be in any danger.

"Can I help you?" the girl asked.

"Are you . . . the psychic?"

The girl giggled and shook her head. "I'm Elvia. Xilomen," she pronounced it *Sheelo-Men*, "is my mom. You want a reading?"

Without waiting for an answer, Elvia called in rapid Spanish and a woman appeared behind her, wiping her lips with the tips of her fingers, as if to brush off crumbs. She didn't wear diaphanous fabrics or heavy eyeliner, and she looked nothing like the hippie healers back home, with their ratty white-person dreads or their milkmaid braids, the crystals warming their clavicles. Xilomen was probably a decade older than Cherry, which meant she had also been a young mother. Too young. Maybe she would get it.

Xilomen was very short, only a few inches taller than her daughter, and though she looked tired and wore no makeup, she was pretty, with a high forehead and a long, regal nose, and dark hair pulled back in a banana clip.

How was it, Cherry wondered, that everyone in LA was good-looking?

Xilomen wore a long itchy-looking green skirt that reminded Cherry of the sponges Ray preferred and a loose brown cardigan. When she stepped forward, the sweater fell open to reveal her T-shirt; Cherry was surprised to recognize the painting of bored cherubs printed across it.

"I'm sorry," Cherry began. "Did I interrupt? I was hoping for a . . . consultation." She paused and gestured to Opal in the stroller. "For her, I mean."

"Take her out of the stroller," Xilomen said.

As Cherry unbuckled Opal, the little girl rearranged the chairs at the table, two on one side, one on the other.

"Your daughter?" Xilomen said as she gestured to the single open chair, its back to the entrance.

"Opal," Cherry said.

"Qué linda," Xilomen said. She sat down, and Elvia climbed into the chair next to her as if it were perfectly normal for her to participate.

Xilomen caught Cherry looking at Elvia and said with a grin, "She doesn't like to be without her mama. Like a baby."

"I am not!" Elvia interjected, but she wasn't upset. She leaned across the space between their chairs so that her shoulder touched her mother's.

For a few seconds, they nuzzled, and Cherry looked away, feeling ashamed. She had come here for a problem Xilomen wouldn't understand.

"Put her down," she heard Xilomen say, and she looked up. Xilomen was nodding at Opal. "She wants to crawl around, and anyway I just vacuumed. She's interested in the mannequins with their fancy dresses. My mother is a seamstress." Was it obvious that Opal was itching to get down and explore, or was Xilomen, indeed, clairvoyant?

Once Opal was on the floor, scooting across the room, Xilomen said, "I'll be honest with you. When someone . . . like you . . . comes in here—"

"Someone like me?"

Xilomen raised an eyebrow. "I do a whole thing. A *production*. Like, turn off the lights and light a few candles before chanting some Mixtec phrases I learned from my mom's *didi*. But I don't speak it. It's a show."

"You're fake?"

"Not at all," Elvia said quickly, offended on her mother's behalf. "She senses the invisible."

Xilomen smiled. "I'm not selling snake oil."

"What are you selling?"

"The Sense," Elvia said.

"Since I can remember, I've had the gift," Xilomen said. "Sense."

"Neat," Cherry said stupidly.

"It's not neat," Xilomen said. "It's also not some hocus pocus family tradition. It's in me. No idea where it came from or why, but Sense chose me." She grinned. "I will tell you what you want to know. I promise. Sense will know."

"Okay." Cherry could hear Ray in her head—*you really falling for this*? And she was. Or maybe it was simply that she had nothing to lose.

"So you agree?" Xilomen asked. "We skip the show?"

Cherry nodded. There was a pause.

"Opal does this thing . . . " Cherry began, unsure of herself. "She goes into these trances, she—"

"Ten dollars first please thank you," Xilomen said.

"I'm sorry. Of course." Cherry handed her the twenty and the woman passed it to Elvia, who got off her chair and ran into the back.

"My daughter, the bookkeeper," Xilomen added and winked.

Elvia returned with two fives. Once Cherry folded the bills into her pocket, Xilomen nodded as if to say, *Go on.* Opal was halfway across the room.

"Like I said, she goes into trances," Cherry said. "Worse than trances. The first one was a couple months ago. They come every week or two." Cherry described how Opal's body froze, how her eyes went blank. She described the melting cabinets, the plastic bed, and how her milk let down and dripped into the waistband of her jeans. "And the room—I can't explain it. It trembles . . . or seems to. No one else can feel that part but me. I feel scared after. Something isn't right."

Xilomen listened closely as Cherry spoke. When Cherry didn't have anything else to say, Xilomen stood and walked to Opal, who was pulling on the mannequin's red taffeta dress and raising herself into a squat. Holding onto the mannequin's calf, Opal stood up, wobbling. Xilomen kneeled down to her level, smiling at the child with tender authority. Opal seemed to regard her thoughtfully. Xilomen didn't say anything. Didn't have to. She was like Mama Ursa in her confident command.

Cherry thought she should get up and help in case the mannequin toppled her child. That's what a good mother would do. She didn't because Xilomen was there, and Cherry didn't want to get in the way.

Xilomen was looking at the child closely, as if examining her. Attentive, discerning, curious, seeking. Sensing.

Sense, that's what she called her gift, didn't she?

"Opal is fine," Xilomen said after a moment.

"She is?"

"There's nothing wrong with her."

"That was fast."

"Sense did not come. No reason to. Sense doesn't waste time."

"So what's happening then? My husband thinks I'm hallucinating. I'm not."

Xilomen let her gaze rest on Cherry, and Cherry's stomach dropped as if she were falling from a great height.

"Is it me?"

"You have had a hard life," Xilomen said, and then she gritted her teeth. "But—"

"But what?"

"I don't need Sense to see that."

"It's how you walked in here," Elvia said, and her mother seemed pleased that her daughter was so observant.

"Come pick up your child," Xilomen said. "Let me see what happens."

Cherry felt Elvia's eyes on her as she stood from her chair and approached Opal, who was still holding on to the mannequin for balance. For the first time, she wished the child would slip into an episode; if Xilomen witnessed its terror, she might be able to interpret it. Cherry sat down next to Opal and put her hands around the child's torso.

Nothing happened when she had Opal in her arms. Her child let go of the mannequin to lean on Cherry, and Cherry flexed her forearm so that Opal could balance, and then she let go of the child's torso. Opal stayed upright, her tiny toes gripping the nap of the carpeting.

Cherry put her free hand on top of Opal's head, petting her soft hair. She hoped that Opal would remember this moment: the heaviness of her mother's palms against her scalp. A mother is close, disgustingly so, until she's gone and that's all you want. To step back in.

Cherry pressed on her daughter's head, the silk of her hair.

Xilomen closed her eyes, and when she opened them, the whites rolled up like a horse's when it bucks.

"Mama!" Elvia cried.

Xilomen shook herself as if she were flinging off a chill, and then she sat up straight, shoulders down, chest out, chin raised. She wasn't the same woman who walked into the room ten minutes ago. When she spoke again, it was with a deeper monotone, a voice flat as a dial tone. "Sense is unhappy."

"About what?"

"This feeling here."

"Sense feels it?" Cherry didn't feel an episode coming on. "Where is it?"

Sense's voice was flat and dead sounding. "Something's between you and the child. It's bad."

The psychic was saying what Ray said and what Cherry always feared.

It's you.

Cherry was the problem. Always had been.

"It's me," she said.

"Not you," Sense said. "It's you *with* her."

Sense let out a big rush of air, an exhale with a moan at the end of it, like she was trying to expel everything inside herself. The lights overhead blinked once.

Xilomen was different now—or back to how she was before, her voice returned to its original tone. "You need to be careful," she said. "Opal needs to be careful. Or else."

"Or else what?"

Xilomen was standing now. "Sense can't see the future. Sense only feels. Feels a darkness hovering over you two."

Cherry closed her eyes. What did this mean? How would she ever explain it to Ray?

She knew she wouldn't. Whatever was between her and Ray when they escaped the mamas was gone.

Cherry didn't immediately notice that the weight of Opal was gone. It wasn't until she heard Elvia exclaim, "Look!" that Cherry opened her eyes. Was it an episode? Oh god, not—

But it wasn't. Opal was taking her first tentative steps, away from her mother, toward the table, staggering like a tiny drunk, arms aloft.

Xilomen cheered her on in Spanish, and Elvia did the same, clapping her hands like they were at a sporting event, like Sense hadn't just delivered devastating news.

It's you with her.

Cherry watched Opal transform from baby to toddler and felt nothing. Opal might as well have been another mannequin. The child could walk now, so what.

"Come back in a few months," Xilomen said. "I give you a discount."

∞

Cherry barely registered the bus ride home. She didn't notice the old ladies cooing at Opal, or the streets westward, the buildings rundown and the people poor, until they were rich, the houses big, and then something between the two extremes: forgettable, modest, middle class. When the bus reached their stop, Cherry pulled the wire and let the driver carry the stroller with Opal onto the sidewalk. She forgot to say thank you, only remembered when she was at the corner of their street, the bus long gone.

At home, it was lunchtime. Cherry let Opal toddle around the house as she prepared their meal, and she did not speak to her as she fed her the buttery noodles, Xilomen's words—Sense's words—careening in her head.

There's nothing wrong with her whatsoever.

It's you *with* her.

After lunch, Opal's cheeks and hands glistened with grease, and she had applesauce all over her chin. Cherry thought, but didn't say aloud, in a fake cheery mom voice, *Let's get you in the bath!*

She imagined how other mothers did it. When Elvia took a bath, Xilomen probably stepped into the water with her daughter. She soaped her back, traced letters with the bubbles, washed Elvia's hair. Xilomen would brush it afterward, too, which was why Elvia's hair was so neat and glossy. Xilomen was a good mother.

In the bathroom, Cherry ran the water, warmer than usual, but not so hot that it would burn the child. She undressed Opal and then took off her own clothes, folding each piece neatly in a pile as she did at the doctor's office when pregnant, her underwear and bra tucked primly under her blouse and pants. As she undressed, Opal walked around the hallway beyond the bathroom; she was naked, her little bottom dimpling with each step.

Opal's walking was already improving, transforming from an inebriated stagger to a straight-legged march. Cherry assessed the child as a stranger would. The child was quite athletic—already walking at ten months. That was almost unheard of. She was tall for her age. She looked like her father.

"Come on, Opal," she called. "Come have a bath with Mommy."

Opal, curious that her mother had stepped into the tub, came toddling. Cherry reached out and heaved the child into the bath with her. They didn't usually bathe together because it reminded Cherry too much of the mamas in the creek—unabashed female nudity—and it seemed like something most urban families wouldn't do. Plus, Opal would only want to nurse.

Sure enough, sitting together in the water, Opal went for Cherry's breasts, kneeling to get her mouth on the left nipple, her favorite one.

"Not now," Cherry said and leaned away. "Sit in the water. Let's soap up." She rubbed the soap between her hands and set the bar on the side of the tub as she washed Opal's torso, her legs, her feet. Opal reached for the bar of soap, which fell into the water.

"Opal, look what you did."

Cherry searched the tub for the bar of soap, splashing around her own bent legs and Opal's, but her hands only moved through water. More water.

It was if the soap dropped into an abyss.

"Where is it?"

Cherry, frustrated, stood up and tried to see the rectangle of white from above, cutting through the water like a sleek submarine. There was nothing but cloudy water and Opal's pale legs, Cherry's own feet and the warm water pouring from the rusted spigot.

"I hate this," Cherry said.

Opal gazed up at her and smiled. If her daughter was smiling at her, was there really something bad between them? Opal's two teeth stuck out of her bottom gums like tombstones.

"Show me what's between us," Cherry said. "Show me how bad it's going to get, Opal."

Cherry felt cold, standing in the tub, so she got out and wrapped a towel around her torso. She felt as she had the night before, with Ray. Like screaming.

"Show me," she said again.

Answering her, the lone towel on the rack shivered a little, as if in a breeze. The window was shut, though, the door too.

The towel on the rack kept trembling. Cherry held the other to her body.

"*Show me*," she whispered.

The towel on the rack—

It was *changing*.

It was growing fuzzier. Like it was growing mold.

Was it—was it growing fur?

The wall contracted and shrunk, like a heart beating.

Why did it feel like the soap was in her hands? Slippery.

Cherry looked into the tub, already knowing what she would see. Opal—

Opal's body was rigid, her eyes blank, her legs straight in front of her. The bath was more than halfway full.

Cherry hurried to turn off the water, her hands shaking, water dripping down her legs. The towel popped open, and she grabbed for it, covering herself once more, afraid.

Without the water, the bathroom fell silent.

The water in the tub was still as glass. Had the water transformed to glass? Her daughter was entombed. The water was glass, the towels were furred like animals, the walls were moving.

"Opal!" Cherry screamed.

This would be the last time.

Outside the little window with its frosted glass was a world without this feeling.

"Stop it!"

Cherry plunged her arm into the water, breaking its glassy surface. The room shook. It felt like it would buckle. Cherry's arm was under the water, feeling for her daughter's body. She couldn't feel it, even though Opal was right there, staring straight ahead, her body still as the dead.

The walls rippled, and Opal was still half-submerged in water, unmoving.

Something heaved into Cherry like a large animal pushing against her. Pushing her out. She had to leave. It's you *with* her. Cherry screamed and backed away from the tub. Her arms were wet and so was the towel. It sucked to her stomach.

She always tried to stay calm during an episode; she would call Opal's name and coax her back, keep her voice authoritative and stable. Breathe deeply until the episode's effects passed, and then she would be soothing and officious toward her daughter.

Not this time.

She wanted to scream again and push out this bad feeling with her own.

"Stop it!" she yelled as she backed away. "You can't do this to me!"

She stumbled out of the room.

∞

Cherry found herself outside in the yard, naked, the towel discarded on the grass next to her. She was on the ground. The lemon tree was across the lawn, and she crawled toward it because it was as far as she could get from the bathtub, from Opal, from whatever *that* was. Her heart beat in her ears. She might choke on her tongue. She was trying so hard to take care of Opal like a mother should. She fed her and changed her, she taught her the names of animals and colors, counted her toes, the birds in the tree. She told her cat starts with *C*, dog with *D*, time for bed, baby. In the middle of the night, she watched her sleep. That tiny body, she kept safe.

Cherry loved Opal. Or she did in the beginning, didn't she?

Cherry sat up, her eyes on the house. The baby. The bath.

She was a horrible mother. She was damaged. She was a *mama*. The only thing that came easily to her, came naturally, was neglect.

Cherry ran.

The child was only underwater for a second or two. Cherry found her, dark eyes open, thrashing, grabbing at the water, and pulled her out of the tub. She brought her to her naked body, hushing her. Cherry held the coughing baby to her chest as Opal began to cry.

∞

That night, Cherry took the cash they kept at the back of the linen closet for emergencies, walked down to Melrose, and used a pay phone to call a taxi. It was 3:00 a.m. This was the right thing to do, the only choice. Her daughter had almost died because of her.

Cherry waited on the dark street, a small duffel bag cutting into her shoulder, and when the cab arrived, she asked the driver to take her to Barstow because for now it would be far enough. Ray wouldn't look for her there.

She would emerge in a new place, with a new life. She would disappear. For them.

Picture it. The desolate street. The taxi pulling away. The numbers on the meter are as red as—cherries. The driver's beaded seat cover. The *tick-tick-tick* of the blinker.

Picture Cherry in the backseat, glistening and vulnerable as a lung. In her bag is a single change of clothing and eleven stones.

With every passing moment, Opal is farther and farther away from her.

Part

THREE

9

Now Opal was fifteen. Ray could hardly believe it: his daughter—a teenager.

Taller than all her friends, with a Barbie watch on one wrist and, on the other, a string of skulls inked with a ballpoint pen, Opal gave catcallers the finger and occasionally stopped by the nearby laundromat to help old ladies fold their sheets. She was a freshman at a magnet high school across town, where she was a straight-A student and had loads of friends; she ran the Dissidents Club. She told Ray they discussed activists and political rebels every Wednesday at lunch. Opal was also secretary of the Seinfeld Club (episode-viewing every Friday) and attended the Vegan Society's potluck lunches. High school in 1996—high school in LA in 1996—was bizarre. A trip, as Opal might say.

Her oldest friend was a goth girl named Fab who'd moved in two doors down when the girls were seven. Fab was short for Fabiola—Fabiola Carlisle, her father from Ireland, her mother from Haiti. Fab, with her black lipstick, her scowl, and the black fishnets she wore as sleeves beneath her black Sisters of Mercy T-shirt, clearly wanted the world to mistake her for a monster, when in fact she was the kindest teenager Ray had ever met. Fabiola went to Fairfax High around the corner, a school that, according to Opal, should be razed. ("You know its architect designed prisons, right?")

Whenever they saw each other, Opal and Fab flashed what looked like peace signs. It meant V-for-vagina, a joke that Ray didn't quite get but which usually sent the girls into paroxysms of laughter. There were a lot of things Ray didn't quite get about Opal and Fab, though he never gave up trying. Why did they buy disposable cameras to take photos of boys at bus stops? Why did they fake Australian accents when they went to the supermarket? Why did they thrust the air with their pelvises whenever Alanis Morissette came on the kitchen radio? He didn't know why they circled full-time job listings in the classifieds with big red markers, or why they called each other Keanu Reeves, or why they put pennies in their Cokes. When they learned they were going to different high schools, they enacted an elaborate ritual and called it The Separation; Ray watched, bewildered, from the bathroom window as Opal buried a creepy doll in the backyard while Fab chanted the *Jetsons* theme song like a funeral dirge. Afterward, he applauded without thinking, surprised to find both girls crying. Opal's eyes met her father's through the window screen. "Da-ad!" she called out, but he could tell she was glad he was there. She was a good kid. He knew it for certain because he made sure he was around to witness her goodness.

The neighborhood had changed. Two years after the Northridge quake, people were ready to live in LA again. To live *here*, in fact—this was a desirable neighborhood. Their house was robbed twice in 1987 and once in 1988, and during the Riots an apartment complex one street east burned down to the ground. But everyone said all that was in the rearview mirror, that things were different. Crime in the area was down and real estate was up. Their own lease was ending. Ray was sure Mrs. Vartanian would raise the rent. He was afraid they would have to move.

Melrose was different now too. Gone were the panhandling punks and the bondage stores. Only one of the old vintage shops remained. A new one specialized in expensive denim with something called Talon zippers, and another resold celebrity clothing: at a Star is Worn, they listed on each tag the name of the celebrity who once owned the blazer or evening gown before it made its way to their racks. Other, seedier boutiques, with cloyingly sassy names like Girlfriends or Sweetheart, opened all the time, their salesgirls smoking cigarettes or talking on the cordless out front as they weaved around the mannequins on the sidewalk. These shops all sold the same cheap, tight dresses and blouses from the garment district; Opal said the fabric dye came off on your skin. She and Fab complained about these stores—their sameness, their shoddy wares—and about the tourists who shuffled cluelessly down the avenue, stopping in the middle of the sidewalk to snap photos of the restaurant shaped like a giant hamburger, which was pretty mediocre food-wise, Opal said.

Nevertheless, every other weekend or so, the girls paid their respects to Melrose. They were still so innocent. They shared a shake at Johnny Rockets. Fab might get her ear pierced (again) or buy those black rubber bracelets from Maya, a jewelry store adorned with carved masks and other tribal accoutrements. Opal saved enough money to get the jeans with the fancy zipper, and she always picked up some plastic bugs at Wacko, which only sold useless novelty items, as far as Ray knew. On Opal's dresser, a line of fake cockroaches paraded toward a pink plastic baby the size of her thumb.

Ray didn't understand any of it, but he loved it. He loved her. Opal was so funny, so smart, so sure of herself. She knew who she was, and she liked being different. Imagine that.

He didn't have to. Here stood Opal at the stove, nearly as tall as he was, shaking bright orange cheese-dust into their macaroni. An early dinner because she would be volunteering that evening at her school—ushering for the musical.

She was handling the main dish tonight. Before leaving for work that morning, Ray had prepared the bruschetta as a side dish, a recipe he'd picked up in all his years of cooking dinner. He even had a special jar for it, and like Ebony from DataComp instructed him over a decade ago, he let it marinade for as long as possible. By now, the tomatoes would be garlicky and slurpy.

"Look at that," he told Opal as he spooned the bruschetta onto the toasted bread. "Slurpy as a . . . snail. An Italian snail."

She cringed. "Um, that makes no sense. It's also disgusting."

"Snails aren't disgusting. Escargot, anyone?"

"It's still bad. You lose."

"Fine," he said. "Your turn."

This was their game. *Bon-Mots*. They tried to one-up each other with clever descriptions of things. It was pretentious; Ray was terrible at it, and Opal was too good at it, at least for a high school kid.

Opal smirked, glanced at the pot of now-orange macaroni. "Alka-Seltzer pack of cheese fizz," she said.

"That's not a *bon-mot*, that's a poem."

"It doesn't work because cheese doesn't fizz. But okay, yes, I'm a poetess."

"*You dig?*" Ray said, and Opal rolled her eyes.

This was exactly what he'd envisioned when she was born: a daughter he could joke with, a child he knew well, a person he enjoyed spending time with. As they played their little parlor game, his mind flew above the scene. He watched it like a movie: Opal, three months into fifteen, her light brown hair unbrushed, her eyes that same rich dark brown she'd first greeted the world with, the daisy-print dress she called a baby doll falling just above her knees, men's white gym socks pulled over her calves. No shoes, though her Pumas waited by the front door.

She hummed to herself, stirred the pasta, tapped the spoon on the side of the saucepan, *rat-a-tat-tat*. Outside, in the yard, the sunflower seeds they planted at the fence were pushing their green stalks from the soil. In a couple of months the flowers would tower over them both; he would make Opal stand next to the tallest one for a photo, and then, as he did every year, he would put one of the photos on the fridge. All summer long, she and Fab would lie out in the back-yard, tanning themselves on the plastic chaise longues Fab bought at Kmart, reading aloud from a book of Anne Sexton poems. "She was a confessional poet," Opal told Ray. "She used to model for a while too. She smoked through her readings."

"Don't smoke," Ray said.

"I already tried it once with Svetlana." That was a friend from school. "Don't worry, it wasn't for me."

Now they carried their food to the small table in the breakfast nook, with ten minutes to eat before they had to leave. Ray tried to be home as much as possible; he still made Opal her school lunch, and if he wasn't working he got up before she left for the bus, even though she said he didn't have to. If he could, he liked to be home for dinner. When Opal was younger and he was still selling microfiche, he was always there to wake her on school mornings, shaking her bed and yelling, "Earthquake!" as she screamed for him to stop, laughing all the while. She used an alarm clock nowadays—and she never hit the snooze button. How had he raised someone so competent? So willing to be out in the world?

"I'll do the dishes after I come back," Ray said.

She nodded in gratitude and didn't stop eating. Hunched over her plate like that, working on her food with the focus of a wolf, she looked just like—

Opal didn't remember her mother. She only knew what Ray told her: that her mother's name was Cherry, and that she left when Opal was very young. There really wasn't much more to say. Opal thought her parents barely knew one another when Cherry got pregnant. Ray told her they never married. That Cherry only moved in with Ray right before she gave birth.

When Opal was five, he said, "Cherry didn't feel well. In her brain."

Opal thought her parents met when Ray first moved to LA, at a party near the airport, the airplanes flying low overhead, the engines so loud that their first conversation was barely audible. Somehow, Cherry managed to hear Ray ask for her phone number. Ray liked the story, though Opal asked for it only once, at age nine, and never again.

Their last conversation about Cherry was when Opal was eleven. Four years ago. They were driving in the car, a searing summer day, on their way to El Matador. The house had been sweltering, air still, curtains closed against the sun. Ray told Opal to hurry and put on her suit. They'd park on PCH if they had to, walk down to the beach.

They were nearing the end of the 10, headed into the tunnel to PCH, when Opal asked, "Why did Cherry leave?"

Ray had been waiting for her to ask that question again—it was normal for a kid to have questions.

"She suffered from mental illness," he said, as planned.

They reached the tunnel, and it snuffed out the daylight like fingers over a match flame. When they emerged on the other side, the ocean would appear like a magic trick.

"She was nervous," he said. "Afraid of stuff. She didn't sleep. I think maybe she heard voices. That sort of thing."

Opal said nothing and he knew she was holding her breath, making a wish.

They exited the tunnel and, as it always did, the water appeared on the left, a line of sweating blue. Ray heard Opal exhale. What was her wish?

The traffic crawled north, everyone in the city seeking relief from the heat. Opal had her window open, and she was looking toward the cliffs, away from Ray and the water.

"I barely knew your mother," he said. "I know that sounds weird."

"That's why there's only that one dinky photo album?"

"That's right."

"Why didn't you take her to the doctor?"

"She refused. She didn't want medication, either, which can help some people."

Opal turned, finally. "Where did she go though?"

Ray kept his eyes on the road. This was the real question, wasn't it?

"I searched and searched for her," he said. "I never found her."

Maybe that scared Opal a little, that Cherry disappeared. Or that her mother was mentally ill. Whatever it was, Ray's answers must have satisfied Opal because she didn't ask about Cherry again. The photo album was just a cheap paperback thing Rexall gave you for free when you developed your film; inside were photos of Opal's first months of life, starting with the hospital room. There were only a few pictures of Cherry, the rest were all of Baby Opal. The album remained in her room, wedged into the bookshelf between a dictionary and a copy of *The Way Things Work*. He used to see her paging through the album, but that was years ago.

In Ray's bedroom, on the table by his bed, next to the little portable television, sat a framed black-and-white photo of two people he called Robert and Marion. The couple stood, arms linked, in front of some sequoias, the sky white above them, Robert in stiff work pants and a plaid shirt, Marion in a sensible-looking dress with a collar and three buttons, her dark hair coifed in that 1950s way. Ray purchased the photo for a dollar at the Rose Bowl flea market when Opal was three.

"My mommy and daddy," he said when he showed her the photo for the first time, right after he bought it, a few feet away from the antique dealer. The lie unspooled so easily. "Their names are Robert and Marion," he said.

He told her later that Robert and Marion died within a year of one another when he was eighteen. His father to cancer, his mother in the house fire that destroyed everything; Ray said his father's colleague gave him the photo. He had no siblings, he said. His parents were only children. He was orphaned.

A fairy tale, and Opal believed it.

"You're my whole family, baby girl," he liked to say. That part was true.

"Ready to go?" Opal said now, and he was brought back to the world: his daughter in the breakfast nook, Friday evening, 1996. He was thirty-eight. She, fifteen. Traffic to her school would be rough but what was a little car time in the scheme of things. Before he knew it she would move out and he wouldn't get to see her all the time. He winced at the thought, a physical pain, imagining the loss.

Opal pushed away her plate and stood. Ray hurried to wipe his mouth with his napkin.

"In a year you'll have your license," he said, "and you'll have no use for your old dad."

"Don't worry, I'll still need your money."

Then she did a little jig, her eyes wide and deranged, and he laughed.

∞

Doctor Dale Howard preferred to be called Doc, and Ray complied, even though it made him feel like he was spending an hour with a salty sea captain instead of a therapist with multiple degrees. Isla Patricia swore by Doc's methods. "It'll seem insane," she said, "but, trust me, you'll feel incredible afterward. Like a marshmallow walking across more marshmallows."

If Ray hadn't felt anything quite that extreme after his first appointment, he *had* noticed a change. As the elevator descended to the parking garage, he laughed at his reflection in the mirrored doors: hair mussed, face reddish, clothes sloppy. His body felt loose and relaxed, as if he'd just smoked some hashish. He hadn't felt that way, not without drugs, in years, probably not since his first months in LA, when Cherry was pregnant with Opal and they found their little house, when it seemed as if his true life had finally begun.

Although the feeling from Doc lasted only an hour or so, it was enough to bring him back for another appointment. Hopefully, this time, the effects would last. Even though Isla Patricia said it could take years working with Doc for Ray's armor to break down (she was five years into her tutelage), Ray secretly hoped it would happen faster. The first time Isla used the phrase "emotional armor" he felt a shock of recognition. That was exactly what it was, like he was encased in metal and could barely breathe. He wanted to be rid of his armor, as soon as possible.

Not that Doc would discuss timelines.

"For now," he said on that first visit, "we'll just get to know one another, and you'll get reacquainted with your breath and body."

It wasn't the kind of language Ray expected from a man who looked like Doc: pushing seventy, portly, his bushy white beard yellowed by nicotine. Then again, what kind of man would he expect to talk this way? Ray wondered what his own father looked like. If he was even alive—Ray didn't know—had he ended up with a dirty Santa Claus beard just like Doc's? His mother never spoke of his father, or not that he could recall. His father—nameless, faceless—was a stranger.

Doc's waiting room was a small antechamber with one rickety chair and one rickety side table. In the corner, a tweed coat hung from a hat rack. The room reeked of wood cleaner, that fake pine tree scent obviously designed by someone who'd never smelled a real tree. Ray felt like he was inside van Gogh's bedroom, which made no sense because that painting was cozy and inviting, whereas this was mere Europe-inspired claustrophobia.

He had to write that down, "Europe-inspired claustrophobia," otherwise he'd forget to tell Opal during their next round of *Bon-Mots*.

"Raymond."

Doc was standing in the open doorway. His previous patient, the same woman as last week, thin and nervous, her dark hair brushed smooth as a mink's pelt, passed Ray on the way to the exit. No eye contact. If she was worried Ray had heard her in there, he had not. The walls of Doc's back room were covered in carpet scraps and egg cartons.

"How's it going?" Ray asked.

Doc grinned. "Surviving, my good man, I'm surviving!" He sighed. "The day is gorgeous, isn't it?"

The thing about Doc was that he seemed genuinely thrilled to be alive. Last visit, he told Ray he started every morning "with a shit and a gag" and claimed it set him up for the day. Could that be the secret to life?

He led Ray into his front office, a book-lined room with a large window overlooking Wilshire. This part of the boulevard was called Miracle Mile; what was miraculous about it Ray didn't know, and whenever he tried to find out, no one ever gave him the same answer. Across the street towered a boring beige skyscraper. Next door was the art museum, not that he'd been in years, and farther down, the now-defunct May Company, the department store shuttered a few years back; it looked to Ray like a bronze soda can. Farther down the block was the Wilshire Tower, its Art Deco architecture pleasing and elegant, though it wasn't visible from the window. Even from the eighth floor you could hear the traffic.

"It's hard to believe mastodons used to roam these parts," Ray said, sitting on the leather chair across from Doc.

"Go on."

"You know—the fossils they found around here . . .?" Doc was waiting for more. "You can see them at the Tar Pits." Doc nodded, his eyes on Ray's mouth. Ray continued. "There are something like a hundred dire wolf skulls on display there." The doctor leaned forward. "I used to take Opal when she was younger, we'd . . ."

Now Doc's ear was angled toward Ray.

"What's wrong?" Ray asked.

Doc chuckled and leaned back. "Sorry! I can tell you're not breathing as you speak. You ever notice that? Probably doesn't bother you unless you're trying to say a lot and by the end you're choking on the words."

"Cherry used to tell me that."

"And you disagreed?"

"She said a lot of things."

Ray waited for Doc to ask him what else Cherry said. After a single appointment, Doc already knew the bare outline of Ray's life. The truth. That he'd been raised by women in a forest, that he met Opal's mother there. He knew the other stuff too, that Cherry wasn't in the picture and that he had recently switched careers. Ray was surprised how much he'd been able to confess about his childhood on the first visit. Even if it wasn't much in the scheme of things, it was more than anyone else knew, including his own daughter. He wondered if he could he tell this man more about Cherry. How her leaving, and the searching for her, was still like a knife in his gut.

Thus, the armor.

Instead, Doc announced that he wanted Ray to practice breathing deeply. Ray was relieved; he didn't want to tell that story.

"Describe what you had for breakfast," Doc said. "Try to be aware of the air emerging as you do so."

"I had two bowls of Cheerios," Ray began, speaking slowly, careful to exhale, though his mind was back on Cherry. More than fourteen years since she'd left and he still thought of her, sometimes multiple times a day. He wasn't able to will her from his mind. Years ago, when they were with the mamas on the compound, Cherry put her hand on his chest and said, "Let it out." It was as if he could conjure the soft weight of her hand on his chest, even now.

"With bananas and skim milk," he said. "And coffee."

Cherry's hands: papery palms, long graceful fingers, chewed cuticles. She bit her nails for years; Ray remembered her gnawing at them in the kitchen doorway back home, Ursa telling her to cut that out. He thought her nail biting was cute, and he also knew no one could ever find out he felt that way. At sixteen, he'd already grown taller than the mamas, and he had a sparse beard along his chin. His voice was deep. It made some of the mamas cringe. Not Cherry though.

"Very nice," Doc said.

"I'm thinking about Cherry now," he admitted.

Doc shook his head. "Say it again, with breath."

Ray tried. "I'm . . . thinking . . . about . . . Cherry . . . now." It did feel better.

"Good." Doc waved his hand through the air. "And it's fine to think of her. How's work?"

"Nothing going, but that'll change. I was busy during pilot season so I just have to remind myself it ebbs and flows."

"Isla Patricia's got your back."

Doc pronounced it incorrectly. It was *Ees-la Pa-tree-cee-a*; the first time Opal heard the name she made it into a little song, dancing around the house. It puzzled Ray that Isla Patricia, the reigning queen of Echo Park, whose grandfather still rode through Altadena on horseback, wouldn't have corrected her therapist on something as essential as her name.

"She's been really helpful," Ray said. "Good thing, too, because I just heard FicheUSA laid off about a third of its salesforce."

"Obsolescence is a bitch, isn't she?" Doc said.

"The biggest," Ray said.

Leaving his steady microfiche job was a wise move, no matter the anxiety he felt every time he balanced his checkbook. The company he worked for was bought and sold three times in the last two years alone. Anyway, the World Wide Web would eventually come for microfiche and all the schmucks who peddled her. Ray would not be a schmuck.

Isla Patricia was a location manager. So far Ray had assisted her on a pilot for a kids' show about the alphabet (shot in Agoura Hills) and then one about a cop in New York (shot downtown). He helped Isla Patricia's old friend, another location guy, on reshoots for some cheap thing, making signs on poster board with stencils and a can of spray paint, stringing them on telephone poles so that the crew knew where to park. Afterward, he picked up trash. He didn't complain; he was determined to keep at it. Locations struck Ray as a noble profession: hands-on yet rarified, requiring a vast well of knowledge about the city (that USC could be Exeter; that Union Station could be a bank in 1941). Finding places for movies to take place: that couldn't turn obsolete, could it? He didn't want to be left behind. Again.

"I haven't worked since the low-budget thing. I'm hoping to assist

Isla Patricia on a Clint Eastwood project," Ray said, exhaling as he spoke. He inhaled deeply and saw Doc look on with approval. "I could use some money."

"I bet," Doc said.

"Cherry liked Clint Eastwood. I remember that. Not that she'd really seen any of his stuff. She caught something on TV. It was her first TV. My first too. She liked it—liked him, I mean."

"I don't care what Cherry liked," Doc said.

Ray had to keep reminding himself that Reichian therapy wasn't like the therapy he saw in movies. He wasn't here to talk to Doc about his loss, about his feelings, about what his upbringing was like. Or not only that. This session wouldn't end with Doc handing Ray a box of tissues and saying, "Let's explore these issues next week." There was so much more to it.

Although Doc had a doctorate and the requisite board certifications, on their intake phone call he wanted Ray to understand that his Reichian practice veered from conventional psychology in important ways. "You won't be lying on a couch for fifty-five minutes," he said.

Ray knew from Isla Patricia that Reichian therapy was named for Wilhelm Reich, an Austrian psychoanalyst who had studied with Freud before setting out on his own. Doc explained that Reich became more radical, politically speaking. "Our man wasn't afraid of the Nazis," he said.

Reich believed that emotional disorders and neuroses emerged from social expectations and cultural structures.

"Our man was a Marxist," Doc said. "They ran him right out of Europe."

Wilhelm Reich believed that trauma was stored in the body. Talk would not help. "Reich began to feel it was a prison," Doc said at Ray's first real appointment. "This is about what the body stores and blocks." He touched two fingers to his sternum. "All that bad energy." He palpated his chest. "It's my job, as the clinician, to help you release it. Are you interested in that?"

"Definitely," Ray said.

Oh, the irony—to be involved in this hippie-dippie shit and to find himself believing in it when all he'd wanted, when he left Santa Cruz, was to never be around such nonsense again.

History repeats itself, et cetera.

Ray preferred the talking part, but Isla Patricia said that was because the not-talking part was scarier. At least at first. She reminded him that talking wasn't what helped.

"Let's go to the back," Doc said now.

He meant the windowless alcove off the front office, where the energy was dealt with. "In here you will unblock," Doc explained on Ray's first visit. "You will release uncomfortable emotions."

The room was drab, illuminated by the same black-and-gold standing halogen lamp everyone seemed to have acquired a couple of years back. Ray had one. Doc kept his on dim. The ceiling was low and felt lower because of the sound insulation. The carpeting was thick and gray; a full-length mirror leaned against one wall. In the center of the room lay two futon mattresses without their frames, each covered in batik bedspreads. They reminded Ray of the beds of his youth, and then of Cherry. Before they came to LA, he and Cherry had never had carefree sex on a bed. Even when they fucked in her room, the encounter was quick and furtive; anyway, they usually met up outside, once in the hen house, the stench of chicken shit almost too much to bear, the birds' beady stares a dare to keep going. If they'd been at all normal before fleeing home, just two lovers in a bed, if they had been able to witness even one healthy romantic relationship, they might have been able to stand real life together.

Cherry had been gone for so long, for nearly all of Opal's life, and yet these memories were still inside of him, rattling around his brain and body. Haunting him. Bad energy, maybe. Falling for Cherry had happened in a past life, years ago. And yet it might as well be days ago. Seconds ago. Time meant nothing in the face of pain.

In Doc's back room, pillows were piled against the wall and tossed across the floor. Last time, Ray had screamed into one covered in pink velvet.

If Opal saw this place, she would likely wrinkle her nose and say it looked like a child molester's grotto. It would be the winning *bon-mot* if he had the guts to use it, which he didn't. Opal would. His daughter had a sick sense of humor—that didn't mean she'd be wrong. The room was creepy.

"Let's start with the looking," Doc said as Ray headed for one of the futons.

Ray nodded and sat up, legs crossed, just like last time. He began looking around the room, into every corner, without blinking. It was possible he resembled a deranged pug, but he knew when he was finished the world would look sharper and he would be fully inside that sharpness, living his life as it was, not how he wanted it to be, or wished it weren't.

He let his eyes follow the carpet scraps up the wall. They'd been stapled in, and the staples were big and rusty. When the scraps gave way to cut-up egg cartons, he felt a little relief because the cartons were curved and soft, almost pretty by contrast. He wondered what the walls looked like behind all this junk, and then he was looking at the ceiling, his eyes deep in his skull, and the thoughts washed out of his head.

"Good, good," Doc said.

Ray didn't blink. His eyes were on the mirror now, past it. The exertion of moving his eyes in all directions made Ray a little dizzy. His sockets felt dried out, and he thought a headache might be coming on, the kind he used to get when he was a kid after he'd cried hard (he hadn't cried in years). Tears didn't come last session, and they weren't coming now.

He let out a breath, a long one, and there it was: that momentary clarity, a kind of release. Already he felt better. Free. (Free as in *liberated*; the sessions themselves cost fifty dollars each, no small amount considering how tight funds were these days.)

"Lie on your stomach," Doc said.

It wasn't long before the doctor was driving his fists into Ray's shoulders; Doc pushed harder.

"Let it out," Doc said.

Ray yelled again. The pain and the powerlessness reminded him of wrestling with Hawk. Poor kid. His friend. His brother, nearly. Ray missed the oafish shit even now.

Doc pinched him, hard. "Where are you, Raymond?"

"Here!" Ray yelled, bucking under Doc's touch, and the image of Hawk dissolved. It felt so good to let him go. The present was what mattered: right here, right now, this futon, this grunting, this pillow, this pain. He was here now. He was nowhere else. That was why he had come.

Doc pinched him again and Ray swore to himself he wouldn't return; why was he paying fifty bucks to be tortured?

He'd told himself the same thing last time.

"Breathe!" Doc urged. He was sitting on top of Ray now, his massive thighs on either side of Ray's back. The doctor screwed his fist into Ray's arm—inside the shell, into the crab meat of him—and said, voice booming, "Don't let yourself get away from this!"

"I'm not!" Ray was panting. "I won't. Please."

"Let it out. Feel from your gut."

Ray tried his best, but his best must not have been good enough because Doc drove his fist deeper into Ray's body. Ray cried out, snot streaming from his nose.

"Don't!" Ray yelled. Inside his brain was white light. Nothing. Light.

Doc let up with the grinding, and now, oh god, he was tickling him. The man's fingers dug into Ray's armpits, and Ray writhed, he had to get away. He screamed so loud it scared him. The white light had turned orange. Peach-colored then. Shimmers.

"Yes! Yes!" Doc said, and all at once he lifted his hands.

Ray felt himself sink into the mattress, everything weak, his breath at once ragged and deep. He pictured where Doc's hands had been, the skin rising back to the surface like pinched dough. Tomorrow he'd have a bruise or two. Isla Patricia called them battle scars. Thank god Opal wouldn't see them; she knew he was going to therapy, but he hadn't told her it was any different than what she imagined. How could he begin to describe Doc's methods to her? What would she think of Wilhelm Reich's ideas? He imagined telling her that Reich was popular in the sixties with writers like William Burroughs. Would she think that was cool? She'd probably roll her eyes and say something like, "Didn't Burroughs accidentally shoot his wife in the head?" Opal was the only person he could think of who didn't have armor. She would never need this kind of help.

He sat up. He cleared his throat. "Okay, um, thanks."

Doc put a gentle hand on his shoulder. "We aren't done yet."

"We aren't?"

"Your eyes and mouth, your voice, are still—"

Ray winced.

"Nothing to worry about," Doc said. "You only just began treatment. This is why you're here, isn't it?" Doc grabbed his own throat and bugged out his eyes. When he spoke again, his voice was squeaky and strangled. "It's stuck for you, Raymond. Right here."

"It is?" Ray asked. "What is, exactly?"

"The orgonic energy," Doc replied, as if he were naming a restaurant everyone had been to, or at least heard of, like Spago, or Inn of the Seventh Ray.

"The orgonic energy," Ray repeated.

"Every living thing emits it. Other people might call it God. Reich didn't."

"Do you?"

"I do not. We want it to move through you, so that you can *feel*. Isn't that what you want?"

Ray nodded even though he wasn't sure.

Doc smiled. "When energy is blocked, so too are emotions."

Ray knew he had blocked a lot. If he could release it with Doc through these weird massages and tickles—that would be ideal.

"What do you want me to do?"

He was to stand and walk to the mirror on the far wall. He was to stand before it and watch himself as he stuck a finger down his throat.

"Go right to the edge," Doc said. "Right to the moment before vomiting."

"What if I barf?" Ray asked.

"You won't. Keep your eyes on yourself."

When Ray got up from the futon, he was surprised that his limbs weren't shaky, that he wasn't dizzy. He felt great. He agreed to these appointments because he wanted Isla Patricia to call him for jobs. He had to admit, again, that he would come back to Doc, work or no.

In the mirror his face was bright pink, his shirt wrinkled. He could smell himself. This was what he was paying for, he thought: to be reminded that he was an animal. He was just a body, and that was nothing to be ashamed of.

"Go ahead," Doc said from the futon and mimed gagging himself, index finger pointed like a witch's, crooked and arthritic looking.

Ray returned to his reflection and drew his finger to his mouth. He didn't want to do what he was about to do, but he also liked the idea of the energy dislodging, and him not having to say a single thing.

He took a breath and stuck his finger inside. When he retched, his whole body seized, as if his insides were going to splash out of himself. He pulled his finger from his mouth. His heart was beating fast, then faster. Panic was rising in him and he felt suddenly afraid.

He wondered if Ursa had been into Reich. Maybe back in San Francisco? Would she have done something as outlandish as gag herself for emotional release? Seemed possible. Maybe it's what all the mamas did together, in secret, in the eastern wing.

Ray didn't want to think about his mother. The mamas. Not now or ever. He wouldn't.

"Again," Doc said from across the room.

Ray didn't even lift his hand.

"Ray?" Doc said.

"I can't," he said.

"Are you sure?"

Ray nodded. His throat felt raw. "I'm sure. I'm sorry—I'm done."

Doc didn't reply for a moment, and when he did his voice was gentle. "All right then, that was good for today."

Back in the main office, Doc told him he'd done well. "Let's try it again at your next appointment. Can you manage it?"

He meant could Ray cough up the dough. It was also Ray's cue to pay him. Ray said yes and handed Doc a fifty-dollar bill. "The other location manager I helped out—Tony—he paid me under the table last time, so . . ."

"Nothing wrong with cold hard cash," Doc said, though he held the bill up to the light.

"I'm actually going to see a house today. Which would ease up the financial pressures until the work gets more steady."

"Oh yeah?"

"It's an estate, not far from the airport. Opal and I could live there, for free."

"Nothing is free."

"I mean, in exchange for my labor. I'd oversee the property. It's only used for locations."

"That certainly sounds copacetic," Doc said as he led him to the door.

"The house overlooks a field of oil derricks. It's on that same land. Off La Cienega?"

"Ah, a pastoral view then, just like in your youth." Doc winked.

Ray startled. It was hard to believe how much he told Doc the last time: the mamas, the land. It wasn't talk therapy, but Ray wasn't deluded. His silence—his lies—had built his armor.

Five minutes later, down in the parking garage, Ray didn't feel the lightness that had followed him out of his first appointment. What was different? He gave his body a pat-down, as if looking for his keys.

It was what Doc said at the end. Comparing a field of oil derricks to the woods of his youth. The suggestion that Opal's childhood view would be apocalyptic whereas his had been bucolic. As if he'd ever willingly put his daughter in danger. As if the woods of his youth were innocent. He hated that place and that's why he didn't talk about it.

He tried to breathe. Doc made a joke—that was all.

Ray should have known not to talk about the mamas. Or Cherry. It didn't take much to turn his whole day sour. From now on, he would stick with the screaming and the tickling. And, okay, the gagging. That worked. He didn't need to confess. That was a myth. Talking was a prison.

He stepped closer to the wall, next to an older Mercedes, and opened his eyes wide like Doc showed him, a real "holy shit!" look, as if he were one of the actors playing a drug dealer in that movie he worked on, in the scene where the SWAT team arrives to bust the operation.

He looked at everything, moving his eyes around just as Doc instructed. Ray saw cars, then a scuffed concrete pillar. He saw an oil stain, an exit sign, and more cars. He kept looking. It was more magic trick than therapy practice. *Whoosh* went the thoughts from his brain.

∞

Ray wasn't sure how Opal would react to the news that they were moving—and to an isolated mansion on a dirt road, among oil derricks. She'd have to leave Fab, for one. The estate was closer to her school, though, and having oil rigs in your backyard would no doubt earn her cred with her classmates. He'd be able to sell her on the views.

The house, two stories, with big windows, sat on a high hill, the land surrounding it dotted with oil wells. These were the rigs spotted on the way to LAX, off La Cienega. Ray had no idea there was this much land; from the road it was just scrub brush and a few rigs bobbing up and down. Opal loved to spot them from the car.

The property manager, Kim, picked up Ray at the oil field's gated entrance. She handed him a permit for his car, which he was to park in the small lot. Once he was in her truck, Kim entered a code on the gate keypad, and the gate shuddered once before yawning open. It felt as if they were heading onto some famous person's compound, or a bomb site, though Ray figured it would sound weird to say that. Instead they made small talk as she drove: her work, his, the weather, the flannelly blue sky. They passed a couple of oil rigs, but not as many as he expected. On either side of the road rolling hills were interrupted only by fan palms and fringy pepper trees, with their bunches of bright red peppercorns. A few minutes passed before the road forked. Kim turned right, and in a moment they reached a second locked gate. Kim got out of the truck to enter a code into another keypad.

"Here we go," she said.

And then Ray saw it: a big two-story house. It looked somewhat like a Craftsman, but also like what a rich person from the nineteenth century might call a cottage. It was made of dark red bricks and had a slate-gray gambrel roof. Olive trees bordered it on either side, and wide, sturdy stairs led to a front porch. Ray pictured Opal lying across those stairs in dramatic fashion, the back of her hand on her forehead. The house was solid, he thought. More than that: it was regal. It made him sit up straighter.

The truck reached an unpaved driveway, short and dusty. Kim slowed as they rocked across it and then pulled the truck in front of a falling-apart garage. She saw him looking at it. "The garage has a dirt floor and so many spiders we've stopped using it for filming. If you can evict the arachnids, you can use it as you see fit."

Ray doubted it; the garage looked like it might collapse at any moment. *Depression-era chic*, he planned to tell Opal.

"Let me show you around," Kim said, holding up the keys as they approached the house.

The inside of the house resembled any decent Craftsman on Wilton or in West Adams—hardwood floors and built-ins, a brick fireplace, glossy wood wainscoting. There was minimal furniture, but it appeared well-made. Ray already loved the deep leather chairs in the living room. A draft of cool air tickled his neck as he moved from one wide square room to the next. He touched the glass of one window with the tip of his finger.

The rooms made Ray want to slow down, take them in. He didn't want to admit it, but the house possessed some ineffable quality, something special, something that felt magical—or adjacent to it. He asked Kim when the house had been built.

"Nineteen fourteen. But I'm told it was designed to look older."

It hadn't been around much longer than the house he and Opal lived in now. And yet this felt more like his childhood home. Like that house, it had history. Like that house, it was special.

"Who built it?" Ray asked.

"We don't know much. Or I don't. Someone rich, no doubt. Lots of stories though."

"Like what?" he asked. Opal would love to know.

She waved her hand. "Typical stuff. Someone's mistress lived here." She nodded at the fireplace. "There's a little hidey-hole in there, for booze during Prohibition."

"Mistress?"

"Want to see the bedrooms upstairs?"

The banister was a marvel. Its massiveness would never let you forget it had once been a tree. Back when Los Angeles was even more country than Ben Lomond and you could build a mansion on a hill surrounded by nothing but more hills, someone wealthy had asked for this banister and gotten it.

Ray turned to Kim. "How soon can we move in?"

Kim raised an eyebrow. "Let's drive the grounds first."

Back in the truck, Kim took them down that first road and then turned at the fork. "The oil is mostly this way," she explained.

There were just over a thousand acres. "It's the largest contiguous urban oil field in the country," she explained with pride as they followed the road that curved around one set of pumps and then another, all but a few industriously dipping their metal heads up and down, up and down. The rigs were on sandy ground, often fenced with chain-link, a utility truck or excavator nearby for some sort of human industry, though Ray spotted no other humans besides himself and Kim. The land surrounding the rigs was beautiful, flecked with sage brush and chaparral, shaded with live oaks and eucalyptus; farther off, a row of palm trees paraded across the land. From the truck, Ray spotted little paths for walking; he and Kim even drove by a stream, a duck tucked into its surface.

"How come no one knows about this place?" Ray said.

"I wouldn't say *no one*. There are fifteen hundred thirsty birds here and they produce over two million barrels of oil a year."

"I guess not a secret then," Ray said, sheepish about his ignorance. "Thirsty birds—is that what you call them?"

"Oh, there are all kinds of names. Thirsty birds, pumpjacks, sucker rod pumps, horseheads, grasshoppers, rocking horses." She paused. "Just don't call them oil derricks. That's for a different piece of equipment."

"I'm learning a lot today."

"Where's your place now?" she asked. When he told her, she said, "You know, there's a pumpjack on Pico. Just west of Fairfax."

"I had no idea."

"That's by design," Kim said. "It's hidden in what looks like a nondescript office building. Personally, I prefer our human addictions out in the open."

"I guess it *is* more honest," Ray said.

Most of the local pumpjacks were painted green; that was why he and Opal called them grasshoppers, though this close you could see that their sides were caked with rust. This close, it sounded like the pumpjacks were whining, the noise metallic, groaning. Kim explained that the pumpers came regularly to gauge the machines, the trucks were always in and out. That Ray would come to recognize the guys, and probably chat with a few. "Good people," Kim said.

They kept driving, across more and more land. There were more rolling hills and shallow crevasses where oak trees sprouted. He counted two hawks and one gopher peeking its head out from a hole.

Doc's joke aside, the place did remind him of Ben Lomond. Ray's keenest memory of childhood was of space, of the privacy it gave him. No one saw you if you didn't want them to.

It wasn't until he and Kim circled back to the outer edges of the field that he could see the cars rushing past on La Cienega below. If it weren't for that traffic, the planes flying overhead, and the distant hikers at Kenneth Hahn, he could trick himself into believing he lived on a farm in Iowa or in a Tuscan villa. "It's been cast as both," Kim said.

He would sign a year contract to take care of the estate: keep the house clean and clear any debris from the road leading up to it. Check the gates every evening. They would provide him with a truck. He didn't have to be there for filming, and it would be Kim's job to show it for locations—unless he was available, and in those cases, they would pay him an additional fee. The position required he make himself available should any emergencies arise. "Put out the fires," as Kim put it. During filming, he and Opal would have to stay in two of the upstairs bedrooms; one of them had a hotplate and sink for this very purpose.

"Filming isn't constant," she said, "if that's a concern."

"It isn't."

The owners—the trust—weren't keen on a minor living at the estate, but they were in a bind and Isla Patricia had recommended them.

As Kim pulled the car in front of the house, she said, "Pretend I didn't say this, but . . ." Her voice trailed off and then she was yanking the parking brake and pinning Ray with a serious look. "You have a kid, so I have to. The health risks. I'm sure you researched them, right? You know—asthma, the potentially noxious gases."

Ray hadn't researched anything. Was this a terrible idea? Probably. But the house was remarkable. It was special, magical even, and so was the land. And he was nearly out of money. They had to move. He couldn't wait to be here. Opal would love it. A temporary place for them, until he got his career going.

"You really shouldn't live here for longer than a couple years," Kim said.

"We won't."

"Isla Patricia says your daughter's a hoot."

"She is. You'll love her."

They could move in on the first, Kim said, provided Ray could be trained beforehand.

Before Ray got back into his car, Kim handed him an envelope. "Inside's the trust's rules. Isla Patricia already warned you, right?"

"No outside cars unless they've been preapproved for a shoot. No parties, not ever."

"And it's well water. People have been bathing in it for decades, but no one has taken a sip since the Johnson administration. I don't advise you buck tradition. You'll need to use bottled water."

"Isla Patricia told me."

"Make sure your daughter reads it too," Kim said.

∞

After giving it some thought, Ray figured Opal would pass through a series of emotions when he told her about the move: disbelief, followed by scorn, then giddiness, then grief over everything she would have to leave. After she wept and described her feelings, there would be a few self-designed rituals to help her let go. She and Fab might light a candle or kiss every sidewalk crack from here to Melrose. After all that, she would be ready. Unlike Ray, Opal's eyes were wide open. She was breathing.

He was correct about the disbelief and the scorn at least.

"It doesn't have an address?" she said.

"We'll have a P.O. box."

They were in the living room. She hadn't even put down her backpack, she was so stunned by the news. More than that. She was pissed.

"There's nothing around? Seriously? Where will I go for a smoothie?"

"We have a blender. Opal, you'll love it. Trust me."

She dropped her backpack and they both watched it slump to the floor.

"Dad, it's in a fucking oil field. Won't I, like, die of cancer?"

Even his teenager knew the research.

"There are some risks," he admitted. "But the house is actually quite far from the rigs, and we won't live there for too long. A year or two. Besides, did you know that all over the city there are pumpjacks? They're not called oil derricks, by the way. The pumpjacks are hidden in these huge buildings we drive by every day."

Deadpan eyes. "Wow. Neat."

"Anyway, the house—it's beautiful."

"*This* house is beautiful."

She had a point. Here, the window that faced the street was shaped like the entrance to a castle. For most of the year, the lemon tree was heavy with fruit. It was the only house his daughter had known.

"There are thousands of houses like this one," he said, which was true.

"I like it."

Opal was wearing her favorite corduroy miniskirt. Across her white T-shirt she'd written the word FUCT with a black Sharpie. She'd even drawn the little ™ sign next to it. Her knees were covered in Band-Aids—her version of accessorizing.

"Are we really that broke?" she asked.

"Yes."

She sucked in her breath.

"Mrs. Vartanian wants to raise the rent by thirty percent," he said.

"Could you have even managed that with the old job?"

"Barely." He didn't want her to worry. To become, as the books said, *parentified*. But he liked being honest with her. Transparent. "Do you wish I still sold microfiche?"

"God no. You need to live your dreams."

"Fly high like an eagle," he said.

"And I am the wind beneath your wings." She stuck out her tongue at him. "But couldn't you, I don't know, manage an apartment building or something, like a normal person?"

"Since when did you want to be normal?"

She said nothing. Ray could hear her breathing—Doc would be proud! He could tell she was letting his question soak in.

Opal turned and headed for the kitchen. Ray followed her, knowing she was after a Fruit Roll-Up. He felt a burst of satisfaction when she pulled one out of the cabinet. She took it out of its packaging and then wrapped the sticky red square around her index finger. He winced as she popped her finger into her mouth.

"I realize this is a big deal," he said. "Let's have an open conversation. I have my own worries too."

"Like what?"

"Like, what if it's just too weird?"

She took her finger out of her mouth. "You already know it is."

"What if there's a fire and we can't get the fire department there in time?"

"Jesus, Dad, and you still agreed?"

"It's a film location. The access road is wide and easy to navigate." She didn't look convinced.

"I'll even call the local fire station before we move in," he said. "You'll see. It's amazing. The banister is magnificent."

When she pointed her Fruit Roll-Up finger at him, Ray was reminded of Doc, explaining how to gag properly.

"Yes, ma'am?" he asked.

Opal was about to respond, then she hesitated. She put her hand down. It was unlike her not to say what was on her mind. She was alarmed: her eyes huge, her lower lip quivering. She looked like Cherry. He could barely stay in the room.

"It'll be okay," he said softly.

"I didn't say it wouldn't be," she said.

"Then why are you crying?" he asked.

Opal didn't have an answer. Tears, silty with her purple mascara, fell down her cheeks. Her nose began to run.

The crying felt too fast. How had she moved past all the other emotions?

"I know you'll miss Fab," Ray said. "You won't be that far, I promise."

"It's not about that," she said and began sucking her finger again. She pulled it out. Her fingertip was poking through now, the chipped burgundy nail polish. The Fruit Roll-Up was disintegrating.

"Opal?" Ray said.

She sighed. "What about . . . *her?*"

Ray started. He might get used to talking about Cherry with Doc—but with Opal? He couldn't imagine it. Except for those handful of conversations, they didn't discuss Cherry, who was a stranger to Opal, whose abandonment was the only dark spot in the entire history of her charmed life. But years had passed since that car ride to the beach, and Opal was older. Smarter. She was bound to ask about Cherry again. How naïve he'd been, to not prepare for this moment.

"What about her?" Ray asked.

"What if she comes back? And we aren't here?"

"Oh Opal." He thought of Cherry—again. Not the Cherry as she was when she left them, but years before that. Cherry asking about her mother. Ruth.

"You think I'm being stupid," Opal said.

"I would never think that."

"How can you not know *anything?*"

"I told you, I barely knew her, I—"

"Have you even tried looking for her? Lately, I mean."

He hadn't. Not for a long time. There it was, another reason the strange house appealed to him, a secret he'd been keeping from himself. Cherry wouldn't be able to find them there. They could disappear as she had.

"I don't want her to find us," he said, finally.

"You don't?"

"Do you?" he asked.

"Is it bad if I do?"

Ray did not offer his first reaction, which was, *Yes, it's bad. Why would you want the woman who left you to come back? She would ruin everything.* Instead, he thought about Doc.

"Not at all." Ray exhaled as Doc would have wanted. "Your feelings are your feelings."

Surprise and relief crossed his daughter's face, one after the other. Ray loved how her emotions were so close to the surface. They were a lesson: if he could feel everything, as Opal did, he would survive. More than that: he could be happy.

"I search for her on AOL sometimes," Opal said.

"Oh yeah?"

"Nothing ever comes up."

"Opal," he said, and she took her finger out of her mouth. She looked up at him, waiting—for what? Wisdom, comfort, assurance, protection, presence, love. It was his duty as a father to give her all that and more.

"It's her loss," he said.

Opal's mouth twitched and her eyes hardened, shutting out their usual softness. It was as if she were trying to move on, to be tough. Was that armor? He hoped not.

By the next morning she was packed.

10

Organic energy was strong on the estate. Ray intuited it right away, and every passing day on the property solidified intuition into certainty. The place crackled with an invisible vigor, that life force Doc alluded to. Whereas Ray's own orgonic energy was blocked, especially in his throat, on this land, the energy was free. It moved. It was strong. It was beautiful.

Isla Patricia said he wasn't totally nuts. All over the world, for millennia, human beings looked for ways to describe this invisible force. *Chi. Prana.* Isla Patricia said some German guy in 1845 called it the *Odic Force.* It was human to feel it, she said, and to want to name it.

According to Reich, orgone energy—massless, omnipresent—coalesced to make every living thing. The smallest units were microscopic. *Bions* he called them. The largest ones could create clouds, even galaxies. Here, the organic energy, the *bions,* flowed from the dirt roads and the humming oil wells into the fences and the palm trees and the fragrant acacia trees with their furry yellow blossoms. It emanated from the squirrels scurrying up the trees and into the gophers twitching and digging underground. It spread into the house, too, through the wide front door and into the airy rooms, into the crack above the fireplace mantel and out of the graying window sashes into the floorboards. And, maybe, if he was lucky, it flowed into Ray too.

It wasn't until he and Opal were settled into the house that he realized how long he'd been holding his breath. For years. Maybe he wasn't used to being a city slicker after all.

That first night when Ray turned off his bedside light, the darkness was complete, the city sounds barely audible. On other nights, there would be helicopters, the occasional far-off ambulance siren, but not this first night. All was calm. Outside, in the fields beyond, the pumpjacks panted; together their chorus resembled the hush of a body of water, moving, rushing.

In the dark, Ray undressed and got into bed. He wasn't afraid. He was relieved. He breathed deeply as Doc instructed. He imagined the energy flowing. He remembered the woods back home, running through a darkness that felt prehistoric, into that rush of sunlight where the trees separated. Wiping the mud at the bottom of the creek across his arms and then down the backs of the other kids. And inside: in the kitchen pantry. Ursa and the mamas called it the larder, but he wouldn't. The spiky scent of cardamom, jars of beans and millet. Warm scent of oat.

Ursa must have had her own word for the energy back home.

Ray shut his mother out of his mind and breathed. In minutes he was asleep.

It took a bit longer for Opal to feel comfortable. At first, she was scared to go to bed and made Ray leave the hallway light on until he was sure she was unconscious. During the day, she seemed cowed by the open space. It made her itch, she said, and at night she was frightened by the owls hooting, the coyotes crying. She said she missed the squealing brakes of garbage trucks and the horns honking on Melrose.

The pumpjacks didn't bother her at least. She called them their neighbors.

She missed Fab, though she also said she couldn't wait to bring her here for a sleepover. "It's going to be epic," she said.

She decorated her room and sewed curtains for its two large

windows "Do you want a serial killer to watch me undress in the two lit-up windows?" she said. "No thank you."

"Don't be ridiculous," Ray said.

He was standing in her doorway, ten days into their new life. It was late June. The estate had a queen bed for her, so they got rid of her old twin and bought new bedding. He had a lot of money in savings now, with all the furniture they'd sold. "You're safe here," he said. He reminded her that not even the oil guys had the second gate's code. The film crews received temporary ones, and after the shoot they expired. If a hiker at the park across La Cienega wanted to, they could glimpse the roof of their new home, but even then they'd have to be searching for it.

"It's a secret out here," he said.

"That's even creepier," Opal said. She paused. "But it is a *bon-mot*."

He cheered and then said, "Give it time. You will fall in love with this place."

He was right.

A few weeks after they moved in, Opal left the house to explore the land. She was gone for so long that Ray worried she was lost. When dinner was ready, he called her name from the porch, and, getting nothing in response, he walked down the road to the gate, his voice growing louder and louder—*Opal! Opal!* —until it was ragged. He got into the truck to find her, his heart thunking in his chest. Something might have happened. An animal could have attacked her. Were there mountain lions on the property? Had someone gotten in and hurt her? Had she fallen and broken her leg? The sun would set soon and then she'd be in real danger.

He told himself to breathe, but it was no good, the air in his lungs thick and black as the oil beneath the land. He sped up, honking his horn, searching for her bright blue shorts in the brown brush.

He finally found her standing among the eucalyptus trees at the far end of the property, petting a trunk, marveling.

"Nature's velvet," she said, making him put a hand to the tree.

If she had been any other teenager, he would have assumed she was high. She wasn't. She was Opal.

"Promise you won't do that to me ever again," he said. "I have to be able to find you."

She promised. She was sorry.

Was she also thinking about Cherry?

∞

It took a while for Ray to fully understand how far out Reich's theories got. The man—*our man*, as Doc liked to say—went from believing trauma blocked the flow of energy in the body to espousing the theory of orgonic bions, which he was certain floated through and created the universe. From there, he built a machine, called an Orgone Accumulator, designed to trap orgonic energy. He believed one could sit inside the metal-lined box and harness the bions. The good, vibrant energy would fill you up. Heal you. Reich claimed he could even cure cancer.

"Didn't take long for the FBI to open an investigation," Doc said.

"Jesus," Ray said. They were in the last few minutes of the appointment; it was always at the end of his treatment that Doc doled out the history lessons, the Reich biography, maybe because Ray was so spent by then, sweaty and sore, his throat raw, that all he was capable of was sitting and listening.

"What happened?" he asked.

"They threw him in jail," Doc said. "Destroyed his papers and any devices he had. This was up in Maine, where he ultimately settled when he came to the States."

"How awful."

"It is. And it isn't. Our man *did* go a little insane at the end." Doc bit his lip, wincing, and stroked his beard like it was a small pet. "It's a shame he went so far. He even believed he had built a machine—not the Orgone Accumulator—that could make rain."

"You're saying he died a quack?"

"You could say that," Doc said. Ray appreciated the honesty.

"Well shit."

"But the major tenets of his theories are sound," Doc went on, rocking in his chair, and Ray could tell he was gearing up for one of his little lectures. "When I say theories, I'm speaking of the body theories, which are now considered if not mainstream, then at least essential to trauma work, especially by somatic psychologists and such. The proof is in the pudding! I've witnessed it myself, as you know. This work helps. It heals. Don't you think?"

Ray had to admit that it did. He was coming to see Doc once a week, as long as work didn't get in the way; these appointments, along with life on the estate, were doing *something*. He felt great. Miracle Mile, indeed.

"Do you have an Orgone Accumulator?" Ray asked. "Not here at the office, I know you don't. At home though?" Ray knew Doc lived in Silverlake, bought a house in the seventies. His house overlooked the reservoir, he said.

"Alas, no. I've only tried it a couple of times at a friend's place."

"And?"

"Felt exquisite," Doc said dreamily.

At a previous appointment, Doc told Ray that bions released through the top of the head, escaping until the body felt depleted, drained. The question was, how to get the energy back? Ray imagined stepping into an Accumulator.

How big was it? Was it scary?

No. Exquisite.

"How can I get one?" Ray asked. "An Orgone Accumulator." Without meaning to, he leaned forward, as if preparing to lift off.

Doc was surprised. "You want one?"

"Is that—wrong—?"

"Wrong? Never. But you aren't a Reichian therapist. You aren't elderly. You don't have cancer or arthritis or any of the other diseases some believe the Accumulator can cure. Honestly, if you *did* have a serious malady, I'd tell you it was just a box."

"And because I don't?" Ray asked.

"It'll feel exquisite." Then Doc squinted. "But you didn't just receive some troubling diagnosis, did you, Raymond?"

"No, no," Ray assured him. "I just want to feel good."

Doc chuckled and began pawing around on the desk behind him, at the piles of papers and books and mail there. Finally he found what he was looking for and held it out to Ray. It was a catalog. Very thin. More like a pamphlet.

"This is from a friend of a colleague. He lives in Maine. The ones he builds aren't cheap, but they're worth it."

The catalog featured photos of what looked like a small closet, a freestanding wardrobe, constructed with cherry-colored wood. In one, the door was open; the interior was made of silver walls. A single chair fit inside.

It said the Orgone Accumulator would arrive unassembled—six panels made of alternating layers of wood, wool batting, and steel wool. There was a phone number with a 207 area code to call for ordering. The Accumulator would be built within two to three months, it said, though it would take the customer only twenty minutes to reassemble. Once it was built, the customer could sit inside, shut the door, and feel the energy collecting within him.

"Can I keep this?" Ray asked.

∞

Summer turned to fall and it got hot, as it always did in September, the sun inescapable and harsh, the leaves on the olive trees paper in the dry air, flashing their silver undersides in the hot-breath breeze. It cooled at night and Ray kept all the windows open. In late October, fall's heat finally unclenched and the olives lay in the dirt; Kim said to leave them be.

One Friday night, Opal and Ray decided to have a picnic on the property. She was now in the tenth grade, taking all honors classes and writing for the school newspaper. The picnic was her idea; she wanted to eat at the foot of 199, her favorite pumpjack. Unlike the others, it was painted a peachy orange, and it perched on the edge of a hillside that seemed to hang over the entire city. They sat on the west side, as Opal insisted, with their backs to the pump, and faced a ring of shaggy eucalyptus trees. Their trunks glistened.

Over four months on the estate and the eucalyptus still impressed her, and today she remarked how the bark peeled off like pencil shavings. They weren't even playing *Bon-Mots*; they didn't do that anymore. Opal was too old for cute rituals with her dad. It happened overnight. Or so it felt. Ray pretended it didn't bother him.

"The tree looks more ominous than that to me," he said.

For this picnic, Opal cooked steak and frozen fries; she steamed carrots. Tomorrow the entire downstairs of the estate would be commandeered by a crew shooting a commercial; they would have to hide out upstairs. Bagel Bites for breakfast, chicken Caesar salad wraps for dinner. Thank goodness he'd be prepping a film and Opal would be at school. Not that she complained—this place had won her over, as he'd predicted it would. Even when it was a pain, even when there was a film crew and they had to be careful of wires and lights and remain quiet during takes, she liked it. Ray was growing a little sick of the phlegmy garble of walkie-talkies and those stupid skater wallet chains all the grips wore; there was the headache of running out of bottled water or toilet paper at an ungodly hour. He kept his complaints to himself because they were petty. He still loved it here: the energy, the beauty, the wild, the secret of the house and its land. He could probably afford to move them to a normal house at the end of the year; he was in the union now and working regularly, but he made no exit plan. He didn't know how he would ever get Opal and himself to leave.

Two weeks ago, Opal had taken off down the dusty driveway

during a commercial shoot, no shoes, hair flying behind her, ripped peasant dress ruffling in the breeze. The director on set stepped into her path and asked if she might want to be in the spot. She laughed in his face. The next day, she stole Ray's clippers and shaved her head. Fab was calling her "Fidel Gastro."

"What does that mean?" Ray asked as they ate.

"She said I looked like G.I. Jane." Opal sighed. "G.I., as in Gastro-Intestinal, Gastro as in Castro. It made sense at the time." She laughed, rubbing a hand over her bald head. The look suited her; it emphasized her big eyes and broad cheeks. To her chagrin, Ray thought, she'd probably be offered a modeling contract by a stranger at the mall.

"Are you going to grow your hair long again?" he asked now as she served the food.

"Why? Do you hate Gastro?"

"Gastro's a cool dude."

"What's shooting tomorrow?"

"Car insurance," he said.

"Riveting." She gave him that little smirk, the same one she'd had since she was a toddler, sassy but not without joy.

They ate as 199 huffed and clinked at their backs and birds called in the trees.

"Isla Patricia told me about the Oregon Robot," Opal said finally, her fork poised in the air. Tines pointed at him.

"What are you talking about?" he asked, even though he knew what she meant.

"Raymond," Opal said. "Don't pretend to be a bimbo."

"It's called an Orgone Accumulator," Ray said.

"In the garage? Really?"

"That production designer, Wallace? She said it's totally sound. And the exterminator came through. It's our space."

"*Your* space, you mean."

"You're welcome there, anytime."

"Isla Patricia said one of these—"

"Orgone Accumulators."

"She says one costs, like, a thousand dollars."

Damn it, Isla Patricia. They'd slept together once, a weekend Opal had spent at Fab's, and now the boundaries were unclear. Did she think she was the stepmother?

"I have the money," he said.

"Not anymore you don't."

There was one piece of steak left on his plate, a hoof of fat. He ate it.

"You're my child, not my accountant," he said with his mouth full. Opal hated when he talked with his mouth full.

"I'm not a child."

He swallowed. "I didn't say you were *a* child. I said you were *my* child."

"The Reich stuff is too weird, Dad."

"Isla Patricia introduced me to Doc. She's normal enough, isn't she?"

"Does Doc get a commission on the orgone thing?"

"No! The guy who makes them lives in Maine. He comes from a family of shipbuilders."

"Wilhelm Reich was cuckoo for Cocoa Puffs. You know he believed he could make it rain by shooting something at clouds?"

"I do, yes."

"There's a Kate Bush song about it."

"Where'd you learn that?"

"I have a library card."

"Show me the books."

"It's called the internet."

"Did the internet tell you that J. D. Salinger has an Orgone Accumulator?"

"Has he even left his house since *Catcher in the Rye* came out?"

Opal seemed distressed as she began to pile their dishes. Pumpjack

199 went up down, up down, clanging, slurping all that rich oil from the earth's veins. How long before there was nothing left?

"Opal," he said.

"Dad," she replied.

"Look, you're not off base. Reich did have some crackpot ideas," Ray said. "Especially toward the end. I didn't order the cloud buster." He kept himself from mimicking Doc's speech about somatic therapy and such.

"Instead you ordered a metal box that cost a thousand dollars," Opal said.

Her response shouldn't have surprised him. She didn't get why he saw Doc in the first place. She agreed that the body held on to feelings and that the mind and the body were connected, but, according to Opal, there was a big leap between that and gagging in front of a mirror for an old man. "And you pay him for the pleasure," she liked to remind him.

Even though Ray knew he shouldn't try to convince her of the Orgone Accumulator's benefits, he wanted to, if only to see her mind race to present new arguments. He also couldn't bear to keep it from her. This would not be a secret.

"Wait until you sit in it," he said.

Opal reached for a lock of hair, no longer there, and her hand paused, floating above her scalp. "No way I'm going in there."

She wasn't in debate mode anymore. She seemed scared.

"Why not?"

"I know how to breathe, Dad."

"I never said you didn't."

"Still no."

"What are you afraid of?"

That was Doc's favorite question, and he had a gift for asking it at the very moment Ray was feeling proud of how loud he was screaming, how hard he was crying. Obviously, his pride was proof he hadn't truly let go; he couldn't dive into the dark waters of his soul if he was too busy admiring his reflection. "Scare yourself, Raymond," Doc would say. "Go ahead. Get scared."

"I'm not afraid of anything," Opal said. "A box cannot collect energy." At the last word, she wiggled her fingers around her face, miming a lion's mane. "I know you're from Santa Cruz, but do you honestly believe in this life force bullshit?"

"I do," he said. "I know it's cool to be skeptical."

"That isn't why I'm skeptical. It just, honestly, seems crazy."

Crazy. The word hung there for a moment.

"Trust me," he said. "I know it how it sounds, but how can part of you not believe in something like orgonic energy? I feel it. Don't you?"

She sighed. "Feel *what*?"

"This," he said, and held his arms out wide.

He could tell she understood by the way she looked out at the view and then closed her eyes, as if to trap what she'd seen inside. He laughed, and then she did too, and he felt so happy.

Cherry used to say that dads were insignificant. "No one cares if they leave," she'd said in their past life, back in Ben Lomond. It was nighttime at the creek, and he was drawing circles on her back. At the time he agreed because it was true for them both. But it wasn't true for Opal. Ray was here for her. He was all she had.

On the drive back to the house, she rolled her window all the way down.

"Why do you need it?" she asked.

What could he say? What could he tell her about *why* he needed it? He didn't want her to know that he wanted to be healed. Cured. Of what Cherry did by leaving them. He needed to unblock the bad energy.

He repeated what he told Doc. "I just want to feel good."

The house came into view and Opal hung her arm out the window to catch the breeze. Cherry used to do that, too, except she'd cup her hand. She would scoop the air like water.

∞

The Orgone Accumulator arrived on a Thursday when Opal was in school. For the first time in weeks, Ray was between jobs and no one was filming at the estate. The land was quiet except for the persistent insect drone of the pumpjacks. That morning, during rush hour, a news helicopter hovered, checking out a car accident on La Cienega heading north, but the tow trucks and cops were long gone, and the roads and skies were clear.

To Ray, it felt like the universe was smiling upon him. He'd taken a chance when he gave the guy in Maine the estate address, which wasn't to be used for regular mail; they had a P.O. box for that. Just like the mamas, he thought—and tried not to. Large packages *could* be delivered to the first access gate, but if no one was home when the driver called the house number listed at the keypad, then he was out of luck. Somehow, though, it worked out perfectly. The phone rang just as Ray was getting out of the shower. He was planning to go pick up some lunch, but he was noodling around, in no hurry. It was like the universe wanted him to be home.

The UPS guy agreed to follow his truck all the way to the house, probably out of curiosity, and he even helped Ray carry the long rectangular box to the garage. Unassembled, the Accumulator was about the size of a piece of IKEA furniture, a kitchen table, perhaps. It felt strangely light. The two of them managed it just fine.

Ray wanted to install it in the garage partly because of its dirt floor. Reich believed the machines worked better when buried in soil, Ray didn't know why.

He wasn't going to leave the box unopened, even if he was hungry for lunch—to do so would be a desecration. Ray ran back to the house for his toolbox and a banana and returned to the garage. His breath was shallow, and he imagined the bions rising out of the top of his head like cartoon thought bubbles as he peeled the banana and tossed the peel through the open door. He smashed the banana into his mouth and fell to his knees so that he could kneel over the box. He swallowed, throat thick. He was so nervous his hands were shaking.

Inside the box were six panels, including the ceiling, floor, and door. When he held them upright they came to his shoulder. He was afraid he was going to need someone's help and that Opal, teenage attitude flaring, might refuse. But the panels were easier to screw together than he expected. The universe, again. The garage was getting hot—and the heat barely touched him.

In less than fifteen minutes, the Accumulator stood upright, as wide as a refrigerator or a phone booth, if not quite that tall. He was almost finished; it was almost ready. The hairs on his arms stood, his skin brailling with goose bumps. It was time to dig the shallow hole.

The dirt was dry and stubborn, root choked. It took nearly half an hour to get anywhere, and by the end Ray was sweating and cursing, his hand sore from gripping the trowel. His back hurt. Finally, the hole was big enough, and Ray dragged the Accumulator into it. The soil only covered about a foot of the structure. Better than nothing. He dug out the dirt at the front, so that the door could open and shut easily.

He did not even wait to find a chair that would fit inside. Did he really need a chair? Was that part of the—what was the word? The *prescription*? *Ritual*?

Only one way to find out.

He stepped inside and shut the door. Inside, it was so dark the world disappeared and then he did too. It was the kind of darkness that swallowed your very body.

What did he hope would happen? He told Doc and Opal he wanted to feel good. That was true, but that wasn't the only thing. He wanted the Accumulator to heal him, to cure him, as stupid as that sounded. And that word, *cure*, only began to approach it because he wasn't sure what was wrong with him in the first place—or what wasn't wrong. A fucked-up childhood, a father he never knew, a messed-up mother, a beautiful, brilliant daughter whose mother abandoned them both, a loneliness, a wound you couldn't see, a sense that everything good in his life had come from hoarding lies. Oh, you know, just all that.

He wanted to laugh. Was there a cure for *all that*?

He closed his eyes and let his breath guide him. In and out. In. Out. The floor of the Accumulator was hard and smooth. His tailbone began to ache but he stayed where he was, breathing. With his eyes closed, he felt unmoored. Floating. He breathed.

In. He was flying through space. Out. He was space.

He didn't know much time passed before he felt something gentle overtake him. A tenderness. Like a hand, cupping his body. A wave of softness. Were those the bions?

When he opened the door, the deluge of light was almost unbearable. He covered his eyes. When he stood, his legs felt strong. He willed himself to open his eyes. See it.

11

THERE WAS THAT OTHER PART OF REICHIAN THERAPY, the famous part, the part people joked about at parties if you mentioned his name. The function of the orgasm—the saucy parts, as Isla Patricia called them. It wasn't enough to ejaculate, Reich claimed. Anyone—any man, at least—could do that. You had to surrender fully into the climax, the release. According to Reich, mental health depended on fulfilling one's orgastic potential. ("Orgastic potential," he imagined Opal saying. "Aren't they playing at the Troubadour on Tuesday?") Unless you were without armor, unless the energy flowed through you freely, you couldn't let go completely. To be able to do that, you had to be willing to accept love. If you couldn't accept love, you were mentally ill.

Reich argued that prohibiting children from expressing their feelings, including sexual interest through masturbation, would cause them to repress emotions and build up armor, which would keep them from being free and happy.

That was what Ursa had done. Ray growing from a boy into a man was treated like a betrayal—he felt her and the mamas' tacit disapproval. Ursa claimed she wanted the kids to be free, and run wild, but the truth was, the children's needs were too much for her and the other mamas, and so Ray had learned not to have needs. Cherry too.

Or they tried.

Ray knew that, for all his flaws, he was a good father. Opal was the most important person in his life, and he wasn't afraid to let her know it. He had never told her to stop crying, or that she was eating too much or too little. She'd been affectionate as a kid, and if she wasn't anymore that seemed natural too—what teenager cuddled with her dad? He didn't know if she had any interest in guys (or girls, for that matter) or if she had even been kissed. For all her swagger, she was private about certain things. At least with her dad. There was probably a world of stuff she would have confessed to Cherry were she around to listen. Motherless girls kept secrets.

Isla Patricia thought Ray should sit Opal down for a serious discussion. "One day soon she'll get pregnant and you'll wonder where you went wrong."

"No way," he said.

"You don't think she's going to have sex?"

"I think if she wants to have sex, she'll get herself on the pill."

Isla Patricia had to give him that. "I've never seen a more self-possessed girl. She'd probably demand an STD test from the guy too."

Opal was at Fab's for the weekend. Isla Patricia had invited herself over—this would be their third tryst. As soon as Ray picked her up at the first gate, he felt a fizzing through his whole body, an urge to touch her, even a simple pat on her tan arm. The way she'd waved at him through the window before flinging her duffel into the truck bed, then hadn't even bothered with the seat belt. Did her body bounce as they made their way through the property? He tried to keep his eyes ahead. He couldn't. Her thighs touched. She wore construction boots covered in dust from a recent shoot in Vasquez Rocks. Her perm was fading, and her hair was longer without the curl, dark with a few strands of gray. She had lips like pillows, a chipped front tooth (nothing traumatic, she said the last time, when he put a finger to it, she had a grinding problem), and a chin that could cut you—him.

Now they were in jackets to watch the sunset from the porch, the sky a deep purple running into hot pink, the descending sun lighting up the colors from within, the tall palm trees in the distance already flat black cutouts. It was psychedelic. Unreal. Was it really true that pollution was what made LA's sunsets so good? Or was it Isla Patricia next to him?

The downstairs was still crammed with lights and wires and tape because the shoot had run over; they had more to do on Monday. The producer was an ass, Isla Patricia warned Kim, but the trust wanted money, and Kim got it.

"I hear he gave ten thousand to Ross Perot's campaign," Isla Patricia said.

"Was that before or after the 'you people' gaffe?"

For dinner, they had heated up Hot Pockets in the upstairs microwave. They were drinking gin and tonics.

"No limes?" she said.

"Home, home on the range," he began to sing, and she shoved him. All it took was that single touch. What was he, a teenager?

She had come over, ostensibly, to check out the Orgone Accumulator. If he weren't working again, and such intense hours, he would use it every day. Isla Patricia wanted to try it.

There was, also, the sex they were going to have. It was an unspoken item on their agenda, and Ray was yawning from nerves. She said, "You can't get tired on me," and winked.

She was divorced, no kids. She knew that before they started seeing each other it had been a long time since he'd been with a woman. What she didn't know was that Cherry had been the only one: his first and, before Isla Patricia came along, his only. A lie by omission.

It was funny how the smallest lie can give you all the power.

He let Isla Patricia believe there had been encounters here and there, no one serious enough to introduce to Opal.

"After Cherry left, it seemed too . . . loaded," he explained the first time they were naked in her bed.

Isla Patricia grinned—as if she were the first woman to pass some test—and he tried to ignore her pride. The truth was, if Opal didn't already know Isla Patricia, there was no way he would introduce them. Isla Patricia wasn't his boss anymore (they were on different productions), but he still considered her, if not a mentor, then at least an important professional contact. It wasn't smart to get involved, especially since she seemed to want more than he did. What was it he wanted?

He'd known Isla Patricia long enough to know he wasn't in love with her. For starters, she was too bossy. Too nosy. She hated soup, black pepper, large dogs, men in sandals, water with ice, and how some people used the word *supermarket* when they meant grocery store ("What's so super about it?"). She couldn't stand the smell of coffee because it gave her headaches—news she repeated each time she saw him drinking a cup. She popped her gum. She refused to take Santa Monica Boulevard. She slept with an eye-mask like a cartoon princess.

Isla Patricia was what Opal and Fab called an "SDP"—small dose person. Other people, they argued, you could hang out with forever. They had a name for those types too: "Feasts." Fab had told him, her voice soft and quivery, as if overcome by her own profundity, "One person's SDP is someone else's Feast." Opal nodded, adding, "It's all about how hungry you are."

Whatever the nomenclature, it was evident he and Isla Patricia would not last. He didn't feel for her what he'd felt for Cherry.

And yet.

Isla Patricia, and his desire for her, made him feel normal. Back home with the mamas, he hid his attraction to Cherry because it was gross and wrong for him to have any attraction—to anyone. That he wanted to sleep with Isla Patricia, and that it was okay to want that, was a solace. He was a person. He deserved to be a person.

He didn't end it, because of Isla Patricia's body, which he liked very, very much: curvy and compact, her ass big, her breasts perfect, nipples the size of Susan B. Anthony coins, strong legs that she shaved from ankle to crotch. She smelled like jasmine. Her bush was carefully trimmed, a dark moss. He needed her again, and she knew he did, which was how she'd wrangled this invitation. Their attraction was uncomplicated, unfettered. She did not make him feel wrong for desiring her.

But she had already complained twice about the Hot Pocket—it was cold in the middle, what was this sugary taste? She would probably bring up the absence of limes at least once more before the night was over. The entire weekend! He was both thrilled by the prospect and, already, annoyed.

Ray wasn't being totally fair. He was glad she was there to try the Orgone Accumulator. He wanted someone to feel as he did. To tell him it *was* working. The bions were filling up, right? That he owned an Accumulator and could use it daily to keep his energy from flagging and his immune system strong was the kind of privilege he wanted acknowledged.

He just hoped they slept together *before* they went to see the Accumulator. It would be the only way to take the edge off. One offhand remark about how stuffy it was in the garage and he wouldn't be able to hide his annoyance. He still hadn't confronted her about telling Opal how much he'd spent on the Accumulator. He probably never would.

Doc thought this relationship, or whatever it was, was good for Ray. He said there was nothing wrong with the setup: they were both consenting adults, and they were friends, comfortable with one another. Doc didn't know just how pathetic Ray's sexual history was, although Ray had admitted it had been a long time since he'd been with anyone. "I'm rusty," was how Ray put it.

"Isla Patricia," Doc said, again mispronouncing her name, "won't care."

"What if it's . . . what if I'm . . . bad?"

Doc sighed. "Raymond. There will be no report card issued. You've been working hard in these sessions. You're so much less tense than when you started. Your armor is falling away."

Was it?

"I just feel embarrassed." Ashamed was the word, but he didn't use it.

"Just be in your body, let yourself be with hers. Enjoy it." Here, Doc grinned. "You said it was fun, no?"

It was fun. Better than that. Isla Patricia was sexy because she was confident, easy in her own body. She looked into Ray's eyes a lot. She smiled. She might bite his shoulder, just a brushing of her teeth against his skin, and then laugh. When it felt good, she said so. When it didn't, she voiced that too. When he went down on her she lowed like a cow, or like a woman giving birth, but from pleasure, not pain. He could tell by her openness that she wasn't ashamed: of herself, of being with him.

Tonight, he took her drink out of her hand and said, "Let's go upstairs."

"Can't I see the Orgone Accumulator first?" she asked. She was already standing.

"No."

"Why not?"

"Because you're driving me crazy."

She took it as a compliment, but he meant it in more ways than one.

He didn't try to mask his eagerness and he didn't want to, because to pretend his desire wasn't about to chew him into pulp would be a lie and he'd told enough of those. If there was a time to strive for honesty it should be now, in his bedroom, with this woman and her body. What was attraction between two people but an urge to turn two into one? They couldn't do that if he put forward some false self. He wanted her in a way that was mammalian and simple, stupid probably, earnest at least, and pure.

Kissing her, he took off her jacket and then her shirt, and then her bra, the wire in one cup poking through; she had a mark from where it had irritated her skin. He imagined their libidinal energy speeding through them. Her lips were reddish pink. She smiled between kisses.

He was holding himself back, thinking stupid things to distract from the pleasure. He didn't want to enjoy this despite himself. Pleasure you didn't let near you wasn't pleasure at all, it was desire, and desire was just an ache that eventually burned itself down to ash. Who needed that? He pulled Isla Patricia on top of him.

Sex with Cherry had never been like this. In the beginning, sure, there was that same eagerness and need, but maybe only on his part. Cherry rarely grabbed for his body; if she touched him at all, it was almost an afterthought, as if she had succumbed to her own pleasures and was being careful not to forget about him. She didn't want his body in the way he wanted hers. Was it his fault? Maybe, but it was the mamas who had messed them both up: everything wrong with him and Cherry was because of them. What did they teach Cherry about desire and her own body? Nothing good, that was for sure. She and Ray had to hide in the purple room, for god's sake.

Even after they were in LA and their relationship was no longer forbidden, they were careful and quiet in bed. Furtive. Once Opal was born, they were hardly ever intimate. He wasn't sure she enjoyed sex with him. Not like Isla Patricia did, who would rock every which way to find the thing she wanted, and when she got it, she would say, "There it is," under her breath.

Now he let himself get closer to the pleasure. He was searching for a resistance. It was as if his body were pushing to find something never found. The search, the pulse, the—

Reich said orgone energy was blue, like the sky, like the ocean, which reflected the sky. This was better than blue. Here it was. Something holy here.

Here.

When he was done, Isla Patricia kissed him once on the forehead. She climbed off him, breathing hard, and kept touching herself. She came moments later with a little squeak.

"Know thyself," he whispered into her ear.

"Shut up," she said.

"I mean it." He did not think to stop himself from saying what he felt now: "I wish I had what you have. You aren't trying to be anyone else except you. You're real."

The words were out before he had a chance to calibrate them. It was the closest he would come to loving her.

∞

Isla Patricia took a shower, and when she was clean, she put on her pajamas, a long T-shirt dress that reached her knees, the words WAKE ME WHEN IT'S OVER printed across the chest, paired with flannel pants. He'd never seen worse pajamas.

"I hope you're wearing that when the four horsemen show up," he said.

She laughed and said she wanted to be comfy for the Orgone Accumulator. She leaned over and grabbed his ass. He moved closer to her, sniffing the slope where her neck met her collarbone.

"You smell good," he said.

"You know it," she replied. And then, "Thanks for letting me see it."

She meant the Accumulator.

He'd forgotten the flashlights, but the house's back porch light illuminated their path somewhat, and, besides, tonight the sky was an ill shade of greenish brown, the fug of a city that always kept its lights on, its TVs blinking. The only sound was the buzz of the wells.

"This place is spooky," Isla Patricia said.

"Opal and I love it."

"So do I."

She took his hand, squeezed it once, as if to say, *I can be like you guys*. Had he led her on? He imagined the bions fizzing out the top of her head. The Orgone Accumulator would trap them in its chamber and Isla Patricia would fill up with them.

They made their way across the lawn that separated the house from the garage, a field of grass so large that a television show had once used it to shoot a cemetery scene, the art department's head-stones looking surprisingly real.

"Just so you know, the seat's not comfortable," he told her.

"Doc told me you weren't sitting on anything before he intervened."

"He did? What ever happened to doctor-patient confidentiality?"

"Relax. He just told me you owe him for the shooter box."

That was true. When Ray explained to Doc that he didn't have anything to sit on, Doc was concerned he wasn't doing it right. He called a friend of a friend, who loaned Ray something called a shooter box. The shooter box was an energy charger that you were supposed to sit on. It looked like a cheaper miniature version of the Accumulator itself, or like a piece of mysterious medical equipment at a Victorian sanitarium. Constructed with layers of steel wool and sheep's wool, its inside was lined with steel, its outside encased in fiberglass. A door opened at its front, and in its chamber one could place objects—plants, food, cosmetics, a hat, anything—to be charged. A long rubber tube sprouted from the front of the box like an octopus leg, and its end terminated in a big black funnel made of steel wool and metal. When Ray went to pick it up the day before, the guy told him to be careful not to place the shooter box anywhere near microwaves, computers, or fluorescent lights and to make sure to put it outside every few days, to soak up the sun.

"It has a million uses," he said, beaming angelically. "Call me when you get your own so I can have this one back."

Ray hadn't tried it yet. Isla Patricia would go before him, and so, as they reached the garage, he told her how to move the funnel to whatever parts of her body she felt needed the orgonic charge. How it would draw energy out of the charger and into her.

"Love love *love* this," she said.

Small dose person, he thought.

He pulled open one of the garage doors. The Orgone Accumulator was set up below the single unlit light bulb. If Isla Patricia weren't with him, Ray would leave the light off, despite the spooky factor, and soak in the darkness. Instead, he pulled the string and the room illuminated. From where they stood, the machine resembled a cheaply made wardrobe, or maybe one of those napping pods for businessmen in Japan. Isla told him about those. The dirt around the Accumulator made it look like something washed ashore.

"Here we go," Ray said.

He wasn't sure what to expect from witnessing someone else's session. In truth, as he sat cross-legged on the dirt floor across from the Accumulator, its door closed, Isla cocooned inside, he felt nothing. A little impatient for his own session to start. Sleepy. Bored.

Twenty minutes later, she emerged, beaming, blissful.

"I feel so loose," she said. "Like I just did some restorative yoga, you know? Ujjayi breath."

She was talking a mile a minute. His thoughts were on the Accumulator.

"I should have brought a book," he said. "Not much to look at if I can't see you."

She smiled. "Thanks for letting me go first—such a gentleman. While you get started, I'm going to pee. I'll come back with a magazine. And a flashlight."

He was already stepping inside the Accumulator to sit on the shooter box. "Wake me when it's over," he said, and he shut the door before she could laugh or protest.

The small space smelled like her. To his surprise, he didn't mind. The scent wasn't overpowering, and it wasn't her shampoo or her perfume—it was Isla Patricia herself. Her skin. Her essence. It was more abstract than that, even; the Accumulator had nurtured someone new, and Ray sensed the trace of that someone's presence. It told him he wasn't alone.

He pulled the funnel to him, aimed it at his chest, and closed his eyes. He breathed as deeply as he could, his lungs expanding with air. He felt it occupying every space, down to his belly and up to his throat. He held the oxygen for a moment and then exhaled as long as he could, until he was emptied like a sleeve. A chill had entered the garage and the Accumulator felt cool.

Eyes closed, breathing, the funnel a pleasing weight on his heart, he began to think about the old house, their rental on Edinburgh. He imagined it as it was the first day he saw it, and on the last: empty of furniture, clean, floors mopped, cutlery drawer wiped of debris, light fixtures dusted, everything still as a painting.

No doubt someone new lived there. They would fill it with their own stuff, their own lives. What might happen to them in that house, under that tile roof, in those private rooms?

Ray breathed in. Out. The metal walls seemed to breathe too. He felt cradled. The funnel was warm in his hands. He lifted it to his neck.

He remembered waking up that morning nearly fifteen years ago. He never thought about this.

Cherry wasn't asleep in bed next to him. She wasn't a great sleeper after Opal was born, and sometimes he found her cooking breakfast before dawn, or sitting on the porch with a cup of mint tea. He didn't dare say what he feared in those moments he caught her drinking the tea—that she was enacting the same rituals as the mamas had. It seemed better to pretend it was nothing.

One time, he found her sitting beneath the lemon tree.

Did she really have to take Hawk's stones with her when she fled? It was cruel how she took that secret, that story, from him.

Somehow, that day, seeing her side of the bed empty, he knew it wasn't a typical morning. Something was wrong. Ray didn't even take a piss before searching the house.

He remembered feeling afraid.

Opal—

She was still in her crib. She'd gone to bed with a runny nose and now she had a soft snore as she slept. He let out a big rush of air, relieved. The evening before, he'd come home from work to find

Cherry oddly calm. "She had an episode in the tub," she said, but her voice was affectless and it spiked a chill down Ray's spine.

"She's okay," he told Cherry, taking the baby. "Looks like she has a cold, that's all."

Opal squirmed out of his grasp and he placed her gently on the floor. That was when she got into a squat and stood. Ray whistled and she turned back to him, smiling and proud. She began to walk, toddling away from him, across the living room. Ray cried out; he could feel himself grinning.

"She's been walking all day," was all Cherry said. Again that flat speech, as if reading instructions from a manual. She went to bed right after putting Opal down.

Inside the Accumulator, Ray squeezed the metal tube in his hand. He imagined the energy coursing through it and into him.

That morning.

He had searched for her, calling her name softly.

What he could still remember now, after all these years, was the frantic feeling that pillaged his body as he moved through the rooms and back and forth across the yard. He headed to the front of the house and walked up the street, and down, calling softly, "Cherry, Cherry." No one answered.

Back inside, he looked for a note. He found nothing. Her keys were no longer on the dining room table. But her purse was still there. She had not taken her purse.

In the bedroom, he rifled through her things. The duffel bag was gone. He couldn't remember her clothes well enough to know what was missing.

Her sneakers, though. She took her sneakers.

He went right to the linen closet and dug furiously through the folded sheets and washcloths, all the way to back. His hand hit the wall of cedar and he knew for sure. The emergency cash was gone.

Cherry had taken it.

She took their money. She'd left them. She was gone.

If Cherry wasn't with him, where was she? And if she was gone, what would become of Ray? Who was he without her?

Was this how his mother felt? Like wanting to die?

In the Orgone Accumulator, Ray kept his eyes closed. The Accumulator was growing warm with his bions and he breathed in and out as deeply as he could. He let the funnel roam down to his navel. He kept breathing. *In, out. In.* He never allowed himself to think about that morning. *Out.* It was too awful to revisit. The shock. The shame. The betrayal. The panic and, under that, dread. Cherry was his only lifeline to his past. She was the only one who knew him entirely. And she was gone.

He had to find her. Would he drag her back to this life, though, if he did? He didn't want it to be that way. What was so wrong with this life they'd made? How could she not see how perfect it was?

Ray was about to call the police when Opal cried out.

Cherry had left Opal. Her own daughter, abandoned.

At least she left him Opal.

Ray squeezed the nozzle and pushed the funnel into his skin. He let out a rush of air at the memory. He thought he heard Isla Patricia return to the garage. A scrape of the door. A clicking—the flashlight maybe. On and off as his breath went in and out. He didn't want her to bother him. The bions were flowing, he was sure of it. He was so closed up, Doc said. Not only at his throat. Everywhere. He was armored, unwilling to let anything in. The bions had to flow through him. The past too. He would let it flow out.

Here it was, the thing he never thought about, Opal, in her room—

He was standing at the linen closet, and discarded bedding lay in piles at his feet. He had to pee so badly it hurt, but Opal was calling for him, he had to get the baby. She was okay. She would be. They would find Cherry, or they wouldn't. Either way, he wouldn't leave, he would be the best father in the world. Even if Cherry was batshit crazy, he wasn't. He was normal. He hadn't let the mamas ruin him.

With a new resolve, Ray kicked at a blanket on the floor and pushed the bedroom door open. Inside, Opal stood at the crib, her chubby hands on the rail.

"Daddy!" she cooed, snot glistening beneath her nose.

"Opalina," he said. "You woke up! Do you have a little cold?"

She didn't babble a response or move.

"Opalina?"

Then the thing happened that Ray tried so hard to forget, to never think about, because it was so scary. Not only that, it was shameful. It defied understanding. He didn't think about it. It went away. Or it didn't.

In the Accumulator, Ray sucked in his breath and let it go.

Just think about it, he told himself.

It happened to you. Don't let it keep happening.

Where are you, Raymond?

Opal reached out one arm and it was as if she was struck in the chest. Ray thought the word *knifed* as she leaned back and seemed to freeze there, suspended.

"Opal?" Ray said, and he knew at once what it was. His daughter's eyes were empty and lifeless. "Opal!"

He remembered that evening months before, Opal a zombie on the kitchen floor, lost to him and Cherry until he clapped his hands, Joy Division blaring on the record player.

That was an episode, and this was an episode too. This was what Cherry was always going on about, what scared her, made her unable to sleep, or go anywhere, or make friends—what made her leave.

It wasn't only Opal who looked wrong: stiff, unseeing. It was the room too. It felt different. Wrong. The air felt—soupy. Like the air was a thickness to claw through. That wasn't all. Ray sensed a blackness inside of Opal, radiating from her, leaking from her, infecting her. He couldn't move, his limbs like cinder blocks. He was frightened.

Cherry tried to tell him.

Something is happening to Opal, and it isn't right.

She'd wanted his help.

The episodes are real.

He didn't listen. He didn't try to help. No wonder she left. He deserved it. It was his fault.

It's been a long time since anyone's been mean to me like this.

"Cherry," Ray cried out. But she wasn't there.

"Opal!" he screamed and clapped his hands like a round of applause.

At that, Opal shook her head and the spell lifted. Back to Earth. The mobile above her bed spun in a lazy circle and Ray felt warmth run down his legs. His pajama pants were soaked with his urine.

He was a coward.

How had he been so dismissive of Cherry? So condescending. So cruel. She needed him to believe her. He hadn't, and now he and Opal were paying.

In the Accumulator, Ray was crying, remembering. The bions were filling him up as he let the memories move through him, as he let them go. The bions were filling him with lightness where before it had been hard and heavy.

Ray didn't know back then that the episode he witnessed in Opal's room would be her last. He would never know what they were or why they stopped, but they did. After that, his daughter was back to being herself. She was perfect. As more time passed, the easier it was to push the experience deep inside himself. Seal it up. He had nearly convinced himself it never happened.

God, those weeks after Cherry took off. The rage and shame. The nights after Opal was in her crib and there was no one else around, the house quiet as a tomb. Was he even alive?

He took two weeks off from work, and when he went back he told a lie about Cherry moving in with family on the East Coast. No one questioned his story: he could tell they felt bad for him, a sucker with a baby to raise alone.

He tried as best he could to search privately for Cherry. He called the nearby hospitals. He and Opal drove to places Cherry liked—the

horse paddocks at Griffith Park, the tony streets of Hancock Park—
to see if they would discover her there, wandering. He didn't want to
open a missing person report because he and Cherry were supposed
to be gone. Cherry had never existed in the first place. But maybe that
was a bad idea. He could have looked harder for her.

He did try one thing.

It was the other unthinkable thing.

It was sealed up. Ray never thought about it, about how, a few
weeks after Cherry's disappearance, he scrawled off a note and ad-
dressed and stamped the envelope. He dropped it into the blue mail-
box up the block. He was asking for trouble but he had to do it if it
meant finding answers.

In the Accumulator, Ray let himself remember.

Sitting in front of the TV after work, the lights dim, his tie slack
around his neck, ice cubes melting in his big crystal glass of bourbon.
It was around seven thirty in the evening and Opal lay asleep in her
crib at the back of the house. During the day, the baby was irritable
without her mother; she rejected the bottle and would only eat orange slices, napped fitfully. But she was warming up to the babysitter,
Miry, who had been staying late to help Ray get comfortable in a
post-Cherry world. Miry had just left when Ray sat down with his
drink. It was easy to play the part of the bumbling single dad, the lost
and grieving young man, and he allowed Miry to assume that Cherry
was dead. He didn't care if she caught him in the lie; she was merely
the first of many sitters those first two years.

The phone rang.

In the Accumulator, Ray trembled. He pressed the funnel back to
his neck. Breathe. *In. Out.*

It rang again.

"Hello?" he said.

He wanted it to be Cherry. God, why couldn't it be Cherry?

He remembered she said, "It's me."

Ursa. He remembered the shock of her deep voice, how the

familiarity of it hit him at the base of his stomach. He had to be careful.

"You got my letter," he said finally—or something like that.

He'd mailed her a single sentence, *Call me*, the words underlined twice, his phone number written below it. He sent it to their post office box, sealed in a thin envelope. Her name and address were typed on the front, no return address.

He didn't remember how Ursa replied, but in the Accumulator he let himself conjure what he could. The scratchy beige and brown couch that Cherry picked out. His cold hands against the cold glass of bourbon. Something was on the TV but he couldn't remember what it was. He remembered Ursa saying she missed him, or something like that.

"Tell me where you are," she said.

He refused.

"Why did you write me?" she asked.

Why *had* he written her? It must have been the fog of Cherry's abandonment. It blinded him. He didn't know what else to do, who else to go to. He was stupid enough to think Cherry might have gone home. Women came to the mamas all the time with troubles no one else wanted to listen to. Maybe Cherry had sought out the mamas, for their understanding and protection.

"You're in LA, I know that much," Ursa said.

His stomach seized once more. Did that mean Cherry was with the mamas? Had Cherry told them where he was? Did Ursa know about Opal?

He didn't know how he replied, but he remembered she was angry at him.

"I'll find you," she said.

He said something—something silly. He remembered he kept shaking the bourbon in his glass as he talked.

Finally, he said what he needed to say: "I'm looking for Cherry."

"Cherry?" Ursa sounded surprised. "Isn't she with you?"

Of course Ursa didn't know where she was. Cherry would never go back to the mamas. How could he even think she would? He hardly knew her.

He mumbled something. In the Accumulator he allowed the memory in. He brought the funnel to his ear like a phone.

On the other end of the line, there was a long pause.

When Ursa spoke again, it was with deliberate slowness. "I could have told you she would leave you," she said. It was as if she were choosing her words carefully, as if she might have said something more hurtful but was holding back as a kindness. She was a killer.

"Go to hell, *Sharon*," he said.

He remembered he called her Sharon more than once, and she was upset, and then she hung up on him. Strangely, that hurt. He wanted to be the one who always did the leaving.

He was back to being alone in LA without Cherry and no clue as to where she went. And his mother knew it.

If Ursa tried calling again, Ray wouldn't know. He unplugged both phones right away and the very next day he had the number changed. She would not find him. He knew he was risking cutting a connection to Cherry, but it was a risk he had to accept to keep Opal safe.

In the Accumulator, Ray kept breathing, but he felt calm now. He had moved through something and returned home. The memories were over—they hadn't killed him. If anything, he let them in, and then out, and now he felt lighter.

He opened his eyes and dropped the funnel. The Accumulator was dark, but the light beyond slipped through the crack at the door.

"Isla Patricia?" he called out.

A rummaging. "Ray? What is it? You okay?"

"I'm great." No—he felt better than that. Exquisite.

∞

The next evening, after a day of walking the land with Isla Patricia and cooking together, and dodging her petty complaints and tolerating her prattle, and having so much sex he felt wrung out, Ray drove her to her car at the first access gate. She suggested they try the Accumulator once more before she left, but he demurred. He wanted to return alone, without a witness. She seemed to understand his reasons, and he felt grateful as he leaned down to kiss her mouth through the open window of her car.

He watched her drive off and then he turned back to the estate, the land bruised and blue in the gloaming, the pumpjacks dark as shadows against the sky.

Something about the Accumulator had changed him. He didn't just feel different—he was different. He had tried for so long to un-think those terrible first weeks of Cherry's leaving. He was certain that turning away from them would make them disappear, and the opposite happened—the memories grew fangs, they bit him. But the Accumulator dragged the monster into the light, tamed it, loved it. He felt capable of love. He was no longer afraid. What was done was done. He didn't avoid the past, he accepted it. This acceptance would allow him to move on. He would heal.

He wound his way back to the house and parked the car. What else was he ready to face? The mamas, his mother, Hawk, the days before he and Cherry took off, how anxious he'd been, buying that car, getting everything ready, knowing he would never see Ursa again.

He needed to be back in the Accumulator.

Heading across the lawn, he peered at the garage. Its doors were closed but the light was on—had he forgotten to turn it off? He thought he remembered pulling the chain to extinguish it. Yes, he definitely had, because he remembered Isla Patricia grabbed his arm at the moment the room fell black and that single touch was enough to want her all over again.

He got closer. "Who's there?" he called.

No one answered.

"Hello?"

He heard something moving behind the door. Was it—

Was Cherry there? Inside the garage.

She was here for Opal.

But that didn't make sense. Maybe it was Kim?

He pulled the door open and his daughter stepped from behind the door.

Opal looked taller than she had the day before. That was how children grew, wasn't it? Not incrementally but suddenly. The fact of how fast time moved could take his breath away; before he knew it, she would be an adult. How could Cherry stand to miss everything? Opal's hair was growing in, and curls framed her face.

"Hey, Dad." She wore the 1984 Olympics T-shirt she'd discovered at the Jet Rag dollar sale, where she'd sifted through mounds of clothing in a hot parking lot. He didn't recognize her bell-bottom jeans. They probably belonged to Fab; it turned out sharing clothing was a way of females everywhere, not just hippies on a commune.

"*Hey, Dad?*" he repeated, moving into the garage. "What are you doing here? You're supposed to be at Fab's until tomorrow. I thought I was coming to pick you up. You scared me."

"How do you prefer I greet you?" Opal asked. Behind her on the floor lay a plastic bag of cut-up mango, her faux-fur coat, and a large flashlight he had never seen before.

"What's going on here?" he asked. That same thought came for him again. *Cherry.* "Is there someone with you? A boy?"

"You think I'd bring a guy to this place? With the dirt floor? Please." She sighed. "Come on, Fab. The jig is up."

The Accumulator door opened and there was Fabiola Carlisle in a ratty black tutu dress and black-and-white striped tights. She was wearing Opal's high-top pink Converse; Ray could tell they belonged to his daughter by their ballpoint tattoos: checkerboard on one toe; the words *little ghost* on the other. Fab wasn't wearing her usual black lipstick. Without its familiar defense, her face looked young, as vulnerable as a baby's.

"It was my idea," Fab said.

"How did you even get here?" Ray asked.

"We took a taxi," Opal said.

"Taxis can't come on this property!" he cried.

"Relax. He dropped us off at the access gate."

"You walked?"

"Yep," Opal said.

"Why?" Ray asked.

"I wanted to see the Oregon Robot," Fab said.

"I told you I'd let you use it," Ray said. "Why sneak in?"

Fab was looking at Opal, as if waiting for her to say something. Opal shook her head and turned her gaze back to him. "I can't tell you that," she replied.

"It's dangerous," Ray said.

"The robot is?" Fab asked.

"I mean it's not safe walking around here in the dark," he said.

"I told you it was this place," Fab hissed. "It's doing it."

"Doing what? What are you talking about?" Ray asked.

"It's safe here," Opal said. "We're fine."

"If you weren't, no one would know," Ray said.

At the thought of Opal in danger, Ray's throat winched closed, as if someone—*Cherry*, squeaked his brain—were turning a dial, tighter, tighter. Above him the garage rafters were cobwebbed even though he'd taken a broom to them just the other day. The patch of mold on the wall, the one he'd scrubbed down to a pencil-dot, was already growing stubble. He wanted so badly to be back in the Accumulator—that feeling of being light and free. Where was it?

"When I saw the light on in here," he began, "I thought—"

The girls were watching him. He wanted to tell the truth. He could feel the words trying to get out, inexorable.

"You thought . . . what?" Opal asked

He shut his eyes and opened them. *Say it.* "I thought you were your mother."

The urge to confess kept coming. Would they make fun of him?

He didn't care. He exhaled as Doc had taught him. The armor—he was breaking it down.

"I imagined Cherry," he said. "Hiding."

"Don't."

"Who knows why. And I felt like I was going to die. Or that I might kill her."

"Holy frijoles," Fab said.

"Fabiola," Opal warned.

"She's here," Fab said.

"Who is?" Ray asked.

"*Fabiola*," Opal repeated, her voice stern.

Fab, no longer sitting in the Accumulator, was standing in front of it, one hand on its door. She smiled; her eyes were wet. The tears were from happiness and wonder, and she was looking at Opal like Opal was a preacher who might rid her of some disease with a tap to the forehead.

"Cherry," Fab said. "Cherry's here."

"You found her?" Ray's stomach dropped; all at once, his breath left him, he couldn't breathe. Opal had seen Cherry. Cherry had seen Opal.

"Has she been to the house? Here?" he asked. "When?"

Opal said, "It's not like you think."

"Is she back in LA? Was she always here?" he asked.

Opal shook her head. "I said, it's not like that. It's something I do."

"I don't understand," Ray said, but he thought maybe he did. Cherry had never left them. He'd never stopped thinking of her. Sometimes Opal looked just like her mother. And sometimes even the smallest thing—the light at dawn, a bad radio ad—would bring the memory of her right next to him.

"I can go to her," Opal said, tapping her head, then her chest. "In my body."

"What does that mean?" he asked.

"Show him," Fab said. "Show him!"

"It's not a fucking performance!" Opal said.

"What are you trying to tell me?" Ray asked.

"We came here so I could stop it. I want to stop it."

"Stop what?" And then, "You came to use the Orgone Accumulator."

"It can help, right?" Opal was practically begging, and Ray saw that she was frightened.

"You said that, didn't you?"

Ray said, "Why don't we go in the house and talk about this," but Opal wasn't listening.

"I had a purple onesie," she said. "When I was a baby."

Ray didn't know. Was there a photo of it in the little paperback album? He didn't think so.

"It was Cherry's favorite outfit for me," Opal said. "She'd put it on me even after it was too small and it wouldn't snap. I'd wear it unbuttoned until you complained and made her alter it to a little dress thing."

Now he remembered the fight. Not a fight really, just a debate about how Opal looked ratty in the too-small onesie, too much like a kid from home. It bugged him, and he'd said so. They'd been in the breakfast nook, and on the table between them were eggs and potatoes and glasses of the pulp-free OJ he'd requested, a miracle of their new life. The crows were circling the sycamore trees outside. Opal couldn't have been six months.

"How do you know that?" Ray asked. "There's no way you remember it."

"I told you," Opal replied. "I can go to her."

"She means to Cherry!" Fab cried.

"I don't understand," Ray said.

"I can get to that moment," Opal said. She took a deep breath. "I can go back in time."

Part

FOUR

12

GET INSIDE THE BOX. COUNT TO FIVE. CLOSE YOUR EYES and hold your breath. Let it out. And go.

Opal didn't have to use the box, but it was more difficult without it, like trying to fall asleep when she was too tired. Inside the box she broke through with only the slightest effort. Opal never called it the Orgone Accumulator, not unless she was talking to her dad.

Occasionally, she would think about how it had felt at the beginning, when she had only just discovered what she could do, before she even understood what it was. She was eighteen now, and she hadn't tried using this power to return to the first time she tunneled. That event was still too close to the present—she didn't know how to access more recent time. Inevitably, though, she imagined, years would pass, and she would one day slip in easily.

She could remember it, at least. She was almost sixteen. A Friday morning in early December, just past nine. In history they were discussing Tippecanoe and Tyler Too, but Opal wasn't in class. She was tucked into the corner stall of the girls' bathroom, first floor, Humanities building. Changing her tampon, her third that morning, no wonder she felt faint.

The room had only one window, and it only opened an inch, its glass beveled and thick. The room stunk of shit and that pink powder soap the tap water transformed to mush. Underneath this, Opal could smell what Fab called "a thousand public school vaginas." Fab said the scent had to be worse at Fairfax. Why would that be? Opal remembered laughing at the thought.

She unwrapped the new tampon and was reading one of the many tags scrawled on the stall door, SNOOPY XVIII, OJ=GUILTY, when an urge to vomit hit her. There was no wave of nausea, no acid rising like molten lava in her throat. It was more like a jolt in her body, a sudden need to retch, followed by that same resistance Opal always felt when she had to throw up: a fear of the unnatural, of the body reversing its course. Her dad would tell her to go with it, that gagging would loosen up the armor of her thorax, that a necessary release would follow, a freedom and alertness that lasted all day once she got the hang of it.

Unlike him she'd never pay a creep in corduroy to tickle her.

"No, no, no," Opal remembered murmuring.

Opal tried to stick to facts. The stall: beige. The floor: pebble-sized gray tiles in grayer grout. The toilet paper, rare to find in any of the school bathrooms: tiny squares that hung from the dispenser, one folded into the next. The tags on the door. She remembered CULVER CITY 13. R.I.P. BIGEE. YOURE SO MONEY. Various declarations of love and spite.

In her memory, the need to throw up made her shudder and then the room went blurry, as if plunged underwater. Something covered her vision. It was like clicking a child's viewfinder, a whole new scene dropping before her eyes, except it was more immersive than that, an entire world surrounding her. She was inside of it. The sick feeling had ebbed, but Opal still felt it threatening at the edges.

She was outside the old house on Edinburgh, on that stretch of concrete where the roots of a tree buckled the sidewalk into a tiny hill. She and Fab used to ride their bikes as fast as they could over that bump, get a little air before skidding to a stop at the corner. She knew the house was on her left, that she was facing north. It was a clear day, and she could just make out the individual mansions stacked on the hills that separated the city from the valley.

Opal knew she was in the bathroom at school, that she was sitting on a toilet. She was holding a tampon, for god's sake. But she was also not there. She was on her old street. It was warm and dark in the bathroom. It was sunny and still on Edinburgh Avenue. Earthquake weather. The rough grass by the curb. Faded street cleaning sign, NO PARKING TUESDAYS 9:00 TO 11:00 AM.

Opal tried to turn to see the house. She couldn't. What was wrong? Something didn't feel right. She could sense the nausea sloshing inside her. She tried to move once more. Still no. All at once she understood. There was no body to move. She couldn't hold her hands out before her, or clutch her stomach, or her throat. She could not call out. She was nothing. She was able to see and feel, but she herself had disappeared. Or failed to appear.

Eventually, Opal would find her lack of a body liberating—*becoming nobody*, she called it to herself—but not at first. At first, dissolving like that upset her, felt like a kind of death, and it frightened her. And then when she finally learned how to have a body in the past, she was clumsy. It took almost a year to teach herself this new gravity.

What else could she do except remain where she was, on her street? She waited. Lucy Chu drove by in her white Volkswagen Rabbit, the one with the blue vinyl seats. The Chus got rid of that car years ago. Some far-off speaker was playing Janet Jackson—she didn't want those nasty boys to ever change. An airplane buzzed overhead and a motorcycle gurgled down on Beverly.

The bathroom was there too. It was like holding two thoughts at once, like remembering a phone number before you had a chance to write it down. Doing a math problem, carrying the one.

Before the moment was swept away, Opal looked back at the black tar. If she hadn't, she might have shrugged off this temporary disembodiment, called it a bizarre waking dream or even a straight-up hallucination. She could have blamed dehydration, menstruation, stress, her virginity, boring AP History. However simple the black tar was, so much less remarkable than her disembodiment, it was what got her. Opal knew that when she was young the city slathered the tar across the little hill, a short-term fix to a larger problem. She couldn't have been older than seven or so. Now the tar was glistening and chunky, as if it had just been lain down. It was fresh.

A second later a figure snagged into her view. A child, walking down the block toward her. Opal knew at once that it was herself—her past self.

Oh, *there's* my body, she thought.

Her hair in two long braids. Her gangly legs and slight shoulders. That red handball, bouncing before her. The ball eventually popped on the last day of fourth grade, right after school, and Opal sliced it in two; she gave Fab one half. That summer, they wore them on their skulls like berets and would only take them off when it got too hot, and only at the exact same moment, like a dare.

An icy apprehension slipped through her. If this were a memory, she wouldn't be watching herself.

As quick as a thunderclap the scene disappeared and Opal was back in the bathroom. Were it not for the sweat dewing the back of her neck she would wonder if she'd been through anything at all. She inserted the new tampon and flushed the toilet. She opened the stall and put her hands under a faucet's rough spray. She looked up. The mirror above the sink was fogged and she couldn't make out her face—only a blur. The bathroom was sticky with humidity.

Opal remembered being very afraid. What was going on? Did she have a brain tumor? More likely, she was losing her mind. This was what happened to her mother, wasn't it? Ray said Cherry was nervous, likely depressed. He thought she might have heard voices. Did she hallucinate? Maybe this was how it began. Was it like this for her mom too?

Washing her hands, Opal felt the urge to flee the bathroom. She didn't want whatever occurred to occur again. She didn't want anything to be wrong with her. She didn't want to be like Cherry. And she didn't want the sudden nausea, or the disappearing body, or the vision of herself walking toward her to ever come back.

She shut off the water and rushed to class.

Then, suddenly, came a second urge: she did want to make it all happen again, because, even from the beginning, Opal had an inkling about what happened: she had gone back in time, as stupid and impossible as it sounded. The dry tar—wet. The cut-up handball—bouncing. The woman—a girl.

∞

At eighteen, Opal felt tender toward her younger self. Back then, she was innocent of what she could do, of how much her life would change because of it.

Before that morning in the school bathroom, she thought she knew how the next few years of her life would go. She would get her license and drive her dad's old Mazda, and she imagined she would drive it to the movies or the beach every weekend, or to whatever party she and Fab deemed the least annoying. She would study like hell, 4.3 weighted GPA, all fives on her AP exams, and get an after-school job. After graduation, she would attend a prestigious liberal arts college that offered hefty scholarships, maybe someplace where it snowed. Maybe she'd major in English. Maybe she'd shave her head again. Lose her virginity. Get an internship.

Some of that happened. Most of it. She went to the parties, she lost her virginity to a valley kid named Owen, and her GPA remained high. She graduated on the honor roll. But she wasn't interested in college anymore. Not yet, at least. Two months after graduation, she signed the contract Kim dropped off, and Ray moved in with Isla Patricia in Echo Park. Before he left, he kept asking Opal if she would be okay, if she really wanted to live out here alone.

"Go," Opal told him. "I'll be fine."

She meant it. Plus, Isla Patricia was his fiancée. They deserved a normal life in a normal home.

He'd been gone for nearly a month. Now only Opal's name was on the lease agreement; now only she was responsible for the house. She promised it wouldn't be for longer than a year. Kim said she wouldn't renew the agreement beyond that.

"You've got to get away from the thirsty birds eventually," she said when she came to pick up the papers.

Ray was so relieved to have Kim on his side he tried to hug her. Opal laughed when Kim reared back, as if repulsed. One did not *hug* Kim.

Opal had the house all to herself now. The land too. The pump-jacks were her only companions and her favorite, Well 199, peachy orange in the late September haze and barnacled with rust, was her only true friend.

She was being dramatic. Fab wasn't dead, and she wasn't even that far away. She was in a dorm at UCLA, hanging out in lame Westwood, eating those cheap ice cream cookie sandwiches. If Opal avoided rush hour she could be there in fifteen, twenty minutes. They could see each other all the time. Not that they did. Out here, it was easy for things to fall away.

For cash, Opal transcribed medical recordings for a few hours a week, a boring if mindless job, and at least now she could spell words like *erythematosus* and *myxedema* from memory. There had been just one shoot since her dad left, and Opal had enjoyed flirting with a dumb but devastatingly handsome PA; she invited him to stay the night when production ended.

Most of the time, she was left to wander the house's grand rooms. She would sit by the giant fireplace, or gaze out the living room windows, or eat her meals on the front porch steps, plate on her lap. She knew the land by heart, and once her dad moved she liked driving around the property with all the windows down, the hot breeze drying the sweat from her neck as she directed the truck around the pumpjacks and into the serene section of the estate where tall grasses

surrounded eucalyptus and oak trees brittling in the heat. At the top
of the eastern hill, she would get out of the truck to stand at the edge.
She spread her arms wide. Sometimes she sang as loudly as she could.
That no one could hear her made her feel powerful.

The box was waiting for her in the garage. Its presence made her
feel powerful too. The tunneling she did in there. *Tunneling* was the
word she used; Fab came up with it.

When Opal got inside the box and hurtled into the past, she
was certain that her only true purpose in life was this: to revisit the
smallest moments, to resuscitate them. She gave them new life. She
held them in her body. She honored them. Reliving them meant they
mattered, that they weren't insignificant. Memories pulsed with life
again. That she could access something that everyone else assumed
was forever lost—it exhilarated her. If she didn't tunnel, what was
she? Just an eighteen-year-old with a high school diploma and a boring job, hanging around an old house.

Not that Opal had tunneled since her dad moved out. She didn't
just do it whenever. There were rules. Two years before, when she
confessed to her dad what she could do, Ray drove Fab home and
returned ready to talk. It was late by then, but he said they couldn't
leave it.

They sat on the porch, the only light coming from the house behind them. She told him again how it started, in the school bathroom, and what it was like. She described what she had seen on her
visits, four so far: first Edinburgh Avenue and the wet tar, then the
beach with Fab's family, then her third-grade classroom. And the argument about the onesie. She told him she'd been a baby under the
kitchen table, playing with plastic cups and her dad's shoelaces as her
parents talked—as they argued. She hadn't *seen* them, she told him.
Only heard them. Heard Cherry's voice.

"You think I'm insane," Opal said.

Miraculously, he didn't.

"I don't doubt your sanity," he said. "I never have."

His answer hung there and she wondered if he was also thinking about Cherry, how she was so troubled she ran away.

"I just wonder if you didn't experience a buried memory," he said. "Is there any way you simply *remember* being that young? It's not impossible. Maybe the Accumulator unlocked your unconscious."

"This wasn't that, Dad. I promise you. I was there. I experienced it again. I—I—felt it."

"Memories feel like that sometimes."

"It wasn't a memory!"

"It just sounds so . . . out there," he said.

"Imagine how I feel. It's definitely *out there*."

"Then again, look where we live."

Opal laughed but her father didn't. He had a solemn look on his face.

"I explored some old feelings in the Accumulator last night," he said. "It wasn't time travel. Or at least I don't think it was."

"Oh—you would know for sure."

"I definitely didn't then."

"What happened?"

"Let's just say, confronting some old stuff . . . it healed me. I opened up to it. I let it out." He combed a hand through his hair and sighed like he did when they ran out of drinking water and he had to get right in the truck to get some, no matter the hour. "I feel more open than I did before I went in. I can't explain it."

"Wow, so it really helped."

"It did. I'm not even sure I need the Accumulator anymore."

"Seriously?"

He nodded. "I guess . . . I guess I'm going to believe in your . . ." He stumbled to find the right word. She didn't blame him. What was it? A gift? A talent? A superpower?

"Your *idea*," he finally said.

"It's not an idea, Dad."

"Your dream?"

"Nope."

"That onesie you had," he said.

"It was a light purple. Like a lilac color? It had those baby-doll sleeves, and a little silk rosebud at the collar."

"And those snaps. The onesie didn't fit you any longer."

"Exactly. It was hanging off me, unsnapped, and one of the snaps was torn off. I'd chewed the hem of the fabric, and it was a little wet from my saliva. You remember?"

"Oh my god, I do."

"Do you remember the argument? I heard you from under the table."

"You loved sitting under there. It was cute." He paused. "I remember that conversation with Cherry, yeah."

"You were saying something about getting her a sewing kit, to alter it, how I looked neglected, and she said she hated sewing, that you knew she hated sewing. Then I dropped out before I heard anything else."

"Jesus." He looked spooked. "If you hadn't relived that—or gone back to it, or whatever we're calling it—I probably would be calling the doctor right about now."

"I get it." She told him how intense the last couple of weeks had been. "The Accumulator helped, but in the opposite way than I thought it would. I thought it would make everything stop. Like . . . cure me. What Doc talked about."

"Doc would say you misunderstood him, that I paraphrased him wrong."

"Good thing he isn't here then. What matters is the Accumulator made it easier. Way easier."

Her dad didn't balk, and she realized he really believed in the box—so much so he wasn't laughing at everything she told him, or freaking out. She imagined him inside the Accumulator, eyes closed, holding that black funnel to his chest. It was so effective he didn't need it any longer. What happened to him in there?

"Unlike you, I'm going to keep using it," she said. "Not in the way Doc intended, obviously."

He didn't reply.

"You'll let me, right? You have to. As *out there* as it seems."

"I guess," he said, and for a flash he looked surprised, as if slapped by some revelation.

"Dad?"

"You swear to me the first time this happened was in the school bathroom?"

"I promise."

"Nothing before then, no inklings of this when you were younger?"

"No, nothing. I told you—this just started."

Her dad was looking beyond the house, into the velvet darkness where the pumpjacks buzzed like cicadas. Her father shook his head, as if trying to dislodge something. He was worried, but wasn't he always? Mr. Protective. Always trying to make up for Cherry's absence. Fab said Opal got two parents for the price of one. And now this new thing to deal with, something neither of them understood.

"Does anyone know about this?" he asked. "Besides Fab?"

"No way."

"Good." He hesitated. "I might tell Isla Patricia. Eventually. If that's okay."

"Did you guys have fun this weekend?"

"So you know about me and her."

"I'm not an idiot, Dad. It's great."

"You're sure you're okay with it?"

"Are you kidding? You were weird for *never* dating. Your first girlfriend! Congratulations!"

"That's enough, thank you," he said, and she punched him on the shoulder.

For a second everything felt normal.

"I have a few rules," Ray said finally, and then he grimaced. "Rules for Time Travel."

"Sounds like a cheesy novel."

He grinned and she knew he was thinking about *Bon-Mots*, their old game, which he'd loved so much it embarrassed her.

"As I said," he said, "don't tell anyone, like at school, random friends. Not yet at least."

"It's the last thing I want to do."

"And keep me in the loop. This can't be something you keep secret from me."

"I told you in the first place, didn't I?"

"Only because I walked in." He paused. "This is so strange. Should we be afraid?"

"I don't think so."

"You're okay, right? You feel all right? It's not painful?"

She shook her head. "Not overly so. First two times I felt queasy. Usually, it makes me thirsty. Sleepy, mostly. I can't push it afterward, but it's not harming me."

"Good."

"What else then?"

"You can only do it when I'm home," he said. "And if you try it when I'm out, I swear I'll take a sledgehammer to the box."

"Wow, okay," Opal said.

"If you're in there for longer than—how long does it take?"

"Fab timed it for me. It feels faster, but it takes about twenty minutes."

"Okay, let's say half an hour then. After that, I'll come into the garage and drag you out."

"Please don't drag me. Degrading."

"And you can't do it all the time, without any limits or schedule. If it makes you feel queasy and tired, that's not good."

"How often can I do it then?" Opal asked.

"What sounds reasonable?"

She thought of the first time, in the school bathroom, the tampon.

"Once a month," she said. "Every thirty days?"

They shook on that.

Then he said, "One more thing. It's the most important."

She waited.

He didn't seem to want to say it.

"Dad."

He didn't reply.

"Raymond."

"I don't want you going back to see Cherry," he said.

"What? Why not?"

"It can't be healthy," he said.

"She's my mother."

"But seeing stuff, as an adult, what you were only a baby for?"

"That's the whole point!"

The surge of anger surprised her—her chest felt hot.

"What if you see Cherry in pain?" he asked. "She was messed up, Opal."

"I know she was. I'm not naïve."

"Yes you are. That's exactly what you are."

"This is unfair."

"Believe me, you don't want to relive it."

"Don't tell me what I want."

"Why would you use your gift to revisit something so upsetting? I don't want you seeing all that, feeling that." His voice shifted into a gentler register. "Or not yet at least. You're too young."

She didn't reply. How did he expect her to react?

He said, "It's a blessing, in a way, that you were too young to remember what happened."

Was it a *blessing*? That wasn't the right word for your mother leaving before you could remember a single thing about her. When Opal thought of Cherry, there was only a blankness, a nothingness. Who was the woman who left? Opal wanted to understand everything she'd lost. Wasn't this how Opal would get to find out?

But now her dad was telling her no. That going back would only hurt. That there was nothing there but pain. Her gift would become a curse.

"It's my life," she said.

"It's mine too," he said.

She didn't understand—or not exactly.

"It was *our* life," he said. "I lost her too. It was hard for both of us." He was looking at her. "Can you control where you go?"

She admitted that she could, and that she was getting better with each try. Turned out, time traveling was a skill like any other, muscle memory and all that.

"You have to trust me on this one," he said. "Just like I'm trusting you."

She didn't want to agree. How could he withhold the one person she wanted to see?

"Opal?"

If she refused, he would take the box away. And he would probably hate her. He would stop trusting her, at the very least.

He had to trust her. And she had to trust him. He was her dad.

He was the one who stayed.

"Fine."

He held out his hand a second time, and after a moment she shook it.

"Thanks," he said, but he was now standing, and she couldn't see his expression in the night.

After Opal had time to think about it, she decided that her dad's rules made sense. It was the only protection from her own power. And, also he was right: she didn't want to see her mother in pain. She didn't want to see her leave. She was afraid to.

Bad memories were worse than no memories at all.

∞

And so, like her dad wanted, Opal tunneled to the good things. Happy moments, or, if not happy, then at least harmless ones that might've been lost until she relived them. She went to places she longed to see again: the swings at her preschool, Fab's kitchen before it was remodeled, her father's old office. She sat on her dad's brown leather desk chair and spun in circles until she couldn't see straight, laughing so hard her eyes watered.

Once a month she went to the garage while Ray stayed in the house. When she returned he handed her a big glass of water, and she had to drink it all, no excuses. He made sure she sat down, too, or even reclined on the couch, to recuperate. He preferred that she eat well beforehand, that she not go in hungry or stressed out or sleep deprived. He was clear that this experiment wasn't going to continue unless she took care of herself. She had to be careful. And she was.

As she recovered from each tunneling, Opal would tell her dad how it went. Ray didn't force her to, but it was nice to talk about it. She described the little details that were returned to her, how distinct the feelings were, and how elated she felt as they rushed over her. Her gift was a gift.

Once, halfway into senior year, she tunneled to a school holiday concert, her first-grade class dressed up as twenty-seven Santa Clauses, white paper plates strapped to their chins with rubber bands. They all wore red shirts too—well, everyone except a kid named Christian, who was in blue plaid because he'd forgotten about the performance. First-grade Opal stood in the back row, hair in pigtails, paper plate beard falling off as she sang, the rubber band twisting against her scalp.

Opal found herself at the side door, watching her younger self. The air was close from the crowd of parents, and the children's voices clanged; the large room hadn't been constructed with acoustics in mind. Opal let it fall through her, all the details she'd forgotten: the brown and white squares of the linoleum floor, the now-closed window from where the cafeteria lady served the chalupas and tater tots during lunch, the groan of the stage as Chantilly shuffled next to her, the paper plate pressing against her chin and then her neck as she sang.

Then she spotted her dad in the crowd. He wasn't visible to young Opal, but it was evident he could see her on stage. He sat at the end of a back row and Opal could tell that he was watching the performance closely. He grinned as he nodded along to the medley of carols that Opal had practiced for weeks beforehand. One of them, "Santa Claus Is Coming to Town," used hand gestures she'd struggled to get right: a wagging finger, fists to the eyes in mock-weeping, a pantomime of stretching out a scroll. Two weeks earlier, she'd cried on the living room floor about it, frustrated.

Now the song was beginning, the musical accompaniment bleating from the room's shoddy speakers, the children taking a breath before opening their mouths. Opal felt the pang of nervousness shooting through her younger self, felt her damp palms, the seam at the toes of her red tights, her tight suede shoes.

Ray leaned forward, craning his neck to see the stage, and then he was moving his hands. He was doing the choreographed gestures, Opal realized.

In the box, she cringed.

Her dad gestured barely, subtly, his hands against his legs before flashing quickly to his face. It was as if he were trying to do them privately, so as not to draw attention to himself—he wasn't some stage mom. Anyway, the kids couldn't see him from here.

He kept going. His fingers poked the air. He opened the invisible scroll. He hefted the invisible bag of toys.

It was as if he wanted to telegraph the signs to Opal on stage.

It was so dorky, and Opal wanted badly to look away. She didn't. She kept watching.

Her dad loved her, and his love, his devotion, was right there, pure and uncomplicated. Her dad knew she had trouble with the song and he wanted to help, to be in it with her.

And Opal got to see it.

Surrounding him were other parents, occasionally with younger siblings pulled out of preschool, or even older ones in high school, skipping class to see the show. Cameras flashed. A mom chuckled, grabbed the arm of her husband, who put his hand over hers. There were a couple sets of grandparents.

There were so many mothers, dozens of them. Some were waving. Some weren't paying attention.

Ray was Opal's entire family. And here he was.

His hands moved and on stage Opal's hands mirrored his, and she was smiling because she was totally nailing it. The pride and thrill surged through her as her fingers twinkled in the air. The song ended and the kids bowed, her father applauding.

Opal came to in the box and then headed to the house. When she stepped through the front door, Isla Patricia, who was cleaning the kitchen, tossed the sponge into the kitchen sink and rushed to fill a glass from the jug of water in the fridge. She let Ray pass it to Opal. By then she'd known about the tunneling for nearly a year, and she didn't doubt Opal's gift for a second. "My first boyfriend was psychic," was her only explanation for her faith in Opal, and then she swore herself to secrecy. "It's not my story to tell, you know?"

Isla Patricia wasn't so bad. She grew on you.

After Opal drank the water and curled up on the couch, she told them what she'd seen. She described the multipurpose room rearranged for the assembly, the room packed with families, and the feeling it gave her to see the linoleum floor, hear the scratchy sound system, and read all the signs about food safety. Her stomach fluttering with nerves from being on stage.

Isla Patricia, eyes shining, said, "It's *emotional* time travel."

That's exactly what it was. Opal moved through the past as it was—and as it felt too.

When she told them what her dad was doing during the song, how he'd moved his hands along with the students, he laughed and Isla Patricia made cooing sounds of adoration. Ray swore up and down he'd never been that uncool, but Opal insisted. The tunneling never lied.

"That's true," Isla Patricia said.

"You're *still* uncool, Dad," Opal said.

She didn't say anything else. How could she describe what it felt like to watch her father watching her? She couldn't, it would sound so corny. The feeling was still inside her though.

She got to see what no child got to see. She had witnessed her dad's love for her—only now she was old enough to appreciate it. There weren't words for that.

∞

Thirty days passed since Ray had moved in with Isla Patricia. Not that Opal was counting.

Before he left, she agreed to keep to all of the rules but one. Now she would be able to tunnel without anyone on the estate. She didn't need her dad waiting in the house, guarding her from afar. She promised she would keep to the other rules, and they both knew she would. She wasn't about to mess things up with her dad, her only family—and his.

The box was still in the garage where her dad had assembled it, the soil still inching up the sides. It called to Opal as it always did, but she was determined to keep to her monthly schedule. Besides, she didn't want to overuse her powers—what if they ran out? She imagined them lined up and waiting inside of her like ova in a baby girl.

In her two years of tunneling, Opal had devised a whole system: a way to sit (legs splayed open, feet flat on the floor), a way to close the door (count to five before pulling it shut). She didn't bother with the funnel and tube, which was *bions* bullshit anyway—sorry, Dad. She didn't want anything to interfere.

In these weeks of solitude since her dad left, she'd been fine with not tunneling. It was an easy rule to follow. She was used to the wait, and she needed to get used to life on her own. She wandered the land. She did her transcription work. She showed the estate to location managers who liked to tell her, as they snapped photos of the dining room from multiple angles, how they knew her dad or Isla Patricia. She showed Craft Services where to set up, ate the Red Vines they offered. She went to visit Well 199, listening to it groan and clank as it extracted oil from the earth.

Tonight, though, was different. Thirty days. The first day of her period. Tonight she would tunnel. She imagined the box waiting for her, the past gathering inside its walls. All she had to do was step in. As soon as the sun went down and the traffic on La Cienega thinned, she would head for the garage.

She decided she would tunnel to early elementary school. She'd spent the spring and summer sessions going back to junior high, and she was tired of it. She wanted younger Opal again. Second grade, perhaps. She wanted to revisit the dollhouse she used to play with, which her dad had repurposed from an old white cabinet. With the doors open, the shelves resembled two floors of an apartment. Lofts, Ray suggested, since there were no interior walls.

As Opal washed her dinner dishes, then swept the kitchen floor, the house around her quiet save for occasional creaking and settling, she thought of the little dolls she used to play with, their perfect furniture. She would go to them.

Because of her dad's rule about Cherry, Opal was deliberate about her tunneling. Nothing from infancy, or anything from the first two years of her life. It was easy enough—it was so pleasurable to slip into moments she recognized: a classroom, the tetherball court, a favorite shop on Melrose, the Beverly Center food court. She didn't know how she got to the specific moment she'd chosen; it was like finding a switch in the dark or untangling a knot in a necklace. She just had a sense of it, the way some people understood the correct turn or direction, their body a compass.

She could steer herself deliberately through time, though she discovered that returning more than once or twice to a specific moment degraded it forever. When she went back again, it didn't feel real; sometimes it was blurry.

At sixteen, Opal was pulled back to the tarred sidewalk two more times, and each visit the vision was thinner than it had been previously—fake feeling, as flimsy as an old dream. Now she wished she hadn't used up that place—sometimes she ached for that first visit. The tar, the sky. She couldn't picture it very clearly; it was like trying to remember something from a book she'd read long ago.

Opal put the broom away. It was dark outside, the lights of the wells dotting an otherwise blank landscape. The box was waiting.

She wondered if she should call Fab, or Ray and Isla Patricia, to tell them she was going in, ask them to call her back in thirty minutes to check on her. She was about to pick up the phone when she stopped. No. She was an adult. This was her life to manage.

She grabbed the egg timer from the kitchen and left the house.

You are a time traveler living alone on an oil field, she thought as she headed across the wide lawn to the garage. No one else in the world knew what tunneling felt like. Talking about it with her dad and Isla Patricia, or with Fab, was a solace, but words would never capture the euphoria she felt inside the box. No one understood how keenly the past sang inside of her. Maybe the worst thing about having a gift was the loneliness. And yet, didn't she love her dad and Fab more for tunneling to them? She got more of them, more of life, this way. That she alone understood this—it gave her strength, and she walked faster to the garage, practically ripped the door open.

The box's interior was confining and dark, and because the day had been warm, tonight the box was as hot as the inside of a sneaker. Sitting in it reminded her of crouching at the bottom of her dad's closet when she was a kid, his shirt cuffs grazing her chin, feeling hidden and safe, giddy that at any moment she might be discovered.

After they'd established the rules, her dad, as predicted, never wanted to use the box again. Opal kept waiting for him to change his mind, but he never did. She had a gift, he said, and this was his gift to her. Opal still worried he thought her tunneling had tainted it, but she never asked him because she didn't want to know. Either way, the box was hers.

She had to give her dad some credit: there was something to Reich's invention. Not *bions* or life force or whatever, but the atmosphere did feel charged. Juicier. Something was accumulating in there—or it was she herself who accumulated it. What was it? Time, she guessed. In the box, the boundary between the present and the past wasn't a wall but a penetrable yolk, and tunneling through it felt better than anything. It calmed her and offered a clarity she found nowhere else. Upon returning to her present life Opal understood in an elemental way who she was, what she had done or not done, said or remained silent about, how the sun felt on her back, the insects sawing away, the truck idling. Memory was, by comparison, a consolation prize.

As she sat down, she barely registered the shooter box's hard, unforgiving surface beneath her, or the warm and stale air. She set the egg timer for thirty minutes and put it at her feet. It ticked-ticked below her; she counted to five and shut the door. She was closing her eyes, holding her breath.

Let it out. And go.

She was in her old bedroom.

Right away, Opal knew she'd dropped into the right moment. Fall 1988. She was seven. She'd been tunneling long enough to recognize time the way people learned to read how old someone was. And it wasn't simply the year announcing itself, though that was here too: the first Bush in the papers, *My Two Dads* on TV, cans of Five Alive juice in the freezer. It was more that the world felt as it had to Opal at the time.

Here she was, in the world, at age seven, a couple of months into second grade.

She hovered at the edge of the bedroom. There it was, the yellow walls and the white baseboards, the Jack-and-Jill light switch cover, the preschool rug with its wheel of ABCs. The twin bed, unmade, its comforter with its rose print, the Winnie the Pooh sheets. Nothing matched. Ray told her he came from a place that didn't care much for possessions. Meaning what? That everyone in Santa Cruz had ugly furniture?

The bedroom smelled like quesadilla, and sure enough, a half-eaten one rested on a plate on the floor. Opal could taste it. The smear of ketchup too.

Next to the plate was her seven-year-old self, kneeling with the dolls. Her hair, bleached from the sun, fell down her back, and the hem of her skirt was coming undone.

When they talked about Opal's gift, Fab liked to say, "Kill Baby Hitler!" It was their joke, but Opal was embarrassed by how little she could actually do. She could only go back to moments she had lived through herself. She could bring a version of her own body to the past, but she could not get inside her past body and make it move. She could not touch or handle objects. She could not smother a monster with his baby blanket.

She could only witness, and experience everything as if for the first time.

Opal hovered at the edge of the room, though it was more like the room was hovering in her. The tunneling felt stronger, more intense, than ever before. Inside the box, Opal wondered if it felt more intense tonight because she was alone on the land. There was no one waiting to help her. Or stop her.

She felt the rough weave of the rug and the dust gathering on the shutters. The thread of her skirt hem tickled her thigh as she leaned forward and placed the mommy and daddy dolls on their canopy bed. It was all inside her. She felt it as she had the first time.

Emotional time travel, as Isla Patricia called it.

But what use was *emotional* time travel?

Opal's past self was giving the dolls voices, and Opal knew what the words would be the moment they emerged from her younger mouth:

"Come to bed, *dahling*, we have big important meetings tomorrow."

"Ooh, baby, okay. Care for a foot rub first?"

In a moment, the dolls' faces would smash together, and Opal would feel their hard, plastic heads, their ripples of painted hair, against her fingertips. Even if her younger mouth didn't make the kissing sounds out loud, she knew that wet smacking would be in her younger head.

Smooch, smooch.

She could stay here and let the moment wash over her, haunt her like the ghost Fab said she was. Instead, she turned toward the hallway.

She wanted to see the linen closet, and though she'd never tried it before, she thought she might be able to discover two rooms at once—if you counted a hallway as a room. Why not try it?

She felt so strong tonight, her body accumulating time, gathering it.

She wouldn't be leaving dollhouse-Opal if she could see her from the corner of her eye.

What if she could roam the entire house?

As soon as Opal met the hallway, it trembled once like a TV losing its signal. She feared the cord would be cut, but then everything righted itself and the new space rushed in. The linen closet door with its glass doorknob, a cloudy lavender color, the scuffed wall and the built-in hallway desk she'd always loved, which her dad called the secretary. There were its bronze drawer-pulls, shaped like lions' faces, with manes and noble snouts. There was the tub to the left of the bathroom door. That curve of white.

Opal was here, oh my god was she here, and, at the same time, she felt herself in the box, taking it all in, gasping.

Now she heard the game from the living room, Vin Scully's classy tenor over the ambient cheers of the crowd. The World Series. After the Dodgers won, her dad had their number changed so that the seven digits spelled out KGIBSON.

Opal tried taking a few steps down the hall, toward the living room, away from her younger self in the bedroom.

She took one step. Then two. Three. Then four.

She had to crane her neck to see younger Opal.

Five steps.

Six.

Seven.

Eight.

She couldn't see the bedroom at all now, only the hallway, and there, just ahead, was the door to the dining room. In a few steps she'd be there. The TV was louder now.

Nine.

Ten.

In the box, a ringing. Shrill. Insistent.

What was that?

Eleven.

The timer. Couldn't be. How could it be time to go?

She couldn't bear to leave—not yet. Instead, she took another step toward the door. It was made of solid dark wood, and its varnished sheen glowed in the dark. Whatever was happening with seven-year-old Opal in her bedroom, she didn't know, she couldn't access it.

Just another step.

Then another.

The door was just out of reach. Another step and she could try to touch it.

The hallway grew bright as a bulb flashing in the dark, so bright it stung.

With a jolt she dropped out.

She was back in the box, her head pounding, motion sick, 1988 gone, the timer still ringing. With shaking hands she bent down and silenced it.

When she kicked open the box door, she half expected that bright hallway light to meet her. Instead, it was dimmer than normal, as though the bulb above were on its way to giving up, as if in a flicker she'd be plunged into darkness. The garage always carried a vaguely dank, mildewy smell, which Opal and her dad blamed on the dirt floor, but the scent seemed muskier than ever: earthy and animal, like rotting fruit or animal hides, like something burrowing underground.

Did it have to do with what she'd done? Because she'd tried to walk down the hallway, away from her younger self, because she'd ignored the timer? No one was here to stop her from untethering from the present. She was trying something, she was pushing deeper into the tunnel.

Was that wrong?

By the time she got back into the house, shaky and exhausted, guilt ticked in the pit of her stomach. She grabbed the cordless and dialed her dad's number. It rang four times before the machine picked up.

She hung up without leaving a message.

∞

The next day, her father was the one to call her. He wanted to know how it went.

"I wanted to be there," he admitted. "But Isla Patricia said I should wait for an invitation."

Opal told him she'd seen her old dollhouse.

"Ah yes, the downtown loft," he said, chuckling. "Glad you're okay."

"I'm fine, Dad. It went fine."

She wouldn't tell him about the timer going off, or about her walk down the hallway. *What if she could roam the entire house?* She didn't want him to know how the garage felt afterward either. She wouldn't say that she was getting better at tunneling, that she was stronger without anyone around.

"Don't worry," she said. She couldn't let him worry.

A few nights later, the box was calling to her. She pictured it waiting for her in the garage. How many more days until she could go to it? Twenty-five. That was so long.

To distract herself, she invited a cute props guy named Ruben to come upstairs after production ended. Later, when they were naked in her bed, thoroughly stoned from the blunt they were passing between them, he said he loved Octavia Butler's books.

"I can time travel," she said. Like that, she broke another rule.

Ruben only laughed, weed smoke puffing out of his nose like a dragon. "Is that so? You're saying you're a witch? Like, Wiccan?"

She pretended it was all a joke.

What wasn't a joke was the heat, oppressive by early October, the air inside the house stale and unmoving. Sweat blanketed her, she couldn't sleep; the fans were useless. It was like the heat wanted to fry her brain so she'd stop thinking about the box, about walking down the hallway, away from her child self. *What if she could roam the entire house?* She couldn't stop thinking about it.

When Isla Patricia called and urged her to come over for dinner, to take advantage of their AC, Opal said okay.

It was a Saturday evening. Her dad poured her exactly one half of a glass of wine at the big table in Isla Patricia's dining room. Isla Patricia came out with bowls of spaghetti carbonara as Ray lit the candles and dressed the salad. As they ate, he and Isla Patricia wanted to know about her work, if anything was shooting at the house, and how it felt there without anyone to keep her company.

"Have you given any more thought to taking some classes at SMC?" Ray asked.

"You know I haven't."

"Tell us more about the tunneling then," Isla Patricia said with a mischievous little smile.

Of course, Opal was still thinking about it, but she wasn't going to let on, just as she wasn't going to breathe a word about her stupid stoned confession to the props dude. She told Isla Patricia the same thing she'd told her dad on the phone. Her bedroom, the dollhouse.

"I could smell the quesadilla," she said.

She didn't say that she walked down the hallway. That her child self hadn't done that. No. Her child self was playing with silly dolls.

"I'm so jealous," Isla Patricia said, which is what she always said. "I wish I could do it! I mean, to get to see some of my old toys again? You ever come across something you played with, like at a garage sale? Your whole body—it shudders." Her eyes were glistening as she took a sip of her wine. "You're so lucky, Opal."

"I know, it's really cool."

"How does it feel, though?"

"Isla Patricia, you always ask me that!"

Her father laughed. "She's like a little kid, she wants to hear the story again. She'll watch the movie every day. You're the movie."

"Okay, fine, sue me. It's fascinating!" Isla Patricia leaned forward, eyes on Opal. "Do you feel different because of what you saw in 1988? Does it change how you feel *right now?*"

"Right now?" Opal tried to keep her voice neutral. "No."

The days since her tunneling *had* been altered, though. The past was present, it was here in her head now, wasn't it? It was following her around.

The present didn't feel quite finished either. Time felt provisional. Or no—what was provisional was her experience of time; she didn't trust the present anymore. It wouldn't be complete until she came back to it. Someday, she might return to this very moment and experience something totally different than she experienced the first time. And it wouldn't just be because she was older and wiser; the better she got at tunneling, the more she'd see, the bigger, the clearer the picture.

For the past two years, she'd used her gift for nostalgia and delight. Just like her dad wanted. But maybe it could be something else.

"What if you can change the past?" Isla Patricia asked.

"Calm down, Gatsby," Ray said.

"Good one!" Opal heard herself saying.

It was like tunneling to the holiday concert. Another visit she couldn't get out of her head. She kept thinking about how it felt to see her dad in the audience. His hand gestures, his grin, his devotion. If she'd spotted him at age seven, she would've died from embarrassment.

But she hadn't see him back then. She saw him when she was ready to. It was like she got two lives.

Was that dangerous?

Ray and Isla Patricia stood to clear the table, and Opal gathered her wine glass and the salad bowl.

Her dad was afraid she'd go back to the past and find pain. That wasn't what she was looking for, but she also didn't want to go back just to relive what she remembered. Not anymore. She wanted to illuminate what she'd never known.

"Dessert?" her dad asked. "We've got ice cream."

She told herself she didn't want to see Cherry.

"Sure," she said.

So why was she thinking of all those moms at the holiday concert?

13

IT WAS THE END OF OCTOBER WHEN EVERYTHING TURNED upside down.

It was time for Opal to tunnel again and she couldn't. The house was dressed up for a straight-to-video horror movie, fitting for Halloween, and they were shooting at night; there was no way she could tunnel in the garage while wardrobe bustled by with various blood-splattered camisole options.

Opal typically didn't mind a shoot. After all these years, it still exhilarated her when a caravan of trucks rumbled down the dirt driveway, a stakebed briefly obscured by the dust it kicked up, its bed packed with equipment, an actor's trailer hitched to the back. She held her breath as a burly Teamster behind the wheel calmly maneuvered his fifty-foot truck-on-steroids into the slenderest of spaces, his forearms thick as ham hocks. She loved congregating under a pop-up tent to watch the electricians and grips push in the carts; someone inevitably groused about the sound guy as he adjusted for the hum of pumpjacks in the background—*he could hear crickets fucking.* She loved when someone from makeup offered to give her a smokey eye, and how a hush fell over the crew when the cameras rolled. Just the word, *crew,* like they were sailing a big ship across the sea. And the house, her house, a location but also an actor, in costume, playing pretend. Her house could fool anyone, be anything.

But Opal wasn't feeling as generous as the shoot went on. When it went over by another night so that thirty-four days passed without her tunneling, she holed up in her upstairs room, skimming books and chewing the skin around her fingernails. Her transcription work lagged and she didn't return Fab's calls, who wanted her to come to some costume party. They were too old to trick-or-treat, and then Halloween was over, it was November. The heat had pressed all it could out of LA, and the city entered a stretch of delicate cool so invigorating that all the new transplants on set, people from places like Connecticut and Indiana, rejoiced at their luck.

On the thirty-fifth day, when the last crew member drove off the property for the night, Opal ran downstairs, combat boots unlaced over bare feet, plaid flannel flung over her pajamas. The living room was still a set: black Duvateen attached to the windows with grip clips, the camera and insectoid lights wrapped in plastic for the walk away; everyone would be back tomorrow. At least Bobby, the actor who played Eviscerated Corpse #1, wasn't still dumped against the wall with his entrails in his hands. He was probably halfway to his apartment in Van Nuys by now. It was nearly midnight—they'd ended early tonight because of some mysterious snafu. A gift.

Opal nearly tripped over electrical cables on her way out of the house. All she could think about was the box waiting for her. She didn't bother bringing the egg timer; she would tunnel for as long as she wanted to, as long as she needed to.

She got to the garage, nearly trembling, and flung open the door. There was the box.

With a great exhale of relief, she went to it.

Get inside. Count to five. Close your eyes and hold your breath. Let it out. And go.

She pushed hard and went.

Here it was—

Her bedroom on Edinburgh—except—

It was more plain than she remembered—

The walls were the same shade of pale yellow, but there wasn't anything on them, and no scuffs either. The preschool alphabet rug was gone too. Instead there was just the shiny hardwood floor and a rocking chair she didn't recognize.

This was *before* the rug, Opal realized. Not after.

There was also a crib in the room.

Her bed probably hadn't been built yet.

She'd dropped into the wrong moment. This was earlier than she intended, though she hadn't planned exactly on where—on *when*—to go. She was too busy jonesing for it.

Opal knew at once *when* she was.

The feeling in the room was more charged than anything she'd tunneled to before. It was miasmic with it, and it surrounded her, weighed on her. In the box her throat hurt, as if something were squeezing it closed.

The bedroom was lit only by a star-shaped nightlight plugged into the hallway and its yellowish beam was without warmth. There was a coldness here, in the glow of the nightlight and the unmarred walls, in the crib bars and the empty rocking chair. It was in the air. Opal could feel it inside of her.

The feeling was loss.

Her mother wasn't here—

Left a few days before.

Her mother's absence was everywhere, shapeless and penetrating as water, soaking everything. It was in Opal's throat and in her eyes, in her stomach, deep in her lungs; she was breathing it in, choking on it, a sadness whose only shadow was panic.

In the box, Opal gasped. Were the walls closing in? The box was a coffin. Fear rumbled through her.

She should get out, she knew she should. Her father was right, she was naïve, she shouldn't see or feel any of this. Mr. Protective didn't want her to go there. But she couldn't leave—a feeling or a force told her it was important to be here. She wasn't breaking a rule. Her mother was already gone.

In the world as a baby. Not even one year old.

So this is what it felt like.

In the crib across the room, beneath a mobile of clouds made of white felt, lay the infant. Asleep. Even sleeping, she knew her mother had left.

Opal walked closer to the crib. It was hard to believe it was herself lying there, only a few feet away, and yet it was. The child was dreaming and the images in the baby's mind—a yellow school bus, a sycamore tree with its leaves rattling overhead, an adult's large shoes and pantlegs—flitted through Opal as she approached.

She looked down and there she was.

Baby Opal lay on her back with her arms surrendered above her head, her hands closed to fists, cheeks pink and cherubic, dark eyelashes curtaining her lids, her little mouth glistening.

Opal recognized her own face in the child's, and yet, at the same time, the baby seemed totally unlike her. She came from Opal—or, no, Opal came from her, but they were separate. The baby was merely someone Opal got to be briefly. Someone to shed on her way to growing up.

The baby panted in her sleep. Dream of picture book, dream of big table, dream of scary dog. Her mouth worked into a suckle. Dream of feeding. Soft and warm. *Suck, suck* went her mouth, and Opal felt her baby tongue pushing at the roof of her baby mouth. The baby whimpered for what she couldn't taste, for what was far away.

Opal stepped away; in the box, tears stung her eyes. Her mother wasn't there to pick her up. To hold her. Her mother left. This perfect child.

Opal was about to leave this place—this wasn't what she was after, her father was right, she wasn't ready for this, this was the opposite of healthy—when she heard Ray's voice. He was talking loudly to someone at the front of the house, his voice reverberating on the other side of the wall. Baby Opal kept sleeping, didn't notice, not even in sleep.

Was someone with him? Was there another person in the house?

"I'm hanging up now," he said.

He was on the phone.

"I only wanted to know that one thing."

Opal headed out of the room, walking backward so as not to lose sight of the baby. Again, she felt the dreams—warm milk, no milk, the big dog—as well as the hard mattress beneath her head. She felt the longing course through the baby like blood. She kept walking. She was in the hallway now. Her father must be in the living room.

Opal knew she was strong enough to get there. She nearly did it last time. Her baby self was asleep but she would go and hear who her father was talking to.

"Go to hell, *Sharon*," her father said, in a nasty tone Opal had never heard before.

Who was Sharon?

Opal let herself forget about the crib and the baby. She walked down the hallway. She could do it again. She could go farther. Further. She needed to hear more. This time, the door to the dining room was wide open. She would step through the doorway.

In the box, the walls felt so close they were breathing on her neck, and she pushed.

A few more steps.

A TV laugh track blared and Opal was yanked away. As 1981 disappeared, here was the box, the garage, the pumpjacks guarding the fields. She was sweating, her throat raw. She was alone in a box inside a dirt-floored garage behind a big old house in the middle of an oil field and both she and the land were being sucked dry.

She opened the door. The garage held that same close muskiness as last time, the same wan light. The bare bulb above her swayed on its string like a pendulum.

As Opal rose from the shooter box and stepped into the garage, the room felt tilted. Like someone had tipped it off center. Opal felt dizzy, and she leaned against the wall for support.

She wanted more than anything to go back inside the box. She wanted to try it again. But that was an awful idea. The garage felt wrong, and it would be dangerous to go back in, to feel the loss of Cherry all over again. This was a *bad* memory.

As soon as she got back to the house, she threw on some decent clothes, put her hair in a braid, swiped on some lip gloss. Grabbed her purse.

She needed to get away from the box before it tempted her further.

This would be the first time she'd ventured into the outside world immediately after tunneling. Even if she was tired from being in the box or even a bit sick from it, so what, she could still drive. A bourbon might settle her. She might dance. She loved dancing. Senior year, she got a fake ID and she'd occasionally go to bars and clubs. Most bouncers barely glanced at her Ohio license before ushering her inside.

If she drove home a little drunk, maybe some future version of herself, Geriatric Opal, would intervene at a key moment, righting the steering wheel, hitting the brake, averting injury or death. With more practice, maybe she would be able to intrude on the past.

Was that the point?

Why go back to feel the pain of her mother leaving if she couldn't make that pain go away? The only thing the tunneling accomplished was showing her that her baby self missed her mom. *Needed* her. Baby Opal needed Cherry and Cherry wasn't there and that hurt the baby. It hurt deeper than Opal ever imagined. It was in her stomach now, a hollow pull, a hunger that would never be satiated. Now she carried that loss with her.

She needed that drink. The bar she headed to was close to her dad and Isla Patricia's house. It was a watering hole for Rampart District cops and the occasional Dodgers fan before the hipsters sniffed out the canned PBR and colonized the place. Drinks weren't as cheap as they used to be. Five nights a week a DJ came to spin records.

It was stupid for Opal to drive so far when there were plenty of places to drink near the estate, except she liked this bar: a dim rectangle with a long bar along the right wall and a pool table in the middle. There was the dark space at the back to dance. In no time, Opal was in her car and headed for the 10. She took it east, away from the ocean and toward the 110, into the smog.

The bar was full when she arrived, nearly closing time. Halloween was over but you'd never know it from the interior: orange lights strung across the room, paper bats wilting in the corners, a plastic cauldron for a tip jar. Behind the bar, polyester cobwebs stretched across the top-shelf liquor. By the door, a pirate skeleton leaned against the wall like a second bouncer.

It was Brit Pop night, not Opal's favorite; she preferred more bass, though she did like the crowd who came to dance, Mexican girls in liquid eyeliner and vintage dresses with big Peter Pan collars, the white guys in tight jeans and pointy boots. The girls always pony-hopped to the music. Most of the men swayed awkwardly and a few did a sort of manic soft-shoe that Opal loved.

Someone vacated a stool at the end of the bar, and she hopped onto it. She ordered a well bourbon and soda as confidently as she could. She still felt like a fraud ordering liquor at a bar; she supposed that's exactly what she was, two months shy of nineteen with an ID that said she was Jennifer Hawes, twenty-two, from Cleveland.

The whiskey the bartender placed before her was flourished with two tiny red straws. Opal removed them and brought the glass to her lips.

She felt better now that she had the drink and this room of strangers, and at least a few miles between her and the box, her vehicle to her past. She took another sip. She could already taste the ice melting, dulling the knife of whiskey. The music was loud and people at the back were dancing. If she leaned from her perch at the bar, Opal could see their heads bopping along to the sprightly beat. She would join them soon enough.

Part of her was mad at herself for landing in 1981. It was too painful, that feeling of her mother so recently gone. She should have ducked out immediately.

On the other hand, she learned something.

Opal finished her drink, and when she caught the bartender's attention she held up an index finger. He nodded.

"None of those next time," she yelled, whiskey-brave, gesturing at the straws he was whisking away along with her empty glass and the sodden cocktail napkin. He smiled as if in approval.

The dancers were moving to a song with a jaunty guitar. Opal's new drink tasted better than the first; either the bartender had mixed it a little stronger or she was already tipsy. The song helped too. Opal took another drink as the music swelled. The horns came in. A moment later, a woman's voice, talking. The dancers were reciting along with her; they all knew the words. Something about a small town, and no escape. Everyone cheered and kept dancing.

If Opal had just stayed in the bedroom with her baby self, maybe the feeling of intense loss would have settled. Maybe she could have worked through it, metabolized it somehow. Processed it.

God—that poor child.

It was her. *She* was the child.

She hadn't broken the rule, and pain still found her.

And then she'd heard her dad on the phone.

The bar was getting hot and Opal's legs were sticking to the stool's vinyl. She adjusted her body and took another gulp from her glass.

Who had he been talking to? Who was Sharon?

Fuck, she needed to get back to 1981.

She finished her drink and left a twenty on the bar. A song she liked came on and she got off her stool.

The dancers were easing into the music, moving sexy or meek, a little slow because they knew the song would get louder and faster and their bodies would respond. Opal swayed a little, easing into it. She loved to dance. She really did. Maybe she'd take a class someday. Do something with her life besides mining what had already happened.

Tears burned her eyes as she walked through the crowd, her arms rising softly until they were by her face. There were more orange lights in here, winking on and off, illuminating and then shadowing the dancers as if they were standing in the glare of an ambulance's flashing light. More fake cobwebs hung from the rafters, so many it was like the ceiling was a bank of clouds. A giant fake spider, its bloated abdomen made of black velvet, perched in the corner.

Opal swayed her hips into the blinking lights. A guy with thick Beatles bangs smiled at her. Two girls were kissing. There was another girl wearing a Joy Division shirt. Opal liked Joy Division. The girl's shirt became orange in the light, then winked into darkness.

The song was turning wild, and everyone began jumping up and down and tossing their bodies around, and Opal was with them, throwing her arms out wildly, a streak of happiness riding across her.

It felt good if only it felt as good as the other thing.

Already she was dancing toward the photo booth. She was warm from the whiskey and hot from dancing and Opal told herself she only wanted to have her photograph taken, four of them in a strip she'd find at the bottom of her purse a month from now. Some record of this night. But she knew that was a lie.

Maybe because everyone was busy dancing, or because to get to the booth you had to weave through the crowd, there was no line when Opal reached it. She pushed the curtain to the side and thrust herself inside. Dropped her purse. The blue curtain behind her was pulled only halfway across the checkered-print backdrop.

Don't do this, don't do this, it's against the rules—

She didn't even bother to fish the cash out of her wallet and feed it into the dispenser. Instead she remained sitting, her legs apart, feet flat on the floor, and breathed in, her mouth tacky from the booze. She held her breath, then let it go.

She began to count.

One, two.

She closed her eyes.

Three.

This was an enclosed space, but it was no box, and here came the wave of nausea, the sweep of wrong. The orange lights spilled into the booth, filling it, she was glowing in the light, sick with it, and the music was so loud.

Four.

Five.

She reached for the curtain and yanked it shut. She didn't hear the music anymore. She was alone in the orange light, in silence, and now it was dark and it felt like her organs might explode.

Opal kept pushing forward.

Her old bedroom came into focus. Here it was. The same details as before, though a few minutes earlier than that previous visit: the pale yellow walls, the dim nightlight, the cloud mobile, the sleeping baby, the absence of Cherry a weight holding everything down.

As Opal expected, there was something tarnished about the scene. It was a little blurry. This might be her last chance to return to this moment. She had only one chance.

She felt the loss of her mother rushing in. For a moment, she watched the baby sleeping. Let herself feel her mom's absence. Her child self—all she wanted was her mother.

God she was beautiful.

Opal could hear her dad on the phone, murmuring from the living room. He hadn't raised his voice yet. She backed away from the crib and at the door she heard the words more clearly.

"You got my letter."

Opal-in-the-crib sighed. Dream table, dream tree.

Opal had to get to her father now. This was her last chance to hear him.

"I won't tell you any such thing," he said.

Opal moved out of the room. Goodbye Baby Opal—the baby's dreams were whisked away as soon as Opal couldn't see her. Here was the linen closet. Here was the glass doorknob, the purple tile in the bathroom. Here was the hallway secretary.

There was the doorway.

Her father's voice, closer now.

"Good luck with that," he said. "It's a big city."

Here was the doorway.

"I'm looking for Cherry," he said.

Opal thought she might pass out, hearing her mother's name.

He'd been looking for her.

Who was he talking to?

She was in the doorway.

She took a breath and stepped across the threshold. All at once, the dining room hit her with the force of its presence. Here it was, as it was. The three French windows that looked onto the front porch. The mahogany table and chairs. A bongo drum in the corner. A hat rack with a single baseball cap hanging from it. On the table: a vase of pink carnations, a pile of mail, keys.

"So you have no information?" her dad said.

Opal turned toward the living room. The fireplace and the high curved ceiling and the bell-shaped light fixture.

And her father.

Dad.

She could only see him in profile. He sat on their old brown-and-tan couch, the one her father replaced when she was around eight or so. He was staring at the television, beige phone she didn't recognize at his ear. He gripped the receiver, its cord stretching across the couch to the wall. A glass of a brown liquor sweated in his other hand.

He was so young, and thin—he looked as if he weren't yet fully grown. His back was slumped into a C-shape, and his suit pants and collared shirt were too big, and rumpled. A tie hung off the edge of the couch, as if tossed there. The light of the TV lit up his face.

"I'm hanging up now," he said.

Spittle flew from his lips and Opal held her breath.

Dad.

"I only wanted to know that one thing."

His hand was so tight on the phone.

"Go to hell, *Sharon*."

Opal wanted to see his face. He was so angry. She moved toward him.

A scrape, and then it felt like she'd been punched.

A hole opened in the floor and Opal fell into it and she and the house were sucked away as if down a drain. When she came to, she was in the photo booth and the music was so loud she heard it in her molars and behind her eyes. It might crack her skull in two.

She pulled open the curtain, purse clutched to her chest, and the orange lights blinked furiously, twice as fast as before, as if to the rhythm of the song just beginning.

This song. It was Joy Division. Opal recognized its thumping drumbeat and then the irresistible bass line. The guitars came in, and the song grew louder, so loud Opal's ears ached. She needed to get out of here. She pushed herself from the photo booth into the mass of dancers packing the center of the room.

The girl in the Joy Division shirt emerged from the group as if summoned. Her eyes were wide open, hard; Ray would say she had an energy block, that all her rage and intolerable feelings were lodged in her pupils, stuck there. She was shaking her whole body to the music: her arms, her torso, her ass. Even her head shook back and forth, as if saying *no no no*. She got closer and closer to Opal, and Opal reared back, tried to yell, "Hey!" but the music swallowed all other sound. The girl shoved past Opal, reeling across the dance floor, possessed by the music, as if dancing against her will. Another girl, in the corner, was vomiting into her drink.

The other dancers were shaking and writhing ecstatically now too, as if the spirit in the song were inside of them. And the room itself was blinking. It seemed to rattle along with the bodies. As Opal pushed through the crowd, the dancers jostled her, their eyes wide, their clothes pocked with sweat. In the orange light, the bags under their eyes deepened, shadowed. They smiled at her, and their gums bled. One woman pulled at the phony spider webs above her, and when the whisps came undone she wrapped them around herself. She tried to dance with Opal, orange teeth, orange eyes, ensnare her in the orange web. Opal pushed her off.

She needed another whiskey.

She reached the bar and held on to its edge, as if it might steady her. The bartender caught her gaze and a moment later passed her a drink. He refused her money and then said something she couldn't hear. The next moment, he placed a water in front of her.

"Drink both," he said.

She downed the water first, thought of her dad forcing her to hydrate after a tunneling. She'd seen him. What was he, twenty-three? Gripping that phone, so angry. He was all alone.

Now she knew what the phone call was about. Her mother was gone. Ray called someone who knew her. Someone he didn't much like. Who was she?

No—he didn't call. He had written. He said, "You got my letter."

Opal finished the water and chugged her drink. She left a five on the counter and headed out before the bartender could see her go.

It was as if the bar were a soap bubble that popped as soon as she was outside. The street was refreshingly cool after the heat of the bar, and calmer too. Normal. Whatever happened inside, that strangeness didn't escape its door. And yet Opal still felt the strangeness inside her: her legs were weak, her head pounded. Were the dancers still throwing themselves across the room in there, senseless and lustful as zombies?

Smokers congregated on the corner, laughing as they blew smoke into the air above. Her car was parked down the block, but she wasn't in any condition to drive. She wouldn't go home just yet. Her dad's house wasn't far.

She—*Sharon*—had called him.

Opal passed a janky florist whose awning read FLORAL AR-RAIGNMENTS and a computer repair store with a handmade poster taped to the window: REMEMBER TO TURN OFF YOUR

COMPUTERS BEFORE MIDNIGHT 12/31/99! This was next to a
new clothing boutique, and then a new vegan restaurant. A woman
was set up on the sidewalk between parking meters, cooking Sonoran
hot dogs on an open grill, people crowding around her, drunkards
and locals alike, hunched over paper plates.

Who was her father talking to?

When Opal turned off Sunset, the traffic and the light fell away,
the night now quiet, the street steep, overgrown bougainvillea tickling her face, the weed stink of a far-off skunk. She felt sleep calling
to her; tunneling twice in one night took its toll and she might pass
out at any moment.

She didn't know how much time passed before she made it to Ray
and Isla Patricia's house, a modest bungalow sandwiched between a
fourplex and a home daycare run out of a shabby Victorian mansion.

Opal rang the doorbell. Twice.

Finally, the porch light came on. Isla Patricia's voice, "Opal? Is
that you?"

"In the flesh."

Isla opened the door in one of her infamous nightgowns. This one
was seafoam green and pictured a teacup with droopy, long-lashed
eyes, the words I DEMAND MY BEAUTEA SLEEP! written in spar-
kly cursive below it.

"What the fuck with those pajamas, Isla Patricia?" Opal drew out
the syllables of her future stepmother's name.

"It's late," Isla Patricia said.

"I was in the neighborhood."

"Your dad has a five a.m. call time."

"He finally got a job," Opal said.

"Thank god. You know how he gets when he isn't working."

"I was at that bar you hate."

"Those white hipsters need to go back to Michigan."

"You're marrying the original white hipster."

"You're drunk."

"I'm tired. Can I just—"

At that, Opal felt her bones get heavy, her eyes closing. Sleepy teacup.

"Your father is worried," Isla Patricia whispered.

"What else is new?"

But she was already slumping into Isla's arms.

∞

Opal woke on their living room couch. It was before dawn. Her head felt squeezed on all sides, a lemon getting juiced.

The light was on in the bathroom. She sat up and saw her father standing over the sink, tongue out, eyes wide at his own reflection. He brought two fingers toward his mouth and then gagged himself, just as he did every morning since working with Doc.

"What time is it?" she croaked.

He jumped at her voice.

"Isla P. let me in. I was at that bar."

"You mean Jennifer Hawes was at the bar."

"She's visiting from Cleveland, came for Halloween and decided to stay a while."

He made her coffee. Isla Patricia wasn't as offended by the smell as she once was; she liked to say it was the most certain sign she loved Ray. Opal sat drinking it as he rushed around her, getting ready. His work bag, his work gloves, his scarf, and a lightweight denim pullover he called a sark. Also, his wide-brimmed straw hat.

The kitchen was your basic tile-and-linoleum LA special, but it got great light and within an hour or two would be bright and inviting, the kind of room that made you believe you could be happy. Her father's favorite Entenmann's pastry sat on the counter, knife handle jutting out of the partially opened box for convenient snacking. Isla Patricia's plants lined the windowsills.

Ray told her he'd gotten the movie about crooked cops. "Every location is seedy," he said. Today they'd be at a liquor store on Pico.

Opal felt hungover and tired, just on the edge of sick. She also felt a thrum inside her. She could go back to the estate. The box would be there.

Close your eyes and hold your breath. Let it out. And go.

Her dad stopped moving. He was watching her.

"What are you doing here?" he asked.

"I was at that bar."

"So you mentioned. Why?"

"Did you ever try to find my mother?" she asked.

"You know I did." The clock above the fridge ticked forward and Ray glanced at it. "I have to leave in three minutes."

"Then I'll get to the point. Who's Sharon?"

He shrugged. "It's a fairly common name."

"Sharon called you."

Ray froze, as if a wild animal had crossed his path.

"You told her you were trying to find Cherry."

He didn't reply, but he was sitting down now at least, ready to talk.

"You were on the couch, watching TV."

He looked up, stunned. She waited for him to speak, and when he didn't, she went on. "The phone was beige. The cord, one of those curly ones, was stretched across the room—the outlet was under the side window, by the speaker. Your tie, it was burgundy. With little blue diamonds. You must've taken it off at some point because it was on the cushion next to you. You were drinking whiskey, or maybe it was scotch."

"How do you know all this?"

"You know how."

"But you were a baby. And you were asleep. I put you down in the crib."

"I heard you, Dad. I *saw* you."

She wanted him to ask her more about it so that she could admit what she'd been up to on the estate. She wanted to tell him how she'd broken the rules. He said nothing.

"Tell me who Sharon is," she said.

"She's nobody."

He was treating her like a little kid—or like she was a stranger. He hardly ever talked about his past, only a detail or two about his dead parents, Robert and Marion, the one in the single photograph, or maybe a little Santa Cruz factoid. Other than that, he acted as if he hadn't existed until she was born. Or after that: he didn't exist until Cherry left.

Was this what he thought a good parent did? Curate a life? Protect your child by hiding everything? By treating your kid like she was the center of the universe? He wanted so badly for Opal to be well-adjusted that he shut out anything unsavory or difficult. Opal wanted to tell him that it didn't work. And not only that—it made it worse. It meant she had to find out on her own, without his help. Without him, she would understand what her childhood was actually like. Was the bad stuff so bad that it had to be kept from her like a secret? He treated it as shameful.

"Why won't you tell me?" she asked.

Opal waited. He wouldn't meet her gaze so she looked away, too, and it was as if the kitchen were a film they were watching. Opal took in the clean plates in the dish rack, the pastry box on the counter. She imagined the custardy innards, the sugar-coated crumbs along its back, the knife's sticky handle. Soon the plants on the sill would glow with sunlight.

"I did try to find her," he said finally and his words fizzed up Opal's spine.

"You mean Cherry."

Ray nodded. "She was your mother and my partner and she left us. I needed to know why, or at least make sure she was somewhere safe."

Opal waited a moment in case he'd give her more. He didn't.

"And this Sharon woman didn't know where she was?"

Ray shook his head. The clock ticked forward once more. The fridge groaned like a ghost.

"Please, Dad," Opal said. "Who's Sharon? Was she a friend of hers? Someone you both knew? Someone from—"

"Sharon . . ." Her father said the name as if it were unfamiliar, as foreign as a word in another language. He winced, grabbed one hand with the other, as if to steady himself. "Sharon is your grandmother." He paused, let out a long shaggy breath. "She's my ma—my mother."

Opal sat up straighter, spine fizzing again. "I thought your mom was dead. In the fire. You told me your house burned d—"

Ray blanched. "I lied," he said, as if he couldn't quite believe it himself.

"You *lied*? To me? But why?"

"To protect us. From her. If she was dead, I wouldn't have to tell you about her."

He didn't say anything more and Opal knew he wouldn't. That story was locked up tight. But why should it be? Hadn't he told her that the box helped him work through stuff from his past? He said the Accumulator *healed* him. Bullshit. He was still hurt by whatever his mother had done, which must have been a lot if he needed to hide the fact of her from Opal.

Across the table, her dad fiddled with one of his canvas work gloves. For a flash she could see the skinny, slouched, twentysomething in him, talking to his mother on the phone, his voice mean, his hand grasping the receiver so hard he might mold it like clay. She thought of the room where Baby Opal slept, dreaming for Cherry, the loss of her in the air. Her father breathed that air too. It was here in this kitchen, all the people who weren't here—but were. Opal wondered how much she didn't know. It went further back than she'd ever imagined.

"Can we talk about this later?" Ray said. "My call time."

"It's at five, I know, but this is important!"

"My work is important."

"You can't be serious. I have a grandmother! Who's alive! What about your dad? Is he there too? Is he just as bad?"

"I never met my father."

"How can I trust you?"

"I swear."

"All this time I thought we were honest with one another."

"Opal, please. You didn't break the rule, not officially, okay, but you *did*. And you know it."

"I didn't!" Her breath was shallow and it was like she was sipping it, desperate for it. He'd asked her to trust him and meanwhile he had a mother, and his mother knew Cherry. There was a whole story there—and he'd been hoarding it. "You lied to me," she said. "Your mother knows Cherry? Did they somehow meet? Did she come down to LA? Did I meet her?"

"No. Never. I would never. Listen, Opal, the tunneling. I'm worried about it."

"I didn't break your rule," she said. "I never saw Cherry. She was already gone."

"I'm still worried." He massaged his jawline with a palm, as if he might rub his entire face away if he pressed hard enough.

"I shouldn't have let you stay at the house," he said. "Even with the rules."

"*Let* me? I'm an adult. And I'm fine." She put her mug down so forcefully that a little coffee splashed over the edge.

"Maybe I should come get the Accumulator," he said softly.

"It's mine," she said. "You gave it to me, remember?"

"It was a bad idea."

"Why? Because I'll I find out more? Because I'll go back to Cherry? You know I will. You always knew I would. That's why you gave me that rule."

"I did it to protect you."

"I deserve to see her. She's my mother. I deserve to see her. You lied to me."

"Only about that. It's just that—there's so much you don't understand."

"Then explain it to me!"

"Everything I did, that Cherry and I did, was to protect you. I'm sorry I lied to you but I did the best that I could. It was just the two of us, and you were so young."

He stood up.

"Dad—"

"My call time."

Opal looked back to the window. How lucky her dad was, to be marrying Isla Patricia, living a new life. He had remade himself, moved on. Unlike Opal who was stuck in the past, her past, obsessed with it.

"There's an apartment, up on Valentine. For lease," he said, gathering his things. "It's a one-bedroom."

"My contract with Kim goes until August."

"You know you can break it." Ray put on his hat. He wanted this conversation over. "I'm your father and you need to trust me on this."

"You're my father, but what about Cherry? She's my mother."

"Oh stop. Sure, okay, she's your mother. But she left! She disappeared the day after you learned to walk. *The day after*, Opal! Let that sink in. I know she was afraid, she was nervous. And I get that. But she saw you walk for a single day, and then she left. Can you even imagine? That's all you can do, actually, because you don't even remember her! You have no idea what it means to miss her."

"I *do*. Now I do."

"Because of the Accumulator."

"Exactly. I miss her."

"Don't even talk about missing that woman!" He was yelling as he struggled to get all his stuff in order, his arms awkwardly full. "I've missed her every day for the last eighteen years! Don't you get that? She was the love of my life!"

"Dad," Opal said, trying to stay calm. "You need to tell me more. The Accumulator makes what I can do easier," she said. "But even without it, I can do it. I can find out."

"You should stop," Ray said. "Please stop."

He wanted her to stop tunneling, to stop asking questions. He had to know she couldn't.

14

HER MOTHER'S CHOICE TO DISAPPEAR REVERBERATED through Opal's entire life. That was obvious now. How could it be any different? When she tunneled, she was certain that every moment in her life was happening at the same time, that chronology was a fiction. Even after she left the box the past stayed with her.

She wasn't special. Fab said it was like that for anyone who had been through something terrible. Why was it that the worst things replayed in the mind on an unending loop? And if not, history repeated itself, tragedy as déjà vu.

Fab was her roommate now. As soon as Opal left her dad's, she drove to Fab's dorm and told her everything: the rules she'd broken, hearing her father talk to his mother on the phone. Fab knew about how Ray lied. She knew that Opal had seen herself as a baby—had dreamed the child's dreams, even. As soon as Opal was done confessing, Fab said she was moving onto the estate. She packed two bags right then. "You need help."

Opal knew Fab's presence would appease her dad. She was still angry with Ray, but she also couldn't help but feel a little guilty about their fight. It was going to be rough between them for a while, how could it not be? And yet she wished it weren't.

Fab was partly the reason Ray stopped harping about the one-bedroom on Valentine. He still wanted Opal to stop tunneling, but at least she had a chaperone again. With Fab there, he wouldn't show up unannounced. Besides, it wasn't as if her dad had much of an argument: *he* was the liar. If he expressed too much concern, Opal would bring up Sharon— and Isla Patricia didn't know of any Sharon. He had no choice but to bite his tongue.

Her dad assumed Opal would follow the rules. Or he probably deluded himself into assuming that. He was sort of correct: she would only tunnel once a month, and she would do so with Fab present. Fab had other rules: no more driving around the estate to sing to nobody, no more heading to bars across town for whiskey. Fab commuted to her classes at UCLA and used their extra second-floor bedroom as a study. They would facilitate the estate's locations together. Unlike Opal, Fab had zero interest in sleeping with a prop guy. Not that Opal wanted to do that again. There was no rule against it; Opal simply found herself longing for something more.

"Love!" Fab cried.

"That, or sex in a house with potable water," Opal replied.

Laughing with Fab was almost as good as tunneling.

Almost.

∞

It was early December now. The city twinkled red and green, and grizzled men with the resigned miens of former addicts sold Christmas trees in every vacant lot, and at every mall Santa's throne was never far from an oversized menorah. Hanukah had arrived early this year; it was already over. Meanwhile, in Beverly Hills, lit-up reindeer high-wired across Wilshire Boulevard, pulling Santa in his sleigh, bright as Vegas, into a new millennium. It was sixty-five degrees outside and dark before dinner.

In Opal's bedroom, she and Fab stood facing one another, their eyes closed, arms out, only their palms touching. The window was open and a breeze nudged the curtains and carried in the huff of the pumpjacks. Fab turned nineteen a few weeks ago and in February

Opal would too. *Make a wish*, they always said to each other on their birthdays. They had known each other for most of their lives.

"Exhale," Fab said, and Opal carved out as much air from the base of her lungs as she could.

"Good," Fab said.

Ray might like to think of Fab as the chaperone but what she was, in fact, was Opal's enabler.

"You need to find Cherry," Fab said that morning in her dorm. She conjectured that once Opal got to see her mother, she would be sated, healed, and her urge to tunnel might fade.

Now she said, "I can hear you breathing. Let it move through you."

Fab's mom went through two decades of self-help, everything from the power of positive thinking to past life regression therapy, and some of that language rubbed off on her daughter. Fab made fun of her mom's searching, but she also lit a candle when she wanted something badly enough, silently putting that wish into the universe. If their roles were reversed, if Fab were the one to time travel, Opal wasn't sure she'd have the same faith for her friend. Fab never questioned Opal's gift.

All the furniture was pushed to the edge of the room, and they stood in the center of a circle Fab had painted blue, their bare feet against the cool floors. Their hands were warm.

They closed their eyes for so long their bodies flew away and it was only their spirits, their minds, floating, focusing.

"Tell me what's bothering you," Fab asked.

It was easier to talk this way, probably because they couldn't see each other, could only hear their disembodied voices. After a minute or two it felt a little mystical, like one of those silly *light-as-a-feather-stiff-as-a-board* sleepover tricks that tipped you off the planet, let you touch some other side of reality. You could say anything to your best friend because you'd crossed over together.

They'd been doing these exercises since Fab moved in: breathing, practicing relaxing, imagining the body as liquid, open. The plan was if Opal could slip into time as relaxed as this, she would be more successful. She would be nubile enough to stay longer in the past and do whatever she wanted there. The theory hadn't been put to test, but they were both interested to see if would work. The thirty-day mark was coming up.

Now Opal spoke. "Do I really want to break the rule?"

"You're worried about Ray." Fab sounded exasperated.

"Well yeah. I promised. I know what you're going to say, that he lied first, but—"

"Two wrongs don't make a right?"

"Exactly," Opal said. "And do I really want to see my mom . . . having a hard time?"

"You tunneled to her before though. The purple onesie! You heard her voice!"

"That was over two years ago. And I didn't actually see her."

"Still. You did it, and you can do it again."

They stood there in silence, breathing.

"Breathe," Fab said again, and Opal did.

"I wish I'd seen her."

"You can. You will, next time you tunnel. You're so much better at it now."

Opal had been thinking a lot about that visit. Beneath the table it was dark, and her father's shoelace was a tangle. Her mother's voice was a little squeaky, unsure of herself, but her father's was impatient. She couldn't crawl yet, and so Baby Opal just sat there; the shoelace was what she liked, and also these two plastic cups. Opal, watching, was squatting under another chair, and she couldn't stay long before the moment dropped out.

Fab breathed deeply, and Opal matched it.

"You're not separate from your past self," Fab whispered. "You *are* your past self."

Opal let her body soften, go limp, insides pouring, and kept breathing.

The truth was, after becoming herself in the crib she wanted to try it again. She wanted to feel new like that. Newer, even. She would tunnel to *before* Cherry left. She would slip into an unknowing that suspended in all directions.

She would cry, and her mother would hear it.

Opal opened her eyes. Her father couldn't stop her.

"Let's go to the box."

"Now?" Fab opened her eyes. She grinned devilishly.

Outside the garage, Opal held both flashlights as Fab wrestled the door open. Opal's heart beat hard, and she was shivering though she wasn't cold. Would the garage be musky and dim, was it still tilted like a photograph slipping from a picture frame? Would the bulb blink as furiously as the orange lights in the bar? Would Opal's tunneling make Fab writhe, wide-eyed? She didn't want to be responsible for all of that; she was afraid she was.

As soon as the door was open, the musty dirt smell smacked Opal, nearly bringing her to her knees. It didn't repulse her. The opposite. She wanted to get inside the box.

"Slow your breathing," Fab said.

She pulled on the light and there was the box. It glimmered.

"Remember, you aren't fighting anything," Fab said. "You're slipping into it. You were already there. You are there."

Fab opened the box and Opal got inside. She hadn't been in here since last time.

Would Fab's presence hold her back?

No. Never—*light as a feather, stiff as a board.*

She closed her eyes softly. Felt her body go limp once more. She heard Fab shut the door.

She used to squeeze her eyes shut; she would push into the past, even though there had never been a need to force it because the box liked her tunneling. With Fab's help she would transform the process into something more graceful, and that lightness would make it easier to navigate. Or so she hoped.

Opal was going to visit Cherry. Her mother. Opal would finally be her mother's child.

"Ready?" Fab asked softly.

Opal felt herself nodding, already receding like the tide.

Close your eyes and hold your breath. Let it out. And go.

Fab was right: this new way of tunneling felt more natural. Opal went back, back, back until she was where (and when) she wanted to be. And then, with a long loose breath, she cut into time. It was as easy as parting meringue with a knife.

Her she was. At the old house, outside. She was on the porch, but along the side of the house, standing so close to the stucco she could prick her finger on its crust. It was morning and the air was chilly, dew starching the strip of grass below the porch. From where she stood, Opal heard the crows cawing from the sycamore tree in front of the house; she could only make out the very top of the tree, but even from here she could tell the birds were darkening the branches, their feathers lacquered black. The sky was gray and overcast but it wouldn't be for long.

Opal couldn't see her mother but knew she was here. Nearby. She already felt Cherry's solid hip against Baby Opal's thighs, felt Baby Opal's back resting against the crook of Cherry's elbow. In the box Opal's heart fluttered.

This was the first time she'd dropped in and not seen her younger self.

Were they inside? Should she go to the yard? No—not that far. They were on the porch.

We're on the porch, Opal told herself.

Opal moved along the side of the house toward the street. It was easy getting closer to her younger self. It was like gliding.

In the driveway was an old, beat-up car Opal didn't recognize, a sheet of dew blinding its windshield. She edged around the corner of the house; in the box she held her breath.

"Breathe," Fab was saying.

Opal exhaled.

There, on the porch, at the top of the stairs. Her mother.

Cherry stood with her back to the house, looking out at the street. She wore a long-sleeve gray T-shirt and jeans, and she was barefoot, even outside in this morning chill, a person who didn't like wearing shoes, whose feet could withstand anything. Her dark blond hair tangled down her back. She was just as tall as Opal imagined, but she was more solid seeming, strong, and her hips looked like Opal's hips.

Opal couldn't see her mother's face, but her mother was holding the baby as Opal knew she would be. Opal felt her mother's arm beneath the baby's diapered bottom and she felt her mother's other hand resting on the baby's leg. She was petting Opal's leg through her pink pajamas.

In the box, the gentle pressure of her mother's fingers through the cotton fabric came through like a signal. It was a language Opal had always understood. She was born knowing. The comforting weight of her mother's hand.

It meant *I'm here with you. I'm here.*

A mug rested on the porch wall, steam rising. So her mother drank tea in the morning. Opal could smell the mint. So her mother was someone who drank mint tea in the morning.

Did she still?

Her mother had not stopped holding her. Her fingers, on her leg. She was here.

The baby wriggled and Cherry's fingers fell from the baby's leg as she hitched the child higher on her other arm. In the box Opal was untethered like a helium balloon and she wanted desperately to be caught once more by her mother's hand. The baby was too distracted to care. She was so used to her mother's hand on her she took it for granted, she assumed it would be back.

The baby was wagging her arms at a woman running down the block. The woman wore nylon shorts, weights velcroed to her ankles. Her socks were bright white, as was the sweatband around her head.

"Hi Cindy!" Cherry called. Her voice was more confident than it was when Opal had heard it under the table. Cindy waved as she jogged past and the baby squealed.

From far away somewhere, Opal heard Fab. "Do you see your mom?" Opal said she did.

Opal longed to get closer. She would tap Cherry on the shoulder. Her mother would turn around. She would show her face.

What did she look like?

What did she look like when she was looking at Opal?

Opal heard Fab's voice again: "You're a baby. She is you. Go in."

Opal stepped closer to her mother and the baby, but as she did so, she concentrated not on Cherry but the baby.

The trick was to let go of the body she traveled in. Lean into her past consciousness. It was already beckoning.

Opal began to tip into the baby. The tree branches above her baby-head shimmied in the wind and the shimmy ricocheted through her. The crows cawed and they cawed in her.

Somewhere Fab was whispering, "There you go, there you go," and Opal sensed herself in the box, nodding.

A massive garbage truck rumbled up the street, its engine coughing and grumbling, and then its brakes screeched as it stopped at the cans lined up at every driveway.

"The truck! Opal!" her mother said.

Baby Opal's breath got short as the truck got closer and louder. She flapped her hands, and Opal felt her careening forward. The baby didn't look at Cherry—too much was happening, something far more exciting than her mother, who was always there.

"You perceive it, baby girl!"

Opal was vibrating with joy—the truck was coming!

Her mother held her so she wouldn't fall.

In the box, Opal was held.

Truck went away. Tender gums, arms tucked in now, a nest, warm. Her person, warm. Opal smelled the nape of her mother's neck.

"Shh," her mother said, laughing. "You just ate." Her laugh was deep and real, and Opal felt it against her own ribs. She didn't anticipate her mother laughing. Ray said Cherry had been so sad and anxious.

Did Ray lie about that too?

"Daddy will be out any minute," she whispered. "He loves this."

Loves what?

"He wouldn't miss the morning ritual," she said, seeming amused. "Shh, Mama didn't say that, did she?" Cherry paused. "Not Mama. Mommy."

Cherry sighed and suddenly the baby was moving, her mother was holding her under her arms, and Opal was—oh, oh, she was flying!—her mother was lifting her overhead.

Opal looked down and there was her mother.

There she was.

Opal had the photos from the album Ray gave her, but they didn't really capture the person here with her. Cherry looked like a kid—she was maybe the same age as Opal was now. Opal saw in her mother's face her own cheekbones. She saw a little scar above her mother's eyebrow, the freckles dusting the bridge of her mother's nose. Her mother's hair, tangled as her own if she wasn't careful, which she wasn't. Her mother's eyes were a rich golden brown and they were shining as they took in the baby above her. In the photos, Cherry was looking at a camera, she was looking at Ray taking the photo.

But now she was looking at her baby.

Cherry smiled, and her teeth were crooked. One of the front ones was gray.

Her mother was smiling at her. This was her mother.

"Luck be upon you, Opal," her mother whispered.

Now there was the rusty squeak. The screen door, opening, Opal thought.

Her dad was coming. He loves this.

"Opal!"

That was her father's voice all right but she heard it from very far off, as if she were swimming in the ocean and her dad were on the shore, yelling her name as she floated away.

Cherry still held the baby overhead. Someone was coming. Far away in the box something else was happening, and Opal struggled to stay with her mother and her mother's hands that encircled her baby chest. Her mother's crooked smile, the dead tooth, her mother's shining eyes.

"Get out of there," she heard her dad say, his voice louder now, and her mother's face dissolved under the fire of a bright light.

For a moment she was back in the box, and her dad was crouched at the open door, red-faced, panting, his khakis dark with the dirt of the garage floor. Fab peered behind him helplessly. It was dark at the edges of Opal's vision, as if she were viewing them through a door peephole. They were inside the rounded lens, and she was on the other side of a door that wouldn't open. She couldn't meet them, even if she wanted to. She didn't want to.

Opal closed her eyes again, breathing as Fab taught her, and went limp like they practiced, her body nubile, liquid, moving freely, and back she went.

In the distance she heard her father: "I need to tell you something. About when you were a baby. The doctors. Your mother was so worried."

What doctors.

"Opal, don't do this! I'll tell you everything just come back."

But Opal was already gone. She was trying to shuttle back to the porch to her mother. She wanted Cherry to lift her overhead again, to smile at her. Her mother.

Her father didn't want her to see her mother. But why?

Fab's hypothesis that Opal would be healed by seeing her mother possessed a neat logic but now the opposite felt true: Opal would never get enough. She would always want to be with Cherry. She was a baby. A baby needed her mother.

Someone was grabbing her legs—her dad.

"Don't," Fab was saying. "Stop!"

"Opal," Ray called. "Opal!"

Opal kicked hard and Ray's hands released. She snatched the door shut.

Off she went.

She tried to slip back to the porch, but it was like trying to find a dream after waking, the story lost, and the past too. She was being carried along a current.

She thought she heard her father murmuring in pain. Fab too. Was the box moving? It felt like it was moving, rattling as the dance floor had. It was like she was hiding in a closet during an earthquake and there was a fault line directly beneath her, and the earth was buckling, roiling, lifting her, shaking everything out of her. She thought she saw a flash of light around the edges of the shaking door. And then the box stilled.

She didn't stop tunneling.

Here she was.

Inside the house.

This wasn't the same day as the porch.

She was in the living room. It was midday and hot, radioactive sunlight soaking the hems of the closed curtains. It looked like it did when her dad was on the phone.

As before, Cherry and Baby Opal weren't visible, but she sensed them nearby. Why didn't she arrive closer to them? Maybe it was a good thing; the looser method gave her the mobility she'd always wanted.

Opal moved away from the couch toward the back of the house. She could feel the baby there. She was older than she had been on the porch. Maybe seven months. She would be lying on the bed. Her hands would be sticky with peach juice as she held her own bare feet. Cherry wasn't holding her, but she was very close, and the baby smelled her mother's perspiration and the funk of her armpits. The baby was in a sour mood, and it itched at Opal in the box.

She reached her father's bedroom. Her parents' bedroom. Her mother had once slept in this room.

There they were.

The baby lay on the bed on her back just as Opal knew she would be, shoeless, grabbing her feet. Fussy. An itchy feeling. Her mother was bustling around the room, a diaper in her hand, a piece of clothing for the baby draped over her arm. Cherry looked tired. Her face glistened with sweat, she was red-cheeked. They'd been outside in this heat. The baby wanted milk but she wasn't hungry she didn't want milk she wanted to be picked up but she was hot she didn't want to be touched she didn't know what she wanted just not this.

Opal writhed in the box, uncomfortable as the baby, and she heard her father's voice again.

"She okay? I don't think she's okay?"

"She's fine," Fab said. "Let her be."

Opal pushed their voices away, tipped into the liquid. The room, her mother.

The room—it was silent. Cherry appeared deep in thought and the baby on the bed watched her mother who didn't watch her back. Look look look. She wasn't looking.

Finally, her mother glanced at the baby.

"Hey baby girl. Hey cutie."

Her voice was all false cheer, and it hurt Opal in the box. Even if the baby had no idea there might be something wrong, Opal knew. This was what Ray had warned her about.

Did she really need to be here?

Opal was about to slip out—she should go have the argument with her dad that he was waiting to have—when a tapping sound startled her.

Was Ray banging on the box? Was he knocking its sides with his fingers, or his fists?

Tap. Tap.

No. Whatever it was, it was in the bedroom with her mother.

Her mother was heading toward the French window. It had slammed open and it was tapping the wall.

That was all—it was nothing—except—

Had something climbed through the window?

Opal suddenly felt crowded, as if someone were in the box with her. She located her body and waved her arms around. There was nothing in her way, except something *did* feel different: the air inside the box was soupy with humidity, the kind of heat that had mass, a skin. She shook her head like the dancers at the bar, *no no no*, and something shifted. The air turned gritty and ashy, fire season air. She didn't want to breathe it in. She had to.

"Hello?" she called out.

No one answered. Maybe Fab had convinced Ray that they needed to leave the garage.

And yet, something *was* here. Someone.

It wasn't in the box, it was in the bedroom. Something was overtaking the room.

The baby.

Something was taking over the baby. Some invisible force. Holding her down.

In the box, Opal felt the weight. It coated her like a brine, a muck. She pushed against it, tightened her whole body against it, tried not to let it in, let it take her. But the baby was going under. It was a buried-alive feeling. No no no no. Look look look look. Mama.

Cherry was at the window, peering through the screen to see if there was something there. She wasn't paying any attention to the baby. Turn around turn turn turn.

Cherry finally felt it. She turned and Opal was catatonic and unseeing on the bed and her mother was frightened, she couldn't reach her. Breastmilk shadowed her shirt.

What was happening?

Opal gritted her teeth. The box was moving again. It shook violently, like someone throwing themselves across the room, like a body wracked with tears. Opal heard distant voices.

save me save me

By the bedroom window, in the corner, a shadow dark as the milk on her mother's shirt caught Opal's eye.

It wasn't a shadow.

It was a figure.

A woman.

She pulsed like a flame.

The figure was older. Tall. Disheveled white hair. A dress like a sack. She had a glow around her. Or no, it wasn't a glow, it was more like the fuzzy black-and-white gravel of TV static, and it surrounded her like armor. She wasn't from this world. Was she a ghost? The heaviness was coming from her, she was producing it. It was a weight, a force, a murk, a brine. She pulsed.

The figure was obscured by the shadows—it *was* the shadow. Opal didn't know if the woman could see her. The walls were—

Wet.

Dripping.

The baby was going under. She'd drown.

Her mother grabbed her and her touch was a knife. It hurt.

It wasn't the same as before.

The shadow pulsed.

Opal screamed and screamed. In the box, her body went stiff as the walls around her, as hard as a dead body before it decays. She couldn't move. She opened her eyes and her mother disintegrated and she was nowhere. She saw nothing, only white, and then gray smoking at the edges. Her eyeballs, silky as larva, slipped into the back of her skull.

The shadow inside her, still pulsing.

∞

Opal woke up on the floor of the garage, cheek against the dirt, her legs still crumpled in the box. She was crying, snot in her mouth. Her arm hurt from where she'd fallen.

"Opal!"

Her father. He was outside, and through the open garage door, she saw him come to standing, dirt all over his face and clothing. Fab lay curled on the grass, and he went to her. He was pulling her to sitting.

Opal tried to get up and she couldn't. She was so weak. She was crying.

She lay in a shallow hole in the dirt, right in front the box. The door of the box was halfway blown off; it hung from a single screw on the lower hinge. The air was so humid. It smelled like rot.

"Dad," she called out.

He rushed to her, limping a little. As he kneeled and heaved her upright, he made a hushing sound like she was a baby. She sat at the edge of the hole, wiping the tears from her face.

"You okay?" he asked. "You're okay. I'm here. You're okay."

"I'm scared," she said, her voice raw. "We need to get out of here."

"You're okay, you're okay. This used to happen when you were a baby. You're okay."

"I wasn't alone, Dad. I saw . . . someone. Something else was there, in the room with the baby and Cherry."

"Where?"

"In the bedroom. On Edinburgh. A woman. Maybe it was a ghost? She was all clouded over. But I could see she was older. White hair. She had on a long dress. The baby was going under because of her. It was her doing it, Dad. She was reaching out for me, my baby self. Like she wanted to snatch me."

The weight, the force, the murk, the brine.

Opal closed her eyes and tried to push out the feelings, the way her eyes had bucked back and the white nothingness, the pulsing shadow.

She needed to sleep before she really felt sick. Her dad could carry her back to the house and she'd be okay. She never wanted to go back there.

"Ursa," Ray whispered, and Opal opened her eyes.

Part

FIVE

15

Ursa was always asking and then answering these questions for herself, confirming the present like checking a door to make sure it was locked. Her *now*, she decided, must matter, or else someday she wouldn't have a past worthy of transporting back to.

It was December 1999. Early morning.

She was still hidden in the woods outside Ben Lomond, California, still drinking fresh mint tea. Mary sat across the kitchen table from her, doing the same.

Nothing changed.

Everything did.

Karin had been dead for three years, killed by lung cancer. She'd avoided all doctors until it was too late and passed on not long after diagnosis in an ugly, plastic-edged hospital room that would have made her *tut-tut* with disgust were she not out of her mind with pain.

But Ursa wouldn't think about that. She wouldn't think about how if Karin were alive, the sixteen young women who filled the kitchen and spilled into the hallway, their mugs steaming, would have her itching. Karin would be even unhappier about the other women elsewhere on the land—the Farm, as they called it now: the ones sleeping in the western addition or working downstairs. Ursa could just picture Karin's raised eyebrow as she took in the young women with their vintage peasant shirts and baggy corduroys balding at the knees. How she would wrinkle her nose at the others too: their tattoos, the rings stuck in their noses like bulls or in their nipples like exotic dancers, their fingernails painted black as their eyeliner. Jenny with the candy necklace? Karin would find her absurd.

Also, all the guns. She definitely wouldn't like those.

But Karin was dead and so her opinions didn't matter anymore. The Farm had a beekeeper and an assistant beekeeper, a cohort dedicated to agriculture, one that took care of the chickens, another that handled the goats. The largest group oversaw the marijuana, which they'd expanded by 20 percent in a little over a year. Business was booming, and Ursa quite liked the dust-and-oak smell of money. She liked the young women, too, who worked so hard.

She didn't call them anything special. They couldn't be the mamas because there were no children. And anyway, they seemed too young for motherhood, though Ursa knew that wasn't the case. She was nineteen when she gave birth to Ray, the same age as Meg. These women had other concerns besides being mothers.

Meg dropped out of UC Santa Cruz after one quarter; she was one of the Porter girls. ("Don't call them *girls*," Mary kept reminding her.) Porter had a reputation for being the artsiest of Santa Cruz's eight colleges, which Ursa hadn't realized when Ray was a student there. Porter College's motto was "Life is short, art endures," though it seemed to Ursa that what endured most at Porter were drugs and hacky sack.

But her mind was getting away from her.

Where was she? *When* was she?

In the woods. In the kitchen of her friend's house. Her dead friend. The eighth day of December, 1999. She was sixty-one years old, and Mary was two years her senior. The other women surrounding them were young and vital. They had ideas—*theory*, as they called it. They had energy, too, and they did not balk at the labor required to run the Farm. Their desire to grow the business, and to please Ursa, was like a motor inside them.

Ursa took a sip of tea and closed her eyes. She noted the slurping sounds, someone blowing across the surface of their tea, someone else's ujjayi breathing. A cough. Yawns, long sighs, mindful humming.

Ursa opened her eyes. Phoebe rubbed her tired face, Maritza bit her fingernails. More than a few were already skunky with marijuana.

It wasn't called *reefer* anymore, or even *pot*. It was *weed*. And Ursa didn't call what they were doing the morning ritual anymore either. It was known, simply, as Tea. Over Mary's protests, Ursa abandoned the silly refrains as soon as the first women moved in. They would find such declarations of timelessness cheesy. Inaccurate, even. "Bullshit," one of them might say. "My tits sag. If that's not time for you, I don't know what is." The young were as vulgar as gapped teeth. Also, Tea wasn't mandatory. Ursa gave the women the choice to attend, which provided the illusion that everyone had a say in what went on here. In reality, only Ursa did.

Her mug was empty, mint dark as seaweed sludging the bottom.

She tapped Angelica on her wrist and Angelica pushed her chair back, tugging at her nightgown, which she wore all the time, like a dress. She stood so that even the ones lolling in the hallway could hear. "There are twenty-four days, including this one, until the new millennium dawns."

"Thank you, Angelica." Ursa remained seated, trusting her voice would carry. "How are we with our plans?"

"Decent," Meg said. "The second generator works great, and we did all that canning last week." She sat cross-legged on the counter, her mukluks pulled over thermal long johns. She was from Eureka, her mother a meth head; who knew who her daddy was? Angelica met her at a walk for Santa Cruz's Take Back the Night; Meg had been weeping and intermittently screaming on the sidelines. "Tweaked out," as Angelica put it. She told Meg about Ursa and Mary, and she helped Meg detox before bringing her onto the property.

"We probably need another cistern." This came from Emily, their beekeeper. She sat on the floor against the oven, her white-blond hair dreaded into sponges. Thank goddess for Emily's upbringing on a compound in rural Idaho. As she was eager to tell anyone who asked, she dropped the racist nationalism but kept the survivalist skills: how to tie knots, how to raise goats (and bees), how to build shelter and a fire. How to store water. The girl was obsessed with water. That and Amanda's pussy—she liked to say pussy was what made her flee Idaho. ("Not the racism?" Maritza asked.) Emily also claimed that nothing prepared you for sex with a woman like learning how to field strip and clean an AR-15 while blindfolded.

"It's going to rain and we'll want that water," Amanda, next to her, said.

"I'm on it," Azadeh called from the hallway. Azadeh had a sometimes-boyfriend in Watsonville, a harmless stoner with family money whom she strung along when the mood struck her. They were able to get a lot from Jameson. Ursa wasn't worried he'd try to get onto the Farm, if only because the others worried for her: these women were more afraid of outsiders than the mamas had ever been. Militant, even.

"And we're all feeling okay?" Mary, ever the den mother, asked. "The year is almost over."

Murmurs. Titters. Hoots.

Most of them feared and welcomed the new millennium in equal measure. For more than a few, it was an obsession.

The big glitch, they called it. The Y2K bug.

Apparently, computers—those soulless gray boxes Ursa had never laid a finger on—weren't programmed to read the year 2000 correctly. As soon as the year changed, this failure would wreak havoc, destabilizing global industries across the world. Banking, travel, education, media. Chaos would descend. Those who didn't prepare would suffer.

Ursa realized early on that to let the women prepare for the worst was the best way to hold their attention. They were afraid and that made them loyal.

From across the table, Sunshine raised her hand as if this were school. Of all the new recruits, she reminded Ursa most of the mamas, with her straight waist-length hair parted down the middle and her initial meekness, how she wore her longing to be loved and accepted like a birthmark across her face. She'd been nervous as a stray dog when she arrived, scared of her ex-boyfriend, it turned out. Guarding Ursa in the eastern wing was what brought her back to life.

"What is it, Sunshine?" Ursa said.

"Explain to me again why we're so worried? Sorry I'm not getting it."

"When the new year happens," Sierra, co-beekeeper, began, "there's a significant chance the computers will think it's the year 1900."

"For real?" Sunshine said.

"We don't know for sure," Angelica admitted. "But if they do, they'll go beserk."

"The computer nerds used just a two-digit code for the year," Amanda added.

"They left out the 19," Sunshine said, pleased with herself.

"That's correct," Mary said, patting her hand.

"But why?" she asked.

"The programs were written in *the sixties*," Meg cut in, and Ursa caught Mary's eye. To these babies, the sixties might as well be the Cretaceous age. "They weren't thinking ahead."

"How shortsighted," Ursa said dryly.

"We should sell all the weed we have," Becks said from the hallway. "We'll be less vulnerable that way."

"Perfect timing," Phoebe said. "Holiday season and all."

"And then we'll have reserves of cash," Amanda said.

"Let's exchange it for gold," Angelica said quietly to Ursa. "In case of a currency crash."

Ursa nodded. Though she wasn't afraid of Y2K, she also didn't think it hurt for the Farm to be totally self-sufficient, an island in the midst of a chaotic world. If the apocalyptic vision did come to pass, better to be ready for it. They would protect themselves. If nothing happened, she would be there to cushion their disappointment.

"What else?" Ursa said.

"I hate to bring it up," Jenny said, talking through the string of her candy necklace, which stretched between her teeth like floss, "but we've got to slaughter Tony."

Tony was a goat. As Ursa expected, a few women protested.

"We'll *need* the jerky," Jenny said over the din.

"I can still feel sad," someone yelled from the hallway.

"You'll be less sad next spring when you're starving."

Everyone laughed; the room filled with their glee.

Ursa thought an outsider would be afraid of what they'd created here, a world onto itself, a place for hidden women to name the animal they would eat. Sure, they had guns, and Emily always carried a knife that she could pull out of her boot faster than a sneeze, but it was their confidence that intimidated, a swagger that the mamas never possessed. Earlier this summer, Angelica spearheaded painting the house a dark green, the windows and eave carvings a light brown, and now the mansion was a giant gleaming tree among trees, and out of it trickled all these women who wouldn't question hurting a stranger if he dared to disrupt their project.

Not that anyone was coming here. The tentacle mazes were in impeccable shape, and it wasn't as if the feds were flying their helicopters overhead. The weed operation was still small potatoes compared to what was going on up in Humboldt; they didn't have hard drugs, which was what the local police cared about. Besides, no one wanted to bother two old ladies babysitting a bunch of pretty girls. Men ruined the world; women just did their hair.

But wait—where was she? *When* was she?

The Farm, 1999. The women were still laughing and going on about Tony.

Someone asked, "Why must we devalue a goat's consciousness?"

"Because," Maritza replied, "Tony's anus releases shit pellets like coins from a winning slot machine."

Someone groaned. Everyone else laughed some more.

These women were strong and proud of their independence, and many of them were educated and cheeky about it, swapping books with titles like *The Ethical Slut* and *Cunt*. They spent their downtime debating the merits of men and the lucidity that a sexless life might provide. They wondered aloud whether sexuality was malleable, and they discussed the irony that technology, though evil, enabled their liberation. What would it mean to give it up, they asked, just as they were doing here on the Farm? They talked about how the big glitch would bring down capitalism once and for all, forcing civilization to remake itself. After the collapse would come regrowth. They wouldn't need the old models. Their ideas passed over Ursa like interesting background music; talk meant little to her.

"Hush now," she said over the hubbub, and at once the room fell silent.

No matter what they thought, they all followed Ursa without protest. In this way, they were exactly like the mamas. These women liked to say, "This is a safe space," but that didn't mean everyone was safe, only those who understood the requirements for entry. It meant it was unsafe to be on the Farm unless you were a resourceful woman, a little feral, too, unless you were beautiful because you deemed it so, unless you were toppling the patriarchy by being joyfully self-sufficient, the silver piercing in your tongue glinting in the sickly light of the weed room. You weren't safe unless you believed in Ursa and what she could do.

"Tonight I will go to the eastern wing," Ursa said.

Another change since Karin's death: Ursa transported whenever she wanted, usually every few weeks. No more open moons. Mary learned not to complain, though she and Ursa still talked like the mamas sometimes, which the younger women found mysterious. To them, the mamas were old-testament-powerful.

Everyone remained silent. They were waiting.

"I'll need protection," Ursa said.

She pointed at Sunshine, her weakling, and Angelica, who was Sunshine's opposite, a natural leader. She nodded at Mary. Like that, her guards were chosen.

"We should be ready to discuss further preparations by Friday," she said, getting up from the table. "Please ask Jenny if she needs help slaughtering and dressing Tony. And everyone, keep in mind what else we need to consider. The year is almost over and we want to be ready should any crises occur." She paused and nodded to Amanda, who led the weed cohort. "Let's get those eighths ready before the students leave for Christmas break."

∞

If Ursa was honest, her only worry about the new millennium was that Ray would be swept into it, be harmed. Even after everything, she didn't want him harmed.

Nineteen years since he'd left—almost two decades without him.

He ran away in the dark of night like he didn't love her, like he hated her, and then, when they finally spoke, all he wanted was . . . information? He would have taken it and given her nothing.

At the thought, Ursa shivered. She wore only a long white dress, and its hem trailed behind her, ghost-like; to wear a puffer jacket over it would look silly. She still had her vanity, even now.

The eastern wing waited for her at the end of the hallway, which the women swept and mopped daily so that its wood floor glistened like a horse's back. Ursa put a hand on each wall, as if to hold her up. She needed to shrug these thoughts off or her transport would be wonky, leave her with a nasty hangover.

Ray had reached out with that note, not because he regretted leaving or because he wanted to come home but because he was out of options. He'd been desperate on the phone, and mean. He didn't care about Ursa. He wanted Cherry.

Did he, over these decades, ever find her? Did Cherry come back to him? Was Ray still alone out there in Los Angeles?

Ursa told herself to stop. Cut it out.

Ray's absence was always with her, pricking her again and again like a tailor's needle forgotten in the waistline of her dress. What could she have done to keep him with her? And where was he now? Did he miss her?

She still had the paper he sent to the P.O. box, the one that read *Call Me.* When she tried the number a second time, she got a busy signal. The next day it was disconnected.

Served her right: she was the one to hang up on him.

Ursa told Ray her old name when he was just a kid. For years he'd had so many questions, about who his daddy was, about why she'd fled Connecticut, about what the mamas did in the eastern wing. *Don't worry about your daddy, Connecticut is too conservative, we're just meditating.* She tucked his long hair behind his seashell of an ear and whispered her real name because she knew it would appease him. No one else had said it aloud since the day she left Mystic.

That name was also a needle—sewing into her. It was the last thing Ray said to her.

Never mind, she told herself. Stop.

Ray wasn't why she was heading to the eastern wing on a Wednesday evening at the end of the twentieth century. She didn't want to relive any of that. Instead, she would tuck herself into the hexagonal room and transport to something that made her happy. To Karin. That first year together was fun, and catching flashes of their newfound friendship helped with her grief, made it tolerable. Ursa had been going back there since she'd brought Karin's effects home from the hospital in a plastic bag. In a way, it was a relief to mourn someone besides Ray.

When Ursa was in a lighter mood, she told the youngsters that they didn't need to fear the big glitch. "All the computers want is to time travel," she said. "They yearn for a simpler time. Can you blame them?" The girls loved that joke, and even the hardline preppers like Angelica and Emily appreciated the symmetry of their situation. Ursa promised everyone that they'd all get to pile into the eastern wing when the clocks hit midnight on January first. As a group, they would witness her power, and inside that power they would be protected by whatever happened beyond the woods.

For now, Ursa only allowed a few women into the room with her. As long as she didn't push it, as long as she left the membrane before it got too intense, the girls felt the same bliss the mamas used to crow over. That bliss turned every single one of them into believers; they would fight to defend this place, they would never leave Ursa.

Allowing only a few into the eastern wing was an ingenious idea. It was the same scarcity model they used when releasing certain potent strands of weed; people always wanted what they couldn't get enough of. The women believed that whoever guarded Ursa as she transported absorbed some of the time-bendy energy. It invigorated them, and the others felt magnetized for a day or two afterward. They even held post-transport sessions by the creek, when the guards hugged the other women, one by one, "transferring the goo." Even the more practical women were into it.

Ursa reached the door of the eastern wing. She paused, gathering her thoughts before entering. It was nearly one in the morning, a few weeks since her last transport.

It might be 1999, but in a short while she'd be elsewhere.

Else*when*, as Karin used to say.

She took a deep breath and opened the door. There was Mary, standing with Sunshine and Angelica. There was no more sage ash, no more malachite or turquoise. The room was empty of anything that might hold Ursa back. Not even the pillows remained.

She sat in the center of the room and the three women stepped back. They did not surround her or lay hands on her. They simply watched and barred the door. Sometimes a girl might lean against the wall if the euphoria got too intense. "That was some orgasm," Emily said once.

It wasn't difficult for Ursa to slip into the membrane. The years with Karin, all that time they'd spent as a trio, treating her gift as sacred, honoring it and fearing its consequences, had its benefits. Her transitions into the past were easy as a blink. Over the years, she managed to get more inside of her own body, to feel as deeply as possible. She detached more completely from the present nowadays. She truly became her past self. Even after Karin's death, she was careful with her power. To abuse it would scare off the young women. That couldn't happen. If they left her, she'd be nothing. She couldn't withstand any more leaving.

"Ready?" Mary asked as she moved around her to shut and lock the door. Sunshine and Angelica held hands and smiled.

Where was she?

The eastern wing.

When?

December 1999.

"I'm ready," Ursa said, closing her eyes.

Whoosh.

She went.

∞

At dawn, Ursa found herself in the turret, locked in, as was her preference, curled up in the cracked leather chair. Her mouth felt stuffed with wool, and her headache from the transport persisted, despite Mary's insistence that she finish her barley tea before they opened the eastern wing and let the time-bendy energy flow into the other women.

Ursa had done what Mary wanted and then she'd escaped as soon as she could. She'd been up here in the turret for hours, dozing in and out of sleep until grim gray light seeped through the windows, signaling it was time for her to wake. A soreness drilled down to her bones, and her hips ached. She felt off, and so did the room around her, a disturbance soaking the land.

In her transport, Ursa had gone back to meeting Karin at the café on Grant Avenue.

She loved being in that moment, 1956 San Francisco, the sidewalk choked with people headed to the jazz clubs and bars, to the Italian restaurants that stayed open late. Near the café was the deli whose wares she often drooled over, the baseball bats of salamis hanging from their hooks, softballs of aged provolone tucked among the tins of fish. She smelled cigarette smoke, car exhaust, urine. A man's pomade, a woman's perfume, powdered makeup.

She'd sat next to Karin's table and her friend came back to her. Her mane of curly hair, and her cup of coffee on its saucer, and her capri pants. The way her very presence lit up Ursa.

There she was, with her hand-rolled cigarette.

Young Ursa wanted to smoke like this woman. Young Ursa had no clue. The Ursa inside the eastern wing, the Ursa who was swimming inside of her younger self, wanted something else.

Thinking about it now, head pounding, tired through her bones, Ursa smashed her cheek against the creased leather cushion.

Karin was smoking and Karin was dead.

That tar, in Karin's lungs. Forty years later, the sink would be flecked with blood from her coughing. Karin would be dead a month later.

In the membrane, Ursa leaned forward, toward Karin. She was close enough to burn the tips of her fingers on Karin's cigarette. She was close enough to swat the cigarette out of Karin's hand. Ursa knew—somehow she *knew*—she could have done it. She was strong enough.

She could have said, "Stop smoking!"

She didn't dare.

If she dared, would Karin listen and stop smoking—when Ursa came to, would her best friend be alive?

It was a silly, childish thought. Transporting never brought anyone back; she kept having to learn that lesson over and over again.

But how she missed Karin.

Now a sound jerked her fully awake.

An engine. A big engine. A truck. Not one of their trucks.

Ursa pulled herself off the chair and went to the windows. Out there, nothing was amiss, though a disturbance remained in her body, burrowed there. Through the scrim of fog, the front yard arranged itself: the vegetable gardens and the rusted wheelbarrow overturned next to the compost bins, the new gardening shed next to the large aloe plant, and the bell that Becks installed to let everyone know it was dinnertime. Beyond that, the sweep of pine and sequoia trees, the brambles of blackberry bushes, the two dawn redwoods, their branches bare until the spring. If it weren't so foggy, Ursa knew she'd just be able make out the meadow from the leftmost window and the scatter of live oaks there, with their comforting canopies and massive climbing boughs, their carpet of brittle tan leaves that cut the heels of women who insisted on traipsing around barefoot. Directly beyond the yard was the wide, unpaved driveway, bordered by massive redwoods. This morning it looked as if it were floating on a cloud of fog. In the distance, the fog was solid white, and it rose like a wall.

No more engine sound. Ursa thought maybe she'd dreamed it; then she heard the whistle: one long call, followed by two short ones.

It was the whistle she and Mary taught the women, the same one the mamas had practiced.

It meant *stranger*. It meant *intruder*.

From the driveway, emerging from the direction of the second tentacle, two people, a man and a woman, appeared out of the fog.

The woman was more of a girl really, tangled hair spilling out of a black beanie, a bright red flannel over jeans. Her black boots were muddy. She didn't look pregnant; that hadn't happened in years. That was the old story.

The girl and the man held up their arms in surrender. They were walking slowly, and the man was trying to say something to the girl, keep her calm maybe. The girl's eyes were wide as she took in the land and the house, her lips parted slightly.

Behind them, Jenny emerged from the fog, candy necklace half-eaten, hunting jacket unbuttoned, as if she'd thrown it on hastily. She held a rifle at their backs. She whistled again, and all at once Ursa heard the women in the house below her, crying out and rustling, shaking the house with their running. They were whistling back. Someone blew the airhorn. More rustling. Ursa heard guns cocking.

The fog was too thick for her to be certain, but as the man got closer Ursa thought she saw him walk with a slight hitch, favoring one leg, and he seemed alarmed but not unaware of what was happening. His sneakers were layered with fresh mud, and leaves and twigs stuck in the cowlicks of his mussed hair. He wore a leather jacket over a sweater, and jeans, and from here, through the mist, it looked like his face was unshaven. She thought she could see his ears, pink in the cold. She remembered, with a start, Charlie's ears. How neat they were, how surprisingly delicate.

The man was saying something, and then he stepped forward, presumably to get closer to the women Ursa couldn't see directly below her. The fog passed by him like a gossamer scarf and in the clear morning light Ursa saw him more clearly.

Ray.

It was Ray.

Ray. He was here.

When was she?

She was now. This was happening now.

"Don't shoot!" Ursa screamed and ran to the door. Her hands shook as she reached for the turret lock.

16

HE'D MISSED THE HAIRPIN TURN ONTO THE PROPERTY. In the truck cab, the defroster blowing loudly, Ray flushed with shame, hoping Opal didn't notice. He imagined Ursa's opprobrium—*what are you, new here?*—and in the next moment he felt only pride. He'd missed the turn because he was no longer part of this place. Neither was Opal, who gripped her seatbelt as if she might tear it apart. She would never be part of this place.

"We have to turn around," he told her, putting the truck into reverse. "It's back there."

She twisted her torso, as if to get a glimpse of something behind them, though the fog was too thick. "We missed it? How did we miss it?"

"It's meant to be invisible."

"When you said that yesterday, I didn't really get it."

"You're about to."

Two days before, once Opal recovered from tunneling and Fab went to bed, Ray told Opal everything. In the living room, as she recuperated on the couch, he finally confessed the truth. She asked questions and he answered, holding nothing back. It was like screaming into a pillow in Doc's office, like breathing deeply in the Accumulator, that same feeling of letting go, how scary and comforting it felt to surrender, to fall from the cliff, to drown in the flood. He felt empty and light, at once vulnerable and invincible.

He told her about his mother.

"Sharon?" Opal asked.

"Everyone calls her Ursa," he said. "Her real name is a secret."

He told her about the mamas who worshiped Ursa in the falling-down mansion in the Santa Cruz woods. There was Mama Mary, who had been there the longest. There was Mama Gertie. Mama Alice, Mama Annie, Mama Joan, Mama Natasha. Others whose names he had somehow forgotten.

"All women," Opal said.

"Except for me."

"Seems so seventies. So old-fashioned."

Was it? He'd never thought of it that way.

There were the kids too. The younger ones who came later were especially grimy and disheveled, and they ran through the woods at every hour.

Had those children even learned to read? Were their teeth rotting out of their heads? Did they still spend hours separating the stems from the nuggets of weed until their fingers stung? When the mamas locked themselves into the eastern wing on cold winter nights, did the children know how to keep the fire going or did they shiver until one bit their tongue?

"They're adults now," Opal said.

"If they survived," he said.

That's when he told her about Hawk. About the stones Cherry tried to place on his grave, how she brought them with her to LA and put them at foot of the lemon tree.

"She took them with her when she left us," he said.

He told her about Cherry's mother Ruth, who'd abandoned Cherry as a newborn. How Cherry was left to be cared for by the women, and how the mamas did the bare minimum to keep her alive.

How they bossed her around and made her do more work than anyone else.

He told her about the weed. About the mamas' weird phrases, and the purple room. About their no-men rule. He had so much to confess.

He said that he and Cherry fell in love when he was in college and she was sixteen. Their love was a secret, it had to be. They ran away when they found out Cherry was pregnant with Opal.

Then he told her about the episodes in LA after she was born.

"And it was Ursa all along," Ray said, his throat sore from talking in the darkened living room, his knee still sore from when he fell during Opal's tunneling. "She found us after all."

Ray realized that Ursa could do what Opal did. So that's what Ursa and mamas did in the eastern wing when the moon opened. They were tunneling. Ursa was. Of course. And, somehow, impossibly, across time and space, his mother had reached his daughter this way. His favorite person in the world had connected to his least by some thread he couldn't see, within a parallel universe he had no access to.

"I think Ursa is why Cherry left," he said, and Opal nodded. She was sure of it too.

It was all coming back to him, even now—especially now—now that they were so close to his old home he might be able to hear the creek if he listened closely enough. The memories came, one after the other, the images assaulting him.

The mamas with their vials of jasmine oil and those nuggets of amber they rubbed across their wrists that could not mask their fungal reek. Their frizzy hair clogged the drains, and during their monthlies their stained cloths hung from the clotheslines like flags after a brutal war. They had coarse, wide-hipped bodies. They had hairy nipples and even hairier mustaches, and their desiccated foreheads reminded Ray of the walnut shells the squirrels left on the north end of the property. He had not let go of his disgust, and he didn't wish to. Until he fled, Ursa put him to work or she sent him off—to play, to risk his life, whatever, he just had to be gone.

"The children, we had to be invisible," he'd said the night he and Opal talked.

It was all in service of Ursa's gift, he realized. She'd used it to push him away. She used it to push Cherry away from her own daughter.

"Ursa can do what I do," Opal said, and Ray wanted to tell her that she was wrong, that her gift was different because she used it to connect to others and to her younger self. She would never use her gift to hurt people.

He didn't say any of that because he knew what Opal was thinking. She had evidence that another person, her grandmother no less, could tunnel, that someone else spoke this alien language, and she wasn't a stranger. Ursa was her father's mother, and she lived only a few hours away. They could meet.

When Opal said, "We have to go there," Ray wasn't surprised. "I need to confront her," Opal added. "I'll do it without you if I need to."

"I would never let you go alone. Anyway, you won't find her without me."

The next day, they were speeding north on the 5, passing farmland. Somehow California would transform from this flat muted openness to a fleecy green. When did the change occur, and would he be able to tell as it was happening?

They stopped in Coalinga to fill the gas tank, and at the first unruly smell of cow shit, Ray remembered with sudden, painful clarity the escape from the mamas, when he and Cherry were giddy over what they had managed to do. How untouchable he felt back then, driving with his lover, who would soon be the mother of his child, and how certain he was that they would remake their lives however they liked. They would unshackle themselves from their upbringing with a single road trip three hundred miles south.

He assumed his mother wouldn't have the know-how to find

them. But she did, and she scared Cherry away, and she tried to ruin his life. How had she done it? How had she found a way to reach them? He didn't know, only that she had, and he and Opal lived with the consequences. And now they were retracing this old route. He was returning to her, just as she wanted.

"We need a plan," he said as they left Coalinga and got back onto the freeway.

"Well, you know the mazes—"

"The tentacles."

"Whatever. You'll get us to the house."

"If we're not shot."

"They'd never shoot us. Ursa wants you back."

"But why are we going?" he asked. "What will we say?"

"I don't know. I just need to see her in person and find out how she did that to Cherry. How did she do it? And why would she hurt our family?"

Opal couldn't hide the urgency in her voice, and Ray wondered if they would be able to manage a confrontation without anyone getting hurt. He couldn't lead Opal into danger; he'd never forgive himself.

He didn't voice any of this. Instead, he breathed in and out deeply until Opal said, "Dad, cut it out. This isn't yoga class."

"It'll be nightfall by the time we reach Santa Cruz," he said finally. "We'll have to wait until morning. No way we're going in the dark."

Well, tomorrow was here, the sun weak beneath the fog, and Ray was turning the truck around to find the entrance off the road, slowing to a crawl. He couldn't delay it any longer.

"Unless you know it's there, you can't make out the entrance from the road," he explained, and suddenly he could see it, the opening like a tunnel made of trees. He knew the PRIVATE—NO TRESPASSING signs would be nailed to posts starting a hundred yards down, invisible until they were right in front of you. No sense in drawing attention. The mamas worried a gate would mark the property. Strangers can't bother what they don't know exists.

Who would be there once he steered them down the tentacle and onto the driveway to the house? His mother. Mama Mary, and the others swaying behind her. The children, grown now—only the girls would remain: they would be mamas too. Would there be new children, naked to the waist even in this morning cold, covered in mud, their hair unbrushed or buzzed bald without care, the stink of weed on their fingertips? Would they be interrupting the morning ritual, with its cloying smell of mint tea?

"You sure about this?" he asked. Opal nodded.

The fog was so thick he could barely see a foot beyond the truck grill, but as soon as they rocked onto the rough dirt road, muscle memory kicked in and it was like he'd just left. He could drive to the house blindfolded if he had to.

"If you go straight here," he said, pointing into the whiteness, "it'll lead you in a circle, right back to the road."

"When the fog parts, wow. It's beautiful here."

She wasn't wrong. Once he got to LA, he'd never allowed himself to long for this beautiful place, this chew of white obscuring a world so green it seemed supernatural. He'd forgotten how majestic the redwoods were, how noble the pines, the purposeful rot of downed trees and animal carcasses. If they opened the truck windows they would hear the trees breathing, the creek babbling.

Ferns and tree branches hit the windows as Ray directed the truck off the main driveway and onto the tentacle. He nosed the truck forward, the fog separating in cottony puffs, revealing a dirt path that curved, serpentine. He remembered it all, the buck of the rough road and the boulder at his left, the way the tentacle seemed to squeeze the vehicle on either side. He slowed to a crawl as instructed so many years ago.

Something slammed against the truck hood.

"What was that?" Opal cried.

Out of the fog: a face, a body. A hand on the bed of the truck. Ray braked.

It was a woman. She was white, and young, early twenties at most.

Her dark brown hair was spun into little buns all over her head. Her face and cheeks were splashed with freckles.

Was this someone Ray knew as a child?

The woman wore an unbuttoned hunting jacket over baggy black raver jeans, the kind Opal made fun of. With her other hand, the one not touching the truck, she held a rifle. When she made eye contact with Ray, she lifted the gun with both hands and pointed it directly at the windshield.

"Don't you know how to read, asshole?" she yelled. "You didn't see the signs? No trespassing!"

The woman wore a candy necklace, nearly all the pastel pieces already sucked off, the white string a garrote around her throat.

"Just follow my lead," Ray whispered to Opal, whose breathing was heavy. She was terrified.

He took his hands off the wheel and lifted them in surrender. Opal did the same.

The woman came around to the driver's side window, rifle still trained on them. She nodded and tapped the gun against the window. When he unrolled it, she leaned in close. She emitted a vegetal musk, and he saw that her freckles were actually specks of blood, splattered and dried across her face. Fear plucked at his sternum.

"I said no trespassing!" she yelled into his face, and Ray startled. "What the fuck, man! Get the fuck out of here!"

"Hold on, hold on," Ray said, trying to keep his voice gentle; mamas did not like a gruff baritone. "Maybe—do you remember me? Are you, are you . . . Kitty? Or maybe you were a baby when I left. Canary? Or maybe you came later?"

"Dude, I don't know what the fuck you're talking about. Get out of here."

"Wait—"

"The new millennium is almost upon us, and if this is some bullshit test run on our property I swear I'll blow your brains out right now and bury your bodies next to the others."

"Please," Ray said. "I used to live here."

"No you didn't." She leaned back, held the gun up once more.

"We're looking for Ursa," Opal said.

"Mama Ursa," Ray said.

The woman looked stunned. She didn't lower her gun, but something in her face softened as she nodded at Opal.

"You might be okay," she said. "Unless—are you pregnant? You can't be pregnant."

Opal shook her head.

The woman snarled at Ray. "As for *you*. You're trespassing."

"You have to take me to Ursa."

"I don't have to do any fucking thing."

She cocked her gun. There was rust-colored dirt under her fingernails. Not dirt. Blood. Her fingertips, Ray saw now, were stained red.

"Please," he said. "We mean no harm."

"Bullshit."

"Ursa is my—" He couldn't do it, couldn't say it.

The gun was so close to his face.

"His mother!" Opal cried out. "Ursa is his mother!"

Ray could tell that this information shook the woman; her tongue darted out, as if searching for a piece of candy from her necklace before returning to her mouth. For a moment she wasn't a woman with a firearm, cursing and angry, speckled and stained with someone else's blood, but a mama, a wounded woman. She had come here because she had nowhere else to go.

"Can you just tell Ursa?" he asked softly. "I can wait on the road."

"Get out of the fucking truck."

They would follow her on foot, she said. Hands behind their backs.

"If you try anything, Ursa's boy, I'll kill you," she said.

It was cold out, the kind of cold that seeped into you when it was early morning and the trees held the fog close. The mist wet his cheeks as they trudged through mud and climbed over fallen trees.

Branches scraped his face. He kept glancing at Opal to make sure she was okay.

"Don't stop," the new mama said, and she pushed the rifle into Ray's back. He prayed Opal would not be hurt.

He'd expected the house to look even more rundown than it had when he and Cherry left, the wood underneath its chipping paint stringy, as rough as the fur of some mythical beast. But what appeared at top of the incline looked like a well-kept mansion, as if it had been renovated recently. It was freshly painted, a green shade that complemented the surrounding trees, and the needle tip of the turret shined in the white sky as if some enterprising mama had climbed up to polish it by hand. Ray knew what it meant; his mother was more powerful than ever.

As they reached the end of the tentacle that led to the driveway, the woman let out a whistle, one he still knew by heart. Opal startled, and Ray tried to tell her with his eyes that it would be okay, though he wasn't sure of that at all. The fog parted when they got to the driveway, and the new mama whistled again.

At that, women just like the one pointing a gun at his back poured out of the house, scuttling like roaches. There were at least twenty of them, maybe more, and they were armed. They were young. They whistled and ululated, waving their guns. Ray recognized no one. Where was Ursa?

A woman with a shaved head, wearing a demure ankle-length nightgown, blew the airhorn. Ray knew the harsh sound was coming, but as soon as it bellowed through the air it hurt his ears, and when Opal cringed, he wanted to rush to her and cover her ears with his hands.

A girl with a thick ponytail of blond dreads held a knife as if she might throw it between Ray's eyes. He had no doubt she would hit her target.

"Twenty-four days!" a light-skinned Black woman called out.

Silver star stickers lined the bags under her eyes. "There are only twenty-four days left and we are ready!"

"We *will* defend ourselves!" someone else screamed.

"What the fuck," Opal whispered, and Candy Necklace hushed her.

"They say they know Ursa," she yelled.

Now the women surrounded them, scowling. So many guns. Fear poked Ray's throat. One woman's jeans were covered in what looked like blood, dried like a brownish-red paint.

"Get rid of him," she said, so quietly Ray might have imagined it.

"No trespassing!" someone else yelled.

"No fucking men!"

"We only want to talk to Ursa," Opal said.

At that, the women cocked their guns.

"Who the fuck sent you?" said the one with the knife.

"She's my grandmother," Opal said.

"Dude says Ursa is his mother," Candy Necklace said.

A woman he couldn't see, hidden behind the horde, called his name.

A rustling, and someone came forward.

"Mama Mary," Ray said, his voice tight, he could barely get the words out. A murmur rippled through the group of women.

When Mama Mary smiled, she looked as she always had, only older, her eyes tired, sad maybe. Her hair was no longer that bright red, it was white, cropped closely to her head. Her freckles were obscured by age, but she was dressed like always, in a long shapeless sack.

"Is that you?" he asked.

"You're here for Y2K!" Mama Mary cried out, clapping her hands.

"Y2K?" Opal said under her breath. "They can't be serious."

"We're here to talk to Mama Ursa," Ray said.

The women were snorting now. "*Mama* Ursa," one of them repeated.

And then the screen door whined open—Ray would recognize

the sound anywhere. At the top of the stairs, presiding like a queen, was his mother.

Ursa wore a long, gauzy white dress. Her hair, now nearly as white as the dress, wasn't so much long as it was uncut, and she held nothing: no gun, no knife, no airhorn. Only herself, which was itself a weapon. She was tall and imposing, ageless in her way.

When Ursa spotted him, she nodded once, as if she'd been expecting him.

"You've come back," she said.

"Mama Ursa," Ray said softly. Why did he want to go to her?

He also wanted to spit on her. And run. Instead he stood his ground, crossed his arms. He wouldn't let her in. He didn't dare turn to Opal because he couldn't bear to see her being enthralled by Ursa's commanding figure.

"Guns down," Ursa called, her voice deep and loud, and like good little soldiers the women complied.

Now, from the porch, Ursa looked away from Ray and set her eyes on Opal. Ray watched the suspicion shadowing Ursa's face as she came down the steps. The women parted so that she could approach.

Ray took a step back and grabbed Opal's hand. He shielded her with his body.

"Hello, Ray," she said when she was only a foot or two away from them. He'd forgotten how tall she was; the years hadn't diminished her in the least. "Who have you brought us?" she asked, and he remembered that she rarely used her hands to speak, that she chose her words carefully and spoke them with an unnerving calm. "This isn't Cherry."

"You know it wouldn't be," he said. "This is my daughter."

"Your daughter!" Ursa said, and her trembling, breathless voice betrayed her shock. But how could she be surprised?

"I'm Opal," Opal said, and she stepped from behind Ray.

She put out a hand, and Ursa took it.

Ray winced as his mother held his daughter's palm. Ursa stood there in silence, eyeing Opal closely. She searched her granddaughter's face as if she were cataloging all its details and features, trying to figure it out, as if she couldn't make sense of the girl's presence, as if she'd never seen it before.

Did she find Cherry's face there, Ray wondered. Every day he saw Cherry in Opal's cheekbones and in her wide, searching eyes. Did she see Ray's mouth? Ursa must see her own face, too, just as Ray had, despite his best attempts not to. Ursa persisted in the slope of Opal's forehead and in her height. And in her gift. Maybe there was also some of Ruth, Cherry's mother—in the shape of Opal's chin, or in certain expressions. Only Ursa would know.

Opal was a time traveler like Ursa, but so was any other child. Like any child she carried all the past within her blood. She would carry it into the future too.

"You're Ray's *daughter*?" Ursa said softly. "My granddaughter."

"Hi," Opal said, and she let out a laugh.

"Who's your mother, dear? Why didn't she come too?"

Opal stepped back, letting go of Ursa's hand. She was confused.

"Cherry," Ray said. "Cherry is her mother."

"You found her?" Ursa asked, turning to Ray.

He shook his head.

"That's why we're here," Opal said.

"I see," Ursa replied slowly. "Not sure how I can help."

The women watched, their guns slack by their sides. The knife was gone.

"Why don't you come inside?" Mary said, and Opal eyed the house like it might eat her up. Did she think the eastern wing resembled a tumor, sprouting off the side? He did. Ray wanted her near him, but she was still closest to Ursa.

Ursa turned to the other women. "Please step back. Our guests pose no threat to the Farm. We will welcome them. This is my son,

Ray. I didn't tell you about him because I didn't think he would ever return." She clutched her chest over her heart. "But he has."

Ray's face burned and he looked away, down at the ground.

Ursa continued. "And this is his child." Her eyes shined with pride. "Opal. What a beautiful name."

The women muttered hellos but it was obvious they were caught off guard, unsure of their roles, the rules.

"For this once," Ursa announced, "we will allow a man inside."

"No fucking way," someone said.

"Yes *fucking* way," Ursa said. "Ray was born in that house right there, unlike any of you. And he isn't like other men." She paused. "He's *mine*."

17

WHERE WAS SHE? *WHEN* WAS SHE?

It was late fall, chilly. Almost at Y2K. Ray was back, with his daughter. Was this real? It was.

Ursa wanted Opal to like her, she wanted that very much. Ursa already liked Opal. She loved her, actually, even though, thirty minutes before, she had no clue the girl existed. How strange it felt, to be so smitten immediately, and how good it felt too. Ursa loved not only the fact of Opal but the little things too: the sound of her voice, her wit, her long eyelashes, her nose in profile. And she was so confident, so self-assured.

Opal was Cherry's daughter—okay. Too bad. Ursa could get past it, she had to.

Cherry turned her back on this enchanting creature? She abandoned her perfect daughter? How could she? It was a sign that Cherry had never deserved anything good. Ursa would tell Opal that, when the timing seemed right. If the girl wanted Opal's help finding Cherry, that was what Ursa would say.

Over the women's protests, Ursa led them into the house. Ray protested too; he only complied because his daughter insisted, said they'd come all this way, and it was clear this trip was her idea. Ray refused to enter through the mudroom, as he had every day of his youth; he said they would come in by the front door, like guests.

Even then, he appeared ill as he crossed the threshold, like he might tip over. He stopped in the hall for a moment and placed his hands on his chest. He inhaled and then exhaled loudly, eyes open wide. He breathed out and out and out, as if he were emptying his body of every feeling, as if he were exhaling his very self so that it could float far away from here. It broke Ursa's heart.

"It's okay," she tried to say, and he put up a hand as if to say *Shut up.* Ray never would have done that before he left.

He looked so much older now. Not only older, different. It was the way he walked; there was that funny limp, which was perhaps a recent injury, but it was more than that, it was how he held his shoulders back, his chin up, the decisive steps. It was the way he talked. Casually. A city way of speaking, maybe. An LA way. It was how he looked at her. He wasn't in awe of her anymore, and he wasn't cowed; he didn't need anything from his mother. He was only angry. For what, exactly, Ursa wasn't sure.

Ray, her son, was a mystery to her, she realized. A stranger. All the transporting to their past had brought her no closer to the man standing before her. He was unrecognizable in some essential, ineffable way.

"Come in, come in," she said to Opal because only she would listen.

Ursa knew the painted interiors would surprise Ray. She watched him noting the sumptuous rugs, the new furniture, the light fixture like a candelabra hanging in the entryway. His head darted this way and that.

"It's different now," she whispered, and he reared back from her as if burned.

"Who's locked in the purple room?" he asked. "I want to see *everyone.*"

Ursa could only laugh. "I told you, it's different. No kids."

"Only drug profits?" Opal said. She was a sassy one.

"What makes you say that?" asked Emily, still holding her weapon. She gripped the knife handle, black as a crow.

"I told her the house would be a shithole," Ray said. "Obviously you've got funds to fix it."

"Many of the women have construction skills," Ursa said. "But, yes, the weed sales are healthier than ever and so we chose to invest in our home."

She'd shooed away most of the women. Only Mary and Emily flanked her as she led Ray and Opal through some of the lower rooms. Jenny trailed closely behind the group, perhaps feeling possessive. After all, she'd been the one to come upon these two outsiders during patrol.

The other women headed to the kitchen to prepare for Tea, or they pretended to garden outside or do something with the marijuana. Ursa could feel their collectively held breath. It was clear that she'd made many of them unhappy. She would have to make it up to them.

She allowed Ray and Opal to peer into the kitchen, at the women separating the mint from the stems, setting up the mugs, putting the water on the stove to boil. Most of them tried to pretend they weren't being watched, but Sierra made a hissing noise at Ray, and Diana laughed, and when Ray shrugged at them, unimpressed, Ursa was struck, again, by how different he seemed. How could he have changed so much? It was like Ursa had been shot forward in time to this moment; all the years in between, the path from then to now, were lost.

"The morning ritual?" Opal asked.

"It's not called that anymore," Mary replied.

"I told you," Ursa said to Ray, "a lot has changed. No one you knew is here anymore. Well, just me and Mary."

Mary smiled kindly and suggested they see the parlor.

"Where do you live, my dear?" Ursa asked, turning to Opal. "In LA, I assume?"

"We won't tell you anything," Ray said.

"I live in a house on an oil field," Opal said.

"Los Angeles certainly does feel like that, doesn't it?" Ursa said.

Behind them, Jenny cleared her throat. "I don't feel comfortable," she said.

Ray let out a little laugh.

"He shouldn't be in here," Jenny said, "and he definitely shouldn't see Tea. He shouldn't be given access to any of this. To our operations. Less than a month before the new millennium—we're vulnerable. To let outsiders in *now*?"

"I know, Jenny," Ursa said.

"Why are you covered in blood?" Ray asked.

"It's Tony's," Jenny said, leaning toward him.

"Tony is a goat," Mary said.

"She's only trying to frighten you," Ursa said.

"Mission accomplished," Opal said. "She put a gun in my dad's face."

Ursa sighed. "I am sorry about that, but your father knows we take precautions here. And, with the new year coming, Jenny is correct: the threats will only grow more intense."

"You don't really believe that, do you?" Opal said.

"She does," Emily said.

"Why don't we go on a walk?" Ursa cut in. "Just the three of us. I know the others, not only Jenny, would feel more comfortable with that. I can understand it."

"Can we go into the eastern wing first?" Opal asked, and Jenny sucked her teeth. Mary looked shocked.

"Of course you can't," Ursa said. She squinted at Ray. "What did you tell her?"

"Everything," he said.

"You led her astray then. You know I don't let just anyone in there."

"You locked out your own child, for instance," he said. "You never let Cherry in either."

"Cherry didn't deserve to be let in."

"We know what happens in the eastern wing," Opal said.

"How?" Mary asked.

Ursa raised an eyebrow. "You do? Tell me then."

Opal said, "You *tunnel*."

One word. *Tunnel.* The word meant nothing to Ursa, and yet she understood. Could it be? Opal had a different word for it—did it mean—? Was that her *own* word for it?

"We need to go outside," Ursa said, and when she snapped her fingers, Jenny, Emily, and Mary scattered like birds at the sound of gunshot.

∞

So Opal could transport. *Tunnel*, she called it. Beyond confirming that's what she meant, Opal wouldn't elaborate—or she might, but Ray kept stopping her, telling her not to say too much.

"Oh Ray," Ursa tried, and he sneered at her.

"Hurts a little, doesn't it?" he asked. "Not to know."

Never mind him. Ursa loved that she shared this gift with Opal. Had Opal inherited it from her? She must have. What a marvel.

Ursa felt another purr of love for Opal. She loved her so wholly. She loved the way she admired the house and the land and how she pointed at a Cooper's hawk sailing across the sky that was turning blue and said, "If I had those feathers, I'd fly slowly like that too. Show them off to everyone."

Ursa wanted Opal to stay. Imagine what they might create together. Two powerful travelers, separated by a generation? The women would flip. Could she pull her granddaughter into her own transport? Perhaps Opal would pull her into hers.

As they headed to the meadow, Ursa was startled by a deep pang of grief. She had already missed so much of this young woman's life, and there was a chance Opal wouldn't come back after today. Ursa felt her throat closing, and she squeezed her eyes shut before the tears could come. She wouldn't cry in front of Opal, and definitely not in front of Ray.

She'd already lost Ray, who was someone else entirely.

This was what it must be like for other mothers. Mothers who were better than she was. Normal mothers. They must feel this—this loss, at once monumental and mundane—all the time. Her gift had inoculated her from the feeling. For all of Ray's life, Ursa had transported back to him. She'd returned to him as a baby, as a boy. As soon as he got older, she went to him younger. She saw him again: as a young adolescent, as a teenager. She'd done it so many times, she was always close to him. She never let him go, and for that he'd left her.

They reached the meadow. Ray walked ahead so that he stood directly beneath one of the live oaks. He was looking up at its branches, the leaves that shivered in the breeze, his eyes closed, and she wondered what he was thinking about. She had no idea.

She'd lost him.

How had she not understood this before? Motherhood and loss, loss and motherhood—they went hand in hand. Your child isn't who they were the day before, they are slipping through your fingers, they can walk, and now they can drive, and, if you're lucky, they survive, they grow up and move on from you. Ursa realized with a sudden, seizing flash that by transporting she'd rejected the central sacrifice of parenthood. She never let him leave her. Because she could hold Ray as a baby whenever she pleased, she had taken him for granted. She'd had no idea how precious he was. She never cared for him in the present, until it was too late.

Was it too late for her and Opal?

"I don't understand why you came here," Ursa said to Opal, quietly enough that Ray didn't seem to hear. Or maybe he did and he was finally letting his child speak for herself.

"How could I resist? You, doing what I can do, in the eastern wing."

"Ray never knew what it was though. We kept it from the children . . . to protect them." That wasn't the truth, but it would do. "Why do you believe I can help you find Cherry?"

Opal seemed to want to say something, but then she glanced at her dad and said nothing.

"Opal?" Ursa said.

"Do you ever tunnel to my mother?" Opal asked.

Ursa could see that Ray was worried by this conversation. He wore his emotions clearly on his face. That was different too.

"I prefer not to." She paused. "Her years here were unremarkable. To be honest, she always bored me."

Ray made a disgusted sound.

What did they want from her? Did Opal have the same thought Ursa had? That they might transport—tunnel—together?

"I really have to use the bathroom," Ray said, as if to defuse the situation.

Ursa motioned at the forest all around them.

"I'll just be behind that tree over there," he said to Opal. He wore a stern, protective expression.

Ursa would only have a minute alone with the girl—

"Where are you staying?" she asked.

"The Surfer. Why?"

"I'll come for you tonight. Two a.m."

"What?"

"Wait in the lot."

"Why?"

She grabbed Opal's hand. "I'll show you the eastern wing. You want to see it, don't you?"

Ursa could tell by the girl's face that she did.

"The others will never let your father in there. They'd mutiny. You have to come alone. Opal, do you understand what I'm offering? We can travel *together*."

18

THE WORST PART WASN'T THE GUN IN HER FATHER'S
face, or thinking he might be killed, or that they would both be
shot. It wasn't the strange girls running at them, armed, stained with
blood, yelling some Y2K nonsense. It wasn't her father's barely suppressed anger at her grandmother or the pathetic way Ursa kept trying to get his attention, his affection. No, the worst part was that her
father trusted Opal so completely that he didn't even suspect that she
might return to Ursa and the women.

He fell asleep in thirty seconds flat and didn't stir in his motel bed
when she got out of her own. She snuck out of the room, her clothes
in a backpack, shoes in her hand. She changed out of her pajamas
right outside the door, for anyone to see. Someone *had* seen, in fact, a
skeevy dude in a van who said, "All right," as he drove by.

If only her father had woken up. Could he have stopped her? Part
of her wished he would come to the window and call her name. Waiting for Ursa, she nearly lost her nerve. It would be so easy to go back
inside and slip into bed; her dad would never know she'd considered
betraying him. But she couldn't. They'd come all this way to find out
the truth and she wouldn't go back to LA without some answers.

Had it been Ursa in the tunneling? Ray was sure of it, and, back
home, Opal thought so too. Now she was less certain. Ursa acted
like she didn't know Opal existed. She could be lying, but that figure

haunting Cherry and the baby was wild-haired and unhinged, nothing like Ursa, who was so in control, so calm. Whatever Opal had seen was in shadows, surrounded by static. Obscured. Could she really know for sure what she'd seen?

Here was an opportunity to return to the house in the woods, this time without her dad to shield her. To see the eastern wing, which Ray and Cherry had been shut out of. Opal would get to see what Ursa could do. She would gauge her power. What had she done to Cherry? Opal would find out.

Ursa said they were going to tunnel together. What would happen? It might not work, and if it did, it was probably dangerous.

It was freezing outside the Surfer, the parked cars silent in their reproach; the red neon VACANCY sign droned like a thousand insects. Opal palpated the room key in her coat pocket; she should go back inside.

Just then, a white truck pulled into the lot. Ursa. Opal had been waiting for over an hour and by now she was shivering. Her hand trembled as she worked the truck door handle.

Ursa didn't look the least bit surprised that Opal had decided to go through with it.

"I need to be back by sunrise," Opal said as she got in, and her grandmother sped out of the parking lot. In moments the motel was out of sight.

They were silent as they wove their way through Santa Cruz. In the daytime, the city was all charming wood-shingled bungalows and pastel-colored Victorians, wind chimes on the porches and gardens of rosemary, flying windsocks and California flags, wetsuits drying on the line. Beyond the residential blocks were rundown apartment buildings and men smoking outside of liquor stores, taquerias, and skate and surf shops, their front windows festooned with stickers. There were shabby health food stores. The university was up on a hill and the ocean glittered below.

At night, though, the little city felt lonely, weathered as pier pylons. It was darker than in LA. More mysterious. Opal smelled jasmine, saltwater, and a deeper musk she couldn't identify. The cypress trees that hung off the ocean cliffs and dotted the sidewalks and front yards weren't beautiful in the dark but menacing, with their ropy roots, their branches and needles black ink stains against the black sky.

Opal held her breath as Ursa drove away from the city and its landmarks of civilization on a highway so dark that only a small wedge of the world, illuminated by the headlights, was visible. It was as if they were in a spaceship. This was some new planet. Ursa exited, and then they were on a road that quickly narrowed, and the trees on either side opened their mouths, as if to bite them.

"If you're nervous," Ursa said suddenly, "why did you come all this way?"

Opal told herself to look out the window, to play it cool, to play along.

"I'm fine," she said. "Just excited, you know."

No reply. The truck was warm from the heater and Opal felt too hot. Ursa was wrapped in a large brown sweater over the same white dress, and she seemed perfectly comfortable. The radio was off and the engine was so loud.

"I call it transporting," her grandmother said abruptly. "In case you're curious. I was a teenager when it started."

Without prompting, Ursa described being sixteen, lying on the ground, looking up, crickets everywhere, going back to the night of her father's funeral.

"I'm sorry your dad died," Opal said.

"Don't be. He was horrible. A monster, really. Nothing like yours."

Opal didn't want to talk about Ray. She felt too guilty. Would he wake up before she returned and find her bed empty? If he came here to get her, he would be shot on sight.

Now the road was tight and treacherous, and nothing was visible beyond the headlights. They were closer to the woods, to the eastern wing, maybe to some answers about why Cherry abandoned her family.

"You don't have to be scared of me," Ursa said. "I know your dad thinks you should be, but he's wrong. I won't hurt you." She turned to Opal before bringing her gaze back to the road. "Can you trust me?"

"I don't think so, no."

Ursa seemed to consider this.

"We're the only people who know what it feels like, to do what we can do."

"It feels amazing," Opal said softly.

"Doesn't it?"

They began to talk about the pleasure of it. The intensity. The way it wrecked them. Opal felt giddy. They were like two drunks describing the taste of their favorite liquor, or two chefs describing an unforgettable dish they'd made a decade ago. It was a shared imagination, an entire kingdom.

Did you ever notice how—

Doesn't it feel like—

"What's your method?" Ursa asked.

Opal wanted to tell her about the Accumulator, but to do so, she would have to tell her about Doc, and Isla Patricia, and the screaming-into-a-pillow stuff. She couldn't. Ursa was dangerous. She had failed to protect Ray. Same with Cherry. She had scared Cherry away and now Opal didn't know her mother. Ursa was the reason Ray had gone to such great lengths to protect Opal. Now it was Opal's turn to protect Ray.

"Nothing interesting," Opal said. "I sit in a closet, basically."

Ursa hooted and thrummed her fingers against the steering wheel, and for a second she resembled Ray. "I used to use an armoire."

"No way!"

"Now you see why we have to go to the eastern wing together," Ursa said.

"What's going to happen?" Opal asked.

"Something magical, no doubt."

By the time, they reached the hidden road that led to the house, the plan was already materializing. They would try it. Just once.

"And do what exactly?" Opal asked. "Like you do it, and I try to come with you?"

"Yes. And I come with you. Isn't that why you're here?" Ursa said. "You came because you needed help with Cherry. She grew up on this land."

Why was it that Ursa only spoke of Cherry as a girl raised by the mamas? Was that Ursa's only access to her? Doubt flashed through Opal again; maybe it wasn't Ursa in the tunnel. She didn't know what to think.

Her grandmother was looking at her. "Opal. Don't you want me to take you to Cherry?"

Opal hadn't thought of that. With Ursa's help, she would see her parents, years ago. She would get to witness them. See her mother as a girl, her father as a boy. The idea was so dizzying Opal thought she might levitate from her seat and bump her head on the cab ceiling.

Ursa slowed the truck; they were almost there.

"And you'll show me LA," Ursa said. "I want to see Ray. The years that I missed."

They had no idea if it would work. Opal didn't assume it would; she didn't want to be overcome with disappointment if it didn't. Still, she wanted it to. Badly. Her father had revealed a lot over the past few days, yet it would mean so much to be able to see his upbringing for herself. She could come back to the motel and tell Ray what she'd experienced. Maybe she would see something that would unlock it all, help them understand Cherry. Finally, she would really, truly get it.

And she would see her mother again—a younger version, but her mother nonetheless.

This possibility took her breath away. It made her life legible. *This* was what her gift was for.

Ursa directed the truck onto the property, and the tight maze led them past a small house—more like a shed or a kiosk—where a woman stood guard. Ursa tapped the horn once and the woman waved. Ursa kept driving.

When they arrived at the house, no one came running, no one blew the airhorn. Two women sat in rockers at the end of the porch, smoking a joint.

"Ursa!" one of them crooned.

"Go to bed, Sunshine," Ursa said, but she said it sweetly, like a mother might.

When they walked inside the house, Mary was waiting in the dark kitchen with a mug of milky-looking tea.

"Opal," she said, eyes twinkling.

"Mary," Ursa said, removing her sweater. "You're still up? At this hour?"

"When you told me you were retrieving Opal to transport, well I—"

"You can't come with us."

"But someone needs to guard—"

"Opal will do it. She will make a wonderful guard."

So Mary had not caught on to what Opal could do. Ursa didn't tell her either.

"Oh, I see," Mary said, and Opal wondered what Mary had been through, all these years, with Ursa.

"Opal will be sure to give you a hug when we're done," Ursa said gruffly and took Opal's hand. Her palm was soft and smooth, and without another word to Mary she led Opal through a corridor that bent at an odd angle and opened a door that met another hallway. It was if the house were a maze, bigger on the inside than the outside; Opal was dizzy, lost. And her heart was pounding. Before her lay the eastern wing.

19

THE LARGE, HEXAGONAL ROOM REMINDED OPAL OF A yoga studio with its shiny wood floors and empty wide-open space. It was free of furniture; at the same time, it was full of something else. An energy that Opal recognized from the garage. Syrupy, fizzy, al dente.

"I know this feeling," Opal said.

"The membrane is ready, isn't it?"

Ursa locked them inside.

"Is this really okay?" Opal asked. "The other women, they—"

"I decide who comes in here with me."

Ursa wasn't sure how they might proceed, and she didn't want Opal to see that she was nervous and then lose her nerve too. The thought of finding Ray, younger, in LA, was making Ursa feel queasy. If they were successful—it would be such a gift. It would mean she hadn't lost those decades of her son's life after all. Not totally.

Opal would have to go first though; Ursa couldn't wait.

"I'd like you to tunnel first." Ursa tried to keep her voice steady. "Then I'll transport."

"Fine with me," Opal said, who felt as she had in the truck, like a helium balloon anchored to Earth by a mere string. It might snap at any moment and send her flying away.

"What if there are consequences for doing it together?" she asked.

Ursa could tell that Opal was upset about something. Anxious.

"There is that risk, yes," Ursa said. "But it'll be worth it."

"As for my tunneling," Opal said. "I won't show you Cherry."

"I don't care about her," Ursa said. "You're lucky Ray's the one who stayed. He's the one I want to see."

"But you'll show me Cherry, right?" Opal asked. "I want to see her."

"You need to see her," Ursa said. "Is that right?"

It was.

"How should we proceed?" Ursa asked.

"I have these exercises I do with my friend. To get me into the tunnel more easily. Maybe that would work?"

"Show me."

They began.

Palms touching, breathing together, Opal closed her eyes. Ursa left her eyes open to unseeing slits.

It took only a moment.

Opal tipped into her own past as she had with Fab. She went as gracefully as possible, without fear or brutality.

At once, Ursa sensed the pull of her granddaughter's tunneling and let it take her, like a leaf surrenders to the wind. It felt funny to Opal, to have her grandmother there with her; it was even a little uncomfortable. It was like being tickled, like adjusting your eyes to light after being bathed in darkness. Ursa felt it too. To her, it was like being pregnant and feeling your baby doing a backflip within you before disappearing into your depths like a fish into the deepest part of the ocean.

Opal carried Ursa with her.

Together, it was different.

Picture a pink room. Or not a room, but a corridor. Not a mouth, but a throat. Picture a birth canal. Ursa and Opal were swept into it. At first, they could not see each other completely in this space: their bodies were grains of white, as if they were made of salt.

In the eastern wing, Ursa and Opal were merely two bodies, emitting a faint glow between them. The energy inside the sphere of light in which they sat was strong, and it was growing stronger. Unseen, it thrummed.

Usually, Opal arrived at a past moment so quickly she saw nothing until she was there. But taking Ursa with her slowed it down, and she was able to glimpse some of her life as it whipped by. She couldn't help but pause. And then she moved on. Wrong moment. Keep going.

Whoosh.

Here she is. Here they are.

Opal at ten. Outside with Fab on Edinburgh. There was the Chu house across the street, that stupid Rottweiler barking his head off two doors down, a helicopter overhead, a far-off ambulance siren. A perfect seventy-degree day, the kind of LA weather that makes you want to weep it's so godly, the air like silk against your bare arms. Opal shivered as the moment soaked into her.

It felt so good that she almost forgot about Ursa. But there her grandmother stood, right next to her, in the same loose dress she'd been wearing in the eastern wing. She was looking around at everything, eyes wet with joy, lips slightly parted.

We did it!

At Opal's words, Ursa turned to her granddaughter.

We did. Look at you there. With your little friend.

That's Fab. My dad will come out in a sec.

They stood watching Opal and Fab play with chalk on the sidewalk. They were writing their names and then drawing objects and making the other guess what it was. Opal let the joy of the game sift through her. Ursa couldn't take her eyes off little Opal.

When Ray stepped out of the house, Ursa gasped. In the eastern wing, Ursa clutched tighter to Opal's palms. On Edinburgh Avenue, Opal smiled at her grandmother.

Ray's hair was short, face clean-shaven. He wore jeans and a button-down shirt with the sleeves rolled up. A wristwatch. He was barefoot. His hands held two juice pouches for the kids, and as he held them aloft, he sang in a high-pitched voice, "La da deeeeeeee, la dee daaaaaa."

Opal knew that because Ursa hadn't watched television in over forty years, she didn't know this was his terrible Julia Child impression.

"Dad!" Little Opal squealed. "Fab, look, Capri Sun!"

Little Opal came running to him to grab the pouches of juice.

Watch this. It's funny.

Ursa did as Opal instructed.

Ray was offering to lie down so the girls could trace him.

"You're dead!" Opal yelled, laughing, and Fab said, "We got a warm one here, folks." And then they were detectives, tracing Ray's corpse, conjecturing where the bullet had come from, if it matched the gun they'd recently found in the lake. Mobsters at it again, no doubt.

A bit morbid for kids your age, don't you think?

Adult Opal grinned. Ursa wondered what it would be like to feel what Opal felt. Safe. Ray lay as still as he could, but Ursa saw that a smirk tugged at her son's mouth. She knew that face of his, the one he made when he couldn't repress a joke, when he was bursting with an idea. He was loving this. He loved being with Opal.

They watched for a bit longer and then Opal turned to Ursa. *Okay, it's your turn.*

Ursa was still looking at Ray, who had stood and brushed off his jeans. He was telling the girls it was almost time to come inside. Ursa felt so lucky, blessed even, to have the chance to see him this way: so happy, so loved and loving. That was Ray, her boy, now a man. A good one. He hadn't wanted her in his life, he didn't want his own mother to witness these years—even now, Ursa didn't quite grasp why—and yet, she did. She was here, and her presence hurt no one. Ray was such a good dad. And she knew it for sure. No matter what happened to Opal, she would be all right because she had Ray. Ursa couldn't have damaged him all that badly if he'd raised Opal so well.

Thank you for showing me this.

Of course.

I did love him. I do. I love him.

I know.

They held hands. Opal trembled. She wanted to see Cherry so badly, as much as Ursa wanted to see Ray, probably more so.

Ursa could give this to her. Just because she had messed up with Ray didn't mean she couldn't do right by Opal.

They closed their eyes and slipped back into the membrane. The plan had been to return to the eastern wing, but as soon as they left Opal's childhood, Ursa realized they could get into her own time without returning to the present. Their pasts, their tunnels, were overlapping, tangling, blurring.

It was easy. There it was.

Wordlessly, Ursa pulled Opal through; she knew she was in her time because it felt as familiar as a hallway in her house.

The pink, the pink, they were salt again, they were going.

Ursa wanted to take Opal to one of the fiddle sessions on the land, one of the only times she was sure to find both Cherry and Ray. It seemed the least damning too. It would be festive, and Opal would see that it hadn't been all tragedy: there had been music and natural beauty and inebriated mamas dancing as the kids threw leaves into the fire to watch them spark, the canopy of the forest watching over them. Ray must have carried some of that happiness to LA and passed it on to Opal. She hoped it was part of the reason they had returned to her.

Why had Ray hung on only to the bad parts of his childhood? He hadn't given Ursa any credit. Hadn't she tried her best? The land wasn't terrible. Not always. Sometimes it was fun, and it was always beautiful.

Opal felt Ursa tugging them through her past, time's mouth sucking them back and back.

It was right here—Ursa was sure of it, one of the fiddle nights, the children laughing as the mamas performed their silly chicken dances, squawking.

But no.

They were hurtling further back than that, pulled by a force stronger than a crowd.

Ursa felt swept away, as if by a current, and it scared her because this had never happened in a transport. Opal didn't know what was going on, only that it seemed to be taking a long time. They were still white as salt. They were salt. Ursa was groaning; in the eastern wing, she was trying to emerge. She wanted to start over, or not try at all, but the pull was too powerful.

Whoosh.

They landed in Ursa's bedroom.

It was gray with darkness.

Ray, a small child in the bed, is just a lump in the blankets. Ursa, a few years older than Opal is now, sits up next to him, pulled from sleep by a sound downstairs. She wears a long white nightgown not much different than the dress she wears tonight, in the eastern wing.

Ursa knows immediately where she is. When she is.

No, no. This isn't right.

She takes Opal's hand and closes her eyes, as if to slip back into the membrane, but Opal keeps her eyes open. They're at the edge of the room, their backs nearly touching the bureau.

What's going on? Look at you. You're so pretty. But you look sad. Is that my dad?

He's younger than I wanted him to be.

How old, you think?

Three.

Wow. I wish you'd pull off the covers so I could see him.

You won't see Cherry here though. I made a mistake. This isn't right.

Ursa tried to close her eyes again and yank herself and Opal out of there. This was not when she wanted to be, but Opal was stunned by the image of her father, just a little boy, and she did not help her grandmother slip out of there.

Ursa-in-the-nightgown got out of bed, listening for something. A noise downstairs. A rustling. Opal heard it too.

After glancing at sleeping Ray, Ursa-in-the-nightgown crept out of the room.

When she was gone, Opal tried to get a better look at her dad—he was so tiny! The quilt covered all but his hair. This was nothing to see, not really, and with Ursa's absence, the room was going blurry. Opal turned to her grandmother.

Follow yourself.

Ursa tried once more to close her eyes and click them out of there, back into the membrane, but it wasn't working.

Opal nudged her.

Why are you trying to escape?

Opal was already walking out of the room. The time no longer belonged only to Ursa.

It was weird to tunnel through someone else's life, like being in a dream, at once familiar and off-kilter. Opal followed Ursa-in-the-nightgown down the hallway. Her grandmother's hair was light brown and scraggly, and she was thinner than Opal expected. Her nightgown was so threadbare you could see right through it. She wasn't wearing any underwear.

Opal wanted to turn back to the bedroom to see her dad again. He was so young. She wondered if Cherry had even been born yet.

This would be her only chance, and she knew it, and maybe Ursa was right to get out of this moment. Too soon. Opal would miss seeing her mother.

And yet, something told Opal to stay.

Someone was downstairs, and it was clear that younger Ursa was confused by the noises. That's what she was doing—investigating.

Behind Opal, older Ursa followed. Her hand skimmed Opal's shoulder.

Stop, Opal. This isn't—

Opal shrugged her off and kept walking, and her grandmother had no choice but to follow.

Ursa knew who would be downstairs in the entryway. Ursa had

never transported back to this moment because she had no desire to relive it. And yet, here she was, forced to—and with her granddaughter. This was a punishment.

Opal got to the bottom of the staircase. There was Ursa-in-the-nightgown, and by the front door stood another woman. She was young, younger than Opal even. Her hair was brown and parted in the middle, knotted as a nest. She wore a blue dress that resembled a pillowcase: loose and rectangular. It hung baggy. Across the chest were two dark stains. She was pulling on her sweater.

Who's that?

We have to get out of here, dear.

Tell me who that is.

Ursa didn't have to answer because her younger self did it for her. "Ruth, what are you doing up? You need to be in bed."

She was just some mama.

No she wasn't. Ruth. I know that name. That's Cherry's mother.

We should go. Help me leave. Do you really want to see this?

Ursa had a point, Opal thought. No memories were better than bad ones.

But no, she'd already learned that lesson, rejected that idea. Her father had been wrong. Her gift wasn't about nostalgia. She had to stay.

Then she saw the baby.

Cherry.

Her mother. At the beginning. A baby. New to this world. Unharmed, unleft.

Ruth had wrapped her in a blanket and set her on the floor. The baby had been laid carefully atop a bag.

"Going somewhere?" Younger Ursa asked.

Her grandmother spoke to Ruth imperiously. Ruth seemed frightened. She was trying not to show it. She didn't pause in buttoning her sweater. She was hurrying.

Ursa tried once more. She grabbed Opal's hand and squeezed her eyes tight, trying to break into the membrane. It was a wall. She could not pass.

"We've got to go," Ruth said.

"At this hour? Where?"

"To find Charlie."

"Oh, honey," Ursa said.

"I'll walk myself and Cherry to the bus station," Ruth said. "Thank you for your hospitality."

Oh my god.

Ursa was still holding on to Opal's hand, and Opal let go.

Now Ruth was bending down to pick up the baby, who started to whimper.

"Did Charlie tell you he loved you?" Ursa asked, and when Ruth didn't answer, she said, "He told me the same thing."

Ruth looked like she'd been slapped.

"You didn't know? Charlie was my lover."

When Ruth didn't answer, Ursa continued: "He's gone, Ruth. Or at least until he drops off the next girl."

Watching herself talk to Ruth, Ursa flinched at her own cruelty. She knew, even as she said it, that she was wrong, that Ruth was right. Charlie wasn't planning on finding another woman. He was in love with Ruth. She'd seen how tender he was with her.

"You're young, Ruth."

"So are you."

"Hardly. I've got a child and this house. No family. This is my life."

The baby was crying harder now, and Ursa gestured to take her. Ruth looked around Ursa, as if expecting another woman to come out to see what all the fuss was about. Opal could tell Ruth didn't want to wake anyone else. Why not? What was she afraid of?

Cherry's whimper became a soft mewl of a cry.

Ursa said, "If she cries any louder, the others will come downstairs."

Ruth handed the baby over, and Opal sucked in her breath.

No, no, no.

Ursa-in-the-nightgown smiled. She began to rock the baby. In a minute, Cherry was calm.

"What's your life look like without this baby to care for?" Ursa asked.

Ruth was stone-faced.

"Go on," Ursa said.

"I was supposed to matriculate at Cal in the fall," Ruth answered softly.

"Wow, that's wonderful!" She paused. "Hawk's still nursing, you know. There's milk here."

"I know."

"You don't want this life. Don't give up everything for this."

"She's my child."

"True, but what will everyone say, a girl meant for college, saddled with a baby?"

Opal felt sick—in part because she understood Ursa's arguments. They were rational. Ruth had gotten into college. Into Berkeley! And she was so young.

But Cherry was Ruth's baby. Ruth did not want to leave Cherry.

Ursa only had to glance at Opal to recognize her distress. Could Opal see through Ursa's intentions? Did she see that they were impure?

Ursa knew that Ruth's instincts had been correct: Charlie would be back for her. Not only for her, but for their baby. He loved Ruth. He'd only left to help out his brother and get some money so he and Ruth and their baby could rent a larger apartment. In her bones, Ursa was sure that if Charlie hadn't died, shot in that bar in Idaho, he would have returned.

In the hallway, the sky graying outside, an owl hooting, young Ursa was already hatching her plan. Charlie would come back, and soon. He'd find his new baby, but not his new girl. Heartless Ruth, Ursa would tell him. Ruth is no woman, no mother, she'd say. She's a girl. Don't pretend. She's different from you and me, Charlie. Her kind doesn't know right from wrong. She just left her baby on the floor by the front door. Could've caught a cold. Or worse.

It would hurt Charlie. But then he might see Ursa in the way she deserved to be seen.

Now, standing next to Opal, Ursa was grateful her granddaughter could only watch what had happened and that she couldn't read Ursa's thoughts, or her motivations.

"It's better for you," Ursa-in-the-nightgown said to Ruth. "And better for her." She gestured at the baby. "You see how happy she is here?"

Ruth nodded.

"You got yourself into trouble. That's all. You can go back. It never happened. Okay?"

Pause.

"Okay?" Ursa said again.

"Okay."

Hearing Ruth give in, Opal let out a little cry. Ruth left Cherry, and then Cherry left Opal. Mothers leaving their daughters. The same story told again and again.

Ruth wiped her eyes with the palms of her hands; Opal wondered if Cherry had done the same thing before she escaped LA in the middle of the night. Did she take one final look at Opal before leaving? Did she try not to cry?

Ruth reached out to hold the baby one last time. Ursa said, "Why torture yourself?" Ruth seemed to understand. She kissed the baby on her forehead and retrieved her bag. She held the door open. The sun was just starting to rise. The owl was silent; maybe it had gone to sleep.

"We'll take care of her," Ursa said. "She's in good hands. Go back to your family."

You think she wanted this?

It was for the best.

Maybe. Maybe not.

Let's go now, Opal. Don't torture yourself.

It was the wrong thing to say. Don't torture yourself. The same line used on Ruth. As if their pain were self-inflicted.

Ruth was on the other side of the open door when something stopped her. Ursa and Opal both sensed her beam of need, of love and duty and animal urge. Her breasts were weeping milk. She wanted her baby. Ursa had known it all along, and now Opal would know it too.

Ruth turned back. She shook her head, reached for the baby. Ursa stepped away, the child at her chest, one hand on the door, ready to shut it. She told herself Charlie would be back.

"No," Ursa said. "Don't turn weak now. Do what's right for your child."

Ruth tried to speak but Ursa held up a hand. "You're leaving."

"No, I—" Ruth said.

Another woman might have tried to punch Ursa, push herself into the house, but Ruth was good, and Opal could see that she was worried that Ursa would drop the child in the skirmish. Cherry could not be hurt. Her baby mattered most.

"Please," Ruth said.

Ursa shut the door in Ruth's face. Opal wanted to scream.

You tried to get us out of here before I saw what you did.

Ursa did not know what to say.

Ruth was out in the cold, locked out of the house, and her child was inside. She began to pound on the door. Then kick. Ruth was going to wake everyone up.

"Ursa," she was pleading. "Let me in."

Let her in, my god, let her in.

Ruth was crying. You could hear her wet sobs through the door. Then they heard her walking down the porch steps.

Opal thought Ruth was gone, but Ursa knew she wasn't. And so, unlike her granddaughter, or her younger self, she didn't flinch when the rock came sailing through the pane of stained glass at the top of the door. Ursa-in-the-nightgown gasped.

"Ursa?"

Mary was at the bottom of the stairs, a blanket wrapped around her shoulders. "Who's here?" she whispered, fear creasing her brow.

Who's that?

Don't worry about it.

"Mary," Ursa-in-the-nightgown said.

"Why didn't you whistle?" Mary asked.

Ursa-in-the-nightgown shook her head and hushed her.

"Take this," she whispered.

The hallway floor was shimmering with green and purple glass and as Ursa walked to Mary and handed her the baby, a shard caught in her heel. It didn't stop Ursa. From the closet, she retrieved their one rifle.

No. Ursa. No.

Ursa-in-the-nightgown was opening the door partway, wide enough to show her face. There was Ruth, on the porch.

Opal tried to step closer to Ursa-in-the-nightgown; maybe she could yank the weapon out of her hand, step between the women. She had to do something. Alter this course. But she couldn't move any closer. She wasn't powerful enough.

"You could have hit Cherry with that rock!" Ursa-in-the-nightgown hissed. "You could have killed her."

"Give me my baby."

"Don't you see this gun? Get out of here before I call someone to drag you away."

"Give me my baby," Ruth repeated.

Ursa said, "What baby?" As if Cherry weren't right behind her in Mary's arms. "Do you think anyone will believe you? You bring anyone here and the baby will disappear."

Ursa cocked the gun.

"Now get out of here before I shoot you."

Opal stepped away from the older Ursa, as if she were contagious with something deadly.

When Ruth didn't move, Ursa-in-the-nightgown said, "I said I'd take care of her. Now go." She slammed the gun against the threshold and Ruth jumped back, terrified.

Ursa shut the door, and Opal watched the younger Ursa limp to take baby Cherry from Mary. She limped to the parlor.

"Go back to bed," she said over her shoulder.

When Mary didn't move, Ursa said, "Now, Mary. This is for the best."

Mary nodded once and turned. She headed upstairs.

Ursa would tell the mamas—she did tell them—that she had been the one to throw the rock, out of anger at Ruth and her leaving.

"I was so angry with her," Ursa would say. Did say. Mary pretended to be as shocked as the others.

Ursa and Opal watched from the window as Ruth ran down the driveway toward the road, the trees golden in the dawn light, until she was gone.

Opal faced Ursa, the older one. The younger Ursa was on the parlor couch with the baby, acting as if nothing were wrong, as if her heel weren't covered in blood red as garnets and she hadn't cast out the mother of the child she held.

My father was right about you.

You don't understand what you saw. There's more to it.

Bullshit. I understand it perfectly. You were trying to hide the truth from me.

Opal imagined her dad, asleep in a motel room. He hated his mother and he didn't even know this story.

I'm done with you.

Opal, listen to me. You must. I'm your grandmother.

So is Ruth.

How dare you!

Ursa was so angry she was juddering, hands shaking, and Opal felt afraid. The air thickened as the younger Ursa held the baby to her chest, her face placid, her heel weeping blood. The room grew cloudy as Opal watched her. It was as if the fog Opal walked through that morning were snaking its way into the house like a poison.

She had to get out of there.

Opal shut her eyes. Her body went slack, and Ursa felt her tugging free. The membrane was letting her slip away. Ursa tried to follow, but by the time she got into the pink, Opal was gone.

When Opal came to, she saw that Ursa was still in the tunnel, her eyes open but unseeing. The eastern wing's walls were cracked, like a spoon had whacked an eggshell. It smelled of burned hair, of rot.

Ursa mouthed indiscernible words, like a person caught in a nightmare. Opal stood quickly. She was lightheaded and very thirsty. She had to get away.

When she pushed the door open, Mary was crouched on the floor, vomiting into a bucket, only inches away. A dread had descended on the eastern wing and into the hallway.

"Something is terribly wrong," Mary said.

Opal didn't bother answering as she pushed past her.

∞

Mary tried calling Ursa's name. She tugged at her arms. The energy in the room was now worse than dreadful—it was despairing.

Where was Ursa?

At first, she was in the membrane—in the mouth, the throat, the canal. In the pink. Calling for Opal even though Opal was long gone. Ursa wished she could spirit her granddaughter to a better past, to the fiddling, to all the cozy wildness and laughter, even as she knew it would be no use. Opal saw what Ursa had done to Ruth. She would never forgive her.

Well, so what? What did Ursa need that ungrateful girl for? Opal left, just like everyone else. Everyone Ursa had ever loved ended up leaving her.

How dare Opal leave?

But Ursa loved her.

She let out a scream, her shaking hands skittering in the air between her and her younger self. She would gouge her own eyes out. The young woman on the couch just sat there, cradling an infant that didn't belong to her. Ursa's fingers ransacked her hair and scratched at her cheeks, she stamped her feet. She wanted to rip her dress off and writhe before her younger self and that worthless baby who had ruined her life. And now ruined her second chance with her son and her only chance with her granddaughter.

In the eastern wing, Ursa's body keened with grief, her eyes now closed tightly as if against a harsh light. Mary tried to bring her back by slapping her and yelling her name; it was like the mamas all over again, that terrible set of days that had nearly killed Mama Alice, what brought Karin back and scared everyone else off. They'd never get past this.

"Ursa!" Mary screamed again, and a wave of nausea slammed into her.

Within seconds the others were at the eastern wing: Sunshine, Phoebe, Angelica, Jenny. They rushed in, disheveled from sleep, or stoned, or hyper with the vigilance of a nightshift. Maritza, with a toothbrush in one hand and a gun in another, followed close behind. Sierra ran in. Azadeh. When they saw Ursa on the floor, they were frightened and confused. And then the nausea that tore through Mary found them too. Their heads throbbed; they felt an unbelievable pressure. Their eyeballs would be crushed like grapes.

They screamed in pain. They called Ursa's name to stop it.

Their entreaties didn't work because Ursa didn't want to come back. In the membrane, she heard their groans, their calls for her to end this, and she wanted nothing to do with them. They had nothing to offer her.

It was when Ursa spun away from the sound of their voices that she realized something was different. While it was true that Opal had left the membrane, her timeline was still there, knotted up with Ursa's.

Ursa could still get inside of it.

Picture Ursa, in her long shapeless dress, lit with anger and grief, discovering she could slip out of her own time, with all its unrelenting pain, and into another's. Picture her as she hurtles away from her past into Opal's, riding through the pink, seeking out the very person Opal wanted to find.

Opal called Ursa a monster. Ursa supposed it was true. And if she wasn't a monster, what she had done was monstrous. There was no difference.

What did it matter if she hurt Opal? she thought. The girl had been planning to leave as soon as she had exacted a promise from Ursa. All Opal wanted was Cherry. Like Ray. Like Charlie.

It was easy to find Cherry inside Opal's time. She was special to Opal and so it was as if certain moments shined brighter than others. Like someone had left on the porchlight.

Here is Cherry. Making spaghetti. Music blaring. The baby on the floor, playing.

And here. Placing the baby on the bed, to change her diaper.

And here. Laughing with a friend in a clothing boutique.

Ursa wants to roar, she is so powerful. How could Cherry, that spoiled brat, that ingrate, run from the mamas? How could she take Ray with her? How could she take Opal, who was part of Ursa? Didn't anyone ever stop to think what *Ursa* had gone through, what sacrifices she'd made? By ten years old, not even Ursa's body had belonged to her.

Well, now Cherry would know how it felt.

Here was Cherry. Making a snack for the baby.

And here. Giving the baby a bath.

Brimming with poisonous thoughts, Ursa got her revenge.

With her rage, she boiled the walls until they glittered with heat.

She pounded into the bedroom that sheltered mother and child.

Her hatred hardened every surface of the room, and the walls damp-
ened with her mold until they dripped. They beaded with her sweat.
They would crumble on Cherry.

Ursa slinked in and everything wobbled. Fuzzed in fear.

Ursa shoved against Cherry.

Out. Get out of here.

Haunting came effortlessly. Perhaps, she thought, this had been
her purpose all along.

In the eastern wing, the women cried. The pain was so great it was
like someone was scratching at their insides with a spike, like the air
would crush them. Something was terribly wrong. They had to get
Ursa out of there, and they couldn't. The walls rippled, and the cracks
that Opal had noticed were cutting deeper and deeper. Ursa writhed.

Again, and again, Little Opal froze at her grandmother's presence, and Cherry read it as a warning. A sign.

Go, Cherry. Leave.

It wasn't until Ursa saw Ray standing at the entrance to Baby
Opal's bedroom, panicked because Cherry had disappeared in the
night, that she realized what she'd done.

Her plan worked. Cherry was gone.

And there was her son. So young. So bewildered, returned to her.

He had no one but Opal.

At the sight of the baby, stiff in the crib, he pissed himself. He
cried out.

That spineless, heartless man. Peeing in his pants like a baby. He
didn't deserve all he had. Did her son have any idea how lucky he was?

"Ursa!" Mary yelled from the eastern wing, sobbing.

Ursa knew she had just vomited, that if she didn't get out of the
membrane, the eastern wing might kill them.

She returned to her own time. Even with all its pain and regret, it
was hers, and she couldn't forsake it for good. She couldn't live forever
in Opal's time. She wasn't a ghost.

She swam away from her past. She would slip back into the eastern wing. She would come to and confess to Mary what she had done. Mary wasn't Karin; she would forgive Ursa her every trespass.

Right here was an opening—

Ursa couldn't do it. Every time she tried to maneuver out of the past, the connection was closed. As locked up as a door.

Picture it. You're inside the birth canal, narrow and dark, but there's a glow just ahead. A promise. Someone's waiting.

Now imagine the glow, the light, going out.

Ursa tried moving one way, then another. The membrane felt as unmembrane-like as ever. It turned from tapioca to chalk. She moaned, trying to push forward to the eastern wing. She felt herself there, in her body, waiting, and then the connection to her body was severed.

Ursa was trapped.

20

OPAL DIDN'T KNOW HOW SHE DID IT, BUT SHE GOT OUT of the house. She ignored Mary, stricken over her vomit bucket. Served her right: Mary was a coward. She was an accomplice to evil.

Opal broke free from the young women who approached her as she exited the hallway. They wanted a hug, asked her if she needed some barley tea, a nice quilt for the night. *No, no,* she muttered. *I have to pee. I'm cool.* From the eastern wing came a moan, and then some panicked yelling, and everyone rushed toward the sound. Unimpeded, Opal kept moving until she was on the porch, panting. The sun was just about to rise, the sky dark gray edged with rose gold.

She recalled Ursa as they were parking in front of the house. Her grandmother had left the keys to the truck in the ignition. A real country move, Opal remembered thinking. Only someone who lived in the middle of nowhere would leave their vehicle up for grabs like that.

Opal got into the unlocked truck and started it. She was terribly thirsty, and she felt weaker than she ever had after a tunneling, but she had to get out of here. If she got stuck in the tentacle, she'd be in danger. When Ursa came to, she would tell them to catch Opal. They would kill her. Or they'd find out what she could do and they wouldn't let her leave. She would be their hostage. Her father would come to find her, and they'd shoot him on sight.

Without looking back at the house, she headed down the driveway.

She prayed no one had seen her, that they were still distracted by Ursa in the eastern wing.

Either the mazes weren't very advanced or Opal remembered when to turn and when not to, because before she knew it she was nosing the truck onto the highway. She finally let herself breathe. With shaking hands, she turned on the heat and then accelerated.

The sun was up by the time she got to the motel. She pulled into the lot and there was her father, waiting outside their front door, his breath smoking in the cold. He had two plastic bottles of water next to him.

Opal jumped out of the truck. "Dad—"

"Drink this," he said, as he always did after she tunneled.

When she had emptied both bottles, she asked, "How did you know?"

"I'm just relieved you're okay," he said.

"You let me go."

"I promised myself you'd be fine. You had to do it alone, or you'd never find out what happened to your mother."

"I still don't know." She wanted to cry.

He ushered her back into the room and they each sat on the edges of their beds as she described what happened. What she'd seen. "You were right, Dad. She's a monster."

Her father seemed struck speechless. Wordlessly, he got up and sat next to her. He put his arm around her.

"I left—I just, I got out. I came to, and I left her there. I was lucky it was so easy. I never want to tunnel again."

"I don't blame you," he said.

"Dad, you saw your mom's face when we arrived yesterday. She was surprised to see me. That wasn't some ruse. I thought maybe it was, but it wasn't. I'm sure of it now. She didn't know I existed—"

She stopped herself. She wasn't ready to say more, to admit that whatever Ursa did to Cherry hadn't happened yet.

She was crying now. "Dad, do you think *I* caused everything?"

He didn't answer, but he didn't let her go either. "Let's just go home," he said.

Part

SIX

21

"LET'S GO BACK IN TIME. LET'S EXPERIENCE SOME OF your earliest memories."

As she spoke, Phoenix leaned back in her office chair until it squeaked, and then she tapped the eraser-end of her pencil against her legal pad.

The pencil's tip was always newly sharpened when Cherry first sat down for her fifty-minute sessions—and it looked dull by the end. During her first visit four months ago, Cherry wondered if Phoenix was a better transcriber than therapist, but then Phoenix stopped scribbling and fixed her green eyes on Cherry and said, "Let's think about what led you here today, on this beautifully chilly morning in December. It's wonderful, Arnette, that you made this appointment for yourself. In fact, it's empowering." Then she did her now-familiar chair lean, her trademark pencil tap. "But tell me: What's the driving force to seek therapy at this time? Why *now*?"

Cherry felt safe with Phoenix, who looked to be in her midfifties, her hair trimmed to an unfussy gray bob, her navy-blue tunic and slacks practical but elegant. On her left index finger was a tattooed wedding band. She grew up right here in Ojai to bohemian artist parents.

"My kingdom for a forgettable name like Susan," she joked when they first shook hands. "That's all I wanted as a little girl."

Cherry knew immediately that she would tell Phoenix Whitlock,

MA, LMFT, that her real name wasn't Arnette Swanson. She knew she would tell her about the mamas, about Ray, about Opal. About leaving Opal. She would tell her how, eighteen years ago, she went to see a dead-eyed man in a trailer park outside Lancaster who sold her, for two thousand dollars cash, a brand-new identity, complete with a social security number.

She would tell Phoenix Whitlock, MA, LMFT, that she never looked back.

Or tried not to. Until now.

On that first visit, she admitted to Phoenix that as the year edged closer to its end, the prospect of a new millennium rippling through town, everyone discussing it with a mix of excitement and trepidation, she experienced a new unease.

"Lately, I've been feeling anxious. Like something isn't right," Cherry said. "I'm having trouble sleeping, for one. And a stressful shift at the movie theater might make me cry, or I'll be hyperventilating. I feel unsteady. I feel . . ." she grappled for the right word. "I feel off. I feel wrong."

"I'm glad you decided to get help."

"A long time ago, I had what I think was a mental breakdown. A psychotic break, maybe? Hallucinations. Paranoia. It was awful."

Phoenix began writing again. "Did you seek help?" She looked up. "A diagnosis?"

Cherry shook her head. "Nothing like that. I didn't grow up going to doctors."

"I see. But you've come to me."

"I'm afraid that if I don't do anything about how I'm feeling, it might happen again." She exhaled, surprised by the tears in her eyes. "I have to do something about my life. Or else. I have to face the choices I made."

"Sounds like a reckoning," Phoenix said, and Cherry said that was exactly right.

She remembered Ray, in LA, when it was really bad, telling her to see a shrink. *You tell your therapist your feelings,* he explained in that condescending tone.

What a tragedy it took her this long.

Four months into therapy, she still had so much to say, to untangle.

Now she squeezed the stress ball Phoenix urged her to use. The therapist had all sorts of helpful tools to make patients comfortable, to calm them, to get them talking: the stress balls and the corduroy throw pillows that felt good to hug. The boxes of tissues. The red plastic eggs that contained tacky nuggets of Silly Putty. There was also the little Zen garden with its tiny rake; Cherry had availed herself of it on one occasion, dragging the rake through the sand as she described how it felt to watch the mamas bury Hawk. There was also a bowl of polished stones—rose quartz, tiger eye—and Phoenix encouraged Cherry to hold one as she talked about tiptoeing away from Opal for the last time.

"Let the gem in your hand ground you," Phoenix said.

This session, Phoenix reminded her that sometimes when people have children, it brings up their own issues about how they themselves were parented.

"Or," she said, "in your case, how you *weren't* parented. It makes sense that this legacy of neglect would reverberate through your own experience as a mother." She paused. "Do you want to revisit some of those earliest moments with me?"

"I'm thinking about the purple room," Cherry said.

Ray reading to her. The younger kids crying. Men's voices down below.

"You felt scared, is that right?" Phoenix said. "I believe the word you used was *forgotten.*"

"I felt that way a lot, even when the mamas were around."

Cherry talked about watching one of the mamas nurse one of the younger kids. Baxter. They were in the parlor and the mama was stroking his hair. Cherry was confused by the desolation she felt, seeing them connect like that. It was worse, and deeper, than jealousy.

"Talking about it now, where do you feel it in your body?" Phoenix asked.

"Here," Cherry whispered, placing a hand on her navel.

"Breathe into that," Phoenix said. "We often hold our feelings inside our bodies."

How the mama pushed her away when she tried to join them.

She breathed.

Phoenix nudged the tissue box toward her.

"I want you to think about Cherry the child," she said. "In many ways, *that* Cherry is still with you. She's still in pain. I want you to do the compassion practice we talked about. Be kind to that little girl. She became a mother without any support, without any tools. That was a lot for her. Too much, you might say. It's imperative that you acknowledge that. Honor it, honor her. Only then can you work on the Opal piece."

The Opal piece.

"How's the anxiety these days? Are you doing the nightly breathing?"

"I am. It helps a lot. I don't feel anything like the episodes coming on. All that feels like ancient history actually."

"Good. I don't hear you currently endorsing any psychotic symptoms. And I'm not seeing any disconnect from reality, either."

"You sure?"

"That was something from your past, Cherry. You're not dealing with that now."

Phoenix glanced at the clock.

"We have to finish up. Before we end, though, I want to recognize the progress you're making. Do you feel it?"

Cherry nodded. "I've never opened up to anyone before. It's helped a lot."

Phoenix beamed. "It's the first day of spring, as you probably know. Even here in California, we're able to witness this annual rebirth. It teaches us an essential lesson, don't you think? About our resilience, about transformation. You're coming back to your body,

Cherry. You're recognizing the wounds there, forgiving yourself as much as you can."

As Cherry gathered her things to go, Phoenix leaned forward. "This week, I want you to ask yourself, what happens once I let go of this guilt? What's in that new, open space?"

"An abyss?"

"You can't change what you did, Cherry, but you can live differently going forward."

∞

As Cherry walked home through downtown Ojai, a little headachy from crying, she pondered Phoenix's parting questions. What if she managed to forgive herself? When she began therapy in December, she didn't think she'd get to this point. She was now able to calm herself when the panic crept in, and she was willing to look at what happened to her as a child. She didn't push it away anymore. She was processing it, Phoenix said. This allowed her to think about Opal and to grieve what she gave up. Sometimes she could do it without blame clouding every hard feeling.

Phoenix was a little hokey, with her gemstones and her mini Zen garden from The Sharper Image, her seasonal metaphors, but a more cerebral approach would have been intimidating. Cherry needed someone approachable, someone a little maternal even. Someone who didn't have to strain to imagine her woodsy, culty upbringing.

Someone who didn't judge what she'd done to Opal.

Cherry reached her home in only a few minutes: a little one-room back house right in town, nestled next to a trio of olive trees. It was a spare yet lovely cottage, with a sturdy wood table by the biggest window and a brass bed she'd splurged on when she moved in. She kept the bed neatly made, two blush-pink pillows flat and smooth as wafers; the plates and the five-piece pots-and-pans kitchen set were always washed and put away. Growing up, she had never been tidy. Now everything had its place.

Her life was quiet and stable, and her job managing the movie theater brought in enough money, so she was happy with it. She no longer
felt sheepish about waking with the sun and drinking tea in silence.
She finally admitted to herself that she hated the taste of mint tea, and
when she switched to Earl Grey upon moving here it was like everything
clicked into place. She could do what she wanted. She used to whisper
we are timeless before she took her first sip until she realized how absurd
it was. No one was around to hear her, let alone say it with her.

Now she said *I am timeless*. Phoenix told her it caused no harm.

Hawk's stones were lined on the windowsill, where they grew
warm in the sun. After her morning ritual, Cherry touched each one
with her fingertips and said, *I perceive this loss*.

In some respects, she'd come a long way. In others, it was like
she'd never left.

"What you did, and what was done to you, will eventually coexist
with how you're living now," Phoenix liked to say. "It won't be forgotten or repressed but synthesized. Part of you."

Cherry let herself into the house and set her bag on the table.
She took in the space, which belonged only to her. This cottage was
a privilege, and she practiced telling herself that she deserved it. The
cool late-March air lapped at the curtains as she headed to bed. She
was worn out from therapy and wanted a nap.

It was her day off, and she could give herself this small pleasure.

Phoenix knew about the 3:00 a.m. cab ride eighteen years ago,
about how Cherry had spent half a year cleaning motel rooms in
Hesperia in exchange for lodging and cash. Her first room had a view
of the rusted dumpsters, and back then she didn't allow herself any
comforts; at dawn she would watch the rats slither out of the trash as
if fleeing a fire. No tea for her; the stones were packed in the closet.
There was no peace, no joy.

Back then, she wondered if Ray would find her. Six days a week
she changed bedding and pulled hair from bathroom drains, working
herself hard so she would be tired enough to sleep at night. She didn't

want Ray to find her, and yet she missed Opal deeply. It was a soul need, a bodily need. Her breasts hardened with milk, and when she expressed it into the shower's prickly stream, she cried at the stinging, stretching pain. It was worse when the milk dried up, as if all messages for Opal, unheeded for long enough, had ceased. Cherry's mother-body was nothing but a dead phone line. She missed how it felt to hold her baby. She missed the scent of Opal's scalp, the drool on her chin, her tiny voice, her laugh, the soft skin of her tummy, her neck, her cry. Cherry longed for Opal in her arms. Her little body.

That body was gone by now—or not gone, but changed, which is the same thing as gone.

Cherry hadn't been the only motel maid without her child. Leah was a recovering addict who was trying to get her twins back. Catalina and Alma were sending nearly every penny to their kids in Guatemala. But only Cherry had taken off like a ghost. Like her own mother had. It was the main reason she had to get away from those women, out of Hesperia.

It was her boss Susa who had instructed how to get the social security card, and after Cherry saved up enough money to do it, she moved away. She had lived so many places since then, always as Arnette Swanson. At first, her new identity felt like yet another trauma; her name was the only thing that tied her to own mother, and she had to let it go.

After a while, though, it became easier to push away that old life. She remade herself, like Ray had always wanted her to. She came from nowhere, from no one.

Occasionally she would dream of Ray. She told Phoenix about these dreams. In them, she and Ray were young again, back at the house in Ben Lomond. They weren't themselves, exactly, it was more like they were pure beings filled with nothing but desire for one another. He'd been older, with more experience, he'd lived in the world, but he hadn't forced her into anything. Or had he? Phoenix was the one to pose that question. Cherry had wanted him, she was certain of that even now, but she'd also been sheltered and needy. That was also true.

Sometimes when she was confessing to Phoenix she felt lighter, as if her history, all her secrets and shame, were a literal burden she was carrying on her back. It was time to set it down. She had punished herself enough, with those menial jobs, this quiet life—being away from Opal the worst poverty of all. *Was she okay had she done well in school did she like to read how old was she when she got her period had she learned to drive had she lost her virginity was she in college was she in love did she wonder why I—*

Opal was fine.

Cherry fell onto her bed and let herself think this for the thousandth time.

There was no way Opal had been possessed.

How could Cherry even think so?

The psychotic break. Was that it?

It was the biggest mystery of her life.

Phoenix said there was something called *depersonalization*. Perhaps it applied to Cherry, though Phoenix couldn't be sure since Cherry hadn't been assessed by a clinician back then. Depersonalization was a disorder. It made the people you know well suddenly seem like strangers. It made it feel like you were observing the world from outside your own body. It isn't a fleeting feeling, Phoenix explained, but a persistent condition. It feels surreal, she said. Upsetting. She said it was more common in people who had experienced trauma.

Maybe that's what happened. Cherry didn't know. For years, she waited for another break to come. The second one would be worse. But none came.

Now, Cherry rubbed her cheek against her thin but soft pillow.

I deserve this, she told herself.

In the small set of drawers by her bed lay the key to the house on Edinburgh. Detached from a ring and others of its kind, it would have been easily lost were it not wrapped in tissue paper and tucked inside an orphaned glove.

For a long time, Cherry carried the loose key in her wallet. Those first few years, she would imagine herself sneaking back to Ray and Opal in the middle of the night, creeping into bed, being there when Ray woke up, as if nothing had changed.

No—that she would never do.

Maybe, she thought, she would let herself in to snatch Opal. And if she didn't have the courage to spirit Opal away, Cherry thought she could at least stand over her daughter as she slept. She would take one good look at her, cataloging all the ways the girl had changed, trying to memorize what she'd missed. But she never did that either.

Cherry had never gone back to Opal. Why, she didn't fully understand. The idea scared her, and what if she endangered her daughter again? She couldn't.

Eventually, she moved the key from her wallet to her dresser. But with every move, every new town, she brought the key with her.

∞

Cherry arrived in Ojai from Hemet a little over a year ago, after reading about the Topa Topa Mountains. Were it not for Marcia and the small library she presided over like a queen, those eight months in Hemet would have been unrelentingly depressing: desert heat like an oven, the job at the dry cleaners and its lecherous owner, a paycheck that barely covered expenses, getting mugged, stepping off a curb wrong and spraining her ankle. One day, a month into Cherry's time in Hemet, Marcia discovered her crying in the stacks, Fiction K–L.

Cherry guessed Marcia was about seventy-five, reading glasses hanging from a beaded chain around her neck, beautiful skin as brown and glossy as an avocado pit. Marcia was so short that Cherry might have mistaken her for a child had she seen her from the back.

"Do you need help, dear?" Marcia asked.

Cherry didn't know how to answer.

She wanted to say to Marcia, "My daughter may be better off without me, but I'm not."

Or maybe, simply, "I'm lonely."

Instead she said, "I need help with my literacy skills."

This was true. Although Ray had taught her and Hawk and a few of the other kids how to read and she could do it well enough to get by, well enough *wasn't* enough. She wasn't a child, she was an adult, and as she got older it seemed more and more a crime that the mamas had not made her capable in this way. She wanted to get lost in a book. She wanted to be able to look up information and understand it as deeply as possible. That's what the mamas tried to keep her from doing. But she knew she was smart.

"I'd love to help you with that," Marcia said and smiled like a kindly aunt.

She and Marcia began meeting regularly to practice blending sounds and spelling. They read books aloud together, and Marcia gave her ones to take home. At first, homonyms in particular seemed to Cherry like a punishing joke meant to trip up the illiterate, until, eventually, she began to anticipate them, remember which word meant what, and then she saw those words as proof of the English language's flexibility, of its tricky genius.

"We all need a little mischief," Marcia said once.

Since the beginning, the librarian tried to pry some information from her. Had she lived in Hemet long, was she married, did she like to cook, had she ever gone fishing?

Marcia must have been able to tell that Cherry wasn't raised like a normal person. Her upbringing, her tragedy, was on her like a bad perfume. She knew Marcia would keep asking questions; Cherry, at that point, hadn't told anyone about her past, and she knew she would eventually tell Marcia something she regretted. It was the same reason she didn't keep any close friends or get seriously involved with a man.

On what ended up being their last lesson, though neither realized it at the time, Marcia handed Cherry a book on the most magical places on Earth.

"There's a fun chapter on California," Marcia said. And then she leaned in and asked softly, "Where you from, Arnette?"

"Nowhere," Cherry said.

That night and the next and the next she pored over the book. She found it fascinating, especially the stuff about California's energy vortexes, places where the planet's magnetic forces converged, retrieved energy or provided it.

Maybe this explained what happened with Opal, Cherry thought. The episodes. Or Cherry's delusions of them. It was because of California. Maybe an energy force had torn them apart.

But there wasn't anything about Los Angeles in the chapter.

Cherry might've given up on the book then, but she didn't, it was too interesting. The science of the vortexes, if that's what it was, eluded her, but she loved the myths surrounding these lands, how people had believed them sacred for hundreds and hundreds of years.

She read about Mount Shasta, where people believed the crystal city of Telos was hidden, its inhabitants seven feet tall and possessing a higher plane of consciousness. The book said there was a convergence of five energy vortexes not far from Hemet, in Desert Hot Springs; at the cleaners, Cherry had met a few locals, buckled with turquoise, their skin tanned to jerky, who wanted to tell her about how special the place was. Many of these vortexes were sacred sites for Native Americans, the book said, and nowadays seekers of all kinds flocked to them. These seekers believed they could feel the magnetic energy of a place, that these forces made their scalps tingle, their hands transmit subtle vibrations. They believed a vortex would amplify emotions and accelerate their healing. As if healing were something you could summon quickly, pedal to the metal, as if pain's opposite were a heavenly destination just up ahead. What a scam, Cherry thought.

And yet she kept reading.

She thought there might be something about Santa Cruz County, if only a mention of the Mystery Spot, that campy tourist attraction not too far from the mamas' land. The tour guides called it "a gravitational anomaly" where balls rolled uphill and trees grew twisted and slanted, though it was only a trick of perception. But like LA, there was nothing about Santa Cruz in the book. Was that possible? There had to be something in those forests. Was it God? Was it nature? Was it Ursa?

Cherry tried never to think of Ursa. Even now, she didn't like talking about her with Phoenix. Somehow, the stories about Ray's mother hurt most of all.

Cherry read the pages on Ojai three times. The book said the word was pronounced Oh-Hi, and that it meant either *moon* or *nest* in the Indian Chumash language. Whether this was error or homonym, Cherry didn't know. The town was only ninety miles north of LA, fifteen miles inland from the ocean, not far from some of the other towns she had settled in.

Since leaving LA, Cherry had only been as far east as New Mexico. California kept pulling her back. The whole state was a vortex. She usually found somewhere cramped and ugly to live, a job that paid okay but not great, her daily life a penance for what she'd done to her daughter.

Until Ojai, there was no desire, only compulsion. But the place called to her; she wanted to go there. It would be beautiful, she thought. It would bring her pleasure. Should pleasure exist for someone like her? Something told her it should. The way the Topa Topa Mountains ran east-west. The seven vortexes. Seven! There were healers there, and good wine, and tiny oranges called Pixies.

"Where you from, Arnette?" Marcia had asked.

Ojai, Cherry imagined answering.

She worked her last shift, packed up her few belongings. On her way out of town, she dropped the book in the library's after-hours slot, a note slipped inside like a bookmark.

Thank you Marcia for helping me. I was raised outside Santa Cruz. Yes I've been fishing.

It felt like progress, revealing that. That was the first step to seeking therapy.

And now here she was, a resident of Ojai, in this back house, olive leaves combing the window screens by her bed, on a street called Eucalyptus, a block from a street called Lion, with a therapist named after an immortal bird. She had a few friends—-more like acquaintances, but still. She read novels all the time, whenever she was alone at home, which was a lot. She loved anything with a detective.

She didn't feel any electromagnetic pulses in Ojai and yet the town welcomed her, and the locals told her their stories. There was the woman whose father had made pornos from their house in the San Fernando Valley. Cherry's neighbor learned to surf when he was three and was now, at forty-seven, afraid to swim. There were a lot of older folks who had settled in Ojai decades ago; a handful had come because of guru Krishnamurti, whose foundation still offered classes, even a school for children. Some locals were Ventura County royalty. A few owned olive farms, or they ran the vineyards outside of town, dirt under their nails, denim shirts frayed at the hem. They accepted Cherry's presence easily; told her about themselves without any expectation of reciprocity. She and Phoenix talked about how she might reveal her real name to these people. Even just saying it was a childhood nickname she preferred would do the trick, Phoenix said. She assured her that this kind of thing—people shifting, remaking themselves—happened in Ojai all the time.

If she wanted to, she could be Cherry here.

Vortex indeed.

∞

That night, Cherry woke with a start. This wasn't out of the ordinary— it was one of the reasons that brought her to therapy in the first place, after all.

But this time, Phoenix's words reverberated in her head.

You can't change what you did, Cherry.

Cherry sat up and switched on the lamp next to her bed.

But you can live differently going forward.

The drawer, the one with the key, was right there.

You can live.

What compelled her to retrieve that key from its nest in the unused glove? To unwrap it from the old crumpled tissue paper? To move it to her wallet?

Cherry didn't know, but she did it quickly and then rushed back to bed. She turned out the light, and in the dark she waited as if something might happen. Nothing did. The room was still. It was three months into the year 2000, a new millennium, springtime, a season of rebirth. All this work to revisit her history, coming to terms with what she'd done, reckoning with it, meant Cherry was hanging on to the past. But it was time to look to the future.

So why not just throw away the key?

The past didn't want to coexist with the present, she would tell Phoenix. It wanted to collide with it.

Cherry lay back in her one-room house, inhaling for five seconds, holding her breath in for another five, and then letting it out for five, just as she'd been taught.

Relax.

Let it go.

Would she need to do this for her whole life?

The next week in Phoenix's office, Cherry said, "I have something to show you."

She retrieved the wallet from her purse, unzipped it, and unclasped the change pouch. She felt for the key. For a moment, it wasn't there, and a string of panic stretched tight across her chest, until, finally, there was the key, adhered to a crusty green penny. Cherry had to pull off the coin before placing the key on the table before them.

"What's this?"

Cherry explained and asked, "Why don't I just get rid of it?"

"Because it isn't only a key for you," Phoenix said. "It means something more, like Hawk's rocks. You carry those from place to place too."

Phoenix was right. The key was a reminder, a talisman. It was proof. It was evidence.

But was it evidence of Cherry's crime against Opal or evidence that Opal existed at all? She had no other connection to that short time with her child.

"I've been thinking about what you said," Cherry said. "About living differently, going forward."

"And what did you come up with?"

"I can forgive myself, or not, but my own blame doesn't matter. Not like Opal's does. I imagine her anger. I understand it because I went through it with Ruth." She paused. "I want her forgiveness."

"But remember, we aren't obligated to forgive those who have harmed us. And that's not why we ask for forgiveness."

"True. But I can't even ask her."

"You're feeling ready to find Opal."

"It's more than that. I *have* to find her. Soon. Now. This key, it's like it's telling me to go."

Phoenix was taken aback. "I don't understand. You want to return—to the house in LA? And use the key?"

Cherry blushed. Spoken so plainly, it sounded foolish.

Phoenix asked if she had someone to go with her. She didn't. If she had some plan in mind. Not really.

"It's been a long time, Cherry. Do you think Opal still lives there? And if she does . . ." The therapist stopped, as if measuring out the correct words.

"Tell me," Cherry said.

"I want to remind you that your daughter might not want a relationship with you. That's her prerogative. Is that something you're prepared to accept?"

"No," Cherry admitted.

"It's good you know that about yourself."

"I still feel compelled to go."

Phoenix's brow furrowed as she bit her pencil.

"Cherry, can we talk about the episodes again?"

"I'm not endorsing psychotic symptoms. You said exactly that. The key isn't really *talking* to me—I didn't mean it like that."

"Are you experiencing urgent feelings again?"

"Yes, but not in the same way. I swear. The episodes . . . they were almost physical." She remembered the melting kitchen, the wet bedroom. The furred bathroom towels, the glassed water of the bathtub where Opal nearly drowned. The pushing, inside of her.

"You're not feeling detached? Are you hearing voices?"

"Only yours. Even when I'm not here. But I'm not *hallucinating* your voice."

Phoenix reached for her bowls of stones and grabbed a jagged piece of black so shiny it was a mirror. "This is obsidian," she said. "My dad would say it offers protection and clarity. I don't know about that. I know for sure that it's volcanic glass. That it's pretty."

She held out her open palm.

"Keep it in your purse. A pocket is better if you have one. Whenever your brain starts spinning away, take it out. Hold it in your hand. It'll keep you anchored."

Cherry didn't move.

"I expected you to reach this decision, Cherry."

"You did?"

"It makes the most sense. It's human. You have done so much work and now you want to return to Opal, try to make amends. But I didn't expect you to want to move this quickly. How you're talking about this, like it's a quest, almost—I'm concerned. It doesn't sound deliberate or prudent. It sounds irrational." She paused. "Will you think just a little longer about finding Opal? We can devote the next few sessions to discussing how you'll find her. Use an intermediary at first, if you'd like. At least to track her down. And at the same time, we can go over the outcomes you hope for, troubleshoot what you might do if things don't go that way."

Phoenix leaned forward, offering the obsidian.

"Here. Take it."

Cherry took the gem, but she didn't promise her she'd wait.

22

CHERRY READ SOMEWHERE THAT HIGHWAY 33 WAS THE least traveled freeway in the state, and she believed it.

It was the very same night, and she going to LA without Phoenix's blessing, passing through little one-horse towns scattered with fast food restaurants and gas stations. A few miles in the other direction, Cherry knew, the two-lane road was lonesome as a country song: an empty curving blackness. That direction was the prison too. Before that, the road snaked through Los Padres National Forest in tight curves.

She should have felt nervous, but she didn't. Was it because this quest, as Phoenix called it, was such a lark that its consequences didn't feel real? Did she have depersonalization disorder? Or was it because this wordless pull toward LA, toward Opal, suddenly felt destined? When she and Ray drove to Los Angeles, Opal smaller than a clove of garlic inside her, Cherry had felt just as placid.

She was listening to AM talk radio. She liked the static that hissed beneath the host's banter. She thought she should ask someone why AM radio came in less clearly than FM, but she also liked not knowing. There used to be a time when it felt like she had nothing but questions, *what's a sports bra, what's a Slurpee, what's a retainer,* but that confusion faded as she had lived in the world, met people, worked jobs, read, got answers to her questions. A year into being on her own, she realized how much Ray was like the mamas: wanting to keep her small and quiet, keep her inside the house. Had he thought she was stupid, as Ursa had?

When the 33 fed into the 101, Cherry began to feel the gravity of her mission.

What was she doing? Maybe Phoenix was right: she should wait, think about it, have a plan.

All she had was an old key and a hunk of obsidian.

She'd been too embarrassed to tell Phoenix she'd actually imagined using the key. She fantasized about walking right up to the front door and opening it. Going right in.

She didn't say that because she knew she would sound unhinged.

She was just going to do a drive-by tonight. She'd pass the house, gather her courage, and then the next day, if it still felt like she had to, she would return.

Phoenix was right, there was a good chance Opal didn't live at that house, even if Ray did, and that wasn't likely either. Opal was nineteen. Couldn't be—how had her baby grown up?

It was one in the morning.

Cherry headed south on the 101, past Camarillo into the valley: Thousand Oaks, Calabasas. The latter had been a small sleepy suburb when she left, but now there were car dealerships and housing developments and, even at this late hour, some traffic. In the distance, a helicopter winked its white light. The sky was no longer dark but gray.

Cherry's palms tingled; the seatbelt was cutting into her neck as the freeway tapered at Hollywood and the road turned potholed. Trash clogged in the brown brush. She was approaching the Melrose exit.

The car eased onto the exit ramp. She was on Melrose now, the asphalt chewed up, the buildings squat. Storefronts sold religion or calling cards, plus a podiatrist, a palm reader. Nobody was walking around. Cherry had forgotten how empty the streets became after dark; she'd forgotten how much she loved it. Some Los Angeles neighborhoods were busy at night, sidewalks crowded with people headed to bars and young women in heels, crossing their arms against the cold. She and Ray had seen them on their early drives around the city when they were trying to figure out this new land. But not here. Driving west on Melrose, it felt like everyone was tucked inside: you didn't know if they were in bed or on the couch or reheating food in the microwave. Everyone was a secret.

The street widened, and as soon as she passed Paramount on the right, the tall studio gates shut for the night, the road turned smooth. She could see the money in the restaurants and the sleek furniture shops, the faceless buildings that were likely production companies or law offices. She passed the Spanish-style house that long ago had been turned into a library. A block north would host more beautiful houses, where people were doing whatever they wanted beyond their flat green lawns.

It looked the same, and it didn't. There were new buildings, but she couldn't remember what had been torn down and replaced.

She headed into the blocks that had once made the neighborhood so famous and sought after. Now one janky boutique followed another. There were stickers on every parking meter pole. The record stores and vintage shops had disappeared.

She was approaching Fairfax, the high school on the left, *had Opal gone there*, and everything felt inconsequential except this mission, this quest. Everything except Opal.

On her left, the neighborhood's only liquor store remained, but the home for the elderly had gone from boring beige to the green of an unripe banana, now a youth hostel. Across the street, the rug store remained; Cherry remembered taking Opal to marvel at the walls fringed with carpet samples.

When she spotted the pay phone she'd used to call the taxi to take her away from here, Cherry gripped the steering wheel.

She turned onto Edinburgh. As the car nosed off Melrose, she felt like she was crossing a boundary into a world she'd vowed never to return to. But she had been the one to draw that border. There was nothing stopping her. She had come back. She was finally here.

The street was dark, and there wasn't a soul outside. The sycamore trees lining the sidewalk looked pitted and stained, their branches knuckling into a whitish night. The dim streetlights barely illuminated what lay ahead, but even in the shadows Cherry could make out the homes that she'd forgotten about until now. Their details pierced her: the storybook house with its slanted roof, the place with the aluminum window awnings, and the ugly, boxy one with shutters. Spanish-style bungalow after Spanish-style bungalow, stucco and orange tile, curtains drawn across big living room windows. Cherry imagined the people inside these houses, frozen midsentence. A fork an inch from someone's open mouth. Hands cupped beneath a faucet, the water solid as ice. Or lying like the dead in their beds, the blood in their veins turned to clay.

Cherry suddenly felt very hot. She thought again about the library book from Marcia in Hemet, about the vortexes. Maybe there was one here, on this very street, sucking the energy from her. She needed to get out of this suffocating car.

Cherry pulled over and opened the door. The air was heavy as pennies.

No, she realized, it wasn't the air, it was her.

Was it? She shook her head.

Was this an episode?

Phoenix had warned her.

She dug the obsidian out of her front jean pocket and clutched it in her fist. She was here. She was anchored. The stone—the volcanic glass—was smooth and warm against her skin.

This wasn't an episode. No. This was different.

The feeling was coming from inside of her, it wasn't being done to her.

In some ways, she imagined Phoenix telling her, the panic she felt, the anxiety running through her, was the most logical response to returning to the site of her leaving.

She held the obsidian and breathed until she felt calmer.

She crossed the street onto the next block. The house would be just up ahead, three more houses, then two, then—

Where the house, with its sloping lawn and concrete walkway, its big front porch and stucco arches, was supposed to be there was a mansion. Or someone's idea of one.

Cherry circled, trying to get her bearings.

Was she in the right place? She was.

The house in front of her was a two-story slab of white concrete with a metal-plated garage door. Three alarm system signs. The lawn was as spiky and green as wheatgrass and so new Cherry could make out lines where one rectangle of sod ended and a new one began.

What had she expected? That the house and the life she'd fled would be here waiting for her, as if all the years between then and now hadn't happened? She had been so arrogant. She was so stupid. Opal wasn't here.

What happens when your mother who abandoned you returns and discovers that the house you lived in no longer exists? Are you unfindable? Did you ever exist?

It was as if the air between her and the house was trembling, like heat rippling off the freeway. No—that was her mind tricking her. She squeezed the obsidian. It was she who was quivering.

She fell to her knees on the gruesomely green lawn. The temperature had suddenly dropped, as it does when night edges to its deepest part. She released the obsidian and it landed on the grass.

Her hands free, she pulled the key from her other pocket. It looked lonely and naked in her palm.

She yanked up a square of lawn. The grass tickled; the soil beneath was dark and wet and stunk of shit.

Cherry wouldn't need the key anymore. It had been stupid to

hang on to it—not even that. It was unnecessary to keep it. The past would haunt her, key or not.

She gripped it between her thumb and index finger and held it in the air for a moment before sticking it so deep into the dirt it disappeared. She didn't know why she did it, or what it meant. It was an offering. A ritual. If a lock has been destroyed, what's the key for? She was sending it back to the land, to the spot her daughter had once lived. Where she had once lived with her daughter. The only place.

Cherry wanted the key to open *something* but it wouldn't, it could merely commemorate what she'd lost. A life, a child, abandoned.

Her hands, covered in dirt, were shaking.

When she got to her feet, her eye caught on the obsidian glinting in the night, and she bent to pick it up. It was dirty, its underside damp from the grass. She thought, suddenly, of the stones the mamas retrieved from the eastern wing every open moon. They would clean and polish them and then carry them back to their secret space, where Cherry was not welcome.

Why had she come here of all places? To LA?

Without Opal, this place meant nothing to her.

It wasn't like that other place.

Home. A kind of home.

LA wasn't the first place she'd run from.

23

CHERRY REACHED SANTA CRUZ JUST AFTER 8:00 A.M. She'd slept for an hour at a rest stop a few hours back and then forced herself to chug a large coffee, but otherwise her stomach was empty, and her eyes burned with fatigue. Before she could chicken out, or pass out, she drove onward, through Ben Lomond and into the wild land without a name.

The road contracted, just as she remembered, and the rush of lush forest beyond the passenger window was as familiar to her as her own body. This was a place that only persisted in her dreams—here it was, untouched, unchanged.

Why had she come? She wished she could call Phoenix and ask her for guidance and clarity, though her therapist would more likely express concern, tell her to turn back.

"The mamas never had your best interest in mind," she might say. "Why would they clarify your trauma for you?"

"This is where it all began," Cherry might reply. "It's why I have this wound. I can't recover until I face them."

"By all means," she imagined Phoenix saying. "Do what you must do."

Her imaginary therapist was much more accommodating than her real one.

EDAN LEPUCKI

Cherry thought she might fall asleep—but then there it was, appearing like a magic trick. The hidden turn. Waiting for her.

The car rocked back and forth as it hit uneven ground. God, she used to love this feeling, tires hitting this rough land, as if the car were an old dog struggling to stand. The fog had already begun to lift, and she could clearly see the tentacle sprouting off the main road. She turned.

She knew she should be frightened, but she wasn't. She was finally facing the past.

Wasn't this what Phoenix urged her to do?

She had to.

Only then would she be able to face finding Opal.

The tentacle was free of debris, if muddy from a recent rain, and as she passed the lookout cottage, she craned her neck to see if anyone was standing outside or peering out the front window. There was no one, and the cottage appeared empty.

Where was the mama, guarding the house?

Cherry kept going.

She reached the driveway and saw that the redwoods lining it were no longer embellished. Why not? She had imagined the glittering eyes in the bark taking in the car, blinking at the sight of her after so many years. Without Ray.

Now there was no one to see her return.

She finally let herself take in the house up ahead. The shock made her cry out. It looked grand through her dirty windshield. It looked magnificent, in fact: painted green and brown, shiny. She got closer and saw that it had a big front garden. A silver bell was installed at the top of the porch. There were two bicycles set up by the garden, shiny as the bell, as the house.

But there was no one around. No mamas anywhere. Hadn't they heard her approach?

She parked, her heart clanging as that bell probably did. She plunged her hand in her pocket to feel the obsidian, as if for courage.

For clarity, Phoenix mentioned.

Protection.

The air outside was just as she remembered: the perfume of dirt and wet bark and who knew what else. She'd missed it so much. For the first time in years, she missed Ray. He was the only one who understood their lives here. It was why she had loved him.

She *had* loved him. Opal came from that.

She never let herself admit that.

The mansion before her was more stately than she remembered, beautiful, but it also felt bereft of something.

No life inside there. No vitality.

It was so quiet.

Was it abandoned? No, look at that garden, those bikes. The house was too well-kempt.

Then there was a woman's voice. It came from the other end of the yard.

"What do you want?"

Cherry turned. Two women were standing by what had to be a rebuilt hen house. One was young, early twenties, long silky hair parted down the middle like a flower child. The other woman was probably about Phoenix's age, maybe older. She stood with a chicken in her hands. The bird was flapping its fluffy wings to get away, bobbing its head, labial wattle twitching, hard gray beak pecking the air. Both women wore jeans under ratty flannel nightgowns. The younger one was barefoot, as if the mud and the cold didn't bother her, but the older one wore green wellies splattered with mud.

Cherry recognized those boots.

She looked more closely at the woman wearing them.

Mary's pale skin was now wrinkled, lines deep as scars. She was no longer beautiful—but it wasn't only beauty she'd lost. Loneliness like a whistling wind blew through her.

In the next moment, Mary seemed to recognize Cherry, and she stepped back. Her arms went slack, and the chicken fell to the dirt, then scrambled away with a squawk.

"Why, hello, Cherry. It's you."

Cherry didn't know what else to do so she squeezed the obsidian. With her other hand, she waved. "Hi."

∞

The younger woman was named Sunshine and she was Mary's only companion. They were officious and welcoming, forced Cherry to sit in the kitchen and eat what Sunshine called gruel, but she gave a little wink as she said the word.

It was almost too much for Cherry. In the mudroom, she'd taken in the familiar brown canvas coat and blue ponchos hanging from wire hangers over the water pipe in the corner, the big metal sink and the mops, and she felt dizzy. There was the pantry to the left, where Ray had pushed down her shorts, biting her ear, while the legumes in their jars looked on. The feelings almost knocked her to the floor.

"Wow," she kept saying.

This place was real, it existed. She realized she'd only half-believed her own life. All this time, doubting her own worst memories. Why did she do that?

It was the same, and it wasn't at all the same. Everything inside the house was new but dusty. Unused. Uninhabited. The house had a gothic feeling. A fairy tale feeling.

Mary and Sunshine lived there alone, not that they had told her that yet. Cherry recognized the signs. There were only two pairs of shoes in the mudroom. In the kitchen sink, only two plates and two forks. On the stove, a small pan webbed with the remains of scrambled eggs. Cherry did not smell any mint. Beyond the kitchen and the parlor, the rooms the mamas had used—for weighing the weed, for the napping babies—were shut tight. Beyond their own murmuring, it was silent.

"Where are the other mamas?" Cherry asked finally.

Mary gave a sad smile. "The ones you knew took off years ago, with their kids."

Sunshine cut in. "I came recently—with some others. Before the new year." She leaned in conspiratorially. "We were preparing."

"Preparing for what?"

"The end of the world," she said.

"Excuse me?"

Mary shrugged.

"Where's Ursa?" Cherry asked.

Mary hesitated and then she said, "It's easier if we show you."

∞

The door of the eastern wing had been torn off, and in its place was a sky-blue sheet, which lifted in the breeze that rushed down the hallway when they entered. It was like someone threw out a sheet on the beach; it buffeted the wind before falling.

"I can't go in there," Cherry said when Sunshine nodded at the doorway.

"Oh, dear, yes you can," Mary said. "Ursa had a gift, and she sometimes shared it with us. You just weren't ready. Anyway, all that's over now."

Cherry blinked and the other two women were on the other side of the sheet, as if they'd disappeared into a portal. She had to follow them.

She closed her eyes and pushed the sheet with her open palms. She let it drag across her face as she walked through to the other side.

"Ta-da," she heard Mary say, and she opened her eyes.

It was just a room. A large one, yes, and as funnily shaped as she used to picture in her mind. But save for an uneven pile of dark-colored blankets against the wall, it was empty.

Cherry stepped in further. This was it, the eastern wing. She had never been allowed in here for the mamas' rituals but there had always been a sense that someday she might be, if she could just prove herself helpful enough, mature enough. That she was no longer a child. She'd been a kitten chasing a ball of yarn; meanwhile the mamas pulled any new boarder into this room.

There was a bad feeling here. Her bones went cold at the dead sunshine that streamed through the skylights above, lighting up the funnels of dust. One of the walls across from her, not far from the bank of blankets, was in disrepair, and patches of sheetrock had already fallen off, the white dust powdering the floor. A crack snaked up another wall to the ceiling, stopping at a skylight; the water had gotten in there, and the ceiling was discolored and swelling.

It smelled like a sickroom, like the unwell or the infirm. Like decay.

You just weren't ready.

They never wanted her with them.

But why had she cared? There was nothing here. Less than nothing. This room gave nothing—instead, it took something away.

What exactly did it take?

Sunshine and Mary looked nervous as Cherry's eyes roamed the room.

"Where's Ursa?" she asked.

"She's right there," Mary said softly.

She and Sunshine were looking at the blankets—which let out a soft little moan.

Cherry jumped back, startled.

"That's—?"

"Yep," Mary said.

"Oh my god," Cherry said, moving toward the body.

Ursa was on her side, facing the wall. Only her face was visible beneath the blanket; it was as if she were wrapped in a shroud, or a fly caught in a spider's web. She was older and appeared comatose, but Cherry would recognize her anywhere.

The broad forehead, the strong chin.

Ursa's eyes were closed and her forehead was furrowed in pain, in struggle. Her tongue lolled out of her mouth. It was whitish and dry, and spittle bubbled at her cracked lips. She smelled of urine. She murmured some gibberish, wincing, and then her face fell suddenly slack before wrinkling in pain once more.

"Is she ill?"

"Not exactly," Sunshine said.

"She's stuck," Mary said.

"Stuck?"

"You wouldn't understand," Mary replied.

"May I?" Cherry said, and, without waiting for permission, she unraveled the blanket. Ursa wore a long white dress, yellowed and stiff with sweat and worse. Her legs, yellowed too, were thin and weak looking, and yet they were stretched straight, as were her arms. They looked as unyielding as metal rods. Like she was fighting something.

Where had Cherry seen that pose before?

"Time to change her," Sunshine murmured to Mary. To Cherry she said, "We try our best to keep her clean. And fed. We give her syringes of water, gruel."

"It won't be much longer, I think," Mary said.

"She doesn't wake up? What the hell happened?"

"She and Opal were in here alone. It wasn't even an open moon. I knew the changes were a bad idea. I tried to tell her—"

Cherry thought she might fall down. "Opal was here? In the eastern wing?"

"Only for a day," Sunshine said. "In December."

"She came with Ray," Mary said. "They were looking for you."

Cherry wanted to cry out. She put a hand to her mouth.

"And then she came back alone," Sunshine said.

"She and Ursa didn't even let me in here with them," Mary said. "Something terrible must've happened because all of us got very sick, and Opal ran away, and Ursa never emerged."

Cherry looked back at Ursa. Those straight legs. Unresponsive. Doll-like. Dead.

The episodes.

"Did Opal cause this?"

Mary shook her head. "It was all Ursa. I'm sure of it. You know how she could be. She went too far and scared everyone off. For the second time."

She scared everyone off—

"Why are you still here?" Cherry asked Mary. "After all this time?"

"I owed it to Ursa. Or I thought I did."

"You were mistaken," Cherry said.

"Doesn't matter. I couldn't leave. My son's here."

"Hawk . . ." Cherry said.

Mary didn't reply but Cherry could tell she was grateful to hear her child's name, to have it float in the air between them. Mary knew Cherry's pain. Hers was far worse.

Just then, Ursa moaned again, her eyes squeezed tight.

"Do you know where Opal went?" Cherry asked. "Can you tell me anything? I'm trying to find her. Please."

Mary sighed. "She said she lives in Los Angeles, in a house on an oil field."

Cherry wanted to cry. That wasn't enough to go on, was it?

Another, finer fracture zippered up the wall, right near Ursa's body. Cherry followed it with her eyes, praying for strength as she imagined the crack biting into the wall, tearing it apart, cleaving it in two. Separated. Maybe forever.

Epilogue

NOW, THE DAYS DISAPPEARED AS SOON AS NIGHT FELL, and then the nights did too, one after the other, matches flaring and then burning to nothing. Opal still wasn't quite used to it, though she tried to remind herself that she'd spent her first sixteen years this way, without the assurance that she could return to this moment, or to that one; she experienced time just like everyone else.

She had given up tunneling. For good. The tunneling with Ursa had been the last. She had no reason to do it anymore. She'd failed to find her mother, and she didn't want any tie to Ursa. Opal vowed to accept the past and move forward, which was the one thing her grandmother couldn't do.

She missed going into the box, and the delicious slip into the tunnel, and the tunnel itself, the never-loss of it all. But now she also liked the feeling of loss, how it made everything special: this cup of coffee, this song, this feeling, this memory of being a baby held by her mother. Remember it, remember it. None of this was coming back, nor was her mother. Opal could finally grieve.

When she and Ray got back from Santa Cruz, she made Fab move off the estate. Their little experiment had failed, and it was time for her best friend to move on, as Opal and Ray were trying to move on. Fab needed to go back to her dorm room, declare a major, fall in love, maybe all three.

Fab was happy Opal had given up tunneling. "Not to denigrate your superpowers or anything," she'd said, "but this has been exhausting."

Opal agreed.

"Get your number listed like the rest of us," Fab said. "If your mom wants to find you, she will."

Opal had never loved her more.

Now Fab was back on campus, dating a guy named Guy, they actually referred to him as guy-named-Guy, and Ray and Isla were still in the house in Lemoyne, apparently in couple's therapy—and not the screaming-into-pillows kind. There was a lot to work through, Isla Patricia said; Ray had a whole past he'd kept secret from his fiancée, and they needed to come to terms with it, together. The wedding was in six weeks.

Opal started taking dance, and she sometimes pushed the downstairs furniture out of the way to practice what she'd learned. It was funny how she counted time now, 5-6-7-8—it was the only manipulation she allowed herself, if you could call it that. How simple and beautiful, to follow time's lead, to dance to it. Her body was the time machine.

She was getting ready to move out of the estate. Kim let her out of the contract early and was already searching for a potential replacement to manage the property, all of them single men. None had a family to bring with them; that era had passed. Opal wondered if the house felt any sadness about her leaving, and then she reminded herself that the house was only brick and wood, that it did not possess consciousness. She still caught herself thinking as Ursa might: communing with a space, feeling its energy, blah, blah, blah, and she had to stop herself. This must have been what it was like for her parents when they first came to LA: so much to shuck off.

Opal would make sure the phone number at her new place was listed, just as Fab suggested. She was moving into an apartment not far from her dad and Isla Patricia.

She was nineteen and it felt like she'd only just started living her life. She was enrolled in school full time. Once she transferred to a four-year college she might major in dance, or maybe something a bit more practical, though what, exactly, she had no clue. Her dad said he'd help her pay for it; he didn't want her to go into debt. He sheepishly admitted he'd been saving up for the past two years.

"Isla Patricia's idea," he said.

Opal would be one of the older college students, though not by much. Everyone would probably assume she had taken a year abroad or was a former party girl, someone who hadn't been able to get her shit together at eighteen. That was true. She imagined her life two years from now (the only time travel she allowed herself) and saw herself as a transfer student at some East Coast college. Fall foliage, salad bar in the cafeteria, brick dorms. Taking the kind of seminars Fab told her about, with clever names like Victorian Sexualities or Comedy and Postmodernism, the leggier girls folded into their desks like locusts. The elusive articulate professor. Opal would go to parties.

And later, once she graduated, she would wish so badly she could go back to that time. She wouldn't go. She would have only memories to flip over and over in her mind, to polish smooth with each telling. She would have only fantasies of the future. And only a right now, to do with what she could. And finally, finally, she would be just like everybody else.

∞

It was after sundown, early April of the new millennium. She thought of Ursa's acolytes, eager for Y2K and the global chaos they were sure was coming. Were they disappointed when the world spun on as usual? Perhaps it didn't for them.

Opal was going through the dining room hutch, six drawers of random junk: scissors and pens and cloth napkins and old postcards from Fab and forgotten business cards from various producers and location people. A yo-yo. A meat thermometer. Sand, a lot of it, as if an hourglass had cracked open and spilled its guts.

Ray had offered to come over and help pack, but she wanted to do it alone, and, anyway, there wasn't much left: just her bedroom and the kitchen and stuff like this. God, she would miss these solid built-ins, even if the drawers did stick.

Opal leaned forward so that she could see into the living room, with its wainscoting and fireplace and big windows. At this hour, it was all darkness beyond the glass. If she stepped outside, she would hear the panting and the groaning metal of the pumpjacks against the oceanic hum of traffic down below. She thought of Well 199. How she'd miss it. She thought of the first time she visited it; she'd never tunneled to that moment, and now she never would. But that's what made it matter so much, didn't it? Just as death transformed life and turned it precious, memories only revealed how unreachable the past was. They were a catalog of losses, even the good ones. Especially the good ones. But it also meant the present was all you had. So take it. Let it in.

The box was still in the garage—calling to her, even now. Ray kept asking her what her plans for it were, if she was certain she didn't want to pass it to Doc or some other Reichian fanatic. She kept deflecting, and then she'd texted Isla Patricia: *ask him to stop asking*

No need to specify what she meant.

The thing was, Opal knew leaving the box wouldn't kill her desire to tunnel completely. Part of her worried, too, that moving off the estate would make it worse. Would she long to travel back to this land, just as she used to ache to return to Cherry? Would she want, desperately, to return to Well 199, to sit in the fireplace hidey-hole with Fab? Seemed not only possible but likely.

And yet—she couldn't wait to be rid of it.

There was one remaining object at the back of the last drawer—maybe that broken hourglass, she thought. But she knew what it was. She pulled out the barbecue lighter. Cackled to herself, went to make a phone call.

"Dad," she said, when he answered. "Did I wake you? I need your help."

∞

Ray was there within an hour. He was dressed in a T-shirt that read
WHY 2 K?

"Ha," Opal said, nodding at it.

He rolled his eyes but looked pleased. "Isla Patricia got it for me
for Christmas."

"She's the best."

When they went into the garage, he said, "This isn't rational." But
it didn't seem like he wanted to stop her.

"I know," she said.

"We need to be careful. Our proximity to oil."

"It's insane, really," Opal said.

"You have the fire extinguisher?"

She nodded. "Just help me."

"Okay," he said. "I'm ready."

Opal hadn't stepped foot inside the garage since they'd returned
from Santa Cruz five months earlier, and now that she was here, wan
light overhead, smell of mildew, her hands against the box, she felt
woozy. Just the chance to go back—

"You okay?" Ray asked.

"Not really," she said.

"It's hard not to want to," he said and put a hand on her shoulder,
let it rest there, gentle but solid, and she nodded.

"Is it Cherry?" he asked.

"It's everything."

"Do you think you'll ever go back?"

She shrugged. "If I do, I think I'd like to work on finding Ruth."

"You could try."

"Maybe. Things are way more malleable than I ever imagined."

Then they both knelt to where the soil met the bottom of the machine. Ray held a small shovel and handed her the second one. The
dirt was hard as concrete.

"Let's get some water," Ray said.

Even after much of the dirt was turned to mud and their hands were caked with it, it took them a good while to dig out the box. Ray finally leaned back on his heels and assessed. Opal watched as he stood and jostled it.

"Is it ready?" she asked.

He nodded. They got on the same side, ready to push the box toward the garage door.

Her father said, "You know what Isla keeps bringing up after our therapy sessions?"

"Should you really be telling me?"

He stepped away, arms falling by his sides. "She says that if things had gone differently, if we never went to Santa Cruz and you never met your grandmother, maybe Cherry would have never left. That in the ideal version of our lives, meaning you and me, *our* life," he gestured to the space between him and Opal, "we would wake up and your mom would be here, as if she'd never left. And Isla Patricia and I . . . would never have gotten together."

Opal had considered this too. If she thought about it too much it made her head hurt.

"Who said it was the ideal?" she said. "It's just different."

There were so many potential ways a life could go.

∞

The box burned as anything does. It wasn't magical.

Something, however, burned inside of Opal. Perhaps that *was* magical. Inside of her, she lit up and sparked, then roared. Then melted and burned. Then was ash. Then was gone. Then there was a space that hadn't been there before. Was it a loss? Or was it a liberation?

Maybe it was both.

∞

After the box was gone, after Ray paid one of his buddies from transportation to pick up the debris, all that remained was a rectangle of charred grass at the center of the meadow between the garage and the house. A couple of weeks passed, and the burned grass disintegrated or blew away, and all that was left was soil.

"Did a spaceship land here?" the future tenant, Adam, asked on the walk-through.

"In a way," Opal said. "Yes."

She did feel better with it gone and, as kooky as it sounded, she felt the specter of Ursa gone, too, as if Opal's resolve were strengthened and that was enough. The old woman could surf the space-time continuum, Opal thought, but she would not be brave enough to find Opal in present-day LA.

When the tour was over, Opal drove Adam down to the access gate. She waved and watched to make sure his little car made it over the particularly troublesome pothole at the edge of the lot—she needed to tell Kim about that before she moved out.

Opal still had some packing to do, but she was already feeling melancholy about this place. She wanted to savor it. She would miss a few things in particular. She was thinking of taking an hour to walk to the dead well at the other side of the property. It wasn't a favorite, but it was a landmark. It had stopped being productive the year they moved in, but there was no sense of urgency to remove it. It was more of a sculpture, or a monument to the fossil fuel industry, than anything. Silent and still, it hulked.

Some days, Opal felt a little like the dead well: without a purpose, gathering rust.

Or not—who said tunneling had been her reason for living? It would not be. She was alive to experience this life as it happened. She liked it best that way.

Opal heard the engine approach before she saw the car it carried. Her first thought was that Adam had forgotten something. But another part of her felt afraid—she didn't know why. Or she did. Ursa had some information about her whereabouts, and who knows what her grandmother had done when she discovered Opal had run from the house. What was stopping Ursa from finding her?

Before the car come into her vision, she ran to the side of the access gate, crouching behind the righthand post. She could hear her own shallow breath.

It definitely wasn't Adam. It was a larger car; she could tell by the engine's gruff. Opal peeked from behind the post and saw that it was an SUV of some kind, an innocuous gray color. A rental, maybe—it was new and clean.

She should run and shut the access gate. But she couldn't move.

The car parked in the lot, and whoever was behind the wheel turned it off. Opal couldn't see the driver from this angle. She would have to step out from her hiding place to see.

What was she doing? Why was she standing frozen like this, so freaked out? It could be a clueless location scout, or a looky-loo who had read about the house in a book about Los Angeles. It could be anyone. She was fleetingly glad she had just finished meeting with Adam and was, for once, dressed appropriately.

Opal stepped out, and, as if in response, the driver opened their door. Opal forced herself to exhale. If it was Ursa, she would be fine. She would close the gate, and Ursa would be locked out. Opal would never let her in.

It wasn't Ursa. Opal saw that at once.

Her hair was short now and she'd gained a little weight around the middle but otherwise she looked as she had in 1981.

Opal marveled at her mother's dress, with its stylish black belt, and her platform sandals. She seemed nervous, but happy, at peace.

"No trespassing," Opal called out, but she was smiling, she couldn't help it. Her body was buzzing, she might float off the ground.

Her mother gave a little start. Opal had scared Cherry, who was obviously not expecting anyone to come jumping out from behind the open gate.

Her mother looked at her as a stranger would. Opal realized Cherry did not recognize her—or that she was just about to. Unlike Opal, Cherry had not seen her in nearly twenty years.

Opal walked closer to her mother. She saw by the goose bumps on her mother's arms and legs that she was cold, or maybe nervous, and that she had on a gold charm bracelet and a delicate gold chain around one ankle. She saw that her mother wore no makeup, that she was beautiful but tired-looking, darkish circles under her eyes. Saw that one of her mother's hands was gripping the driver's door like a person hanging from a cliff. Opal watched understanding descend upon her mother's face. The way her eyes got large and then squinted closed with the shock of it, how her mouth contorted. It wasn't pain, Opal saw, but it wasn't not pain. There was joy too. But not only.

Opal knew that in a time not long from now she would understand how her mother got here. They would go up to the house and sit across from one another and Cherry would tell Opal how she figured out where her daughter was. Opal imagined her mother telling her where she'd been all these years. And that wouldn't be it. Opal would have her own stories to tell, about tunneling, and about what Ursa had done. Opal would tell her what had happened with Ruth, why this cycle of mothers leaving their daughters was repeated.

And there was one question she would ask her mother: "Why did it take you so long to come back?"

But she wouldn't ask it yet. That would come. With time.

Here, right now, her mother raised her arm and gave an awkward wave and Opal saw the chalky white of deodorant lining her mother's underarm. It wasn't a detail she would have ever expected, nor her mother's shoulders as they began to shake, and Opal realized that nothing in the tunnel had ever compared to this moment. Her mother. Right now.

"You found me," Opal called out.

Her mother, right now, is crying. Right now, she says, "I did. I found you."

Acknowledgments

This book would not exist without guidance and support from so many people. It's a privilege to thank them here.

My agent Erin Hosier never gave up on this novel and its "cosmic bulimia." Erin, my boo, thank you for believing in me and my work, and for always making me laugh when I need it. Thank you to everyone at Dunow, Carlson & Lerner, including Arielle Datz, whose emails I love to get. Thank you as well to Amy Schiffman at Echo Lake Entertainment.

It's an honor to be published by Counterpoint. I'm lucky to work with this smart and enthusiastic team of experts. Thank you Megan Fishmann, Rachel Fershleiser, Yukiko Tominaga, Nicole Caputo, Dan López, and Laura Berry for your care in bringing my book into the world. Thanks also to my copy editor Sue Ducharme.

I owe an enormous thank you to Dan Smetanka, my brilliant editor at Counterpoint. Mama Dan! You are a legend for a reason! I'll never forget our phone calls and the excitement we shared as we solved this book. We really did surf the membrane together, didn't we? Thank you for seeing what this novel could be, and for challenging and inspiring me. Working with you has been the gift of my career.

I'm grateful to my earliest readers, who gave me the courage to keep writing: Kara Levy, Lydia Kiesling, Kate Milliken, Yael Goldstein

Love, and Madeline McDonnell. Thank you to my friends who took the time to read an entire draft and offer their insights: Rufi Thorpe, Anna Solomon, Mike Reynolds, Meaghan O'Connell, Rebekah Henderson, and Laura Warrell. Fabienne Leys, thanks for reading—and for letting me use your name! Julia Whicker, you understood this story on a cellular level; you convinced me not to give up.

A writer who is also a parent simply cannot write without child-care. Thanks to the many teachers, caregivers, and family members who made sure my children were in good hands while my husband and I worked. A special shout out to Annie Kemper for being there for us in 2020–2021.

Thank you to Jessie Durant at the Santa Cruz Museum of Art and History for pointing me in the right direction.

I wrote (and rewrote) much of this book at Dorland Mountain Arts Colony. Thanks to Janice Cipriani-Willis and Robert Willis for the time and space there to create and daydream. Darcy Vebber and Kristen Daniels: I cherish our special Dorland evenings together.

I raise a (martini) glass to my fabulous group of LA writer friends: Janelle Brown, Jade Chang, Stephanie Danler, Cynthia D'Aprix Sweeney, and (again!) Rufi Thorpe.

Diana Samardzic was my unpaid consultant on all matters related to psychotherapy and Santa Cruz. She's also my best friend. Kathleen Potthoff, thanks for growing up on Edinburgh with me. Doug Diesenhaus and Molly McDonald, my favorite brains, I write to impress you. Thanks to my coffee buddy Mark Haskell Smith for all the good advice.

To my friends near and far who checked in regularly to ask how my book was going, your interest meant—and means—a lot.

Thank you to my sisters Lauren Lepucki Tatzko, Heidi Cascardo, and Sarah Guzik, and to my brother, Asher Guzik, who answers my questions about plants and trees in a fictional universe. Thanks also to my stepfather Mitchell Guzik, my "stepmother" Keitha Lowrance, and my in-laws Kam and Art Brown.

My mother, Margaret High Guzik, is always supportive of me and my writing, going so far as to buy me big, glamorous "writing rings" to help my creative process. I was able to go away to write because she could pick up my kids from school and care for them. Thank you so much, Mom.

This novel is dedicated to my father, Bob Lepucki, who dropped whatever he was doing to answer my calls about microfiche, movie sets, LA in 1980, and Wilhelm Reich. It was a lot of fun to collaborate in this way. Thanks, Dad.

Thank you to my wonderful children. Dixon Bean Brown, you beautiful, smart weirdo, I don't know why you wanted me to narrate this entire story to you, but you did, and your feedback was so helpful! Ginger Dean Brown, your otherworldly poise as an infant was the novel's first inspiration; you always bring the magic and the mystery that I crave. Mickey Ocean Brown, my baby bear, if only I could time travel to the moment I held you for the first time; then again, why would I? You're just as remarkable in the present. You all are.

My husband, Patrick Brown, is my first, last, and best reader. Thank you for everything you do for me, for our family, for this life we share together.

© Ralph Palumbo

EDAN LEPUCKI is the *New York Times* bestselling author of the novels *California* and *Woman No. 17*, as well as the editor of *Mothers Before: Stories and Portraits of Our Mothers as We Never Saw Them*. Her nonfiction has been published in *The New York Times Magazine*, the *Los Angeles Times, Esquire Magazine*, and *The Cut*, among other publications. She lives in Los Angeles with her family. Find out more at edanlepucki.com.